LAWRENCE BLOCK

This special signed edition is
limited to 750 numbered copies.

This is copy 411.

COLLECTIBLES

COLLECTIBLES

Edited by
Lawrence Block

SUBTERRANEAN PRESS 2021

First Edition

ISBN
978-1-64524-045-7

Subterranean Press
PO Box 190106
Burton, MI 48503

subterraneanpress.com

Manufactured in the United States of America

TABLE OF CONTENTS

The Elephant in the Living Room (an introduction) — LAWRENCE BLOCK — 9

The Evan Price Signature Model — JUNIOR BURKE — 17

Blue Book Value — S. A. COSBY — 31

...from Otto Penzler's Mysterious Obsession (1) — 41

A Collection of Friends — JANICE EIDUS — 45

Lost Shows — LEE GOLDBERG — 53

Bar Wall Panda — ROB HART — 73

God Bless America — ELAINE KAGAN — 91

...from Otto Penzler's Mysterious Obsession (2) — 111

Resonator — KASEY LANSDALE — 115

The Skull Collector — JOE R. LANSDALE — 133

A Bostonian (in Cambridge) — DENNIS LEHANE — 157

Miss Golden Dreams 1949 — JOYCE CAROL OATES — 179

...from Otto Penzler's Mysterious Obsession (3) — 191

The Green Manalishi with the Two-Pronged Crown — THOMAS PLUCK — 195

Devil Sent the Rain Blues (Pm 13040) — DAVID RACHELS — 211

Chin Yong-Yun Meets a Mongol — S. J. ROZAN — 225

The Demise of Snot Rocket — KRISTINE KATHRYN RUSCH — 245

...from Otto Penzler's Mysterious Obsession (4) — 277

First Appearance — ALEX SEGURA — 283

Collecting Ackermans — LAWRENCE BLOCK — 293

About Our Contributors... — 315

THE ELEPHANT IN THE LIVING ROOM

BY LAWRENCE BLOCK

*B*EN: Ah, there you are. Just the man I've been looking for.

JERRY: Who, me?

BEN: Absolutely. I'm able to offer you something I know you'll love, and at a remarkable price.

JERRY: What? I've got everything I need.

BEN: This you haven't got.

JERRY: So? What is it?

BEN: An elephant.

JERRY: An elephant? Are you out of your mind?

BEN: But—

JERRY: I live in two rooms on Pitkin Avenue. Two small rooms on the fifth floor. I got no room for a goldfish, never mind an elephant.

BEN: But—

JERRY: There's no backyard, just ten square feet of garbage cans. There's no front lawn, just a stoop. And out in front there's a fire hydrant, so you couldn't even park a Ford Escort there, let alone an elephant.

BEN: But—

JERRY: So where would I put it? I got no place to put it, and if I did I wouldn't be able to keep it alive, because I'm lucky I can afford to feed myself. I couldn't feed an elephant, and if I could, how am I gonna clean up after it?

BEN: But—

JERRY: And what would I want with it in the first place? You think I'm gonna ride around on an elephant? You think I'm gonna walk it on a leash? I got no use for an elephant, I got nothing to feed it with, I got no place to put it, so I ask you again what I asked you in the first place. Are you out of your mind? Because why in God's name would somebody like me want to buy an elephant?

BEN: You put it that way, Jerry, sheesh—I guess you wouldn't.

JERRY: That's what I've been trying to tell you.

BEN: I hear you, and I have to say it's disappointing. Because what I didn't get to mention is that I've come into possession of not one but two elephants, and I could give you a very special price if you were to take them both.

JERRY: *Now* you're talking!

Now it's true that Jerry's not so much a collector as he is a bargain seeker, but I have a feeling most ardent collectors would get the point. And another conversation between the same two gentlemen has its own point to make:

BEN: This whole retirement is horrible. I got nothing to do and too much time to do it in. I'm going nuts.

JERRY: That's natural. You worked hard all your life. You were always busy with one thing or another, and now you have nothing to do.

BEN: Isn't that what I just told you?

JERRY: It is, and there's an answer.

BEN: Oh?

JERRY: You need a hobby.

BEN: A hobby?

JERRY: A hobby.

BEN: What, like collect stamps and paste them in a book? Do jigsaw puzzles? Crochet lamp shades? That's gonna fill my days with joy?

JERRY: I'll tell you something. It doesn't matter what the thing is that you do. What matters is that you're doing it. You take an interest, you get caught up in it, and your life becomes a pleasure instead of an aggravation.

BEN: I think you're serious.

JERRY: I am. Hundred percent.

BEN: And you? You also worked hard all your life. Now you got a hobby?

JERRY: As a matter of fact, I do.

BEN: Yeah? You care to tell me what it is?

JERRY: I keep bees.

BEN: You? My old friend Jerry? You keep bees?

JERRY: Yes, I do. As a hobby.

BEN: Bees. How many have you got?

JERRY: Well, it's not like you can stand there and count them—

BEN: Round numbers.

JERRY: Round numbers, probably forty thousand.

BEN: Forty thousand bees.

JERRY: More or less.

BEN: Forty thousand bees. You live in two rooms on Pitkin Avenue. Where the hell do you keep them?

JERRY: Well, as a matter of fact, I keep them in a cigar box.

BEN: Forty thousand bees in a cigar box?

JERRY: So?

BEN: So how can that be good for them? Don't they get all crushed and crumpled?

JERRY: So? Get a grip, Ben. It's only a hobby!

On reflection, I'd say we can all be grateful these two guys moved to Vermont to make ice cream. Let's move on. Let's talk about *Collectibles*.

Once I'd settled on the theme for this anthology, I got busy dragooning contributors. Their stories, I explained, could be in any genre or no genre at all, and could concern any sort of collectible item.

What I wanted, what I always want when I'm wearing my anthologist hat, is to provide a grain of sand that will sufficiently irritate a writer to yield a pearl of a story. And, I'm pleased to report, that's precisely what's happened here. The stories don't need me to speak for them. They require, as one might say, no introduction.

So what am I doing here? Besides recycling old jokes that were briefer and more to the point when I first heard them?

Well, I ought to explain the one byline that appears not once but four times in the Table of Contents. The name is Otto Penzler's, and a well-known name it is, although the affable fellow who bears it is not a writer of fiction.

In the fall of 2019, when *Collectibles* was just beginning to take shape, Otto was good enough to send me a copy of *Mysterious Obsession,* a new memoir he'd published that centered on favorite books he'd collected over the years. He was, as you may know, not only an authority in the field of crime fiction and an editor and publisher of some of the best of it, but without question the world's foremost collector thereof. His is a book to be taken in small doses, made for sipping and savoring, and I knew as much—but what I found was that once I'd picked it up myself I couldn't put it down until I'd drained the metaphorical glass—to the dregs, I might say, but there was not a dreg to be found.

It seemed to me that a chapter extracted from *Mysterious Obsession* would be a welcome addition to *Collectibles.* But which chapter? There wasn't a one that wouldn't suit...nor was there one long enough to constitute a full chapter in my book.

You can see how I solved the problem.

Otto's are not the only words in this volume to have already appeared elsewhere. There's also a story called "Collecting Ackermans," appeared in *Alfred Hitchcock's Mystery Magazine* in 1977. The author was, um, Lawrence Block.

I always feel that any anthology with my name on the cover ought to contain a story of mine. This is an ideal often honored in the breach, especially of late, when my own creative juices have gone largely dry. This figures, after all; one embraces the practice of anthologism because it offers one a chance to appear writerly without actually writing anything.

Except, you know. Introductions.

So what I did, as usual, was enlist enough fine writers to fill a book. I get to decide for myself just how many that is, but somewhere along the way I seem to have settled on seventeen, and I've been compulsive enough to stick with it. Not like barnacles to the hull of a ship, or iron filings to a magnet. I've put together books that have exceeded or fallen short of that number. But I shoot for seventeen, and hit it most of the time.

I totted up my acceptances and was relieved to see that I had eighteen acceptances, or nineteen with Otto's contribution. So *Collectibles* could get along without a Lawrence Block story.

Then Covid, and a world turned upside-down. And a couple of writers found themselves unable to produce stories. I was down to fifteen stories, sixteen counting Otto's.

Could I write one?

I thought about it, and kept being struck by the fact that I'd already done so, that "Collecting Ackermans" was an ideal choice for the book. I read it to see if I still liked it, and guess what? I thought it was just fine.

Seventeen!

I've been a collector of one thing or another for most of my life. In childhood I amassed no end of collections. I netted butterflies in vacant lots, I soaked stamps off letters, I checked pocket change for dates and mintmarks. When reading became important to me, I collected books; when I started writing crime fiction, I collected the magazines that published it. Whenever I acquired an object that interested me, I wanted to add others that were of its ilk but slightly different.

I could list some examples, and then we'd have a collection of nouns.

The impulse has been with me in one form or another since childhood. Only recently has it abated, and after I sold my stamp collection a few years ago, there's been nothing I've felt the need to collect.

I can only assume it's age-related. Ecclesiastes would understand. I've grown beyond the time to gather stones and reached the time to cast them away.

Good job I'm not in a glass house.

COLLECTIBLES

But let's end where we began, with the elephant. My Uncle Jerry Nathan, the younger of my mother's two brothers, had collected stamps as a boy, and had been an ardent ornithologist as a young man, but I don't recall his having collected anything in adulthood. Until perhaps his sixtieth year, when he announced with satisfaction that he'd begun collecting elephants. Not living ones, not the kind you'd house in two rooms on Pitkin Avenue, but the sort of carvings you put on one of those shelves designed to hold, um, carvings.

And indeed he had a couple of shelves in his living room, and there was a set of elephants on one of them. All the same elephant, really, in graduated sizes. I think he bought that first set, and then it became something to give him. "Oh, there's an elephant, I think I'll get it for Jerry." And so the collection grew. Not to any great size, really, and I don't remember anything noteworthy about any of the elephants, except that some were wood and some were not.

Never mind.

It must have been a couple of years after Jerry came down with his mild case of elephant fever when my cousin Jeffrey Nathan announced he'd begun a collection. (Jeffrey was the younger son of my Uncle Hi, my mother's other brother. You don't need to remember this. It won't be on the test.)

I asked him what he was collecting.

"Giraffes," he said.

A commendable choice, I told him. And we agreed that the giraffe was an attractive and distinctive and noble beast, and eminently collectible. And even its name was appropriate; *Jeffrey* and *Giraffe* were well suited to share space in the same sentence. He talked for a few minutes about his collection, the aptness of it, the opportunities it afforded. He confided that it had been several months since the idea came to him, several months since he'd become a collector of the long-necked creatures. And then I had a question. I asked him how many giraffes his collection contained.

"None," he said.

None?

He explained that he hadn't yet found a specimen that was quite up to the standards of his collection.

A couple of years later Lynne and I came across a giraffe somewhere and thought it was too good to pass up. Perfect for Jeffrey, we agreed, and bought it, but it was not without a degree of trepidation that we mailed it off to him. His collection, still without a single specimen, was pristine and perfect. Would we be lowering its tone?

Jeffrey called to thank us for the gift, and was quick to lay my concern to rest. "It fits the collection perfectly," he assured me. "It's just right."

Well, really, what else could he say? But I'm still not sure we did the right thing.

The Evan Price Signature Model

BY JUNIOR BURKE

I opened The Fret Gallery mostly to have a place to keep my instruments. When I went from being a full-time musician to a part-time musician to a once-in-a-blue-moon musician, my wife Marlene inquired, at first occasionally, then with more frequency, *did I really need twenty-two guitars?*

Truth was, I'd never sold a guitar, never traded one in. Every time I hooked up with a new group, I'd get a fresh one. For a rock cover band, another electric; a bluegrass ensemble, another acoustic. I bought them used, always a Gibson, Fender or Martin, each one now more than thirty years old. If I'd owned a guitar, played it on the bandstand or in my music room at home, it became part of me. Sound waves never die and those guitars were the chatter of my life.

"You have to open a store to sell them?" Marlene asked. "Why not just put them up on eBay?"

What I wasn't telling her was I had no intention of selling them, not any of *those*. Guitar manufacturing had gone much the way of the auto industry. What was now termed classic or vintage guitars were American, made before the final decade of the twentieth century. The ones for sale would be new, most of them assembled in Mexico or Japan; China or Korea. Mine would hang on their own wall, to be looked at, taken down and played, not part of the commercial inventory.

COLLECTIBLES

Being in Dillard's Grove, thirty miles south of Chicago, a town of forty-two thousand, I wasn't expecting to make a fortune. A few years in, I was banking more than I was spending, largely because I augmented the guitars and their accessories with vinyl. That, like the offshore guitars and amplifiers and effects pedals, was what the kids wanted.

One afternoon I was in the shop when Tad Kilmer came in. While he held a guitar case, his visit struck me as random, as I hadn't laid eyes on him in ten, fifteen years.

We expressed our pleasure in seeing each other, then Tad said, "I didn't know where else to take this, Andy. The family finally sold the motor lodge, in fact it's being torn down tomorrow. I found this in a shed out back, buried under a stack of boxes."

The case appeared spanking new. Tad set it flat on the counter, then we both flipped up a couple of latches. The guitar was cherry red and shiny, silver hardware gleaming; a dual-pickup, semi-hollow single cutaway, with rosewood neck and bridge. The name on the headstock said Gibson, although I'd never seen one like it.

"How long have you had this?"

"No idea. Nobody in my family plays guitar. I'm hoping you'd be willing to sell it for me. How much you think it might be worth?"

"Let me look into it and I'll put it up on consignment. Just give me a day or two." Then I added, "Sorry to hear the motor lodge is going away. Besides being in your family for so long, it's a piece of rock n' roll history."

Tad smiled and shook his head. "Andy, you must be one of the few guys on earth who still cares about something like that."

That may have been, but the Hillcrest Motor Lodge was infamous for a night in August, 1980, when The Scavengers came to play Crazy Cal's Teen Club, a converted skating rink east of town.

Crazy Cal was a famed Chicago deejay and entrepreneur who presented local, sometimes national and even international rock bands. The Scavengers were a five-piece English group whose standouts were singer Thomas Byron Thomas and lead guitarist Evan Price. They hadn't broken any singles, but their second album was generating a great deal of FM airplay.

This was the summer after graduating high school and Marlene and I went that night to Crazy Cal's on one of our first dates. I was astounded by Evan Price's plaintive tone and amazing fluidity, like he was playing slide even though he wasn't.

I went to sleep that night, ears filled with riffs from Evan's Les Paul, and was astonished the next day when it came over the radio that Evan, while taking a late night dip in the Hillcrest pool, had drowned.

I refreshed my memory by perusing the internet. It was immediately assumed that Evan Price was drunk or had taken too much of some chemical cocktail, but the autopsy revealed no alcohol or substances. Most likely, investigators decided, he'd had one of his frequent asthma attacks and couldn't make it out of the pool to his inhaler which he'd placed on a towel atop a nearby lounge chair.

The Scavengers went on with their tour (Evan would have insisted, said Thomas Byron Thomas) and Evan Price's body was shipped to the UK for burial.

I stepped over to the vinyl bins. In the miscellaneous *S* section, there they were, The Scavengers. Evan Price looked exactly as I remembered him on the last night of his twenty-seven-years-young life. The Scavengers ambled on after that, a few more albums of Chicago blues covers and unremarkable original songs, before fading.

Tad's visit reminded me of another time I'd had done some guitar-related detective work. Some sketchy guy came in wanting to sell me a '54 Stratocaster he claimed had belonged to Tater Hardin, one of the last of the great Chicago bluesmen, who'd passed away several years before. It was not inconceivable that this guy had, as he claimed, been given the guitar in lieu of a gambling debt, but the whole thing didn't feel right. I said I didn't have the cash to buy it right then and urged him to bring it back in a week or so. I also wrote down his license number as he pulled away.

The Cook County Sheriff's Department was pleased to hear from me, as the guy had rented a couple of storage spaces to house his stolen goods. The Hardin family was *very* pleased because the Strat had been the legendary blues man's most beloved possession. Tater's grandson Lawrence even came to The Fret Gallery to thank me in person and to drop off a card for Real

COLLECTIBLES

Real Blues, a South Side club he'd just opened. "Come by sometime, Andy, and you'll drink on the house." On his way to the door, he'd smiled. "That guitar was part of my granddad's body and soul. One time his apartment caught fire and he rushed back in and grabbed it. That's what you call love, man. Tater Hardin *loved* that guitar."

As for Tad's discovery, the thing to do, I knew, was to contact Gibson headquarters in Nashville to see what kind of light they could shed. I sent an email to customer support, along with a picture of the guitar, then followed up with a call. I was passed through a couple of levels, until I got to Marty Ingber in the restoration department.

"This doesn't line up with any guitar in our records," he told me. "My guess is, somebody crafted it at some point, then tried to pass it off as one of ours. Sweet looking axe, but you can bet your life it's not a Gibson."

I called Tad with that not-so-wonderful news. We agreed on the price of $500, The Fret Gallery taking 20% of any sale. I hung it beside the made-in-China Epiphones.

With little hope of a flood of customers, I closed twenty minutes early that day. As I locked the front door, I realized I'd yet to plug in the mystery guitar. I thought about taking it home and testing it out, then decided I'd do that when I returned in the morning.

When I got there at ten a.m., the front door was ajar. Somewhat frantically, I looked around and everything seemed in order. I breathed a massive sigh of relief until I saw the empty space on the wall.

My hands were a little shaky as I got Tad's number off the claim check.

"Hi, it's Andy."

"Great seeing you yesterday."

"Listen, I know this sounds… Is there any chance you came back after I closed? Maybe I didn't leave the door locked…"

Empty air, then, "Are you all right, Andy?"

"I'm okay, I guess. It's just…that guitar you brought in, it's gone."

"Gone?"

"I hung it on the wall, I'm sure I did. I'll pay for it, Tad. I've never had anything like this happen."

All that day, I couldn't let go of it. Somebody must have slipped in somehow, but why would they only steal *that* one? I dragged those questions home, didn't even try to explain to Marlene what had happened because I couldn't explain it to myself.

"Since you won't talk about what's bothering you, I don't want you moping around," she told me. "Isn't there music at Vince's tonight? Why don't you go and try and shake off whatever it is that's making you ruin the night for both of us?"

———

Vince's Tap was a pizza bar in what there was of downtown Dillard's Grove. With very little in the way of décor, it did, however, have a stage against the far wall equipped with a basic p.a. system and a pair of standing microphones. There was a drum kit permanently in place, as Vince himself was a drummer, although I never saw him behind it. Also onstage were a small electronic keyboard and a few combo amplifiers. The setup was for the Thursday Night Blues Jam, hosted by a blond-haired local kid named Barry Saltz, (Bluesbarry to his enthusiasts) who blew a bit of cross-harp and would bring on guest vocalists and guitarists to be backed by the house band. While it was called a blues jam, much of the material was more in the realm of classic soul and R&B. This night had drawn a modest crowd of around twenty.

As I took my seat, the band appeared to be vamping, Barry Saltz blowing notes with very little conviction. A stringy-haired guitarist, thin and pale, was perched on a stool, hunched over, right hand drooping near the strings, left hand gripping the neck, neither hand forming a chord or plucking a note. While this surprised me, the next realization ignited my brain like I'd stepped on a land mine.

The guitar the guy was wearing but not playing, was the Gibson knock-off that vanished from my store.

As Barry Saltz concluded his hapless solo, he stepped over to the lost-looking guitarist, leaned down and said something into his ear, clearly in the line of *if you're just going to sit there and not do anything, get yourself off the bandstand.*

COLLECTIBLES

The guitarist, like someone wandering from the scene of an accident, drifted to the edge of the stage and gently placed the guitar in its case.

At first I felt it was only a resemblance, but as the young man floated toward the door, I realized, as though he'd stepped out of that album cover, the dazed-looking guy leaving the club looked *exactly* like Evan Price.

I got up from the table, then exited the club. When I hit the evening air, standing in front of Vince's Tap, guitar case at his side, was the vacant young man who'd just been kicked out of the jam. Maybe the non-playing imposter was some nut who'd come across The Scavengers on the internet and fashioned himself after the band's late virtuoso guitarist. It had been an extremely difficult day. Most of me wanted nothing more than to drive home. But the guitar inside that case belonged to Tad Kilmer and had been lifted from my store. Not knowing what I'd say, some sputtering engine eased me into motion. As I came up beside him, what came out was, "Evan Price?"

Let me remind you that I'd only been in Vince's a few minutes and had nothing to drink. Hadn't smoked weed in years, had never dropped acid, so I wasn't having a flashback. Wasn't taking psychotropic drugs and didn't feel I was undergoing a psychotic break. *Do you believe in ghosts?* was a question I'd never thought seriously about. But a few minutes after approaching him, I knew the answer, because now I was in the front seat of my car, listening to one.

Evan Price was spilling his truth. Clearly, what was coming out had been bottled too long.

"I didn't want to go on that tour. Our idiot manager had booked it well before our second album's release and we were playing venues far below what we should have by that time.

"The other thing, Thomas Byron Thomas had stolen my girlfriend Rose just before we left London. She came with him, with *all of us,* on the tour, was at the bloody motor lodge, the two of them banging in the room right next to mine. Madness... The only reason I came was this guitar."

I said nothing, simply waited for him to continue.

"I felt it was time for a new guitar hero. Clapton was well established; Jimi, nearly ten years gone. I reached out to Gibson before the tour, sent them my own specifications and design and convinced them to build a production model, a cross between a Les Paul and a 335, suited for jazz as well as blues. I fancied I could be like Les himself, have my bloody name on a guitar and rake in a percentage of every one sold. Not have to go on tour with The Scavengers, which is what they were, that lot.

"The guitar was to be presented to me before that gig, to get my approval. Gibson was located in Michigan back then. Not all that far from here, right?

"A bloke from the company drove down but missed the sound check. Arrived right before we were to go on. Except the bloody roadies wouldn't allow him backstage. The bloke was so furious; didn't want to leave the guitar with them, didn't even want to stay for the gig. He found out where we were staying and dropped it off at the bloody Hillcrest with a note for me to ring him the following day.

"When I found out he wasn't let backstage, you can imagine how angry I was. I went straight to the motor lodge. All I wanted was to try out that guitar. I told the two roadies, Liam and Marv, that I would cool off in the pool while they were to get the address of the best blues club in Chicago. Then they'd bloody well drive me there, so I could jam the rest of the night.

"They didn't want to take me, didn't want to wait around a club while I tried out my new guitar. So they hatched some kind of scheme. I was in the pool when they turned up, both of them pissed on drink, all grinning and goofy, saying they fancied a dip as well.

"You have to understand, those two didn't like me, not at all, and that's putting it mildly. I was a rock star who ordered them around. Any groupie hanging backstage was keen for one of the band, not a pair of yobs like them.

"I wanted to get out of the pool and get going but Liam and Marv stripped down to their pants and started splashing and horsing around. At first I wasn't worried but soon I was terrified. One of them dunked me while the other leaped from the side of the pool onto my shoulders. I remember lying on the bottom, surrounded by blue shadows that kept growing darker." Evan let out a deep sigh. "And that's where I've been ever since."

"The bottom of the pool?"

He turned with a look of displeasure. "No, mate, the bleeding Hillcrest Motor Lodge. I wanted to leave, but not without that guitar. Been there for what, half a bloody century?" He drew a big breath. "When I saw one of the owners and realized it had been found at last, I didn't let it out of my sight. After you closed your shop and I got hold of it, I could feel my arms and legs and all the parts of me that had been behind some kind of curtain for all that time, taking shape and growing heavier. When I got outside, people would look and I knew they could see me."

There was a moment, then I asked, "Why didn't you play tonight?"

"I wanted the first time with that guitar to be special." A fresh look of disdain descended. "They call that a bloody blues jam? Those wankers know nothing about groove and dynamics which is what the blues is all about."

I leaned forward and turned the ignition, then I told Evan Price, "There's a place I need to take you."

Chicago's south and west sides, before, during and after the middle of the twentieth century, was where you'd hear the blues. Pepper's, Theresa's, Big Duke's Flamingo Lounge, you'd catch Muddy Waters, Tater Hardin and Howlin' Wolf. At 48th and Indiana, the same block where Theresa's used to be, Lawrence Hardin ran his club. *Real Real Blues* said the red neon sign out front.

There was a coat check right after you stepped through the entrance. I had on a sweater, but no coat or jacket. The young woman in charge had bright, lively eyes. "Wanna check that, hon?" she asked Evan, glancing at his guitar case.

"No," I jumped in, "he'll hold on to that. Is Lawrence around tonight?"

A curious smile. "Lawrence is around *every* night. What would you be wanting with Lawrence?"

"He told me to come by and see him."

"And who shall I tell him came by?"

"Andy, from The Fret Gallery in Dillard's Grove."

She pulled out her phone and texted. After a moment, she said, with mild surprise, "Go on in. Mr. Hardin will meet you at your table."

We stepped into a hallway. On the left, just before you'd enter the club, was a mounted glass case, a glowing light at the base, displaying its contents. Although Evan seemed only vaguely aware of his surroundings, I stopped to look at the chipped and faded gold Fender Stratocaster that had once been in my shop. The white pick guard had yellowed. The guitar had never been refinished, never had the worn-down frets replaced, and there were grooves all over the maple neck. A bronze plate at the bottom said: *This was the main guitar for all performances and recordings of the legendary Tater Hardin, from 1955 until his passing in 1997.*

We entered the showroom, me leading the way, Evan trailing sheepishly. Lawrence, in suit and tie, was standing beside a small round table near the front. Very few empty seats. It was clearly between sets, as there was no one onstage. "I was hoping you'd come see us sometime," he said, the impeccable host.

"Lawrence, could I talk with you a moment?"

Off to the side, I told him that the young man with me was an incredible guitarist who'd come all the way from England to experience some authentic blues.

"Experience *how?*"

"He has his guitar with him. It would really mean a lot to him and to me if he were to sit in on a couple of numbers."

Lawrence assumed a grave expression.

"That's asking a lot, man. This is Real Real Blues, not America's Got Talent." He looked at me, looking at him. "I do know that Marva Armstrong, tonight's headliner, brought in a sub instead of her regular guitarist. Maybe she'll agree to make room for a guest artist. I'll ask her, man, but if she says no, it stands."

———

Marva Armstrong was around fifty, her band a mix of younger and older players. The drummer looked to be the oldest and was clearly the pulse of the group, laying down tempos that never rushed, taking a roll only when essential; splashing the cymbal only when called for. The bass player, the only female instrumentalist, looked to be Marva's daughter. She took cues from the kick drum, locking in precisely to nail down the groove. There was a massive Hammond B3 onstage, the hefty guy at the keyboard driving it skillfully. The sub guitarist was left-handed and played much more rhythm than lead. When he did solo, it seemed like somebody telling a story, who didn't have all the details.

Marva made up for anything lacking in her ensemble. Her voice was a wonder, reaching high when it needed to, dipping low when she wanted to go there. As she captained the stage, mic in hand, the audience knew they were in the presence of someone who'd been to class and paid attention.

Forty minutes in, Marva said, "We got us a guest artist tonight who come all the way from London, England. My understanding is he's a pretty hot guitar man. Let's get Devon Price up here!"

Cradling his guitar, Evan ambled to the lip of the stage, took a step up and stood with the look of a prizefighter who'd just pulled himself up from the canvas. He glanced down at his guitar as though trying to remember why he'd brought it with him.

The bass player handed him the end of a cable, then shoved the other end into the amp directly behind him. The band started a breezy shuffle and Marva shot immobile Evan a look before she took the mic.

I got me a man who's five foot tall,
Got me a man just five foot tall,
But he knows how to dance, and that ain't all…

Putting Evan up there, I realized, was a huge mistake. The look Lawrence held when he turned to me said everything I was feeling. But then a single note rang out like no other note played that night, no other note Real Real Blues had heard in many years. Two more notes, three, springing from some wellspring of power and resonance.

The band responded, making more room for each dazzling statement pouring out of Evan's guitar. Throughout the solo, the organ player padded the chords to support Evan's melodic testimony. Marva stood, not in any hurry to break the spell by returning to the mic. When she at last reclaimed it for the final verse, the band swelled as though they were a troop about to plant a flag on the peak of a mountain.

The crowd cheered ecstatically. The band slid into a slower tempo, as Marva dealt out the lyrics, about her lover doing her wrong. When it came to the solo, there was no doubt who was taking it. Yet as Evan caressed and bent each note, sculpting them into figures, each of his clusters was now supported by octaves and harmonies, thirds, fifths, as deep and true as what Evan himself was playing. The left-handed guitarist was not laying down anything that could have produced such virtuosity, just kept up a chunky rhythm. Lawrence turned to me again, lips trembling and eyes saying, *What the hell is going on here?*

I didn't even try to answer. But I did do something in response to the astounding duet pouring from the stage. I left the table, and went to the case that housed Tater Hardin's Stratocaster.

It was empty; Tater's guitar wasn't there.

The song ended to delirious applause and the band eased into an even slower blues, a minor key this time. I remained where I was, effectively guarding the empty case, captivated by the mournful harmonics pulsing from the showroom. The song finished to no applause, just reverent silence.

Evan Price walked out the way he'd come in, brushing by me on his way to the door.

My eyes followed him, but then I turned back to the glass case and there was the gold Strat, hanging proudly and silently in its place of honor.

I was shaken out of my reverie by Lawrence's voice at my shoulder.

"What the hell *was* that, man?"

I looked back at him, unable to form a coherent statement.

"The guitar that dude played," he sputtered. "Does it have some hard drive hid inside it? Some recording on some kind of loop?" He seemed shaken and vaguely angry. "I been listening to my granddad's tone all my life. It's in my DNA. How did that dude get hold of it and have it play double like it did?"

"I wish I had an answer for you, Lawrence," was my tepid reply. "Thanks for letting us come see you."

As I walked down the block to the car, I half-expected to not see Evan anywhere, but there he was, standing beneath a street light. Already pale, Evan appeared to be even paler, his scrawny form even slighter. But for the first time, he was smiling.

"I can't bloody believe it. Did you see him up there?"

I hadn't, but I surely knew who he meant.

"*Tater Bloody Hardin,* with me like bees on honey, every bleeding note." He shook his head in amazement. "I kept thinking he'd take the lead but it seemed he just wanted to play along." Another astounded head shake. "Playing with *me,* Tater Hardin was."

We stood there a moment. Evan's joy from just a moment earlier was fading.

"I haven't a clue where to go now," he uttered. He seemed to be addressing himself, working something out. "The motor lodge being demolished, perhaps I'll just stay around this club and soak up the music." He laughed but there was no pleasure in it. "Maybe I'll get to sit in the way Tater Hardin just did with me."

I didn't know what to say except "Goodbye, Evan. I'm glad I got to hear you again. You were fantastic."

"The guitar, Andy. Do you want it back?"

Although the guitar case looked as solid as before, there was no longer any doubt. Evan was more ethereal than he'd been in the club. "You keep it, Evan. That's your guitar."

And that is the story of Evan Price and his one-of-a-kind instrument. Being the teller of it, the keeper of that memory, I know the story should end with his displaced spirit, having for a moment reclaimed its passion and purpose.

Will he hang around for the next *half-a-bloody-century,* having tasted the real, real blues? Will he ascend to some finer plane to seek out other gifted players to join in some eternal jam? Will he drift down to some rural crossroads and strike whatever deal is struck at such places, whose details are always different but whose bargain is forever the same?

No, let's leave Evan Price as I left him, and end this story as so many stories end, on an unspectacular, even mundane note.

The next day, my phone chimed the opening bars of The Thrill is Gone.

"Fret Gallery."

"Is this Andy?"

"Yes it is."

"Marty Ingber, from Gibson. I dug out some paperwork about that guitar. It was in a manila folder from decades ago, that's why it's not in our database. Pretty interesting. It's a prototype, made for a departed rocker named Evan Price. Ever heard of him?"

"I have."

"Apparently there were plans to do a run of them, The Evan Price Signature Model. The only thing left to do was to put his name on the headstock, but… well, you know what happened."

"I do."

"Bad for him back then. But the good news for you is, that guitar is likely worth some major money."

He clearly expected me to say something,

"No idea how much," he continued. "You'll have to talk to Christie's or some other auction house, but collectors will definitely be interested. John Lennon's Gibson went for two-point-four mil, but that's John Lennon. Still there?"

"I gave it away."

"You what… Who'd you give it to?"

"A friend."

"Wow, that's unfortunate. Any shot at getting it back?"

"No, it's his to keep."

The conversation was clearly over, but then he said, "Must be quite a friendship, Andy."

"It is," I told him. "It really is."

Blue Book Value

BY S. A. COSBY

*T*rey stepped over the narrowest part of the creek while balancing his shotgun on his shoulder. A cool wind slipped through the pine trees as he made his way up the hill following the blood trail. The sun was a pale chunk of quartz in the morning sky.

Who wings a deer with a shotgun? Oh, that's right. My dumbass. The deer, a huge buck with a medium-sized rack, had covered a hundred yards before Trey could scramble down out of the tree stand and pick up his trail. Just like most things in his life, the tree stand didn't really belong to him. It sat in a tree on land owned by his friend Randy Wright's aunt. Randy had given him a handshake's worth of permission to hunt in his stand while he was on the road in his rig.

Trey had misjudged the width of the creek or the water had saturated deeper into the shore than he thought because his foot was now soaking wet. He didn't stop to clarify who the culprit was. He couldn't let that buck get away. He had to run him to ground before he found someplace to lie down and die that was miles away. He wasn't out here trying to get a new pair of antlers to put on his wall. He needed meat. Tonya and the girls needed food. A big buck had sixty or seventy pounds of good venison on him. Salted and saved, they could make it through the winter. Or at least make it until he could find another job. Maybe get one that didn't test your piss so often.

31

COLLECTIBLES

Trey crested the hill and dropped to his knees. Tracking a blood trail across the moist detritus that littered the forest floor wasn't easy—unless you were like Trey and had been raised to track a deer before you learned how to tie your shoes. His old man had taken that shit seriously. Was a strict disciplinarian, was Jay Gowens. If Trey flinched when they were field dressing a deer or cleaning a fat rabbit he got two hard claps to the side of the head. If his knife slipped cleaning the bladder out of a squirrel and ruined the meat, he got a full-face slap.

Trey shook his head. Jay Gowens was ten years dead. The only beatings he was handing out were in hell.

He dropped to his haunches again. He touched a drop of blood that lay gently on an oak leaf. Up here on the ridge, oak trees ruled. The pine trees didn't dare encroach upon their territory. The blood was still warm and tacky. That buck couldn't run much further. Not with his heart triphammering in his massive chest, pushing his essence out the hole in his flank.

The trail stopped just near a clutch of wild boxwoods growing on the western slope of the hill. They looked like they should be separating a property line, not out here in the middle of nowhere.

Trey swung the shotgun around and placed the stock against his shoulder. *Come on out, boy,* Trey thought. *Time for you to meet your maker.*

He heard the snap of a twig to his left.

The buck was charging him. Eyes rolled back so far in his head all you could see was the white. Nostrils flared wide like a bull at a rodeo.

"Shit goddam!" Trey shouted. He pitched himself forward and to the side in an effort to avoid the buck. His body crashed through the boxwoods and careened down the side of the hill. He slammed to a stop when his shoulder and upper back smacked against an unyielding hunk of metal. He heard the buck run off to die in a place more to his liking.

"Goddammit!" Trey yelled. His voice echoed back around mocking him, or so he thought. He sat up then got to his feet and started looking for his shotgun. With his luck it'd be spread across the base of the hill in two or three big bulky pieces. As he turned in a slow circle he kicked at the object that had stopped him from tumbling.

A hollow metallic sound reverberated through the forest. Trey kicked at it again. Another lonely metallic thunk. Trey took a step backwards. There were more boxwoods here too. Thick ivy vines were laced between the branches. The boxwoods had grown tall and wide engulfing something made of iron or steel. Trey saw a flattened path that slithered through the pine trees and out towards Helen Marshall's house, Randy's aunt. Trey could see how the woods thinned further up ahead on the path. The path itself was dotted with pine cones and saplings. Trey turned back to the shape.

A feeling halfway between curiosity and frustration filled his gut and moved his hands. Branches bent and broke as he cleared away the brush and vines. When he saw what the boxwoods and ivy were hiding he felt his own heart begin to thud like a drum in his chest.

"Well I'll be damned," he said.

Trey knocked on the door of the two-story farmhouse. He'd hiked back to his truck in a double-time march, then put the truck through its paces to get back to Mrs. Marshall's place. After he'd seen what was in the woods, the speed limit was the least of his concerns.

A tall woman came in answer his knocks. She wore a blue sweatshirt over her narrow shoulders. Thick gray hair spilled down the nape of her neck. Her brown skin crinkled near her eyes. It was the only concession her body had made to Father Time but Trey was sure she was pushing sixty with both hands.

"Hello, Trey. Something I can do for you?"

Trey had thought about going into town and finding his cousin Benny… Tell him to bring his wrecker out to the woods. He could have bypassed Mrs. Marshall completely. Just taken what he'd found and put a wad of money in his pocket. That thought had only flamed in his head for an instant. Legality and etiquette demanded he talk to Helen Marshall before he dragged Benny and his truck a mile deep into the woods on her land.

"I was wondering if I could talk to you for a second."

"All right. I just made some tea. Would you like some?"

"Uh, no ma'am," Trey said. "I'm not much of a tea drinker." Mrs. Marshall nodded and turned, and Trey followed her into the house. The interior seemed to be frozen in a time warp from the 1970s. Mrs. Marshall's furniture was covered in plastic. Her walls were covered in oak paneling. Trey saw lamps that hadn't been produced since *The Waltons* were on network television.

Mrs. Marshall sat in a threadbare burgundy recliner. Trey sat on the love seat across from her. The plastic groaned and gasped under his weight.

"How's your mama doing? I heard they took her leg off."

"Yes, ma'am, they did. She's up in Lake Castor now at the nursing home."

"Oh Lord. Well, tell her I'm thinking about her next time you go see her."

"I will. But what I wanted to talk to you about was something I found out in the woods while I was hunting."

Mrs. Marshall sipped her tea.

"I didn't know you was hunting back there, Trey. Randy letting you use his stand? He could have told me."

Trey sucked his teeth.

"I thought he had said something. I'm sorry, ma'am."

Helen waved her hand, dismissing the slight with good old Southern hospitality. But Trey knew for the rest of the week it would be kindling for conversations at the IGA where Mrs. Marshall worked.

"What did you find out there?"

Trey sat up straight.

"I was trailing a big old buck that I nicked when I tripped and fell down the hill. I found something at the bottom of that hill. That's what I want to talk to you about," Trey said.

Mrs. Marshall took another sip of her tea. "And what was it?"

Trey thought he saw her hand shake. His mama's hand did the same thing. A gift from old age, he supposed.

Trey leaned forward and sat on the edge of the love seat.

"I'm no mechanic but I know a little bit about cars. Mrs. Marshall, I think you got a '71 GTO Judge out in them woods there. Was that your car? Or did it belong to Mr. Marshall?"

As soon as the words were out of his mouth he bit down on his bottom lip. Harold Marshall had run off with a sassy old girl by the name of Magdalena Smith back when Trey and Randy were still tying their sneakers with fat laces. Nobody in Red Hill County talked about him that much anymore and when they did they made sure Helen Marshall was out of earshot.

"I'm sorry," Trey said. "I don't mean to bring up bad memories or nothing."

"It's all right. I'm not glass, Trey. I won't break because you said his name. I do have to admit I hadn't thought about that car in years. Lord, did he love that thing."

Trey shimmied his shoulders as he fidgeted on the love seat.

"Yes, ma'am. Now I was wondering if you'd be willing to let me take that car off your hands. My cousin got a wrecker and we could up take it up to Red Hill Metals and sell it for the scrap."

Not true. He had no intention of selling that car for scrap. Not now. That had been his first thought when he'd seen the sky-blue paint that peeked out from under the wide patches of rust like a nervous child peeking around his mama's leg. But then he'd done some research on his phone as he was coming down the road. The Judge was one of the rarest goddamn muscle cars in the world. It came out in '71 and they stopped making it in '72. Even one beat to hell with branches growing through the floorboards could be worth a whole hell of a lot. Maybe ten or fifteen grand. That was a lot more than the big fat zero that Trey was staring at in his bank account right now.

Helen Marshall put her cup of tea down on a coaster on top of the pressboard coffee table. "I don't know, Trey," she said. "I don't really want nobody coming through my yard tearing it up to drag that old hunk of junk out."

"I'd give you half the money from the scrap yard. For real you'd be doing me a favor and I'd be doing you one."

"How you figure you doing me a favor?" Helen said. Her eyes were so brown they appeared black. They were bearing down on Trey in a way that made the back of his neck itch. He didn't like those judgmental eyes. They reminded him of his daddy's eyes.

"I mean I'm dragging away an old ass piece of junk off your land."

"A piece of junk that ain't bothering a soul back in them woods," Helen said. There was a finality in her voice that sounded like a door being shut.

"Look," he said, "I don't know if you heard but I got laid off at the plastic factory. My wife is just getting a few hours at the McDonald's. We got two little girls and we coming up on a couple of big ass bills. This would really help us out."

Detailing just how precarious his family's situation was left a bad taste in his mouth but he didn't have much of a choice.

Helen tilted her head to the right and shook it mournfully.

Trey felt a pit open in the bottom of his stomach. That was when he knew she was going to say no.

He was starting to dislike this woman. She didn't need the damn car. She had a house, not a trailer. She had a nice station wagon in her front yard, not a pickup truck one oil change away from falling apart. Why couldn't she just let him get the fucking car? Yeah, he was playing a game of okey doke with her but she didn't know that.

"I heard. And I'm sorry, Trey. I really am. But I don't think y'all need to be back there messing around with Harold's car. Who knows but Davion might want to do something with it? It was his daddy's car, after all."

Trey squeezed his hands into fists.

Davion was Randy's cousin. Helen's son. Trey heard he was out west. Had gotten an accounting degree and pulled up stakes out of Red Hill ten years ago. What the hell was he gonna do with a GTO stuck in the woods behind the house of a woman he hadn't visited in a decade?

You fucking bitch. But what he said was, "All right, ma'am. I just thought I'd ask."

The night had fallen hard over Red Hill. Autumn was rapidly putting on its winter coat. Trey sat in his truck with a bottle of the cheapest liquor he could find between his legs. He'd left Helen Marshall's and gone home to two screaming kids and Tonya giving him all kinds of attitude. He moved her out of his way as he turned right back around and went down to Danny's

Pub. He'd taken the last of his cash and drank shots of peppermint schnapps until his head swam. He was asked to leave there around six. He'd stumbled over to the liquor store and stolen a fifth of vodka. Then to cap off his night he'd slipped over to Benny's shop and asked to borrow his tow bar.

"What the hell you gonna do with that?" Benny had asked. "It's almost ten o'clock." Benny lived in a back room at the shop so he was almost always there.

"I gotta move a car. Duh." He didn't tell Benny his plan because he knew he wouldn't go along with it. And if he had lied and told him that Helen had given them permission to take the car, Benny being Benny would have wanted to hear it from her own mouth.

"All right, but I need it back by the morning."

Trey had made promises that he thought he might be able to keep and driven off with the attachment rattling in his truck bed. His plan was to go to Helen Marshall's and back his truck down the lane and just take the goddamn car. If she came out the house he'd just ignore her. If she tried to stop him he'd move her aside like he did Tonya.

He kinda hoped she would try and stop him.

Trey pulled down the lane hitting every mudhole as he did. He swung around and backed up to the opening of the path at the tree line of Helen's backyard that led to the GTO... He thought he could back up to the GTO then attach it to the tow bar. He had some hedge clippers and a machete in his truck and he could use them to cut away the vegetation.

He knew the car was likely heavy as hell but if he could get it hooked up he'd drag it out on those dry-rotted tires and take it back to Benny's. Then find some rich retired white guy who'd watched *American Graffiti* too many times.

"All right, get it together," Trey mumbled as he began backing down the mouth of the path. Saplings bent but did not break as he rolled over them. Trey's head rocked forward and hit the horn. He'd backed into a full-grown tree.

"Shit...come on now," he slurred. He put the truck in Drive and pulled forward, then put it back in Reverse. He crept down the path at a snail's pace.

Minutes ticked by as he negotiated the hundred-yard-long path. Finally, he heard a metallic scraping.

Trey peered in his rearview mirror and saw the GTO in the blood-red haze of his brake lights.

Fuck, I'm gonna tear it apart before I even get a hold of it. He put the truck in Park and opened the driver's side door. The soft earth kissed his face as he tumbled to the ground. Cursing, he pushed himself up and listed to his left, bounced off his truck and walked around to the tailgate.

He'd backed into the trunk of the GTO. The boxwoods had proved no match for the bumper of his Chevy. The lid of the trunk had sprung open like the maw of a gigantic demon. Trey used the railing that ran along the edge of the truck bed to keep himself upright. He fumbled around in his pocket, got his phone and hit the flashlight app. A pale blue light battled against the inky darkness that held sway this deep in the woods.

Trey was trying to see if he could attach the tow bar to the rear of the car. A vague voice in the back of his head whispered that wasn't the way tow bars worked when he noticed the brown mass in the trunk.

Trey moved closer but the bumper of his truck was pressed against the bumper of the GTO so he had to lean forward and to the left to get a better vantage point.

"What the fuck?"

The brown mass was a decrepit moldering blanket. Trey knew if he was to touch that blanket it would crumble like newspaper in his hands. He wasn't planning on touching that blanket or anything else.

Sticking out from under the edge of the blanket were a weathered pair of men's work boots. Soiled remnants of denim jeans stopped just above the tops of the boots. In the space between the bottom of the pants and the top of the boots Trey could see a tobacco-colored shaft. He realized with mounting nausea that it was a leg bone.

Moving his light across the width of the trunk, his eyes lit on a pair of woman's red pumps laying at haphazard angles next to the blanket.

"Fuck this," Trey said. He spun on his feet, almost fell again, and grabbed the edge of the truck bed to steady himself.

The beam from a powerful flashlight filled his field of vision.

"Who that? Who is it?"

"You know, you remind me of him," Helen said.

"That you, Helen?"

"You walk around mad at the world and taking it out on anybody that gets close to you. You think people don't notice Tonya wearing long sleeves in the summertime? I notice every time she come through my line."

Trey lurched forward.

"Crazy bitch," Trey said. A couple of shuffling steps got him to the door to his truck. The machete was in there.

"Yeah, you just like him. Think you can put your hands on people. Think you can take and take and take and when ain't nothing left you can just pull stakes and move on."

Trey couldn't see her face but her voice sounded tight as a drum. Each sentence she spoke was clipped and sharp as a razor.

In the distance a whippoorwill's lonely call echoed through the night. A lone holdover from the summer that stayed behind as the leaves began to fall. The call cut through the alcohol-induced fog in Trey's mind. He wondered if the bird was hurt. Was that why it hadn't flown south for the upcoming winter? If it was injured, a long and miserable death awaited it during the unpredictable Virginia winter.

Helen pulled a small black .38 from the pocket of her jeans.

"You know he had the nerve to bring her with him when he came to pick up his clothes on his way out of town? Brought that woman to my house. Slapped me in front of my baby boy. Got behind the wheel of that car like bullets couldn't touch them through glass," Helen said.

Trey couldn't see the gun. But he heard the shot. He felt the slug roll and spin as it sliced his pectoral muscle and ricocheted off his clavicle. It exited just under his left ear, perforating his carotid artery as it did. Trey stumbled backward and fell. He landed half in the trunk and half against his own bumper. Blood poured from his chest and stippled onto the bumper of the GTO.

A few drops fell onto the ground, destined to be lost among the fallen leaves except to the most well-trained eyes.

...from Otto Penzler's Mysterious Obsession:

INTRODUCTION

*I*t was just after college that I started to collect books. Although I earned only $42 a week ($37 after taxes), I had decided that I wanted to collect English and American literature—*all* of it. Fortunately, a wise old bookseller convinced me to narrow my vision and, after a couple of years of specializing in British adventure fiction and World War I poets, I found my future when I focused on mystery fiction.

I'd read virtually no detective stories when I was younger but wanted to read books that would be fun and that didn't hurt my head. I started with *The Complete Sherlock Holmes* (which should be required reading in every high school in America—or maybe in the world) and followed with four or five Golden Age novels a week, loving the puzzles designed by Agatha Christie, John Dickson Carr, Ellery Queen, Anthony Berkeley, and their devious compatriots.

However, after being introduced to Raymond Chandler and Dashiell Hammett, I realized that there were some crime fiction authors who could and should be taken as seriously as literary figures. I enjoyed reading the books and they seemed a good niche for collecting as there was very little competition in that field. New York City's famous Fourth Avenue booksellers' row (with more than sixty bookshops within a few blocks of each other) flourished

back then and it was easy to find a half-dozen first editions in collectable condition within my five-dollar-a-week budget. As my salary increased, so did the
quality of the bookshops I came to know, and the number of shelves I had to
erect to hold ever more books.

In 1979 I opened the Mysterious Bookshop in midtown Manhattan and
broke what I had been told was the cardinal rule of bookselling—never compete with your customers. We sold new and used books, like most mystery
specialty stores in the country, but I was especially interested in first editions
and the people who collected them. Thousands of books came through the
door in some months and all purchases were brought into my office where
they were sorted into two stacks: one for the store, one for my private library.

My office was beautiful! It had floor-to-ceiling shelves that I calculated
could hold nine thousand volumes which, I was certain, was more space than
I'd ever need. Just to be insanely safe, I had them built wide enough to be
two rows deep and, since book collections are like gas, expanding to fill the
space available, they eventually became inadequate as the number of volumes
approached twenty thousand. With no end to the torrent in sight, I built a
large house in the country to hold them. The library wing of the house would
comfortably contain about seventy thousand volumes so, as the collection
hit the sixty thousand mark, there was still plenty of room to grow. In the
year 2000, I decided to stop collecting every new book published, as they
were rarely of bibliographical interest. Instead, I focused on upgrading titles
already on the shelves and filling in the many titles that I still hadn't found.
I owned most of the major titles and therefore concentrated on searching
for the obscure and arcane volumes that had proven elusive, with only mod-
erate success—particularly in the area of paperback originals published in
England and Australia.

Every first edition that came into the store was compared against my
copy. I upgraded books constantly, being obsessed with having the best possible copy, as well as checking for variants, which I thought important for
bibliographical purposes. It is not hyperbolic to state that some titles were
upgraded a half-dozen or more times, which is why the books in my collection were, mainly, in outstanding condition. Because I saw so many books

and had a convenient way of disposing of my duplicate, unwanted copies, I had a distinct advantage over most collectors.

When I was about twenty-five years old, a very sophisticated collector told me that a collection is measured by the condition of the books and by the amount of original material it contains. Sadly, a limited budget left certain things out of my reach (a Sherlock Holmes manuscript, a *Beeton's Christmas Annual* for 1887, which contained the first appearance of Sherlock Holmes, among too many others) and forced me to sell some books that I just couldn't afford to put in the "Otto" pile. A superb first edition of the three-decker of *The Woman in White* haunts my memory thirty years after I had to sell it.

If I couldn't afford all the manuscript material I coveted, I did manage to acquire some, and they were among the most precious to me because they were unique. Among them were a G. K. Chesterton Father Brown manuscript, a short story signed by Agatha Christie, a rare Prince Zaleski story by M. P. Shiel, notebooks and sketches by R. Austin Freeman, and original works by Carolyn Wells, Cyril Hare, James M. Cain, and Stephen King, among many others.

My books and manuscripts went off to be auctioned late in 2018. Selling these books was among the most difficult decisions of a long life. As they were being packed up, I felt that my world, my identity, was being taken from me. The only consolation, slight as it was, is that I felt confident that they would be in good homes. Long-time collectors have been finding rarities that they feared they would never see while newer collectors have had the opportunity of getting off to a flying start with the best copies in the world of many titles.

Over the years, I've had the good fortune to show off the collection to friends and fellow bibliophiles, telling them the stories of where and how I found certain books, various booksellers and fellow collectors who enabled me to acquire them, and other anecdotes that I hoped would make the visit more entertaining than had I merely pointed a finger and said, "there's a copy of *The Maltese Falcon*." Before the books were packed and taken away, my friend and colleague Charles Perry suggested that he take pictures of particularly interesting volumes and that I should write down the anecdotes to accompany them.

A few references are made throughout these narratives on more than one occasion so, rather than describe that repetitively, here are a few definitions:

Frederic Dannay was half the Ellery Queen writing team, along with his cousin Manfred B. Lee, which produced the classic novels and short stories that bear their collaborative nom de plume. On his own, Dannay created *Ellery Queen's Mystery Magazine*, was a serious collector of mystery fiction first editions, and wrote *Queen's Quorum*, a bibliographical checklist of the 106 (later expanded to 125) greatest short story collections in the history of detective fiction.

The Haycraft-Queen Definitive Library of Detective-Crime-Mystery Fiction, which lists the most significant books in the history of the genre, beginning in 1748 with Voltaire's *Zadig* and concluding in 1948 with William Faulkner's *Intruder in the Dust.*

For the vast majority of the American public, hearing stories about the manner in which a certain volume found its way into my library is about as thrilling as a non-golfer being told how someone's bunker shot came *this* close to dropping into the cup.

This book is for the vast minority of the public that has been inflicted by the collecting mania that the great bibliophile Nicholas Basbanes has defined as a "gentle madness" in his masterful study of many of the world's greatest book collectors.

A Collection of Friends

BY JANICE EIDUS

L inda. Genevieve. Blossom. Doreen. Me.

In seventh grade, Linda's doting mother gave Linda whatever she demanded. A gold charm bracelet. Platform shoes with high heels like the older disco crowd wore. Dance lessons: tap, ballet, modern, Broadway.

I thought, *You are so spoiled.* Deep down I coveted everything Linda had, including the doting mother, so unlike my own.

By ninth grade, Genevieve wasn't a virgin. She offered us nuggets of advice: "French kissing is *way* better than regular kissing. But *never, never slurp!*"

Linda, Blossom, Doreen, and me—we hadn't even *"regular kissed,"* let alone French kissed. We hung on her every word.

I wore the same Charlie perfume and Revlon lipstick Genevieve wore, so why did the boys prefer her to me? I envied her sexual experience. I anxiously awaited my first time. Which didn't happen until college sophomore year with a drunken frat boy who *slurped very, very* loudly.

Blossom's parents were poor. They lived with Blossom's grandma. To save money, Blossom wore dowdy hand-me-downs, and her mother cut Blossom's hair into a lopsided wedge.

"Why is Blossom's family poorer than we are?" I asked my mother.

She shrugged. "We're *middle* class. They're *lower* class. That's the way the cookie crumbles."

She poured herself the first of what she called her nightly "hit-the-spot cocktails."

I stormed into my bedroom and slammed the door, waiting for her to come, but she didn't.

Doreen was so timid that when Mr. Rodriguez, the Spanish teacher, forgot to call her name during attendance for an entire week, she wept silently in the back of the room. After school on Friday, I approached him. We thought he was one of the meanest teachers in our Brooklyn public school. "Mr. Rodriguez, you're hurting Doreen's feelings."

He looked at me in surprise. "Thanks for telling me." He sighed. *"Poor Doreen."*

Walking home, I thought, *I'm a good person. I rescued Doreen.*

And me... I was "the smart one." I had the highest grades, at least until tenth grade when my parents divorced and my mother moved on to *three* nightly "hit-the-spot cocktails." "Your father is a piece of shit," she told me.

My father took me out for pizza near his office in midtown. He said, "Your mother is a lush and a leech."

I thought, *I hate you both!*

Linda let me borrow her charm bracelet. Genevieve gifted me with private advice: *"If the boy has bad breath, hand him a breath mint."* Blossom baked my favorite vanilla cupcakes. Doreen helped me to focus on homework.

In eleventh grade, my father remarried and moved to Connecticut. My mother got a job as a secretary and embarked on a long-term affair with her married boss. She cut back to *one* "hit-the-spot cocktail" a night. My grades shot back up.

Linda, Genevieve, Blossom, and Doreen loved me more than my parents ever had, I was sure.

Linda's now married to a tech guru. They own homes in Chappaqua and Palm Beach. She hasn't worked a day since her wedding. Thanks to Botox, she looks thirty-five instead of forty-five. I work around the clock running my own boutique talent agency. So far, I've resisted Botox, a rarity in showbiz circles.

Linda keeps vaguely in touch with us all. Occasionally we meet for brunch. Over a glass of cabernet, she's faux-humble: "My children! Both Harvard grads! I feel *truly* blessed."

I think, *Blessed? Not so sure. But definitely spoiled.*

Genevieve is a literary critic at Oberlin. I know nothing about Harold Bloom and Susan Sontag; she could care less about the world of showbiz. Sexually, she's still *way, way* ahead of me, indulging in threesomes and foursomes with both men and women. She smiles mischievously: "I'm the default dominatrix."

Me… I'm the monogamous, vanilla type. I like to cuddle in front of the TV. I've loved just two men: a Mexican chef and a cable TV news anchor. I broke the chef's heart. The news anchor broke mine.

Genevieve visits often. We have tea in my apartment. We reminisce:

"Remember when we thought Mr. Rodriguez was mean, but he was really nice!" "Remember Linda's crazy platform shoes!

"Remember the no-slurp rule of French kissing!"

I think, *If only we shared more than memories.*

Blossom is a *"feminist-post-feminist photographer,"* known for her black-and-white "Coven" series of women in witch's garb straddling broomsticks. Above their heads, she inserts text: *"We are the granddaughters of the witches you couldn't burn."* Her wife, also a photographer, does editorial work for upscale fashion magazines. They help Blossom's parents financially, and dote on their adorable seven-year-old son.

I see Blossom once a year at her annual November *"Friendsgiving."* She also invites *Linda, Genevieve, and Doreen,* but I'm the only one who shows up. The rest of the year, she isn't in touch. Inevitably, after a few glasses of wine, she reaches for my hand and says, *"You're family."*

I think, *Family you choose to see just once a year.*

———

More than a decade has passed since Doreen wounded me by not responding to my emails and calls. A year ago I ran into her sister in my dentist's waiting room. She stage whispered, "Doreen has schizophrenia. She lives with our mom."

Spontaneously, we hugged. I thought, *Poor Doreen.* This time I couldn't rescue her.

———

Me… I love my work and my clients, mostly hardworking character actors. Sometimes my life is glamorous—screenings, galas, travel. Much of the time it's just endless calls, emails, and texts.

Recently, I made the biggest decision of my life—to adopt a child. The paperwork is done, and soon I'll hold my darling baby girl in my arms. I'll be loving, kind, and present for her.

I think, *So unlike my mother.*

———

Ruby. Daphne. Pilar. Me.

In college, Ruby wore vintage eyelet dresses, tweed newsboy caps, and black lipstick. "I hate my parents! They made me go here instead of FIT!" Frowning, she swept her arms to indicate the sterile campus of the state school we attended upstate.

I was as miserable there as she was. My father had been downsized, and private college was out of the question. I thought, *I don't feel any sorrier for you than I do for myself.*

Daphne smoked weed all day long, although it didn't mellow her much. Every night into the wee hours, she paced up and down the dorm, talking nonstop of her dream to start a small publishing house dedicated to "peace and justice." She said, "I'll publish the next Maya Angelou! The next Barbara Ehrenreich!"

I was enthralled. I thought, *If only I were as passionate about something— anything!—as you are about Maya Angelou.* It wasn't until a few years later when I worked for a talent agent with slippery morals that I discovered my calling—although I planned to maintain my integrity.

Pilar was the first of her Mexican family to attend college. She worked part-time as a nanny to help pay her family's bills. She wore a rosary around her neck. Every morning, she crossed herself and said, "God willing, I'll one day take care of my parents as they take care of me."

She swore that she wouldn't have sex before marriage with her nice Catholic boyfriend. "In God's eyes that's wrong."

Agnostic since tenth grade, I thought, *You're just too religious.*

Ruby's a fashion designer in Paris. She dropped the rest of us immediately after graduation. Her signature style is romantic yet edgy: puffy sleeves on a clinging bandage dress; gingham overalls with a plunging, leather-bordered neckline. One of my clients buys up Ruby's metal-studded peasant blouses like mad. I think, *If you only knew what a nasty piece of work your favorite designer is.*

Daphne moved to Santa Fe, founded the publishing house of her dreams, and married a fiery progressive radio host. I've seen her just once since college. "I still love my weed. It helps me stay calm," she laughed. Although she spoke breathlessly and nonstop about herself: "I make a difference! I publish books that matter!"

I admire her dedication to social justice, but I thought, *You're not enthralling. You're a total narcissist.*

Pilar teaches fifth grade and lives with her parents in New Jersey. A year out of college, she married a firefighter who died on duty before they could have children. She attends church twice a day and still wears her rosary. I learned all this from Daphne, with whom she inexplicably stays in touch.

Pilar hasn't spoken a word to me since her nice Catholic boyfriend confessed to her that he and I had once slept together—something I'm not proud of, and for which I apologized profusely. I kept reaching out until she sent me an email: *"Bitch, leave me alone!"*

I thought, *When Pilar curses, it's time to let go.*

Me… I work as hard as ever, but I make time to prepare for my daughter's arrival. I've painted her nursery a buttery yellow so as not to gender stereotype. I shop for neutral baby clothes, take CPR classes, and watch tutorials on calming a colicky baby.

Amanda. Shushie. Me.

I wouldn't be me if I didn't have new friends. Blonde Amanda was my very first client. She plays the ditzy next-door-neighbor on a famous sitcom. Her sixteen-year-old daughter calls me "Auntie."

Amanda and I talk for hours and hours, never growing bored, discussing our careers, our aloof mothers, her miserable first marriage and happy second marriage, my exes, and my impending motherhood. We call each other "besties."

I think, *We're having a great ride.*

At eighteen, Shushie fled her Hasidic community to escape an arranged marriage. "He was cruel." Her mother shunned her, shouting "You're dead to me, dead to us all!"

Shushie says, "I was suicidal for years until I became a physical therapist. Helping others saved me." We met when she cured me of my plantar fasciitis.

Shushie is engaged to another "Ex-Hasid," as they call themselves, a sweet guy in law school. Their wedding will be friends only—no family. "My children will be free to be themselves," she says, leafing through bridal magazines.

I think, *As will mine.*

Me... I'm now dating a bearded cardiologist. On our first date, he told me, "I'm going to be upfront with you. I'm divorced with two kids and I don't want to become a dad again."

Which is just fine with me. My daughter won't need a father. A loving mother will be more than enough. It would have been for me.

Gilda Lucille.

I'll name my daughter Gilda Lucille, after Gilda Radner and Lucille Ball, two performers who've given me so much laughter and joy through the years. I would have loved to be their agent and friend.

I picture Gilda Lucille playing with her friends—*Emma. Jennifer. Ashley.* Emma might be the spoiled one, Jennifer the precocious one, and Ashley the sweet, vulnerable one.

Gilda Lucille will believe these girls will stay by her side forever, and she by theirs. She will not envision betrayals, boredom, mental illness, or disgust leading to hatred. It will be my job as her mother to protect her from the ache that accompanies such loss. Gently, I'll explain that friendship, like everything else in life, doesn't last forever. Although I won't say what my mother once said to me: *"That's the way the cookie crumbles."*

On the other hand, how can I know Gilda Lucille's future? Maybe she and *Emma, Jennifer, and Ashley* will be forever friends. Or maybe Gilda Lucille will be so loved by me that she won't feel the need to collect friends over and over for herself.

I think, *This mother will not say a single word.*

Lost Shows

BY LEE GOLDBERG

I collect old TV series. The cliché about guys like me is that we are morbidly obese, have bad skin, never get laid, and live in our mother's basement, surrounded by DVDs and videotapes, jerking off to that famous poster of Farrah Fawcett. There's a lot of truth to that, but thankfully none of it applies to me. I'm physically fit, enjoy as much sex as I'd like, and I have a nice, secluded home of my own with a state-of-the-art theater capable of screening shows in any format. I do have that poster of Farrah Fawcett, signed by her and framed on my bedroom wall, but so far I've resisted the urge to jerk off in front of it.

As a collector, I'm only interested in lost shows, scripted series that lasted only an episode or two or, better yet, were produced but never aired. For example, back in 1963, Robert Taylor and George Segal starred in a series called *330 Independence Avenue* about special agents for the department of health. Four episodes were shot for NBC and were never broadcast. I have them.

To find these rarities, I go to The Talent, the actors, writers or directors who made the lost shows. They are the ones who are the most likely to have the film or video that I'm looking for, or know where it might be, if it even still exists. But that's not the only reason I go to them. My collection wouldn't be complete without someone to tell me the stories nobody else knows about the shows nobody remembers.

COLLECTIBLES

Some collectors go to autograph shows or the back alleys of the internet to find what they want. I go to the Motion Picture and Television Hospital and Country Home in Woodland Hills, California. A lot of elderly actors, writers, directors, production designers and other industry people live there and those who don't will stop by to see their primary care physician for check-ups and referrals.

Years ago, before they put a wall around the property and added a guard gate, I would wander the grounds looking for talent, or I'd sit on a bench at the hospital's front entrance and wait to see who'd show up. Julius Harris, the big black actor who played the hook-handed bad guy in the James Bond film *Live and Let Die,* spent his days on a bench there, greeting visitors, until he dropped dead. Now his name is etched on the bench. It's his final credit.

These days I go to the shopping center that's across the street from the MPTV Home. I'll get there around 11 a.m. and find a seat on the patio that's shared by Starbucks, Subway, and a pizza joint. It gives me a good view of The Talent wandering over from the home, or taking the golf-cart shuttle, to do their shopping. I once saw an ancient actor, who'd primarily played priests, rabbis and popes on TV, come doddering out of the CVS with a big box of Depends and a pack of ribbed condoms in the basket of his walker. I'm not sure whether he was eternally hopeful or tragically nostalgic.

―――――

It was almost 12:30, and I was at my usual outdoor table, finishing an over-priced cup of Starbucks coffee, when a BMW exited the MPTV property, cut straight across Mulholland, and drove into the shopping center. The car parked in the handicapped spot in front of the patio and a woman in a halter-top and skinny jeans got out of the driver's side. I guessed she was in her thirties, but it was hard to be sure. She'd been under the knife too many times. Her face and body had a lot of sharp angles and no curves. She reminded me of one of those rock'em-sock'em robots I had as a kid, only with breasts. I know I'm dating myself with that reference, but I'm a guy who does a lot of his living in our cultural past.

She marched around to the passenger side of the car, wrestled a folding walker out of the back seat, and set it up while the old man in the front passenger seat rolled down the window, opened his door, and used the windowsill for support as he tried to stand. That's when I got a good look at his sunken face, the chapped lips around his piano-key teeth, and the scattered tufts of grey hair poking out like weeds on his age-spotted head.

I instantly recognized him. He was Buddy Dinino, a character actor who'd guest-starred in hundreds of TV shows, from *Gunsmoke* to *Diagnosis Murder,* over a career that had spanned fifty years. He'd started out playing the angry young man, bucking authority, before getting typecast as a bad guy. He showed up in every series Quinn Martin, Aaron Spelling, and Stephen J. Cannell ever produced until they died and took his career with them.

Buddy wore a loose-fitting track suit, which was ironic, since he had trouble just getting to his feet from the car.

"Oh, for God's sake," the woman said, in a tone of voice that not only conveyed her frustration, but also the cosmic unfairness she was forced to endure each day. She grabbed him under the arms, lifted him up with ease, and placed him behind the walker. "Can't you do anything for yourself? Now you've aggravated my sciatica. I've got a shooting pain from my ass to my toes."

"I could've stayed in the car."

"So you can shit on my leather seats again? The hell with that."

Buddy hobbled along slowly, leaning heavily on his walker, toward the nearest table. "It wasn't my fault that time, Dora. You said you'd be gone for five minutes. You were in the nail salon for an hour."

"It's always about you. How about thinking about someone else for a change?" Dora pointed a finger at a table. "Stay here while I get us lunch."

He lowered himself into a chair. "I'm not hungry."

"There you go. *Me, me, me.* Did it occur to you that I might be hungry? That I have needs? Of course not. You think that taking you to your doctor's appointment is the highlight of my day. I could have been on my Peloton."

Dora shook her head and marched past me into the Subway. Buddy slouched in a chair, the walker in front of him, and picked idly at one of the many scabs on his arms. His skin was dry, taut, and almost translucent.

COLLECTIBLES

He'd nearly become a star back in 1975. He was cast as the lead in *Pete McShane*, a TV series about a Vietnam vet, physically and mentally scarred by the war, who becomes an unlicensed PI and struggles to fit back into a society that would rather forget him. Four and a half episodes were produced before CBS got cold feet and canceled the show without even airing it. Instead they put on *Switch*, starring Robert Wagner as a conman and Eddie Albert as a retired cop who team up as private eyes. Buddy guest-starred in an episode as a Vietnam vet who kills hookers. I always wondered if that was an intentional fuck-you from CBS.

I picked up my empty coffee cup and approached him.

"Mr. Dinino? I'm sorry to disturb you, but I had to say hello. I'm a huge fan."

Buddy looked up at me, baffled. "You know me?"

I often get that reaction. Nobody ever recognizes The Talent that I'm interested in.

"Of course I do. I've seen everything you've ever done, except *Pete McShane*, of course. I'd love to see that show."

Buddy shook his head. "The only TV you can see that on is mine."

My pulse instantly jacked up. I tried to keep my voice steady, nonchalant. "So you have the show?"

Buddy looked past me and his eyes widened in fear. "Give me something to sign, quick."

All I had was my cup, so I handed it to him, then reached into my coat pocket and gave him a pen. That's when I sensed the woman coming up behind me.

"What the hell are you doing?" Dora snapped.

I turned, and gave Dora my most winning smile. She gripped the top of a Subway bag in her fist and glared at Buddy, who was writing on my cup with a shaky hand. I wondered if his shaking was palsy or fear.

"Giving a fan an autograph," he said.

"You don't work for free."

"It's an autograph."

"It's work." Dora faced me and held out her hand, palm up. "That will be twenty bucks."

Her demand startled me. "What?"

"That's what Buddy charges for an autograph, or did you think you could just take advantage of a crippled, senile, incontinent old man?"

Buddy winced with shame when Dora said "incontinent" and she saw it, too, and that sparked a wicked little gleam in her eyes. It made me want to punch her in the stomach. But instead I reached into the pocket of my slacks, took out my Louis Vuitton wallet, and handed her a crisp twenty dollar bill.

"I'm sorry. I didn't know."

"Now you do." She shoved the bill into her pocket, grabbed Buddy roughly by the forearm, and lifted him to his feet. "Let's go."

She practically dragged Buddy and his walker back to the car. I picked up the cup and pen that he'd left behind on the bench. There was an inscription on the cup. Two words written in light, quivering cursive:

Help me.

While Dora loaded Buddy and his walker into her BMW, I walked casually out to my comfortable and dependable Toyota Camry and got inside. I jotted her license plate number on the cup, started my engine, and waited for her to pull out.

And then I followed her.

———

Dora led me about five miles north to a sun-bleached Canoga Park neighborhood of little low-slung stucco-box homes on a pot-holed street with cracked sidewalks and overgrown trees. The cookie-cutter homes were mass-produced in the 1950s and had ranch-style façades with birdhouses built into the pointed eaves above their garages. I'm sure lots of people have lived in those homes, but not a single bird.

Dora parked in the driveway of the worst-kept home on the street. The front yard was dry, hard dirt. The house's weather-beaten, wooden façade was cracked and peeling and the stucco everywhere else looked like it had been painted with a coat of piss. A black tarp was stretched over part of the roof and a loose corner flapped in the breeze. The windows were barred and the front door was behind an iron-mesh screen. The security precautions struck me as ridiculous, given the condition of the house. What thief would hit that dump?

I parked mid-block, jotted down the address on the coffee cup and watched what happened.

Dora got the walker out of the car, opened the front passenger door for Buddy, then trudged up to the house to unlock the front screen and the door behind it. Buddy wasn't moving fast enough, so she marched back to the BMW, grabbed him with one hand and the walker with the other, and dragged them both into the house. She came out a moment later and slammed the front door behind her. And then she did something unusual. She locked the front door and the screen door from the outside, as if there was nobody home. That's when I realized the bars weren't there to keep anybody out.

They were there to keep Buddy in.

She backed out of the driveway and sped off.

I was right behind her.

Dora drove a few miles west to a 1990s-era, Spanish-Colonial tract home in West Hills that overlooked Valley Circle Boulevard and another tract home community on the opposite ridge. There was a Mercedes, Audi, Porsche or a BMW in every driveway. There must have been a rule in the CC&Rs that required residents to own and display German cars.

She got out of her car and was greeted at the front door of the house by a guy who had to be twenty years younger and two inches shorter than her. He wore a tank-top and gym shorts to show off the muscles he'd built up to compensate for his puny height and, perhaps, other physical shortcomings. He kissed her, slapped her granite ass, and they went inside. He probably went straight to the freezer to put ice on his sore hand to keep it from swelling.

I jotted down their address and drove back to my office.

I own a small three-person accounting and business management firm in Calabasas, in an office building about a block away from the MPTV Home, which is one reason why I can spend so much time stalking the place. Most of my clients are in the entertainment industry in some form or another. We do their taxes, pay their bills, and when they die, we often handle the financial affairs for their estates. I know all about the residuals and retirement benefits provided by the trade unions and guilds. Buddy Dinino had a couple hundred acting credits and was certainly fully vested in his pension plan. He had to be making enough money each month from residuals, his pension and social security to afford a better place to live than the dump in Canoga Park.

Between my contacts at SAG, AFTRA and Actors Equity, and my membership in several background-check websites, it only took me an hour to learn the details of Buddy Dinino's situation.

Dora was the daughter of Buddy's third wife, a former Vegas stripper, who was killed ten years ago in a car accident that left him with a broken hip, broken collar bone, and a perforated kidney. That's when Buddy, who had no children of his own, gave his step-daughter Dora power-of-attorney to handle his affairs.

The home in West Hills and the BMW were both in Buddy's name. All of his residuals and pension benefits went directly to Dora, who controlled his bank accounts and had repeatedly refinanced Buddy's house to withdraw the equity.

The munchkin with muscles was Floyd Dettmer, a self-proclaimed "personal trainer to the stars," who owned the Canoga Park home and was renting it to Buddy for three times the market value. Floyd had been arrested a few years earlier for assaulting a previous girlfriend but the charges were dropped.

Buddy was obviously the couple's ATM machine and he'd keep giving them cash even after he was dead. It was a sweet deal for them, but not so great for Buddy.

Fortunately for him, he had *Pete McShane*.

I prepared and printed out the necessary paperwork, grabbed my notary kit, and drove out to Canoga Park.

COLLECTIBLES

I walked along the side of Floyd's house toward the backyard. The windows were in lousy shape, their wood frames peeling and cracked. The bars could probably be opened from the inside without much effort. But Buddy was in no shape to make the effort, or to climb out, and had nowhere to go even if he could. Dora was legally in charge of his life.

The backyard was all dirt and weeds. There was a single chaise longue, the sun-cracked cushion covered with rat droppings. An oasis.

I could hear voices from a television. The sliding glass door to the family room was open behind iron bars. I walked over and looked inside. Buddy was sitting in an old, vinyl recliner, his walker in front of him, watching *Garage Sale Mysteries* on Hallmark. I felt like I was looking at an animal in a zoo exhibit: Old character actor in his natural habitat.

"Hello, Buddy," I said softly.

He jerked in his seat and twisted around to face me. "Who are you?"

"Your biggest fan. We met this afternoon. I paid twenty dollars for an autographed cup."

Buddy leaned forward, held his hand like a visor over his eyes, and squinted at me. He recognized me now. "You almost gave me a heart attack, though that might've been a blessing. What are you doing here?"

"I read your inscription and I'm ready to help."

Buddy shook his head. "I don't know what I was thinking when I wrote that. Forget it. Go away. There's nothing you can do for me."

"I can free you from Dora and Floyd and give you your life back."

He gripped his walker, and pulled himself up to his feet. "What do you know about them?"

"I know your entire situation."

"And you can get me out of it?"

"I can. I'm a certified public accountant."

Buddy hobbled over to the bars and studied me. "Then you know I can't pay you anything. I don't have any control over my money."

"I don't want your money, Buddy."

"Then what do you want?"

"Pete McShane."

"It was a great show, way ahead of its time."

"That's what I've heard."

"CBS wanted to water it down, make it another fucking *Mannix,* a do-gooder schmuck in a sport-coat, something they could air after *Cannon.* I wouldn't do it. It was like asking me to cut off my balls. So they killed it and I was blacklisted forever as a series lead. But I have no regrets. What did Mike Connors do after *Mannix?* Jack shit, that's what. Couldn't get a decent part. Why? Because eunuchs can't act, though supposedly they can sing pretty good."

"Do you have any episodes?"

"I have them all, even the one we were in middle of shooting when those spineless cowards shut us down. They're in a couple of cardboard boxes in the garage with the rest of my worthless shit."

I tried to maintain my cool and keep the excitement out of my voice. "What format are they in?"

"Sixteen millimeter film and ¾ inch cassettes, not that there's a goddamn machine around you can play them on anymore."

I had one. And a 16 millimeter projector. And the equipment to transfer the episodes to any existing format. I just hoped the film and videos hadn't rotted. It was a gamble I was willing to make.

"Here's the deal, Buddy. I'll get you free of Dora forever. In return, I want you to screen the episodes with me. You have to promise to answer all of my questions and to share every detail you can remember about the experience of making the series."

"Are you writing a book or something?"

"No, I'm just a collector."

He hesitated. "Will I ever get to see the show again?"

"It's your show, Buddy. I'll just be holding it for safekeeping. You can see it as often as you like."

He thought about it for a minute and held his hand out to me between the bars. "Okay, we have a deal."

"I'll need more than a handshake." I opened my briefcase and took out the paperwork for him to sign. "You need to sign these papers."

"What for?"

"To give me your power-of-attorney."

Buddy laughed. "You're wasting your time. The vultures have already picked all the meat from this bag of bones. There's nothing left for you. You chose the wrong old fart to swindle."

He turned his back to me and started to hobble to his recliner.

"I told you, I'm only interested in *Pete McShane*. The power-of-attorney is the first necessary step in setting you free." He gave me the finger. I was going to lose him and the show. "Okay, let's say it is a scam. Look at the shithole you're in, Buddy. Could things really get any worse for you? Isn't it worth the risk just to screw over Dora and shrimp boat?"

Buddy stopped, looked over his shoulder at me, and gave me the same, cocky smile that he'd flashed to E. G. Marshall and Robert Reed fifty years ago in his TV premiere in an episode of *The Defenders*.

"Where do I sign?"

When I want sex, I put on a wedding ring and go to a nice hotel near an airport or office park. I get a room, then go to the bar, order a drink, and check my email. Indifference is the key. I rarely make the first move. I don't have to. I'm a prime catch for traveling business women of a certain age who are interested in a hook-up but aren't comfortable with dating apps. I have photos of some teenage kids and golden retrievers on my phone that I use as bait.

A few hours after Buddy signed the papers, and I notarized and submitted them to SAG, AFTRA, Actors Equity and his bank, I was at the bar at the Burbank Airport Marriott, scrolling through the photos on my phone, sipping a martini and eating the salted nuts. I wanted to celebrate.

A blonde woman in her forties sat two stools over, nursing a glass of white wine, when one of my photos caught her eye.

"Are those your kids?" she asked.

"Yes, Dick and Sally," and our conversation naturally evolved from there, following a predictable script I could have written word-for-word before I got there.

She had kids, too, and she moved to the stool next to mine to show me photos of her two girls. They looked like her, but full of the youth and hope that she no longer possessed. But she'd kept her figure. Her name was Carole and she warmed up to me fast because I listened more than I talked and maintained eye contact. She was in logistics, lived in Louisville, and traveled a lot, helping companies figure out how to get stuff from here to there. Carole was on her second glass of wine when she asked me my occupation.

"I am in the furniture business. In fact, I deal mainly with hotels. You'd be surprised by all the subtle and meaningful ways that hotel furniture is different from what you'd find in your own bedroom."

"Like what?"

"It's hard to explain. It would be easier to show you."

Now she had a decision to make.

Carole took a sip of her wine and thought about me.

I'm clean-cut, have a warm smile, and a vague sadness in my eyes. It suggests that I'm a complex man with some secret pain who needs comforting, which appeals to her mothering instinct. I've also presumably been married for eighteen years, which means I know where to find and operate a clitoris, but I'm probably frustrated and eager for some erotic adventure, which appeals to her desire for a good fuck. Which is all I'm likely to want out of this encounter, too. After all, I have a spouse and kids to get home to, just like she does.

I'm safe.

She turned and gave me a smile. "I'd like that."

———

The sex was warm and satisfying for both of us. At 1 a.m., she gave me a good-bye kiss and went back to her room. I checked out of the hotel a few minutes after that and drove to West Hills. I was limber and totally relaxed.

Thank you, Carole.

COLLECTIBLES

I parked on Valley Circle, put on gloves, slipped on a small backpack, and climbed up one of the concrete swales that checker-boarded the hillside below Dora's house. She didn't have cameras but I was sure that many of her neighbors did.

I scaled her low, wrought-iron fence, and crossed her backyard to the house. She had tropical landscaping, an infinity pool and Jacuzzi, a fire-pit table, and an outdoor barbecue island with a marble countertop and a refrigerator. It must have been a wonderful place to relax and entertain.

The kitchen had a sliding glass door that opened to the backyard. Fortunately for me, Dora had one of those basic alarm system that are triggered when a door or window are opened. No motion detectors, infrared lasers, pressure pads or vicious dogs.

I took a slim-Jim out of my backpack and ran the flat edge slowly along the seam between the sliding glass door and the jam until I felt the slight, magnetic tug from the alarm sensor. I duct-taped the slim-Jim in place so it would remain against the sensor when the sliding glass door was opened. The latches on sliding glass door are simple, usually keyless, and notoriously easy to pop open, which I did with the deft use of a paint spackle tool. It's amazing what you can learn on Google and YouTube.

Once I was in the kitchen, I took a hammer out of my backpack, a bottle of chloroform and a rag. I soaked the rag with chloroform, then I took the rag in one hand and the hammer in the other and walked quietly down the hall to the master bedroom.

The door was ajar. I could hear light snoring and an occasional fart. I peeked inside. Dora and Floyd were both naked in their king-sized bed, the sheets twisted around their waists. He was on his back, snoring. She was on her side, curled in a fetal position, her back to him.

I got onto the bed and straddled Floyd, using my knees to pin down his arms, and I pressed the chloroform-soaked rag against his face.

On TV shows, chloroform instantly knocks a person out. In reality, it takes a few minutes to do the job. Floyd woke up, and started to thrash around a bit, and that disturbed Dora. I let her roll over and get a look at me before I smacked the side of her head with the hammer, breaking her jaw. That put her down again.

Once Floyd was unconscious, I got off of him, wrapped his right hand around the hammer, and repeatedly pounded Dora's head with it.

The human skull isn't a watermelon. It's harder than you think it is. It took a few good whacks before it caved in. It probably would have gone faster if her head was against a hard surface rather than a soft mattress.

I left the hammer in the bed and dragged Floyd to the kitchen. By the way, he was much better endowed than I'd given him credit for.

I draped him over the farmhouse sink, spent a moment admiring the herringbone-tiled backsplash, and took a knife from a cutlery block on the counter. I wrapped his right hand around the handle of the knife, pulled his head back, and slit his throat, careful not to get any blood on myself.

I let his body drop to the marble floor, went out to the backyard, removed the propane tank from under the fire-pit table and brought it back into the kitchen. I turned on every gas jet on the stove, each burner automatically igniting with flame, then I went to the propane tank, opened the valve all the way, gathered my things together and hurried outside.

I closed the sliding glass door, removed the slim-Jim and the duct tape, then dashed across the yard. But as I passed the barbecue, I couldn't resist an added touch. I backtracked, opened the grill hood, turned on all the gas burners to full-blast, and I ran to the hill, practically sliding on my ass down the swale.

I was in my car, driving south on Valley Circle, when the house exploded in two massive, thunderous blasts that felt like an earthquake. It must have looked great, but all I saw was the flash in my rearview mirror.

Oh well, you can't have everything.

Even so, I thought it was a very pleasant night.

The police only took a few days to come to the conclusion that the powerful explosion, which decimated the house, was a "murder-suicide." I helped advance that theory by contacting the police as soon as I heard about the blast on the news.

I told the detectives that earlier the previous day, at the Subway in Woodland Hills, Buddy and I had informed Dora that her power-of-attorney was revoked. We'd also told her that we intended to pursue a criminal investigation of her mishandling of the estate.

Based on the information I provided, and the evidence at the crime scene, the police believed that Dora went home, told Floyd the bad news, and he went into a rage, beating her to death with a hammer. Distraught in the aftermath, and seeing no way out for himself, Floyd opened up the propane tank, fired up the stove, and then slit his own throat.

It was a reasonable theory and there was no evidence to contradict it. Floyd had a history of violently abusing women. The home alarm wasn't deactivated or triggered, nothing suspicious showed up on neighborhood security cameras, and if there had been any detectable trace of chloroform in Floyd's mouth, nose or lungs, it was obliterated when his body was blown apart and burned.

Case closed.

I know what you're thinking. How can he be so cavalier about killing people? Has he done it before?

Yes, of course I have. I'm a serious collector.

I picked up Buddy at the Canoga Park house a few days after the blast. I'd kept him there because I wanted the police to see the squalid conditions he was living in. I figured they'd hate Dora and Floyd for it and they'd have zero inclination to investigate further.

I was right.

The first thing I did when I got to the house was load my trunk with the half-dozen cardboard boxes that contained the lost episodes of *Pete McShane*. Not only did Buddy have the episodes on film and video, he'd also kept the scripts, shooting schedules, and production budgets. As far as I was concerned, those cardboard boxes were treasure chests overflowing with gold.

I helped Buddy into the front seat of my car, stowed his walker in the back, and we drove away.

"I've got no place to live," Buddy said. "My house blew up and Floyd's family is evicting me."

"Don't worry about that. You can stay with me as long as you'd like. I've got a nice room prepared for you with a private bath."

He gave me a sneaky, sideways glance. "Hell of a thing that happened to Dora and Floyd."

I wondered if that was his roundabout way of asking if I'd killed them. I was tempted to answer the implied question, but instead I said: "Yes, it is."

"Almost makes me believe in God."

"Almost? What's holding you back?"

"If there was a God, *Pete McShane* would've been a big hit, I would have moved from TV to movies and had Steve McQueen's life, before he got that basketball-sized tumor in his gut and died on a butcher's block in Mexico trying to get it cut out."

Buddy had a point.

———

I live in a sprawling, one-story ranch house on a large property that's nestled deep in a secluded canyon in the Santa Monica mountains. It's hard to tell from the front just how large the house is. I drove along the crushed-gravel motor court to the front door, where we were met by Guillermo, an illegal immigrant in his fifties from Mexico, who helps me maintain the property. That's not really his name, but that's what I call him because he reminds me so much of Jimmy Kimmel's sidekick. Sometimes, to amuse myself, I also call him Rochester, which is another reference that dates me.

I popped the trunk and waved Guillermo over. "Can you please take these boxes to the projection booth?"

Guillermo nodded and I went to the other side of the car, got out Buddy's walker, and gently helped him up out of his seat.

"Quite a spread you've got here," Buddy said as he got his footing.

"It's my Southfork."

"I did a *Dallas*. I made a pass at Barbara Bel Geddes and Jim Davis slugged me. Damn near took my jaw off."

"Did you make the pass on or off-screen?"

"Both," Buddy said with a grin. "What is it with you and old TV?"

"I don't know, but I'll bet it has a lot to do with my father."

"Always does."

Guillermo started lugging the boxes into the house and we followed him inside. Buddy moved slowly, but that was fine. We weren't in any hurry.

"He used to edit those TV listing magazines that were stuck into the weekend editions of local newspapers," I said. "They had titles like *TV Week*, *TV Times*, that kind of thing."

"I remember. Used to dream of seeing my picture on the cover."

"We had no control over that part of it or you would have been. Anyway, he worked out of this tiny office in Van Nuys. I helped him prepare the programming grids for each issue in each individual market. This was before computers, so it was a real chore. Lots of graph paper and index cards. Every city had a different schedule. I kept track of every show, every air date. I really got into it. But the company he worked for got bought out, he was fired, and that was the end."

"What did he do after that?"

"Drove his car into a tree at seventy-five miles per hour," I said. "I still have every issue we published. I've kept them since I was a kid."

"I'm not surprised."

I led him through the front door into the foyer, which is impressive, not in the sense that's grand, but because it opens out to a big, inviting living room with a view of a pond surrounded by old, well-groomed shade trees. The interior design is Contemporary Rustic Farmhouse. Lots of leather and wood and rugs. It looks like a page out of a Ralph Lauren home-furnishing catalog, minus the hunting trophies, because it is. That's true of the whole house.

"Would you like to see your room?"

"Sure."

I led him down one of the two hallways off the foyer. The original owner of the house had four kids, and the west wing was for them, but I'd renovated and expanded it over the years. I opened the door to the second guest room and beckoned him inside. He navigated his walker through the doorway.

The bed was huge, with a thick comforter and lots of pillows, and a little wooden step ladder to help him get inside. It was very inviting. It even made me want to take a nap. There was a flat screen TV on the wall and a stone fireplace that worked, but was mostly for show. The open door to the bathroom revealed a walk-in shower with a rain-head and a wide, built-in seat with handles on the wall to make it easy to get up and down.

Buddy went to the bedroom window and parted the shade to see what was outside. His room overlooked the colorful flower garden and the little creek that ran through it. Everything was in bloom and the creek had a nice soothing burble as the water rolled over the rocks. Guillermo did good work. When Buddy turned back to me, there was a big smile on his face.

"This is the Ritz compared to how I've been living," Buddy said. "I may never leave."

That was nice of him to say. "Would you like to rest for a bit? Or would you like to see the screening room?"

"Give me the grand tour."

I led him back to the foyer and into the other long hallway, which led to a set of ornate double doors. "This house once belonged to a TV producer who basically ran his studio from here. He built the original screening room at the end of the hall to watch dailies and rough cuts. I thought this would be the perfect place to exhibit my collection."

I swept my hand to indicate the lighted, built-in display cases that lined the paneled walls on either side of us. Buddy's attention had been focused on our destination, the double doors, and he hadn't noticed the walls. Now he did.

He froze and I saw the flash of fear in his eyes.

"Are those...urns?"

COLLECTIBLES

This is always the tricky part.

"Yes, they are." I said it as gently as I could. I didn't want him to have a heart attack. I knew from past experience that it was a real possibility.

Each shelf contained an identical urn, each labeled with a brass plaque inscribed with the name of the lost series, the number of episodes aired or unaired, the year of production, and the name of the deceased. There were forty-two urns in alphabetical order and room for many more.

I pointed to the first one. "This is *Adams of Eagle Lake.* They only made two episodes in 1975 and I have them both."

Buddy pointed at the urn. "And that guy."

"The producer. He never stopped believing in the series." I noticed that Buddy had gone pale. "Don't worry, you're not in any danger and you're not a prisoner. You're free to go any time you'd like. But I'm hoping you'll stay with us."

"As part of your home mausoleum?"

I smiled, in an effort to reassure him, but also because I know how creepy it seemed. I'd been through this forty-two times before. "This is only part of my collection. Let me show you the rest. I think you've worked with some of them."

I cracked open one of the double doors to the screening room, releasing the low hum of conversation from inside, and motioned for him to take a peek. He approached cautiously, leaned on his walker, and looked inside.

The windowless room was inclined toward a huge movie screen and was furnished with twenty-five reclining theater seats, half of which were occupied by elderly men and women, all of them Talent. Writers, directors, actors and editors.

"I did an episode of *The Magician* directed by that guy in the wheelchair. Can't remember his name. I thought he'd died years ago." Buddy turned back to me. "Why are they here?"

I closed the door. "This is where they live now."

He shook his head, confused. I didn't blame him, it was a lot to take in. "I don't understand. What exactly do you collect?"

"I told you, lost TV shows."

Buddy tipped his head toward the theater. "But those aren't shows. Those are people."

"And without those people, The Talent, shows are just meaningless images. It's not enough for me to simply watch the episodes. That's fleeting and superficial. Anybody can have that. I want to have the history and the memories, to know what it felt like to make the show, only to have it broadcast for an instant or never be seen at all. I want to know what it means to be the last person who remembers and cherishes it. When I have all that, then I truly own the show."

"The way I do with *Pete McShane*."

"The way they did with their shows," I said, gesturing to the display cases. "The way I do now that those people are gone. If I don't, who will?"

I thought it was a very compelling argument.

Buddy looked back at urns, at all the lost shows and the people who'd never let go of them. He was free to leave, but the fine print in the irrevocable power-of-attorney that he'd signed said I got to keep him and his assets when he died. Buddy was beginning to understand that now without having to read the contract. But it's always better if they think they are making the decision themselves.

He gave me a little, accepting nod and sighed. "So what happens now?"

"We're all eager to see *Pete McShane*." I held open the door to the screening room for him. "What do you say?"

Buddy smiled and hobbled into the theater, where he was greeted with rousing applause.

Seven months later, I had a new urn in my collection.

Pete McShane
Four and a half episodes. Unaired. 1975
BUDDY DININO

Bar Wall Panda

BY ROB HART

*T*ommy nursed his second whiskey, wishing he didn't have to drink at all. But you can't sit at a place like Rhine and order water. Especially when it was packed. He wished he could be closer to the far wall, but all the high-tops were occupied by rowdy kids celebrating a birthday, their happy-hour pitchers of beer still half-full.

So he settled for a seat at the East Village bar, sizing up the job in the reflection of the mirror. At least he had a good view. He could see the entirety of the drawing—a cartoon-style panda bear drawn in thick black marker on the sheetrock. It was set behind a square piece of clear Plexiglas, with heavy duty screws in each corner. There was a small light installed next to it, casting a yellow glow so you could see it clearly in the dimness of the space.

The drawing itself was roughly eleven by twenty-four inches. Given the location there was most likely a stud behind at least part of it, which meant screws. Tommy hoped none of the screws were behind the ink. If they were behind the bare wall, he could pull them out with a sharp drill bit and patch the holes. If he pulled up any of the ink, that might be a problem.

All told, he wanted to remove it with about six inches of clearance around each side, being sure to preserve the signature. At that size, it wouldn't be too delicate to handle. Not that a piece of drywall is easy to remove and then transport intact. He hoped it wasn't too thin. Three-eighths of an inch would be perfect. Smaller, it would be fragile. Thicker, and it would be heavy and tough to remove.

He had all the tools he needed. A rotary saw to make the cuts, magnets to locate screws and nails. He considered throwing a clear paint of lacquer on it, but the owner may have done that, and even if not, it would take a half-hour to dry and then forty-eight hours to cure.

Tommy glanced around the bar. There were old, beaten cameras in two corners. Easy enough to knock those out. He had been worried about getting in. There was a side door, on a bright street, facing an apartment building. Not ideal. But there was an old smoking patio behind the bar that sat inside an alcove of buildings. No easy way in or out, and while the door was locked, it wasn't alarmed. As long as he could get to the roof, he could make it inside.

After a few nights of watching from Tompkins Square Park, it seemed like the bar crew cleared out most nights around three a.m., unless it was a weekend, when it was closer to five. With the sun set to rise around seven a.m., that meant he couldn't do it on a weekend. Even though this wasn't a high-traffic street, this was still a city that was not fond of sleeping.

He had considered bringing another person in to help, but this seemed manageable. He took a sip of whiskey and walked through it in his head. Starting a little after three, that would be ten minutes to get in (hopefully), five to cut the cameras (if that), ten minutes to lay out his tools and remove the Plexiglas. Ten minutes to remove screws, which usually only takes a few minutes but he would go slow and do it right. That's…thirty-five minutes. He wanted to be out by five a.m., after last call but before the bread trucks.

That was reasonable.

Tommy was considering whether he should bring some heavy-duty cardboard to wrap around the drywall, give it a little added support and protection, when a voice cut through the din.

"Need another one, buddy?"

Tommy looked down at the jumble of melting ice in his glass. And then up at the bartender, a barrel-chested yeti with machine gun arms who seemed annoyed Tommy was taking up prime Saturday night drinking real estate.

Tommy threw a twenty on the bar and said, "Keep the change."

The bartender offered a harsh smirk. "Those were twelve each, my friend. And you're not pretty enough for a buy back on the second round. Maybe the fourth."

Tommy sighed. Dug a ten out and dropped it on the twenty. Now his pocket was empty. He weaved through the crowd, headed for the door, figuring it was a good investment.

After Tommy finished explaining how he would do the job, the man he knew only as Niles—and that probably wasn't even his real name—sat still as a statue, like he was waiting for Tommy to start talking.

Everything about the man looked designer. From his stiff well-tailored jeans, to his mirror-polished boots, to his scrubbed and glowing skin. He looked like he was wearing a hairpiece, though. Tommy was pretty sure it was a hairpiece. That mop of golden blond hair just seemed to sit wrong on his head.

Tommy lingered in the uncomfortable silence, looking around the expanse of the office building where they'd been meeting. It was still under construction, and most of the walls hadn't gone up yet, so he could see from one side to the other, and it was all dust and drywall and painting supplies. Thirty stories up, and there was a brilliant view of the Empire State Building outside the window, nearly blinding in the morning sunlight. He was pretty sure Niles owned the building, or at least the few floors that were under construction, which meant it would be easy enough to pull the permits to find out what his real name was.

But Tommy didn't care about his real name.

He cared about the money.

"So there's virtually no startup cost here," Tommy said, "since I have all the tools. And I'm pretty sure I can do it by myself, so there's no need to bring in another set of hands, and…"

"When?" the man asked.

"When will I do it?" He shrugged. "A week? It's got to be a weeknight. That gives me time to gather a little more intel and do some prep."

"Good," Niles said, getting up and brushing off his still-clean pants, like the act of being there had sullied him.

"We haven't talked money," Tommy said.

Niles nodded. "Twenty-five should cover it."

Tommy did a quick analysis in his head. That bought him a little over a year of mortgage payments, which would get his head above water on a few other things, but it didn't seem like the risk was worth the reward, so he said, "Fifty."

Two and a half years of mortgage payments.

Niles glared at him for a moment before nodding.

"What is this thing to you, anyway?" Tommy asked.

Niles smiled. "I like the piece. I like the artist. I had an intermediary offer to buy it—my name wasn't connected, of course—and the owner of the bar refused to sell. It's the only piece by this artist I can't easily procure, so naturally, I must have it." Niles gave a derisive little laugh. "I wouldn't expect you to understand."

Tommy didn't like the way he said that, like a construction manager couldn't appreciate art. He liked art just fine. He has a reproduction of van Gogh's *Flower Beds in Holland* hanging in his living room. Which, granted, was a poster he bought on the internet and placed inside a $14.99 Ikea frame, but he felt like it classed the place up.

A cartoon panda, though, he couldn't figure. It looked more suited to hang in his daughter Chloe's bedroom.

"Just don't damage it," Niles said, "and do not forget to include the signature in the corner. That's the most important part."

Tommy nodded, a little annoyed, because during his spiel he specifically referenced the signature, confirming that Niles was barely listening, but he didn't feel the need to say anything. He just needed to focus on the job and get it done.

"You sure you don't want me to try and, I don't know, redraw it?" Tommy asked. "Swap it out or something? Otherwise they'll be looking for it."

"It has to be clear the piece has been stolen," the man said. "How else will it be clear I have the original?"

Without saying goodbye, Niles turned and left, disappearing down a darkened hallway. It didn't need to be said; Tommy would wait for a few minutes and leave separately, so they wouldn't be seen together. Plenty of eyes and cameras on the midtown sidewalk.

He wandered the space, giving Niles a head start, being careful where he stepped—the floor was unfinished, and at a few points there were just some flimsy layers of plywood laid down, balanced on the I-beams. He nudged one aside with his boot and found a two-story drop. That should be more clearly marked off. It was a safety hazard, and would probably end with someone getting written up.

Again, he wondered if he was doing the right thing.

The job came to him through a friend. Though, really, "friend" was too strong a word for Ralph.

Ralph was another tradesman Tommy had worked with, who said he had a high risk-high reward gig that Tommy would be perfect for.

Why don't you take it yourself then? Tommy had asked, as the two of them shared a cigarette during their break, outside a teardown in Tribeca.

Needs a steady hand, Ralph said, holding out his own meaty paw, which shook a little, and would continue to shake until he got a drink in him. *Just kick me a finder's fee. Ten percent?*

Damn it. Tommy forgot about that. Okay. Two years of mortgage payments. Still, not bad.

———

Tommy woke from a restless sleep. He stared into the sunlight spilling across his bedroom ceiling. If he woke up on his own that meant Chloe was still asleep. Small mercies. It was always nice to have a few minutes of quiet to himself, before their small Bay Ridge row house was filled with frenetic five-year-old energy.

Two days until the gig. Two days until he'd stop being Tommy Quinn, construction manager, and become Tommy Quinn, art thief.

It'd be funny if the thought didn't make his heart race.

Just this one time. In and out. Buy himself a little breathing room. It wasn't for him. It was for Chloe.

Chloe, who'd be stuck with his sister if he got popped for this and went to jail.

So the trick was to not get popped. He'd laid out his gear in the garage. Gone over the plan so many times he had it memorized. Picked a Tuesday night, when it wouldn't be busy. He even built a display case for the panda—dark wood frame with rabbet joints and a glass front. Maybe Niles wouldn't like it, but woodwork was a good repository for nervous energy.

The tempo of his heart began to pick up, so he vowed to put the job out of his head. It was Sunday, the Lord's mandated day of rest. Even better, it was the day of his people—St. Patrick's Day. Which meant beers and burgers at Uncle John's house on Staten Island. Chloe could run around in the back yard with her cousins, and he could just relax and enjoy the afternoon.

By the time he reached the porch, to pick up his copy of the *Daily News,* he was feeling a little better. More still when Chloe padded out of her room in her pink polka-dot pajamas, bleary-eyed, and asked for butter on cold bread, before running for the living room to put on cartoons.

After Tommy delivered her breakfast, and accepted an "I love you Daddy" in return, he made his coffee and some eggs, then sat down with the paper, flipped it open, and his heart went from zero to sixty in the time it took to get to page three.

Right there was the panda.

He read through the story so fast he couldn't process it; he needed to stop, force himself to slow down, so he could understand it.

Niles never actually explained what the drawing was, and Tommy never bothered to look it up. But apparently, it was drawn by a Japanese street artist named Hiromasa Sato nearly ten years ago. He sketched it on the wall one night after a gallery showing. At the time, Sato was an up-and-comer in the art scene, and the owner of Rhine thought it would be a fun little piece of history.

Since then, Sato had risen in acclaim, and—*American Endpoint,* a take on *American Gothic* that featured the nuclear-blasted silhouettes of the classic farmer couple—just sold for $24.9 million at auction. Which brought newfound attention to the drawing. Rhine's owner refused to speculate on the value or availability, instead chasing a *Daily News* reporter out of the bar, threatening to break her neck for printing the story.

But according to the paper, several experts predicted the doodle, given the age, uniqueness, and location, could be worth at least ten million, possibly more.

Tommy did the math in his head. He was getting less than one percent of that. He wondered how much he should ask for when he heard a buzzing from the kitchen drawer.

As if on cue.

He pushed aside the thick pile of past-due bills and pulled out the burner phone Niles had given him. There were no pleasantries when he flipped open the little plastic brick. Just: "It has to be tonight."

Tommy's chest tightened. "It's Saint Paddy's. Busiest drinking night of the year. No way do they get out of there before five, five-thirty. And even then, the city is going to be full up."

"You saw the paper," Niles said. "Someone else could get there first."

"Yeah, about that." Tommy peeked into the living room, where Chloe was still engrossed in her cartoons, the buttered bread sitting in front of her untouched. "About that. This thing is worth ten mil? And I'm getting fifty K?"

"Maybe you should have done your research," Niles said. "That was the price we agreed to. Are you not a man of your word?"

"Don't hand me that," Tommy said. "You knew the value of this and you knew you were low-balling me. Which is bad enough. But if you want this done tonight, then the price just went up. Hazard pay."

Silence on the other end. So long Tommy wondered if maybe Niles hung up and decided to go with someone else, which frankly at this point, would be a relief. He didn't have much sunk cost into this and...

"Five hundred thousand."

Tommy's knees went momentarily weak. He leaned against the kitchen counter. That was...the rest of the mortgage, plus some. That was Chloe going to a private school, instead of the crumbling public school around the corner.

That was the kind of security he never thought he'd be able to give her after Nellie died.

"Do we have a deal?" Niles asked.

"Yeah," Tommy said, almost on reflex. "We have a deal."

The line went dead. He folded up the phone and placed it back in the drawer, then went to the living room and sat on the couch next to Chloe, who curled into the nook of his hip and tried to explain what was happening on the show, where the cartoon characters were on a treasure hunt or something, but Tommy couldn't follow. His head was somewhere else.

Liz poured herself a nip of whiskey, neat, from the bottle of Jim Beam that she kept stashed in the cupboard. Tommy never touched it himself, but noticed that she'd bought it last week and it was already mostly empty. He didn't love that Liz drank while she was watching Chloe, and he considered saying something, but this was the tenth night now that he'd asked her to stay over.

"How much longer is this job going to go?" Liz asked, a little green shamrock glittering on her cheek. Chloe's handiwork, Tommy suspected.

"Should be done after this," he said, stashing his cell phone behind the toaster. No sense in having a tracking device with him in case things went sideways.

Liz took a sip from the glass as she turned to him. She was already a little tipsy, and annoyed about leaving Uncle John's party early. But there was something else too. Her dark eyes were scanning him, like there were words written on his skin and she was trying to make them out. Tommy knew exactly what those words were; the story of his guilt.

"Tell me again what this is," she said.

"Just an overtime thing," Tommy said. "Building owner wants a job done, has a few guys pulling all-nighters. We don't have the permits, so we have to keep it quiet."

"Why are you lying."

"How do you know I'm lying?"

"I could always tell when you were lying," Liz said, holding up the glass and pointing at him. "Ever since you were a kid I could tell. You don't look me in the eye."

"I'm just tired."

"Hmm." She took another sip. "Be smart, okay?"

"C'mon, you know me."

"Yeah," she said, with a little laugh. "That's why I'm telling you to be smart."

Tommy crossed the kitchen and kissed her on the forehead.

"Thanks," he said.

"Anything for that little girl," Liz said, retreating to the living room. "And you, of course, but mostly the girl."

Yeah, Tommy thought. Anything for her.

A few minutes after five thirty a.m., and finally the yeti was pulling down the roller gate. From his bench on the other side of Tompkins Square Park, Tommy cursed under his breath. He was going to have to move fast.

He'd already stashed his gear on the roof of the building to save time. The street was so crowded he took the risk, slipping into the apartment building down the block alongside some drunken kids. It was a simple matter of taking the stairs to the roof, crossing building over building, and leaving his bag in a dark alcove, and then returning to his spot in the park to wait.

The drunken lunatics, at least, provided him a little cover. The cops were too busy chasing the green-garbed revelers puking and pissing in the street to pay much attention to a man on a bench.

Tommy crossed the park and kept his head down, concentrating on his shoes as he hoofed it back to the apartment building he'd gotten into before. There were no cameras, so it seemed like the safest entry point. He hit a few bells and an angry voice blared out of the speaker before someone too lazy to check buzzed him in. He made quick time to the roof, outside and across, to the apartments that sat atop Rhine, where he pulled on a ski mask and a pair of gloves. There was a fire escape tacked on to the back of the building—useless, since it led down into a concrete box, and probably a remnant from when the building first went up. He had been worried it might be corroded and not hold his weight, but he noticed an ashtray on one landing, some laundry hung out on another, so it seemed people ventured onto it. Still, he went slowly, so as not to rattle anything, or draw the attention of anyone who might still be up.

At the bottom, he found the ladder had been removed—or fell off—and the drop was a little more than he would have liked. He lowered himself down as far as he could safely go and dropped. He landed on the wooden deck amidst empty beer kegs and weather-beaten furniture.

The door was locked with a simple deadbolt, and Tommy made quick work of it. As the metal cylinder slid aside, he took a deep breath, thankful that this was smooth. Glad that he'd put in so much planning. Annoyed at himself for doing it in the first place, but knowing that this one act would set up his daughter for life.

And anyway, it's not like he was hurting anyone.

But as he stepped into a darkened hallway, enveloped by the smell of stale beer, he knew there was a problem, because the first thing he heard was a loud *bang*.

And then another.

His gut told him to go. But he'd come this far, and he wasn't even sure if he could get back up the fire escape, so he crept down the hallway, past the bathrooms, and looked into the bar space, where he saw two men in clown masks. They'd already pulled down the Plexiglas, and one of the men was beating around the panda with a hammer, leaving sloppy holes in the drywall.

"What are you doing?" Tommy blurted, more out of frustration with the carelessness of the job, and then realized his mistake.

The two men turned. The clown masks were hard to distinguish in the darkness, but one man was a little taller than the other. Tall Clown said, "I guess you're here for the drawing too? Beat you to it."

"Don't antagonize the man," Short Clown said. "That's not productive."

"Can it, Billy."

Short Clown hung his head. "Could you not use my real name?"

Tall Clown shrugged and reached back with the mallet, ready to drive it into the wall, and Tommy said, "Will you please stop that? You're going to ruin the piece."

"What are you, like an expert on walls or something?" Tall Clown asked.

"Actually, yes, I am, and you're going to destroy that thing if you're not careful. Have you checked for studs and screws?"

The clowns looked at each other.

"No," Short Clown said.

"Okay, what's your plan for transport?" Tommy asked.

"We have a garbage bag," Tall Clown said.

Tommy sighed, running his hand over the cloth and foam case hanging from his shoulder. It was meant for a circle lighting rig. But it was exactly the size he needed, it was padded, and it had a strap. A last-minute addition to his kit, and even though it meant buying a hundred-dollar light he'd never use just to get the case, it was worth it.

"Okay, first of all," Tommy said, striding over to the wall and pulling a magnet out of his pocket. "You get the cameras?"

"Yeah, of course..."

"Good," he said, running the magnet over the wall, finding two screws that had to be removed, both thankfully behind blank wall and not ink.

"Wait wait wait, you think we're cutting you in on this?" Tall Clown asked. "I said we got here first."

"C'mon Richie, guy seems to know what he's doing, and..."

"Hey, what did you say about names?"

Billy laughed. "Yeah, my bad, I guess."

"Listen, both of you shut up," Tommy said. "I'll make you a deal. Fifty K if you help me with this."

That shut them both up quick. They looked at each other and even though Tommy couldn't see their faces, he could tell they were smiling.

"Great," Tall Clown—Richie—said. "Pay up and let's get to work."

"What do you mean, pay up? I don't have that kind of money."

"So, what, you're work-for-hire?" Billy asked. "Didn't you take something up front? Standard is half."

Tommy was suddenly flushed with embarrassment. "Well, no, I..."

"Jesus, this guy is a shitty crook," Richie said. "Look, you have to understand, why should we believe you're going to make good on this? What are you going to do? Give me your Venmo? That's not how this works."

"Look," Tommy started, "the longer we're in here…"

He paused. There was a sound coming from behind the bar. Groaning? He strode over and found an older, balding man, hands and mouth duct-taped shut, blood blooming from a wound on his skull. He looked up at Tommy with helpless eyes and yelled something through the tape.

"Who the hell is that?" Tommy asked.

"The owner," Billy said. "I guess he was getting the security beefed up after that *Daily News* article? But the company couldn't come out until tomorrow so he was going to sleep in the bar with a bat."

Tommy's chest hurt. He threw up his hands and headed for the back, figuring he'd risk the fire escape.

"I'm out," he said. "Good luck, guys. This is too heavy for me."

A metallic click stopped him mid-stride. He turned and found Richie pointing a gun at his back.

"Nah, you're going to stay," he said. "We don't even have a fence for this. And whatever you're getting, we get half. That's because you seem like a nice guy." Tommy exhaled. He deserved this. And if this was the penance he had to pay, so be it.

"Keep an eye out at the windows," he said.

And he got to work. Pulling the screws carefully to leave the smallest holes possible, then cutting around the piece with a rotary saw. He went slow, making the cuts as even as he could, though he was sure he would have to sand it down to straighten it out once he got it back to the house.

As he worked, his heart rate slowed. This, at least, brought him a little peace, and allowed him to put out of his head the mess he was currently standing in. Two-fifty was still a large portion of his mortgage, and while it would mean no private school for Chloe, at least he could get her a tutor or something.

Once the cuts were made he used the careless holes that Richie had knocked into the wall and pulled down the square, his breath frozen in his chest until it came free intact. He took a moment to admire it. Crazy that this thing was worth so much, but hey, in the eye of the beholder. It was certainly aesthetically pleasing. It reminded him of the characters on the cartoons that Chloe watched, and…

"You done or what?" Richie asked.

Tommy slid the section of drywall into the carrying case and cinched it over his shoulder. "Yeah."

"Good," Richie said. "One last thing."

He reached the gun over the bar, aiming at the owner. Tommy was ready to dive for him when Billy pulled him away.

"He didn't see our faces," Billy said.

"But he knows our names."

"Hey," Billy said, looking over the bar. "You going to remember our names?"

Tommy couldn't see the man's response, but it seemed to placate Billy, who pushed Richie toward the side door. Tommy followed. Billy opened it a crack, looked around, and ducked out. Richie followed, and Tommy went after them. They moved quickly across the street, toward a parked car with no license plates on it. Billy opened the door and waved for Tommy to get in. He climbed in the back, onto the torn-up leather seats, and before he'd even gotten the door closed, Billy had the car started and jumped away from the curb.

They drove a few blocks, toward the Lower East Side, parking on an empty street. Billy got out, and from the sound of it, got to work reattaching the license plates.

"So, when's the drop?" Richie asked.

"This afternoon."

"Great," Richie said. "I know this great little diner uptown. Waitress knows me. We can get some pancakes and some coffee and wait."

"Can't I just call you?"

"No you can't just call me," Richie said, as Billy climbed back in the car, pulling off his clown mask. Richie took this as a sign he should remove his too, and then he slapped Billy on the arm. "Guy says he'll call us."

"Let's go to that diner," Billy said. "What's it called? The one uptown?"

"I got somewhere I need to be," Tommy said, thinking about how Liz needed to leave in the next two hours to get to work.

"Then we're coming with," Richie said.

"No," Tommy said.

Richie turned, and for the first time he got a good look at the man's face. It was dark and angular. The face of a man who meant what he said.

"This isn't exactly a debate," Richie said.

Billy turned. His face was softer, slightly less threatening, but no less serious.

"Yeah man, you have to understand the reality of this, okay? So let's just all play nice, everyone goes home with a fat payday."

Tommy wondered if he would even walk away with half—or his life, at this point. The risk was too high. Chloe had lost one parent. He wasn't going to let her lose another. Not because he'd made such a dumb, dangerous decision.

So he made one more dangerous decision. Hopefully the last one of these he would have to make.

"Okay," he said. "How about this. The drop is in a building that's under construction. We can get inside and wait there. It'll only be a few hours."

Silence from the front.

Then Richie said, "See, that makes sense. You're getting the hang of this."

———

Tommy had been worried about the night watchman, at his little booth at the front of the site, but the man was asleep and they didn't even have to try to sneak past him. They took the elevator to the thirtieth floor, the whole time, Tommy fidgeting, ants marching under his skin. He couldn't believe how calm and collected these men were, talking about where they'd get breakfast after this.

And right after they beat a man bloody.

Tommy had to remind himself of that. That they'd hurt someone who didn't deserve to be hurt. Or maybe he did deserve it, after threatening to break that reporter's neck. Still, Billy and Richie were ready to kill the guy.

He reminded himself of that, to justify what he was going to do.

Through the window across the under-construction floor, the first rays of the morning sun hit the Empire State Building. But the space was still dim. Over his shoulder, Tommy said, "There's an office set up in the back, got some couches and stuff, and I think maybe a coffee maker. It'll at least be comfortable."

"Well if it ain't working, one of us will run out and get some," Richie said. "See? We're not so bad. I'll treat. Won't even come out of your cut."

"I'd like a Danish, too," Billy said.

"How about a box of donuts?" Richie asked.

"A box of donuts and a Danish."

"It's nearly seven in the morning, Billy. Where am I going to find a Danish?"

"Probably any place you can also find donuts."

As Tommy walked, he thought of Chloe, curled up on the couch next to him, watching cartoons as he reminded her to eat her breakfast. The warmth of her little body, and way it felt for her to fit into the grooves of his side.

The way it felt to protect her.

Anything for her.

He made for the plywood planks he'd seen earlier, aiming for the middle, where he knew the I-beam would be. He walked carefully and calmly, holding tight to the bag on his arm in case he lost his footing.

"I'll tell you this much…" Richie started, before there was a cracking and a crash and Tommy felt the boards shift underneath him. He dove forward, toward finished floor, careful to keep the drywall safe, and when he turned back there was just an I-beam and a gaping hole.

He looped around and headed for the exit, but risked a look down into the chasm. Billy and Richie were lying two floors below. They were still, and Tommy wondered if they were alive, but then the pair began to writhe and groan.

"Guy snaked us," Richie said. "Maybe he is a pro."

That was all the confirmation he needed to run and keep running.

"We need to change the location of the drop," Niles said over the phone. "Some kind of accident at the building last night. Can you meet tonight? Twenty-fourth, beneath the High Line?"

Tommy knew he couldn't ask Liz for another night, and no way was he taking Chloe.

"Can't do tonight," he said. "Tomorrow during the day is better."

"Are you kidding?"

"No."

Silence for a moment, then, "How'd it go?"

"All good."

"Okay then," Niles said, and hung up.

Tommy sat in his garage, Liz off to work, Chloe watching her cartoons, and he stared at the panda, now safely set up in the wooden frame. Crazy that this thing could be worth so much money. Not even mortgages—houses. At least twelve in this neighborhood, maybe more depending on the state of the market.

And it was just a panda that some guy drew on a wall ten years ago.

He moved his chair a little closer, examining the swooping lines and the dark ink. The most valuable thing he'd ever held in his hand, but also the most worthless. Because it wasn't like Niles could sell it. He'd have to keep it hidden away for what, ten, twenty years, before he could even try?

But maybe selling it wasn't the point.

Maybe it was just about owning something precious.

Maybe it reminded him of something.

There was a knock at the door, and a soft voice asked, "May I come in, Daddy?"

"Yeah sweetheart," Tommy called out, happy that Chloe was developing good manners. Especially important, given all the tools lying about.

She opened the door, in her green and white turtle pajamas, and he wondered if he should throw a tarp or something over the panda, but then thought, she's five, what is she going to do? See it in the paper and then rat him to the cops?

Instead, she did something worse. She crossed the room, and stood in front of it and let out a long, "Woooooooow. Is this for my room Daddy?"

Tommy sat back. Looked at the panda, then around the garage, at the spare drywall and the black paint markers and pretty much everything else he needed for his original plan, to swap the drawing for a facsimile.

"Yeah kiddo, it is. Can you let me finish it up for you? Why don't you go put on a movie?"

"Okay," she said, before she wrapped her arms around his waist. "You're the best daddy I ever met."

He kissed her on the top of her head and she ambled off, to watch *Toy Story 3* for the millionth time, and Tommy got to work, cutting down a piece of drywall to the right size.

As he did it, his heart calmed, and he even risked a laugh.

Tommy Quinn, art forger.

And yet it wasn't about the money.

It was about something more precious than that.

God Bless America

BY ELAINE KAGAN

Somebody keyed the car!" Joe shouted as he came in the front door, slamming it behind him.

"What?" Connie yelled. She was in the kitchen. The water was running. She was filling the big pot to boil the eggs and you couldn't hear anything when the water was running, which she had told him countless times. "I can't hear you when you're in the hall talking to me and I'm in the kitchen, Joe."

"Goddamn it!" he shouted, throwing his car keys on the dining room table. They skidded across the polished wood like a pinball smashing into her Aunt Eleanor's blue-and-white platter.

"What was that?" she said and exhaled. She carried the pot of water and eggs to the stove, set it on the back burner, wiped her wet hands on the sides of her slacks and pushed her hair back from her face. It was probably 90 degrees already and it wasn't even noon.

"Both cars," he hollered, practically galloping into the kitchen, colliding with her in the doorway. "Jesus Christ, Connie!"

"What?" She gave him a look. "The water was running! What's going on?"

"Some bozo keyed the cars, both cars." He gave the refrigerator door a yank and took out a beer. He popped the tab at the top of the can and drank half of it.

"It's not even noon," she said, stepping in front of him and closing the fridge door. You could hear the soft sound of bottles hitting each other and various china dishes filled with condiments and covered with Saran Wrap that she had shoved into the packed shelves. She still hadn't decided on which coleslaw—the one with the mayonnaise or the one with the vinegar and sugar. Someone didn't like mayonnaise, but she couldn't remember who it was. Joe's Aunt Margaret? She sighed. You had to keep everyone happy. She looked at him. "What do you mean keyed?"

He backed up. "Keyed, you know, with a key!" He chugged the rest of the beer and threw the empty can into the trash.

"What do you mean?"

"For crissakes, Connie, I mean, you take a key and you hold it out in your hand and run it down the side of a car. Hard." He stepped around her, opened the fridge, took out another can of beer and popped the top. "From the goddamn front headlight, along the fender, across the doors and the back until you get to the tail lights and the end of the car!" He took a gulp of beer. "Wah lah!" he said. "Keyed!" He looked at her. "Both cars."

She frowned, pushed at her hair. "Who would do that?"

"I don't know, my Uncle Max, your mother...some Dominican kid who doesn't have anything else to do. I don't know."

She shook her head. "There's no reason to think it's someone from the Dominican Republic."

He looked at her and burst out laughing.

———

The garage was his bone of contention. Or probably their bone of contention, which she had to look up after her girlfriend, Gloria, had pointed it out. *An ongoing argument on a certain topic or issue.* Well, you could say that again.

The boxes. The boxes stacked in the two-car garage where the cars should have been. "Rather than on the street where any fool can get to them," Joe could go on and on.

She could hear him now on the phone in the living room carrying on with the insurance guy about the key business. She still had to boil the eggs. She had slipped little notes detailing what she was going to put inside each bowl or platter so she wouldn't forget except, of course, on the deviled egg plate, which her mother-in-law had given her years ago. You couldn't put anything in that except deviled eggs. She ran her finger around the porcelain ovals.

"What the hell do we need all this stuff for?" Joe had said last week when she'd asked him to get the boxes of decorations for the Fourth of July out from under the boxes of Valentine's Day décor and the boxes of turkey things for Thanksgiving. Through the years she had collected several painted porcelain turkeys of various sizes along with little Pilgrims and Indians. Of course, the whole idea that we had taken the land away from the Indians was a terrible blemish on America and she'd thought about not using the little Pilgrims and Indians on the table last Thanksgiving, but she hated to give them up.

"You gotta get rid of all this crap, Connie," Joe had said, schlepping in the boxes. "If you think I'm going to park my new Tahoe on the street you've got another think coming." He had no idea that she knew the Tahoe he wanted to buy would not fit in the garage. She'd looked it up online and measured.

———

She decided on the coleslaw with the vinegar. She got up from the dining room table, pushed the chair back into place, went into the kitchen and got the red and green cabbages out of the fridge. It's a wonder why no one makes red and green cabbage for Christmas. It would be so festive.

She turned the burner on under the pot of eggs.

———

"You didn't have all this stuff when we got married," he'd said, wiping his face with a dishtowel after he'd carried up two boxes.

"Give me that," she said, reaching for the dishtowel. "Don't you have a handkerchief?"

"Not on me," he said, smiling. "You want to check my pockets?"

"Don't start with me, Joe. I have things to do."

"Uh huh," he said, taking her hand and dancing her around the kitchen.

———

COLLECTIBLES

It began with the first Christmas ornament, which is probably the way it begins in every family. You get married and then you get the first ornament for your first tree together and you put it on the tree, and it has meaning on top of the meaning of Christmas. And then after Christmas you wrap it carefully in tissue and put it in a box in the middle of wads of crumpled newspaper. A small box. The next year there's another ornament and it goes in the box. And before you know it there are two boxes. Even Jewish families, some of whom she knew personally, could have a box of something they put up at Christmas—nothing with Jesus, of course, or the wise men or anything that pertained to His birth—certainly not a crèche—but maybe a Santa or some plastic reindeer in flight across their front lawn. Her friend, Sherilyn Rubin, who was not only Jewish but worked chronicling historical documents in the library at Temple B'Nai Yehuda, told her that every Jewish person, even if they were Orthodox, secretly felt gypped out of Christmas. "After all," she said, "Hanukkah can't hold a candle to Christmas," and then she and Sherilyn had practically fallen over laughing because Hanukkah is all about candles—they light a candle every night until they have the whole candelabra ablaze with candles. Right? A menorah, it's called.

She got her big white bowl out of the cabinet and filled it with chopped cabbage.

And she was sure Jewish people probably felt the same way about their first Hanukkah together as she did about her first Christmas with Joe. Collecting memories was how she felt about the treasures in the boxes. She could look at the first ornament and remember that she had on her new winter coat and it was spitting sleet and Joe was holding her hand. The first ornament was a little French horn—just a little brass colored French horn with a thin red ribbon to hang on a branch. They were in Little Italy walking through slushy snow and he saw it. "Look at that," he said, spying it through the window of a dusty antique shop. "Looks like the real thing," he said. And they bought it. It should have been a drum instead of a French horn since Joe was a drummer, but the first ornament was the little French horn.

The water was boiling; she checked the clock and set the timer on the stove for ten minutes. "No more, no less," she could hear her mother saying.

Her mother, who was possibly clairvoyant or whatever it was when someone knew what you were doing when they weren't even in the same neighborhood, would probably call in ten minutes to tell her to turn off the eggs.

The second Christmas ornament was a little red drum. That was the year they did the tree in red—red bows and red plastic ornaments because the red glass ones were way too expensive, and red beads that they strung in loops on and off the branches. They were in a box she had labeled RED. That was the year she had the miscarriage. Joe was out of town. It wasn't like he was far away—he was only doing a club date in Philadelphia and she was going to go up on the train and then she wasn't. He'd just started playing with Louie Massimino then. He came home from Philly as soon as he heard and then he went right back—it was a five-night holiday gig and there was no way he was going to lose it and she was too broken up to go with him—so there she was by herself on New Year's Eve looking at the tree with the red lights.

She took the vinegar and sugar and oil out of the pantry. They were still in the apartment then; the tiny one-bedroom Joe had in Jackson Heights before they got married. If you walked too fast when you came in the front door you went right out the back. Talk about a lousy Christmas.

Seven minutes on the eggs. She mixed the sweet and sour dressing in a small bowl and tasted it on her finger.

"It might not be worth it to use the insurance," Joe said, striding into the kitchen, "with the deductible." He opened the refrigerator door and stood there looking inside. "Or it might be. I gotta see. Marv says he's got a guy in Newark who can polish out scratches so you'd never know. Says the guy's an artist. I'll believe it when I see it," he said. "I'll get an estimate. What are you making?"

The timer on the stove binged. "Take the eggs off the stove, would you, honey?" she said. "Sweet and sour dressing for the coleslaw."

He didn't move.

"Joe? What are you looking for in the fridge?"

"A cheeseburger," he said. He shut the fridge door, lifted the pot off the stove, moved to the sink, poured off the hot water and took handfuls of ice cubes out of the freezer and dumped them into the pot on top of the eggs. "Wait a minute. You're not making the coleslaw with the mayo dressing?"

"Nope," Connie said, smiling.

"What's so funny?"

She didn't answer.

"What are you doing with these little bitty flags on the toothpicks?"

"I'm putting them next to a bowl of olives. Then people can stab an olive without putting their fingers in the bowl."

"I see," he said, looking at the plastic bag. "Toothpicks adorned with American flags. Who would have thought such a thing existed?"

"Gloria found them. Somewhere in the city."

He shook his head. "The next thing you know they'll bring back crepe paper."

She looked up, her lips slightly open. "They don't make crepe paper anymore?"

"Oh, brother," he said, "I was kidding. Is Gloria coming?"

"Of course, she's coming."

"With that bonehead?"

"He's a perfectly nice man."

"Uh-huh. What time?"

"Four. Everyone's coming at four. You're being very grumpy."

"I am not."

"Yes, you are. Is it because of the cars?"

"Can I have an egg?"

"Absolutely not," she said.

He walked to the sink, took an egg out from under the ice cubes, cracked it and peeled it. He took the saltshaker out of the cabinet.

"Not too much salt, honey," she said.

He sprinkled it with salt and ate it. "I don't know...the cars, the goddamn garbage man..."

"What's the matter with the garbage man?"

"Does he have to throw the cans? What is it? His job to announce the dawn?" He moved behind her, his arms encircling her waist. "You want to take a nap with me?"

Connie laughed. "You must be kidding."

"If you change your mind, you know where to find me," Joe said and walked out of the kitchen.

———————

They bought ornaments for the baby's first Christmas. They named her Catherine but Joe said she looked like a sax player he'd worked with in Toronto named Ching so he'd always called her Ching. The whole first year it made Connie crazy.

The Halloween boxes began when they bought the house. Catherine was five and Tony was three. The four of them had been stuffed into Joe's tiny apartment that whole time. Stepping around drums and sticks and cymbals and snares. Tripping on toy trucks and Barbies. And then there was the time the baby only wanted the cowbell from Joe's drums. "Bell, bell, bell," he would scream. Stepping around the highchair and the stroller and the changing table, the two of them sleeping on a pullout sofa-bed with the kids stuffed into the one bedroom with a crib for Tony and a cot for Catherine— Joe called it a nun's bed. "You can't even turn over on this," he said when he was bolting it together. And they saved and scrimped and did what young couples do and bought this house and Connie thought it was a mansion. Twenty-three years ago.

She looked around her kitchen—some of the cabinets needed paint and especially the stain on the ceiling, which reappeared approximately six months after Joe painted it—every time—because the shower above the kitchen still leaked. How many times could you have that fixed? It was a brick house in East Elmhurst, which was a pretty classy neighborhood to her then. A brick with three floors—if you counted the basement which no one did—and a porch and three spacious bedrooms—well, two were nearly spacious—a front yard and back, and a two-car garage. A mansion. It didn't matter that the house was the mirror image of the house next door and every other house on the block. Whoever built up East Elmhurst had built the same house over and over, block after block. It didn't matter to Connie.

Catherine wanted to be a mummy that Halloween. The first Halloween they had the house. She was five. And she was stubborn. Connie's mother called her *Miss Stubb-Bore-Onn.* "A mummy? What's the matter with her?" her mother said. From the time she was two Catherine never wanted to be anything pretty like a princess or a ballerina or any costume that had to do with tulle. Even when she was older her choices were crazy to Connie. Like the year she was twelve. "But Ophelia is so cool, Mom. The whole time she's drowning she sings! Can you imagine?" Her costume that year was at least pretty because women in Hamlet's time wore gowns, so Connie had cut up one of her old silky nightgowns and sewed on pieces of faded ribbon. The part that got to Connie was that Catherine not only wanted to look dead; chalk pale face—she had to take the train into the city to find that white powder the geishas wore—and charcoal hollows under her eyes, etc., but she wanted Connie to come up with something that looked like seaweed that was wrapped around her throat and choked her when she fell into the river. "Wouldn't you rather be Ophelia before she drowned?" Connie asked, and Catherine, giving Connie one of those eleven-year-old eye-rolls, said, "Where's the drama in that, Mom?" and left the room, the nightgown dragging behind her.

The year they bought the house Tony wanted to be a fireman. That was easy—go to the store and buy a cheapo fireman costume for a three-year-old, including the red hat. That was in a box. Unfortunately, the mummy costume—which was strips of white sheets that Connie had cut and wound and partially sewed onto Catherine—had disintegrated.

She carefully peeled the eggs under a soft stream of water and cut them in halves lengthwise, scooping out the yellows.

It was Joe who was all about Halloween that year. "We'll make it haunted." "What?"

"The house. We'll make it haunted. You know. Cobwebs and skeletons and stuff. Scare the crap out of the kids in the neighborhood. It'll be great."

He carved pumpkins with mean faces and even got a tape made with witches cackling. They didn't exactly sound like witches—Connie knew it was the guys who played with Joe. You could definitely tell one of the witches howling was Louie Massimino. And, who had witches cackling accompanied by a piano, bass and drums? Catherine loved it. Tony, on the other hand, was a mess. "It's okay, son," Joe said, "it's not real. See?" he said, holding Tony up to look face-to-face at the skeleton. Tony let out a shriek you could hear over the bridge.

"You've lost your mind, Joe," Connie said. The skeleton was in a box.

She mashed the yellows with mayo, dry mustard and a little white wine vinegar, salt and pepper. Gloria's secret was a dollop of sweet pickle relish, she'd said, but Connie was sure that wouldn't go over with Joe. "What the hell is this?" he'd said, the time she'd tried a little relish in a tuna salad. "Pickles? No one puts pickles in tuna. Look at this, Ching," he'd said to Catherine, pointing out a speck of pickle. "Your mother's gone berserk."

She spooned the yolk mixture back into the white halves, taking care not to get any stray yellow on the whites. She fashioned the yellow into little mounds, placed each egg into the ovals in the porcelain dish, sprinkled them with paprika, covered the dish with Saran and carefully slid it on top of several other things in the refrigerator.

Her dad had bought her the big blow-up leprechaun that they put on the front porch for St. Patrick's Day. "Looks just like him," Joe said, which Catherine thought was hysterical. "It does, it does, it looks like Grampa," she whooped, running around the porch. "Where's Grampa?" Tony said.

She walked through the dining room and studied the platters and bowls and the slips of paper determining what would go where. She had to go set the table. It was probably a scorcher outside. "It'll cool off by four, kid, and by five they'll all be drunk and won't give a hoot. You worry about it every year," Joe said, giving her butt a little pat. "Stop worrying." You could hear him snoring upstairs. Like a faraway lawn mower. She pulled out a dining room chair and sat down. *Take a load off, Fanny,* Connie thought and smiled.

And what about all the Valentines? How could you not save them? Joe went out of his way every year to find her the most mushy corny large Valentine with long poems inside that would make them both laugh. "Did you see the part about your eyes?" he would say, looking at her. "I mean, I could have written that—right?" She loved them. She set them on the hutch in the dining room, opened like two-sided picture frames, where they stayed until probably the end of February. And the ones from the kids. Both of her children, little heads bent, sitting at the dining room table, cutting and pasting and the damn sparkles that you couldn't get out of the rug until probably summer, and more red marker on Tony's face than on the hearts he'd cut out of construction paper. "That's not a heart," Catherine taunting him. "Can it, Ching," Joe said, "be nice to your brother." His hearts did look more like clouds than hearts. What was she supposed to do with all those Valentines? Pitch them?

She wasn't sure what other mothers did—she'd never asked. She was sure her mother had dumped the Valentines she'd made. She hadn't even kept the little animal statues Connie had made in art. Not even the giraffe.

She picked up the slip that said apple pie and the slip that said cherry pie and switched them. Thank you, Jesus, that she wasn't the one who was baking today. Even with the air conditioning you didn't want to turn on the oven, and Sherilyn was really good with pie. Her crust was perfect. Connie was never a baker. She gave that up a long time ago. She baked a cake for Joe the first year they were married. A disaster. Not only did it not want to come out of the pan, but she had tried to fix it with icing. Like you fix a crack in the wall with Spackle. Don't ask.

She ticked off the things she still had to do. You couldn't make hamburgers and hot dogs until it was time to eat them. The beans were in the big pot. She'd already arranged slices of tomatoes and pickles and cheese on a plate. "Maybe we should make chicken this year," she'd said to Joe. "You know, something different." He gave her such a look. "You don't have chicken on the Fourth of July, kid, that's like sacrilegious."

Her eyes drifted up and across the wall—framed photographs through the years. Taken by the same photographer. Looking in the same direction. The Queens Photo special. Framed photographs of the four of them. Framed photographs of the three of them. Connie exhaled.

"We can't take a photograph without him!" Catherine was screaming in the back seat of the car, sobbing and screaming. "I'm not doing it! I'm not, I'm not! Daddy, tell her." She had already been yelling at Connie—*she wasn't going to get dressed, she wasn't going with them, she wasn't going to sit still, she wasn't going to have her picture taken!* Connie looked straight ahead. Joe's fingers clenched on the steering wheel. "We still exist, Ching," he said softly to his daughter. "We're still here, kiddo. Tony isn't here, but we are." Joe's eyes intent on Catherine's in the rearview mirror. Connie put her hand on his knee. She didn't look at him. If she looked at him, she might have to throw herself out of the car.

And what about that box? The box with Tony's soldiers that she couldn't part with—after you give away the clothes and shoes to the church and change the drapes and bedspread from a boy's room navy plaid to a guest room's flowered comforter? What do you do with the little metal soldiers that he'd carefully painted? With special metallic enamel paint and special brushes. And all the research. The colors of the uniforms, the hats, the feathers. He loved that. "You see this guy, Mom? This guy was Michel Ney, one of Napoleon's eighteen original generals and they called him *Le Rougeaud* because he had red hair and was red-faced. *Ruddy*-faced they called it. Is that cool, Mom? *Le Rougeaud* is French."

"*Oui,*" Connie said.

"Ha ha ha. Good one."

"It's very cool, honey."

"I need a light, Mom. You know? Like miners wear?" he'd asked, his head lifted but his eyes focused on the tiny soldier he was painting. "Like a helmet with a light in the front? You know. Can we get one?" The backs of his sneakers banging against the chair legs.

Connie's eyes moved from photograph to photograph.

He was a regular boy.

He didn't want to brush his teeth. He shot baskets in the back yard. He thought most green vegetables were poison. Was cucumber a vegetable? He had lots of friends. He told jokes. He said he was going to grow up and be a comic and study with Billy Crystal.

"Oh sure. How would you find Billy Crystal and why would he talk to you?" Catherine, always with a tone. "You're such a jerk, Tony."

"That's enough, Catherine," Connie said.

"Well really, Mom, he's going to *find Billy Crystal?!!*"

A regular boy.

With big feet. And little shoulders.

"Hey, Dad, my heart did this really funny thing."

She was squeezing oranges at the kitchen sink. Trying to catch the seeds.

Joe turned a page of the Daily News, took a swig of his coffee. "What do you mean? What did it do?"

"I don't know; it like skipped a beat."

"You mean like a rhumba?" Joe said, smiling. "Come here, kid." He put down the paper and held out his arms.

Tony didn't make it across the kitchen floor.

———

She was in the ladies' room at St. Gabriel's when she'd heard them talking—right after the funeral mass—two women who'd come out of their stalls and were washing their hands and one said, "Well, at least it was fast, you know, they didn't have to watch him wither." Connie put her hand over her mouth. You could hear the rip of a paper towel out of the box on the wall. "I never heard of a child having a heart attack."

"Well, it happens, Mary," the other woman said. "You never know. You have to be grateful for every minute. Hand me a towel, would you?"

Connie couldn't believe the woman had said *wither*. Somehow it was wildly funny to her. But, of course, that year she was mostly hysterical. Laughing, crying, or both at once. Like a pressure gauge going off. Like a blow-out on a tire.

———

She moved her eyes off the photographs, studied her hands. Her diamond needed cleaning. Was that egg? She could hear her father say: *Okay, missy, you better get on it. Enough with the dilly-dallying.* Connie stood up, slid the dining room chair back in place, pushed her hair behind her ears and headed outside.

Well, it was hot all right. Boy oh boy. She ran her hands across her cheeks. She looked across the yard. There was maybe a tiny breeze if you watched the leaves on the oak and there would be shade later where Joe had set up the big metal table. Her cell phone rang. It was in the pocket of her slacks and she'd forgotten she'd put it there and she nearly fell down the porch steps when it rang. "For crissakes," she said, pulling it out of her pocket, "Hello?"

"Hi, Mom," Catherine said.

"Oh, hi, sweetie. How are you?"

"Good, we're good. So, did you already do *everything?* Did you set the table two days ago? Are the drinks in the big bucket of ice?" Catherine had always been intent on teasing Connie about preparation. "Is Daddy taking a nap?"

"Yes. I didn't set the table yet."

"What? Are you all right? Do you have a fever?"

"Ha ha ha."

"Did you make the mayo coleslaw or the sweet and sour?"

Connie sat down on a porch step, slipped off her Keds. "Sweet and sour."

"Daddy likes the one with the mayo."

"I know."

"It's raining here. Raining in Southern California. On the Fourth of July!"

"Oh, that's a shame. What are you taking to Mary Lou's? Is she moving her barbecue inside?"

"I don't know. I'm taking the coleslaw with the mayo. I don't know if we'll even go. Stephen has a sore throat. So, I said, honey, if you have a sore throat we shouldn't go, and he says it's only a sore throat. And I said, well, why did you tell me if you didn't want me to react? He's so blasé about medical things."

"Probably because he's a doctor."

"Right. If it isn't about cancer, Stephen is not interested. I should have married a horn player."

Connie laughed.

"Well, I wish we were there."

"It's okay. I wouldn't want to get a sore throat."

"Ha ha. So, okay, I'll call you tomorrow for the gossip. Kiss Daddy."

"Okay."

"Bye, Mom."

COLLECTIBLES

Connie put her shoes on, picked up the box of Fourth of July stuff and moved to the big table. She took the lid off the box, reached in for the red-white-and-blue tablecloth and napkins and was face to face with the Christmas angel for the top of the tree.

She heard the toilet flush as she moved through the house. "Joe!" she yelled at the bottom of the stairs.

"Connie!" he yelled back.

"Very funny. You brought in the wrong box."

"What?" He was doing a semi-gallop down the stairs.

"Be careful. You'll fall."

"I haven't fallen since I was six years old. And that was the bike's fault."

"I don't see why you can't hold onto the banister."

"Oh, brother."

He followed her outside and into the alley to the garage. "What's going on?"

"I need the tablecloth. You brought up the wrong box."

"Am I allowed to wear shorts to this gala?"

"Which shorts?"

"I don't know, the beige ones."

"You mean khaki?"

"What's the difference between beige and khaki?"

They raised the garage door together. They'd never put in an electric garage door opener. It was another bone of contention. Connie said it was because *she* was the garage door opener and Joe said right; he was going to attach a remote to her cute butt.

And they pulled up the door. And they stood there.

Connie's hand flew to her chest. "Jesus Mary…"

"Holy shit," Joe said. He took a few steps forward and stopped. With arms raised, hands outstretched and mouth open, he turned in a circle like the ballerina in a children's jewelry box, staring at his empty garage.

The cops arrived right before Connie's mother who had driven Connie's Aunt Margaret and Margaret's neighbor lady because she didn't have anywhere to go on the Fourth of July because *her people were all dead*. That was how Connie's mother had wrangled the invitation. Aunt Margaret was cradling her famous lemon pie with the graham cracker crust and the neighbor lady was clutching a dusty bottle of some sweet liquor that she'd probably had in her kitchen since 1942. Sherilyn and her husband, Barry, were right behind them carrying the cherry pie and the apple. Barry had a can of whipped cream sticking out of each of his front pockets. Gloria and her new bonehead boyfriend, whose name was Bob, were right behind them. Bonehead Bob, who appeared to be in excellent shape, was carrying a case of Heinekens and Gloria had a bottle of Chianti in each hand.

They came right in; the front door was open. Connie and Joe were on the couch in the living room. Officer Lee and Officer Williams were in the La-Z-Boy chairs across from them.

"There's a police car in front of your house!" Connie's mother hollered, her hand on Aunt Margaret's arm, practically shoving her into the house. "Oh, dear," Margaret said, clutching her pie. "Hello, everyone," the neighbor lady said, practically twinkling. Both police officers stood.

"Ma'am," Officer Lee said to Connie's mother.

Officer Williams nodded at the people following her mother through the front door. He didn't say anything, and Connie thought, well, what could he say: Happy Fourth of July? She folded the wet Kleenexes in her hands.

"Hey," Joe said to all of them, "we have a little predicament here. Maybe you guys could all go in the back? Barry, maybe you could start the barbecue?"

"Sure, Joe."

"What's going on?" Connie's mother said.

"We'll take care of everything," Gloria said, giving Connie a nod and getting a grip on Connie's mother.

"Not to worry," Sherilyn said and Bonehead Bob gave a little positive gesture, kind of lifting the case of beer.

COLLECTIBLES

It was like a parade, Connie thought as they filed through.

"Sit down, guys," Joe said to the cops.

Officer Lee cleared his throat as he sat. He looked at her. "So, Mr. Caccavelli, as we were saying, it's a crime trend in the neighborhood. You're the fourth house…well, actually the fourth garage that's had a burglary."

"Oh my," Connie said. "Four robberies?"

Officer Williams leaned forward. "It's actually a burglary, ma'am. A residential structural burglary. A robbery is when someone tries to take your property by force or fear."

"Oh my goodness," Connie said.

Officer Lee nodded.

"Yes, ma'am," Officer Williams said. "They got a Tabriz Persian rug worth like seven grand on 94th Street, and a Ducati Monster 1200, worth more than twenty-two thousand, maybe six blocks from here."

"You're kidding," Joe said.

"No, sir."

"A Ducati?" Connie said.

"It's a motorcycle, ma'am."

"Twenty-two thousand," Joe said.

"Yes, sir. Customized."

Connie shook her head.

Officer Lee smiled. "So, Mrs. Caccavelli, do you have any idea what your boxes were worth? I mean, considering what was inside the boxes? Their value?"

Well, how could you explain that? She opened her mouth and closed it.

"Nothing was insured?" Officer Williams asked.

"No," Joe said.

"No receipts? Nothing with a serial number? That someone could pawn?"

Connie shook her head, swallowed what was probably a sob.

Joe pulled her closer to him; he had his arm around her. "It was just…" he said and stopped, "you know…things…"

"That are irreplaceable," she said softly, tears moving down her face, "but not worth much. Does that make sense?" She looked at Officer Lee. He was clearly Asian. Maybe Japanese, maybe Korean. She didn't know. She ran the

Kleenexes across her cheeks. "Officer Lee, does your mother keep things? I don't know what holidays you celebrate but does she keep things that she takes out...or maybe the drawings you made when you were little? Or the bear you slept with?"

"Yes, ma'am," he said. He blinked. "It was a lion."

"I didn't mean…"

"Of course not," he said, looking at her.

Nobody spoke for maybe a half a minute.

"Well, that's what we had," Connie said, her voice trailing off.

"I was born in Brooklyn, ma'am," Officer Lee finally said.

Joe smiled. "Well, there you go."

"I'm from Jersey," Officer Williams said, though no one had asked him. "Newark."

"Newark," Connie repeated.

Officer Williams sat back a little in the La-Z-Boy chair and it snapped back further, and the footrest zipped up, catching his big black boots and raising his legs out in front of him. His hat tilted over his forehead and he quickly pushed it back in place. "I'll be darned," Officer Williams said, giving a little laugh and struggling to get his legs back down.

"I was supposed to get that fixed," Joe said. "Sorry." Joe extended his hand to the big black cop, pulling him forward in the chair, the footrest lowering.

Officer Williams cleared his throat, adjusted his hat, and set his boots on the rug firmly in front of him. "So, Mr. Caccavelli, did you hear anything?"

"No," Joe said, frowning. "You mean last night? No. Just the garbage truck this morning—the guy barrels up the alley and throws the cans. I mean, *throws* them. He must have wanted to be a ball player."

"Mr. Caccavelli, it's the Fourth of July," Officer Lee said.

"Right?"

"There's no garbage pick-up on holidays."

It took a minute. "Oh, dear," Connie said, her eyes wide.

Joe shook his head. "Well, I'll be damned."

Officer Lee nodded. "So, you know, we have to wait for the detectives to get here to make a report, see if there are prints and everything."

Nobody moved.

"Oh, don't be silly," Connie said, wiping her nose. She stuffed the wet Kleenexes into her pocket and stood up. "Everything is probably over the border by now," she said, giving a little laugh, "you know, like in the movies." She took a breath, gave the two officers a long look. "Nobody is ever going to find those things. Really. You shouldn't waste your time." She lifted her hands and shrugged. "We just have to let it go." She raised her shoulders. "And think how upset the robbers must be. If this was a movie you would see them, right? Taking the lids off the boxes. Hysterical!" She smiled at Joe. "What do you think they did when they saw the skeleton?" She turned to the police officers. "Gentlemen, if you would excuse me," Connie said, pushing at the wave in her hair and moving toward the kitchen. "I have things to do."

The three men sat there a minute.

Joe shook his head. "Well. Isn't she something?"

Officer Williams struggled out of the chair. The three of them stood facing each other. "We'll be out front, sir," Officer Williams said as he and Officer Lee turned to the front door.

"Wait a minute, guys," Joe said. "Why don't you come out back and have a burger?"

"Well, that would be good," Officer Williams said.

"Yeah, we've only had coffee."

Williams gave Lee a look. "One of us had a donut."

Joe laughed. He took the lead as the men followed him through the dining room and into the kitchen, batons clanking, boots hitting the linoleum.

Connie was moving wrapped dishes out of the refrigerator and on to a tray.

"The officers are going to have a burger."

"Oh, that's good," she said.

"You know, Mr. Caccavelli," Officer Williams said, "I saw you once. Well, saw you and heard you."

Joe turned. "You did?"

"Yeah, at Small's." The three men stopped in the middle of the kitchen.

"Small's in the city," Connie said.

"Yes, ma'am. Must have been in the nineties." He shook his head. "Hell of a jam. Probably two, three in the morning. You played, Jimmy Betts played. Then you played again. Everybody who'd done a show uptown…"

"Ended up at Small's," Joe said, grinning. "Yeah, man, well those were the days."

"You play a mean set of drums, sir."

Joe shrugged and smiled. "Thank you very much. You guys can't have a beer, I guess."

"No, sir," Officer Williams said, laughing.

"So, Mr. Caccavelli," Officer Lee said, leaning against the kitchen counter, "you're gonna put your cars in the garage from now on, huh?"

"Oh, yeah," Joe said, "I'm getting a new Tahoe."

"Good car," Officer Williams said, nodding.

Officer Lee looked at Joe intently. "You know, Mr. Caccavelli, you better measure—I don't think a Tahoe is gonna fit in your garage."

"I was going to tell him that," Connie said, smiling.

Joe looked at her.

"Take these outside, will you, honey?" she said, and handed him the big pot of beans.

...from Otto Penzler's Mysterious Obsession:

MÉMOIRES DE VIDOCQ
FRANCOISE-EUGENE VIDOCQ

*F*rancoise-Eugene Vidocq (1775–1857) was an extraordinary figure who had equally active careers as a criminal and as a policeman. His adventures as a soldier were well-documented but, when it became clear that some of those exploits were too dubious to be countenanced by his superiors, he left his military career to become a full-time criminal. He does not appear to have been very good at it because he was imprisoned several times and spent many years behind bars.

In 1809, he offered his services to Napoleon as a spy and was soon rewarded with a position as the first chief of the Sûreté—the world's first official police department. The department was composed mainly of former members of Vidocq's criminal cohorts and other ex-convicts who engaged in highly dubious practices. When their activities became a little too suspect, Vidocq was forced to resign. He began a private detective agency in 1832 but his methods continued to be questionable, so the police harassed him to the point that his business was ruined. He died impoverished and forgotten.

He did manage to produce a memoir, though the imaginative Vidocq did not feel compelled to remain strictly factual. Many of the criminal exploits were exaggerated and his brilliance as a detective probably did not exist at all, though his ghostwriter did his best to make the wild stories as credible as possible.

The full title of the book, issued in four volumes between 1828 and 1829, is *Mémoires de Vidocq, chef de la Police de la Sûreté jusqu'en 1827, aujourd'hui propriétaire et fabricant de papiers à Saint-Mandé* (*Mémoirs of Vidocq, principle agent of the French police until 1827: and now proprietor of the paper manufactory at St. Mandé*) and is of such historical (if not literary) significance that it was selected for the Haycraft-Queen Definitive Library of Detective-Crime-Mystery Fiction.

Perhaps surprisingly, it is not a dramatically rare book. The first three volumes had been signed by Vidocq and it is likely that the memoir was preserved for nearly two centuries because of the importance of the author. Most books in France, as is still common to the present day, were issued in paper wrappers, but these volumes were produced in elaborately decorated boards. The fact that it was issued in four separate volumes with the author's signatures and the much costlier boards made it too expensive for ordinary readers to buy, so the sets were rebound in leather exclusively for the libraries of the wealthy, thus more likely to survive than other books of the era.

Note that I mention the rebinding of books into leather bindings, which was the de rigueur practice of the time. There is, however, one copy known that survived the bookbinder's handiwork. It came from the home of an aristocratic family that had a magnificent and enormous library, broken up and sold about a decade ago. Books had been bought for generations, accessioned with a small library label at the base of the spine, and placed on the shelves exactly as they had been produced.

One afternoon I received a phone call from Peter Stern, my colleague and friend of more than four decades. A life-long Bostonian, he is as low key as anyone I've ever known, displaying a paroxysm of uncontrolled joy with a small smile, and enthusiasm for a book of singular rarity by admitting that it is "nice." He had called to say he had a book that I ought to buy. Since he had done this so unrelentingly frequently through the years, perhaps as often as three times, he had my full attention.

He had acquired Vidocq's *Mémoires* in the original boards in perfectly new condition, aside from an armorial bookplate and a label on the spine. He quoted his price and it broke my heart to decline the offer because it was well out of price range. He insisted that I take it and suggested a payment plan that went far enough into the future that I pulled the trigger and, of course, never regretted it.

It had been common for Peter and me to pile into a car and go book scouting together. We would pick a section of the country and spend a week to ten days visiting every bookshop or dealer who sold books from his home and buying what we could for our customers.

On one of these occasions, Peter was driving down from Boston to pick me up in New York. When he walked into my office, he handed me a handsome check. I asked what it was for, knowing that he didn't owe me any money. He said he had stopped along the way and bought a good collection of John Dickson Carr first editions. He made another stop further along the drive and sold them. The check was my half of the profit. But, I protested, I had no involvement in either transaction, neither buying nor selling them. No, he agreed, but his position was that our scouting trip began when he started to head down to meet me. If he hadn't sold them, he assured me, he would have asked me to pay for half the books.

This little episode never leaves the front of my mind when dealing with him (and we have bought and sold a lot of books to each other through the years) and resonated powerfully when he insisted that I buy Vidocq's memoir. I wouldn't have bought it if he hadn't twisted my arm and, I recognize, I'd have had regrets for the rest of life. This remarkably handsome book has been one of the select titles that I always pulled off the shelf to show to the bibliophiles who visited my library.

Resonator

BY KASEY LANSDALE

So what were you in for?" Cathy Day asked.

I struggled to wrap my claw fingers around the neck of my rented banjo into a dreaded bar chord and said, "Helping a friend."

"Sounds like you need better friends."

"Can't I just use a capo? Mr. Spencer always lets me—"

"Do I look like Mr. Spencer?"

I debated on whether or not to answer. A few weeks back my usual teacher, Mr. Spencer, had gotten sick. Some new flu was going around and let's just say he was having some gastric issues. I didn't want to know that, but that didn't stop him from telling me when he called earlier that day to let me know I would have a substitute teacher by the name of Cathy Day for the foreseeable future.

That was fine by me. Could be a three-toed sloth for all I cared. I just had to participate, get my gold star, and turn it into my anger management counselor as part of the judge's mandate to find an outlet where I might channel some of my pent-up rage. My probation officer, who had a familiarity with my family, had once suggested music lessons. Said just because I was born into the zoo didn't mean I had to act like one of the animals.

Anger management was pretty much like it was in all the movies. Sitting around in a circle, sharing our stories. I was the only woman there, which seemed to be a personal affront to all the men, but Jerry most of all. To be fair, it was less about my being a woman in the group, and more about my just being a woman.

Jerry had been accused and convicted of causing bodily injury to a family member. Two weeks after that trial, the bodies of his in-laws were discovered on a routine welfare check when a neighbor called about a foul smell coming from the house next door.

They found the mother-in-law rotting in a bedroom closet and the father-in-law propped up in the bed like he was watching television. They'd been dead for several weeks. They couldn't prove it was Jerry, but rumor said there was insurance money involved. Jerry hadn't helped his case when he'd shown up to court in a brand new, bright red Mustang.

Anyway, I'd really thought this time I could clean up my act. Maybe become a traveling musician. Rumor was that sort of thing ran in the family. I'd heard from my cousin I was staying with that my mother had toured with the Rolling Stones as a back-up singer in the eighties. I couldn't be sure, as I didn't really remember her.

What I did know was there'd always been something complex and mysterious between me and music. Each note was like an echo of a darker past. A memory trying to escape the depths of my brain since before Thorazine.

I was about to ask Cathy Day another question, anything to avoid that bar chord, but she cut me off.

"Listen, stay mediocre if you want to. But if you don't try, then I won't fill out your paper saying you did. Now stop talking and play."

We worked our way through the tune, the banjo calling out like a dying bird until Cathy Day was satisfied by my efforts.

"Now that was all right. Try again."

I watched her watching me. Then she came around behind me, placed her hands on my shoulders like a boxing coach in the ring.

"Again," she said.

I tried to visualize the chords like she'd told me. I took a breath and moved my hands. My fingers slid into place with ease and the sounds that came out of that banjo were unlike any I'd made before. Slow and soothing at first, then they picked up speed. Now I was moving my hands faster than I ever thought they'd go. The notes rumbled, tumbled, and drifted out of that instrument like an eagle in flight.

I felt a jolt of energy burst through me and my breath caught. The rims of my eyelids burned and from out of nowhere I felt the warmth of tears push back against them. Now the sounds had turned guttural, piercing. The veins in my neck jutted out against the thin skin of my throat. I stopped moving my hands, jerked them back from the banjo. It tumbled to the floor with a loud clang.

"Why'd you stop?" Cathy Day asked. She took her hands off my shoulders, scooped up the banjo and walked around to face me.

"I think I'm done," I said.

Cathy Day studied me a moment with her dark eyes. I could tell she wanted to say something, but she just nodded her acceptance. I wasn't sure what had just happened. Cathy Day had tapped into a side of me I didn't like.

I grabbed the banjo from her, put it back in the case, and exited the rehearsal room. I went hurriedly to the counter where a small man sat behind a cash register. He opened the case and examined the instrument, looked from it back to me, and once he decided things were okay, rang up the charge for the rental.

Cathy Day stood in the doorframe at a distance. I could feel her watching me. I paid the money and left in a hurry.

It's a half hour to get to the cabin if I take Interstate Ten directly, but if it weren't for my probation, I wouldn't go there at all. Some distant cousin had arranged with my PO to let me stay there while she was abroad for something or other, and I wasn't in a position to argue. It was a requirement of my parole to be released into the supervision of a family member. I was running out of those.

The phone was ringing when I walked in the door. I rushed over to it, the last land line known in existence, and answered, expecting my probation officer on the other end.

"There's a little saloon out near you—"

COLLECTIBLES

It took me a moment to realize it was Cathy Day. I tried to think of something smart-assy to say but was at a loss, so instead I said,

"What do you mean near me? How do you—"

"It's in your file. We always request the file of anyone we're expected to be locked in a room with for an hour." I nodded like she could see me. "Anyway, it's a little place called Pappy and Harriet's. Sort of a locals' joint, but everyone who's anyone has passed through there. What do you say I come pick you up and we go listen to some music."

"Well as nice as that sounds, I can't. I'm on a curfew."

"About that. I put in a call to your PO. Offered to take full responsibility for you. We're all set. If you want… You still there?"

"Why are you doing this?" I asked.

"Let's just say you got the gift," she said. "You just don't know it yet. I'll be there in an hour."

I wondered what else was in my file, but she hung up the phone before I could respond.

———

That was how it went for a while. I upped my lessons to twice a week with Cathy Day and they became more like therapy sessions between good friends than mandated activities from the courts. I opened up to her about all kinds of things. Told her of my family's past, what I knew of it. Surprisingly, she had a similar story. I told her about Group. What each asshole said and what each asshole used to justify it. I mentioned Jerry and what had happened to his former in-laws and my suspicions of his expenditures. There seemed to be no topic off limits.

We were finishing up our lesson when Cathy Day told me she had a surprise for me.

"Really?" I said. "You've already done enough."

"That's true," Cathy Day said, "but there's something I want to give you."

She turned in her chair and reached for a black case propped behind her against the wall.

"It's an old resonator banjo. You can keep it. Practice at home. No more rentals."

I took the case and laid it across my lap, popped open the metal latches and peered inside.

Stationed in my lap was a 1928 Gibson Florentine original tenor.

"It has some finish wear," Cathy Day said, "and it's missing one jewel on the peg-head, but otherwise it's good as new. Even installed a pickup for you."

It was a thing of beauty. Scenic Florence inlays, original tuning pegs. It had to be worth a fortune.

"It's been in my family for a long time," she said. "I want you to have it." I looked at her stunned, felt movement from deep down. "I see what's in you. I've got it too. But it's coming out in all the wrong ways. Believe me, the banjo is the instrument, but you're in control. It does what you want it to do."

I set the case aside and strummed gently, afraid I might break it.

"Don't hold back," Cathy Day said. "You're working too hard. It's music, not math."

I let out a long sigh and tried to clear my head. And as she predicted, it would happen that once I'd quit trying and worrying, something would move through me that instinctively put my fingers where they needed to go. It was like time was passing by in warp speed and I was standing still, playing that banjo.

Everything that had ever gone wrong in my life up to that point became inconsequential. Every disappointment and heartache poured out of that banjo in a beautiful, resounding wail, like my whole life was designed to lead me to this exact moment in time.

Then again, maybe I was reading too much into that D-minor riff. Cathy Day called it flow. She never did charge me for the extra lessons. Afterwards, we would head to Pappy and Harriet's to catch whoever was playing that night. Paul McCartney even dropped by on occasion. There was no sign of him this time, but we saw some damn good pickers every week.

After a while, we stopped playing the sheet music for the standards like we'd been doing and Cathy Day encouraged me to write my own stuff. Said it didn't matter how good it was or it wasn't, it was just the two of us and I should try. Most of all, I shouldn't let that banjo go to waste.

COLLECTIBLES # COLLECTIBLES

I sat home one night, like I always did if I wasn't with Cathy Day, and started to work on a new song. I called it Flight to Cosmic Nacogdoches, though I wasn't sure why.

When I stopped playing it was almost morning time, and I realized I'd been in flow all night long. I called Cathy Day as soon as the sun was up and told her I had been working on something special. She didn't seem too mad about my waking her. I made a cup of coffee but I was already hopped up. I decided I'd record what I had in case the moment passed and I lost the melody.

I pulled out my phone, started the voice memo application and pressed the big red button to record. Then I popped the quarter-inch cable into the pickup on the banjo connected to the amp and began to play. I felt that same deep feeling, just like in the rehearsal room that first time I'd met Cathy Day.

Let me tell you. I've never played so well. I rode that bass line like a jockey on a wild bull. The strings cried out and the minor chords screamed and the beat drove hard into the bone. As I rounded that last chorus I felt the walls of that tiny cabin shake and the floor shift and wobble. A trickle of sweat rolled down my cheek like a lone tear as the house moaned in response to the vibrations.

I clawed out that last note and hung on like my very life depended on it, let the echo work its way through the house and into that tiny microphone until the final moment when the sound melted into silence and I knew I could finally rest.

I stopped the recorder, put the banjo down and went to turn off the amp. As I approached I noticed the red light wasn't glowing. I had forgotten to turn it on. I looked down at the banjo Cathy Day had given me, and that was when I knew.

———

When I got to Group, I was still high off the excitement of the music even though it had been hours. I tried to be attentive to the other participants, but the idea of hearing yet another man say he didn't mean to hit her wasn't sitting well with me.

In my fever and desperation to change subjects, I let slip that I had written something that would blow their socks off, make them forget all their troubles back home. In fact, by the time I was done talking, I had gone from pariah, to Mariah Carey, sans the vocal ability.

They started asking me all kinds of things. Where'd I get my ideas for the songs. Who had taught me to play? My enthusiasm was now theirs. It's possible I might have embellished a few things, being caught up in the moment and all.

I told them about my mom, that she had been on tour with The Stones. That Jagger was rumored to be my dad. I told them about Cathy Day and the room full of expensive instruments I had at home. I even told them how one time, I'd played with Paul McCartney.

Said we had gotten so chummy that Pauly, as I called him, had signed my banjo, my charts, and as if that weren't enough, he'd given me the Abbey Road album signed by every member from the Beatles.

"And then he told me, it goes like this. The fourth, the fifth, the minor fall, and the major lift."

By this point, I was just talking in Leonard Cohen lyrics, but these idiots wouldn't know Cohen from Mickey Mouse, so I kept on, enjoying my moment in the spotlight.

I figured that was all pretty close to the same as having passed Mr. McCartney on my way to the bathroom. I mean, I'd almost said something.

"Sounds like horse shit ya ask me."

I turned to see Mike, another natural-born Mensa member with his arms crossed at his chest and his knees splayed open like a dog in heat.

"Well," I said. "No one asked you."

"You're just like the rest of them."

"The rest of who?" I asked.

"All you women and your lying souls. It's 'cause of women like you I'm here in the first place."

"You don't know my soul," I said.

"Women all have the same soul."

It was that moment that Bill, our moderator, decided to step in and steer the conversation back to the music.

"Have you felt music to be a helpful tool for your rage?" Bill asked.

But before I could answer, Jerry said, "So you're telling us, that you have stuff signed from the Beatles. The Beatles?"

"That's right," I said.

I watched him consider this a moment. He ran his hand through his scraggly beard then said, "What's something like that worth?"

I pretended to look shocked, as though the mere thought of selling pained me. "Why Jerry," I said. "You don't sell that sort of thing. It's priceless."

I glanced back to Mike, but he had already lost interest.

When I left Group I headed over to the music store for my lesson. I felt pretty good about what had just transpired in that musty old room in back of the Main Street Church. Served them right to be lied to. They'd spent a lifetime lying to everyone else. I couldn't wait to tell Cathy Day, and to play her that song.

Now with Cathy Day sat next to me, that wild sensation that had crossed through me that morning happened again, but this time, Cathy Day joined in.

Talk about taking things to another level.

I was holding down the rhythm like one might hold down a cat for nail trimming while Cathy Day played her own licks on top of the beat. I was the cone and she was the milky, soft-serve goodness that coiled and rested ever so gently on top. An almost solid, shifting in the heat running freely down all sides.

Our session was almost over when I started singing along to the melody. Words were coming to me, bubbling up in my throat like phlegm out of nowhere. They shot out of my mouth and bounced around that tiny room just as we were bringing it home.

I looked over to Cathy Day.

The look on her face was pride and fear and lonely and heartbreak all rolled into one. I know that sounds like a lot, but there you have it.

I sang like I had good sense and then some. Then I saw Cathy Day's eyes shift and her slight grin melt to a tight-lipped frown.

I couldn't tell you why, but by the time I looped my way back around to the final chorus as I had done that morning, there wasn't nothing coming out of my mouth but gurgles and a hiss.

"Stop!" Cathy Day shouted. "Shut up!"

Never one to be told what to do, I countered.

"Who made you the…"

Like a toy drained of its batteries, I felt something inside me reposition and pull, then a strain against my throat until I was unable to make any sounds at all.

"Don't say another word." This time I listened, but only because I had to. "Get your stuff, let's go."

And so I did, and so we did. As we pulled out of the lot, I thought I saw a red Mustang behind us in the rearview.

———

We got to Cathy Day's place a little after lunch time. She pointed me to a recliner in the corner, told me to leave the banjo near the wall and keep quiet as though I had a say in the matter. She'd certainly gotten meaner in the last hour. After all this time, it was my first visit to her place. I watched as she called to me over her shoulder, pulling book after dusty book from its place on the shelf and thumbing furiously.

"Now you're going to think this is batshit," she said, "but this has happened before." I listened, as there wasn't much else for me to do. "I had a great-great-aunt, suffered a similar situation. Not the same, but similar. And believe me, what I'm about to say is not anything I ever wanted to ever say out loud."

I braced myself for what was coming.

"I think you got the curse." I looked at her with dead eyes. "That banjo," she said, "it was hers. My aunt's, from the fifties. Short of it is, she was in a rockabilly band, there was some bad juju, and then a homecoming concert that did not end well for all involved. I thought it was just a story…"

Now Cathy Day stopped pulling books and looked back at me for the first time. "I sensed something that first day, but I couldn't be sure. I thought the banjo at best would be a gift and at worst, well…"

I jabbed four fingers of my right hand onto my chest and tapped.

"Why you? That's what you're worried about?"

COLLECTIBLES

I nodded frantically, pointing at my throat like I was banging out an S.O.S. Cathy Day thought for a moment. "The only thing I can figure," she said, "if the legends are true, is that bad things happen to bad people."

I threw my hands up in a who-me? gesture, to which Cathy Day said, "Which one of us is on parole for helping a friend?"

I rolled my eyes to one side, tilted my head to say good point, then pointed back at Cathy Day. She had no trouble understanding me.

As the day pressed on, Cathy Day told me more about her great-great-aunt and the tales that had passed through her family line.

"In fact," she said, "it was those stories got me interested in music in the first place. Rumor was the women on my mother's side were descendants of Greek Sirens and Salem's witches."

She may as well have thrown in the Superman curse while she was at it. I knew she was sincere but she sounded insane, and none of it was all that helpful in the moment.

Day turned to night and after hours of searching, Cathy Day enlisted my help to go through more of the books. She'd even pulled out some white banker boxes shoved in a back closet and set me down in front of them to search.

"These were in my mother's storage when she died. I'm not sure what we are looking for exactly, but you'll know if you find it, I think. You hungry?"

I was on the floor surrounded by boxes and Cathy Day was in the kitchen making dinner. She hummed from the kitchen as I searched.

Show-off.

I had made it through about a third of the boxes by this point when I noticed an old Bible with different paper clippings sticking out of the top of one of the boxes. I scooched over on the carpet to bring the box into my lap and pulled out the Bible. The leather showed enough age that Jesus himself might have done the binding job.

I got up, then took it back over to the recliner with me. When I sat it in my lap, I let it fall to its natural opening. The pages were yellowed, and in between various scripture rested worn newspaper clippings.

The first few made mention of some odd occurrences, almost in passing, but as I thumbed deeper into the book, the more detailed the articles became and the more familiar they felt. A chill passed through me like a mole burrowing its way into the dirt to die, and that was when I saw it.

"Concert at local high school ends in electrical fire. Traps and kills hundreds."

When Cathy Day dropped me off back home, she gave me stark instructions to stay put, as though I had big plans, and that she would be back soon.

"I have an idea," she said. Her face showed worry, but it faded as quickly as it had come. "Here, you hold on to this."

She gave me the Bible and off she went. From the bedroom window I watched her taillights fade into the distance like all the dreams I'd had, then thumbed through the Bible again in hopes of finding anything. When nothing new was revealed, I moved to the chair to think. I didn't feel much like playing. Even if I'd wanted to, I'd left the demon banjo with Cathy Day. I thought I might should shower, but I didn't.

Instead, I grabbed a throw from the back of the chair, moved over to the bed, closed my eyes and tried not to think about things. Cathy Day hadn't been gone long before I heard the knock at the door. I got to it by the time the third knock came and swung it open to see what she had forgotten.

"Where is it, Jill?" Jerry asked, as he scrounged through the desk drawers. "Where's the record?"

I knew, but I wasn't talking.

He tidied up the stack of papers he'd withdrawn from the drawers and slipped them back inside. He closed the drawers, then turned to look at me. I licked at the swollen place on my lower lip and tasted blood. My hands were tied together, the cord looped repeatedly through the base of my office chair. He had taken off my shoes and tied my legs together with a second restraint.

The good sheets.

"Listen," Jerry said, "it's going to be easier on everybody if you just tell me where it's at."

I wanted to ask him who was everybody.

He sauntered over, presumably in an effort to appear more threatening. It wasn't necessary. Jerry had not taken to heart the old adage to never hit a woman. The swing of his jacket revealed the Smith & Wesson that hung at his hip like an extra appendage. He was just as scary now as he had been when he'd overtaken me at the door with an uppercut and a gut punch.

Jerry asked again, and once more I didn't answer. He didn't realize my reluctance to share wasn't that I was unwilling.

I was unable.

It was nighttime, so for once it wasn't hot. The winds were still and the night critters scuttled around outside. I'd always hated the desert. This wasn't improving my opinion.

I could hear the cicadas like a vortex of hundreds of tiny violins. I'd always hated them, too. Anytime cicadas showed up, bad juju lurked nearby. On second thought, maybe that was locusts. Close enough. Jerry stood in front of me now, unaware of the insect debate running through my brain.

Suddenly, Jerry cocked his head to one side.

"You expecting someone?" He waited a moment, then moved towards the window. He pulled the curtain back and peeked outside. There was a long silence, followed by the sound of the front door swinging open as Cathy Day stepped inside.

Her brown hair was pulled back in a loose ponytail, exposing the grey at her pale temples. Her brown leather bomber jacket hung open atop her white button-down blouse. She was holding the banjo like a sawed-off shotgun. Cathy Day looked like she could wrestle a bear and welcomed the opportunity.

The neck of the banjo was aimed at Jerry, and for a moment I saw fear. She walked towards him, her eyes never dropping from his.

After a closer look at her weapon, Jerry's shoulders relaxed. He laughed, then pulled back the flap of his jacket, releasing the gun from its holster. He stepped towards her, hurried as the next ice age.

"You come here to play me a concerto?" he asked.

Cathy Day strummed the steel strings as he spoke. Still moving towards him, still aiming the neck of the instrument at him like a scope.

Her hands plucked slow at first, then picked up steam. Then a wild, fiery melody echoed out from the bronze wires as though escaping through the gates of hell.

Jerry stopped, raised his weapon and aimed it at her. He was tired of playing.

He yelled over the music. "Think-can kill-with guitar—"

Confusion from the realization of what he'd said showed on his face. He stepped closer to her, then tried again, as though proximity had been the problem. All he could get out this time was, "Instrument."

"Just keep on talking, motherfucker," Cathy Day said.

He tried, and her right hand pumped furiously up and down on the banjo strings. The melody rose and fell. Veered left and shot right.

Béla Fleck had nothing on Cathy Day.

She looked at me, and I nodded. She nodded back. She struck a chord that King David himself couldn't have played and that's when Jerry's eyes turned black like his pupils had sprung a leak. His cheeks started to swell and his teeth chattered and gnashed together. We watched as they broke into shards and fell to the floor in front of him.

Jerry swerved and tumbled. Staggered and stumbled all the while Cathy Day kept the neck of that axe aimed right at him. He clutched his throat and let out a gurgling howl that made my butthole pucker.

Then he collapsed on the floor as the notes absorbed his spirit and carried it away.

"It's a banjo, asshole."

But by then he was still. Cathy Day quit strumming and looked at me. It was then I realized the words were my own and I felt surprise and relief, and there was a swoosh of air like an impossible wind and the sense that I was whole once again.

She rushed to my side and propped the banjo up next to me at the wall, grabbed a pair of scissors from the desk and used them to free my hands. She was about to cut the sheet wrapped around my legs but I stopped her.

"Not made of money, ya know," I said.

"Not yet," she said.

COLLECTIBLES

I staggered to my feet, allowed the blood flow to return to me before taking another step. I leaned against my desk for support, pocketed the scissors Cathy Day had just used to free me and shot a glance over my shoulder to Jerry.

For a moment I felt sympathy. It passed.

"Come on," she said. "Help me get him out of here."

"How do you suppose we do that?" I asked. She looked at me, then over to the sheet she had just freed me from. "Goddamnit," I said. "These are from Macy's, not Target."

"Just get the sheet. Why does everything have to be a thing with you?"

I repeated what she'd said in an annoying baby voice. She looked at me, then at the banjo. I quit talking.

We wrapped Jerry up in the sheet as a makeshift stretcher and dragged him outside and into the backseat of her car. There was no one around for miles, so we didn't need to be stealthy about it.

Cathy Day went back inside and grabbed the banjo and I waited in the car.

We had been driving for a while, me with the banjo held between my knees, Jerry laid out in the backseat like he was taking a nap, Cathy Day hunched behind the wheel. When we finally turned left down another dirt road and crossed over a cattle guard, I squeezed my thighs together to keep the banjo in place as we thrashed around, careful to hold the strings still.

She kept driving a little further until we pulled over at a small hill with a metal structure like the kind cows hide under in the heat of day. Cathy Day seemed to know the spot well. I didn't inquire.

We waited a moment to gather our thoughts, and by that I mean for Cathy Day to light up a cigarette. She instructed me to grab the shovel from the trunk as she remained seated and fussed about with her lighter. I opened the passenger side door, delicately situated the banjo in my place, then got out.

The dry desert air whipped across my skin and I wished now I had remembered to grab a sweater from back at the cabin. I pulled the trunk handle and the hatch rose with a sound like a whooshing of air.

"You just carry this thing around with you?"

I held the shovel up towards the rearview mirror where I knew Cathy Day could see me, watched her take a long drag, then blow little ringlets from her ruby lips.

"As a matter of fact," she yelled over her shoulder.

She took a final drag, then tossed the cigarette on the ground, opened her own car door and got out. She walked around the back to where I stood and stared at me for a moment longer than what was comfortable. She was like that.

She finally broke gaze and closed the trunk. We walked around to the back door pointed away from the roadside in the very far off distance and yanked it open. There was Jerry, still wrapped up like King Tut. I thought for a moment of my childhood mummy fascination, then drifted to Steve Martin on Saturday Night Live. I considered saying something, but thought better of it.

I peeked over the body towards the front passenger seat, noted the banjo where I had left it, decided to transfer it to the trunk, then went back to the matter at hand.

"You grab his feet," she said.

"Why me? Why are you in charge here?"

Cathy Day didn't answer and I didn't push it. We both knew why.

I crawled over Jerry's body. Cathy Day pulled and I pushed with as much finesse as was warranted until he was out of the back seat and onto the desert earth. He was no heavier than a herd of pregnant elephants. I made an ouch face when his head bounced on the step rail, then again when he hit the dirt.

"Goddamnit," I said.

A small bloom of red spread across my high thread count sheet where the back of his head rested.

"What?" Cathy asked. "Were you actually planning to use it after this?"

I didn't answer.

She had him from underneath the shoulders, more or less, with my hands wrapped awkwardly around his swathed ankles. As we struggled against his weight, his left hand slipped out from an opening in the sheet and flopped towards the ground like a flaccid penis. His fingertips grazed the dirt as we walked, leaving a small trail. We had made it several minutes down a dark path before I realized we'd left the shovel back at the car.

As though she were reading my mind, she said, "We'll make a second trip." It was that kind of eerie shit that made me wonder who she really was.

"Are you worried about the banjo?" I asked.

"Nope."

We made it to a dip in the terrain and put Jerry on the ground next to some shrubbery like we were setting aside our morning coffee mug on the kitchen counter. There were no clear markers around, but this didn't seem to bother Cathy Day.

"I'll go back and get it," I said. But I knew it would be me whether I offered or not.

"I'll make sure this asshole stays put."

"Tough job," I said, and turned back towards the car.

––––––––

We arrived back at my place just before sunrise, went inside and sat at the kitchen table. I held the banjo, not too keen to let it far from my sight.

"So what now?" I asked.

"Nothing. It's done. Jerry got what he deserved and no one's going to be crying over his absence."

"I know that. I mean us. The banjo."

"You should keep it."

"I'm not so sure that's a good idea," I said.

She smirked, and shifted in her seat. "Maybe we take this little act on the road. Just like you wanted."

"Maybe," I said.

She pushed her chair back, stood from the table and walked around next to me. She patted me on the shoulder, then left.

I sat there for the rest of the day thinking. About Jerry. About the stories of his in-laws. About what Cathy Day had said about hitting the road. I wondered what would become of Jerry's Mustang. If there really was something to the banjo knowing good from bad and why it had spared me and taken him.

By the afternoon I decided I'd done enough thinking and took the banjo to the bedroom. I positioned it gingerly on my lap, this time with a new appreciation for all it had seen. I wished I could know what really happened that day at the school auditorium with Cathy Day's aunt.

"Can you really tell the soul of someone?" I asked this out loud, in the voice that had been given back to me.

No answer.

I strummed the strings gently and hummed. I guess there was only one way to find out.

The Skull Collector

BY JOE R. LANSDALE

There were three of them, but the guy in front of me did most of the talking.

"What I'm thinking here, sweetie, is you aren't telling us all you know."

"You're thinking that, are you?" I said. "That's where you're wrong. You do all this, hurt me enough, scare me enough, then I'll tell you something, but it won't be the truth. I don't know the truth. You're wasting your time, and mine."

That was a lie. I knew where what they wanted was, but I figured once they knew, I could kiss my ass goodbye.

"Like I care about your time, sister."

"I like to get my nails done on Wednesday, so time matters to me."

"You're a tough broad, I'll give you that. Here's what I'm thinking, though, about that lie part. We find out you told us a lie, then we got to make it harder on you. Being tied to a chair and slapped around, that isn't going to be all of it. We think maybe we might have to start carving you up. Oh yeah. This is Wednesday, and Wednesday is done."

I wasn't actually that tough. I was hoping to die of a heart attack. I feared what they might do to me, feared it to the point of a possible surprise bowel movement, but there's something in me besides shit, and it makes me a smart mouth when I'm in danger. And frequently when I'm not. It's like the skunk that when frightened sprays stink. I'm frightened, I run my mouth.

"You can look all kinds of places, but I don't have it. Turned out there wasn't anything in the grave. And by the way, where'd you get that after-shave? It's making my eyes water."

"Oh," said the tall one leaning against the wall, "she's got a sharp tongue." This guy was probably six-one and he was a guy went in heavy for the hair product. He had enough oil in his dark locks to soothe all the squeaky hinges in creation with enough left over to grease a transmission.

"Tongue won't be so sharp if I cut it out," said the main one, the talker.

"Then you won't get to know what I know is nothing, not unless I lie to you in sign language. And I don't know sign language."

"Oh, shut up," said the man in front of me, the talker. "You're not funny." He had on what at first looked like an expensive suit, but the way it hung on him proved different. It was more like a man tent without the mosquito net. I had just noticed that. When he had been hitting me my powers of observation had been limited.

"I think she's funny," said the third man, a fat fellow with a crew cut and checkered pants that he must have bought via a time machine trip to the nineteen seventies. He had on a shirt so green Irish grass would have been embarrassed to grow.

"Just shoot her, cut her throat, get it over with," said the tall one leaning against the wall. "She don't know nothing. She'd have said by now."

The tall one eyed me carefully. I believed him when he threatened to carve me up. After hours of being tied to a chair in the basement of an abandoned high school, I feared that heart attack wasn't coming to put me out of my misery. I was way too healthy for that.

"I say we get right to cutting her," the fat man said. "A little at a time. Everyone talks when you do that. We can get lies out of the way quick. She don't know nothing, well, we get to carve her anyway. How do you like that idea, baby?"

"Not all that appealing," I said.

The main talker nodded. "What I think we're going to do, missy, is do just that. We're going to cut those clothes off of you, put you on the floor there, and start carving. But we'll do it slow, just in case maybe you do have something to say. You talk, well, we can get it over with quick."

"What a treat," I said.

That's when I heard the door open and Ruby stepped in. Her dark hair was done up in a bun. She was wearing jeans and a droopy brown sweatshirt, holding a sawed off ten-gauge shotgun. She looked like she could eat floor tacks and crap an anvil. Ruby's about five-five, but in that moment, she was Wonder Woman carrying a cannon.

My interrogator, who was focused on me, looked up just as Ruby cut down with that sawed off ten-gauge. There was a roar like a lion and my interrogator's head went away, and what looked like a flight of bloody bees smashed into the wall. The body dropped right in front of me, getting blood on my tennis shoes. I liked those shoes.

The tall one against the wall started to rock forward, reach under his coat. I heard the sharp snap of the shotgun being pumped, and the lion roared again, and suddenly the tall man had a wet, red hole in his middle. Like my interrogator, he collapsed.

The fat one made a dash for the door on the far side, but the lion roared, and the shot caught him in the lower back. He hit the floor and tried to crawl, but he couldn't do it. Ruby pumped the shotgun, walked over to him and fired. Pieces of him and the shot from the load bounced around the room like someone had dropped a box full of ball bearings and a can of red paint.

Ruby put the shotgun on the floor and took out her pocket knife. She cut the ropes around my ankles and feet, then the one around my neck that was fastened to the back of the wooden chair. Oddly, it wasn't until then that I realized my ass hurt.

When I tried to stand up, I had a hard time. I didn't know if it was from being tied so long, or if it was fear. I decided it was both.

"You nearly shot me," I said. When I spoke, I could hardly hear myself. My ears were ringing from all that shotgun fire.

"No, I didn't."

"Did too."

"Don't start crying, Crystal. We haven't time for that."

"Screw you. You took long enough."

By then we were already moving toward the door.

Most of my Wednesdays aren't like that.

I guess I ought to not start in the middle of a true-life story, or maybe it's not the middle. Hell. I don't know. But let me tell you how I got to that chair, and then I'll move beyond.

What I do for a living is I work—worked—for a fence. What the fence does—Ruby is her name—is she buys stolen goods and resells them for a profit. She works out of a pawn shop she owns, does legitimate business too. But when it's the right stuff, she does another kind of business. She knows what's stolen and what isn't, of course, and though there are some things she won't deal in (stolen show dogs), there are a lot of things she's glad to buy and resell, and she's been known to act as a go-between and do all manner of things that having nothing to do with pawn shops or fencing.

Weirdly, she once fenced some stolen bull semen from a prize bull, and this rancher guy bought it, came back later, said it turned out to be a dud. The heifer didn't fatten with calf. He wanted his money back. He was a tough old guy, Ruby said. Big, could crack walnuts with harsh language, chase a squirrel up a tree with bad breath. She had to use an axe handle to sort the guy out a little. It wasn't too bad. He was able to leave on his own, though not without a certain amount of pain and difficulty, one hand on his bleeding head, the other pressed against his broken ribs. That's when I realized not only does Ruby deal in stolen goods, she deals in violence, if the need arises. Her and her brothers, Pooty and Boo-boo.

Actually, that's not their real names. Their names are Arnold (Arnie), he's Pooty, and Benjamin (Ben), and he's Boo-boo. They're two big guys, arms like Popeye, faces like car wrecks. They were always nice to me, though. I should point that out. Of course, Ruby and the boys, as she calls them, are my cousins, so they feel a bit obligated. Cousins once removed; I think. Hell, I don't know exactly. I get lost in the weeds when you get that far into family backgrounds. Dad once said, "In our family tree about the only thing you'll find is monkeys and broken limbs."

Here's how it started.

So, I'm hanging out at the house trying to read *War and Peace* and learning I didn't like it, when the phone rang, and it was Ruby. That's how it started, with a phone call and my boredom with *War and Peace*.

"Hey, want to make some money?" she said.

I was as broke as my ethics, so I said, "Does a bear shit in the woods?"

"What if they live in the zoo?"

"Yes, Ruby, I want to make some money."

"This is a special job. It doesn't require contacts or even a lot of smarts."

"Then I'm perfect for it," I said.

"It's really not a biggie. It's not a fence, and it's not a pawn."

"Is it big enough for me to get out of bed, leave the house?"

"I meant what you have to do is no biggie, but yeah, it's big enough to get out of bed, go out to the graveyard in the middle of the night and make a whole lot of money for a short amount of digging."

I laughed.

Ruby was silent.

"Wait a minute," I said. "You're serious? A graveyard?"

"Serious as a yeast infection."

That night Ruby picked me up in her black van and away we went. I was, as Ruby suggested, wearing work clothes. Had on boots, jeans, and a chambray shirt, hair tied back.

I looked over my shoulder to see what was rattling in the back of the van. Two shovels. A ten-gauge shotgun, a couple of beer cans.

"This is kind of out of my line of work," I said.

"I can do it by myself, but what I thought, while I'm digging, you hold the shotgun, you're digging, I hold it."

"Shotgun? What the hell, Ruby? This seems more like a job for Pooty and Boo-boo, not your petite cousin. I was thinking digging was out of my line, but gun work, way out of my line. I think you can take me back to the house."

COLLECTIBLES

"First, my brothers are out of town. And I take you back, you'll be giving up five thousand dollars for one night's work. Not even a whole night."

I thought about what five thousand dollars could do. Keep the lights and water on, pay the rent, buy some real food. And I needed new underwear. I washed mine much more I'd be wearing lint.

"As long as we don't have to shoot the caretaker, groundskeeper, whatever they call those folks, then I guess I'll stick."

"It's nothing like that. It's just that, well, there could be competition, and I like to be able to discourage them. Also, there's no groundskeeper. I did some research. There's a lot of old stones and some weeds, and Etta Place."

"Etta Place?"

"You know, Butch and Sundance. At the end of the Old West days. They had this pretty school teacher with them when they were robbing banks and trains. Or maybe she was a prostitute. No one really knows. Maybe she was a palm reader and a part-time ukulele player for all I know. Anyway, the skull collector wants her head."

"Wait a minute. Katherine Ross?"

"She played her in the movie, yeah. But Etta, she was real. She left them in South America and came back to the States, disappeared. It's one of history's mysteries. Like why people used to wear turtlenecks with medallions the size of hubcaps.

"Anyway, she came back, and no one had a lead on her. Not the Pinkertons, who looked all over, not the historians. No one. But there was a rumor she had ended up in Texas, where she may have been from originally. That her name was really something else, that she went back to that name and worked in a brothel, later became a school teacher. All kinds of stories. And then the diary turned up. Not hers, but her sister's. There were answers inside."

In a nutshell, this is what Ruby told me. What Ball told her, and what she surmised.

Seems Etta Place, whose real name was Ethel Dodgers, was actually a former music teacher who got bored with teaching brats to play "Chopsticks," and ran off with Butch and Sundance, then returned to Texas. She told her sister, Eunice, about her adventures with the robbers. Started teaching music again, died of what might have been the Spanish flu, and was buried in a cemetery just outside of Tyler, Texas, which was not too far from where we lived.

After her death, Eunice's diary ended up in a pawn shop, was bought by one Seabury Ball, who collected such things. Ball read it, and believed it. Knew from reading it that there was something he wanted. He wasn't called the Skull Collector for nothing. He wanted Etta's skull, one of the most renowned lost-to-history individuals there ever was, and he might be the only person in the world at that moment in time who knew where she was buried, and he wanted her dug up and delivered.

This, by the way, is also called grave robbing and it's not legal. But Ball had the money to buy his collector's items from the right people, and he was good at hiding his purchases. For example, rumor is he has the skulls of the Apache warrior, Geronimo, the noggins of Billy the Kid and Jimmy Hoffa, and rumor was someone ought to check Lincoln's tomb.

Problem was, Ball, an elderly gentleman, had a sugar baby, and one night when he was working on greasing the weasel, his enthusiasm for her, and for the skull, led him to make with too much pillow talk.

He told the girlfriend about the diary, the Etta revelation, but didn't mention the exact graveyard. Being someone who was out for herself, and expecting her Sugar Daddy to go toes up soon, she snuck around and told Repeat Pete, another old man with money, and like Ball, he was a collector of unusual items. A man who could hire people to do most anything. Including shelling peas and killing folks. He also had a rivalry with Ball. Ball wanted it, then Repeat Pete wanted it.

Ball's girlfriend ended up in a graveyard herself, but not Etta's. Rumor was Ball had her whacked when he found out she had spilled the beans about the skull, but it could just as easily have been Repeat Pete's crew, him not wanting Sugar Baby Blabber Mouth spreading the info around any more than she already had. Anyway, she got run over by a truck. Several times.

"So, we're good. Right? I mean, Repeat Pete's crew doesn't know where the graveyard is?"

"That's right. But…"

I didn't like *but*.

"You see, they know it's an old graveyard, and Pete has hired a crew to keep them checked out, or so Ball thinks."

"Checked out for how long? Why not wait six months, see if the observers thin out, then dig her up? And why not use his own folks instead of us?"

"He may not trust them, and me and my brothers have a good reputation with him. Or he may not want to lose his own folks in the process."

I didn't like the sound of that. "So we get killed instead?"

"I doubt anything so dramatic. But, yeah. Maybe. As for waiting, Ball wants the skull now, not six months from now, and he's got the money to get it now. It's not us digs her up, it could be someone else gets that ten thousand dollars."

"Maybe it ought to be."

"I got a vacation planned. I want to go somewhere where I can put my toes in the ocean, and I don't mean Galveston. I thought I might find a pool boy or some kind of good-looking fella at a hotel who doesn't mind making some money on the side, the hard way, if you know what I mean."

"You're pretty awful," I said.

"I am. You still in?"

"Why the hell not?"

The graveyard was down a long dirt road where the trees gathered thick on either side and the shadows fell over the road like a blanket of night. The headlights seemed to have trouble cutting through it, and it was starting to mist, and the mist beaded on the window like little knots of pus. Finally, Ruby turned on the wipers and waved it away.

We came to a gap in the woods and there was a trail made of gravel, just wide enough for the van. Branches rubbed the sides of the van like lustful lovers. We got to the end of the gravel where we had to park. We walked in the dark and the mist, Ruby leading the way with a tow sack thrown over her shoulder, carrying a huge rubber-wrapped flashlight that could have been used to beat a tiger to death, and in her other hand, a shovel. I had the shotgun and a shovel, plus my penlight in my coat pocket.

No one was waiting there for us, other than the dead. So much for needing the shotgun. That caused me to breathe a sigh of relief. Way it looked to me, unless you had the information in the diary, you'd never find this place.

"How old is this graveyard?" I said.

"Old. Look for a stone with Ethel Dodgers on it."

I placed the shotgun on top of the tow sack Ruby had stretched on the ground, placed the shovel on the ground next to where Ruby had placed hers, got my penlight out of my jacket, and we split up, flashing our lights around. I found some really old gravestones, and some graves that were unmarked, but no Ethel Dodgers. Then I heard Ruby call out.

"Bring your shovel. I've found our gal."

It was a grave that had collapsed a little, and there was a broken marble stone lying on the ground where it had fallen over due to erosion or vandalism. It was damp with moisture and the color of old horse teeth in the glow of our flashlights. It was hard to see at first, but chiseled into the stone were the words Ethel Dodgers, a date of birth and a date of death. There was something else written there, but it was so faded I couldn't make it out.

Ruby laid her flashlight beside the grave where the light would shine on it. I turned off my penlight and put it away. We grabbed the shovels and started digging. The air was still misty, and the ground was damp. There were quite a few roots, so it was serious work. In time we hit a few fragments of dark wood. Then we came to pieces of bone, and what might have been bits of cloth, but could have been old, blackened leaves. We got down on our hands and knees and pushed the dirt around. I could feel the dark earth chunking up under my fingernails, causing me to remember I had skipped my manicure today, and then I came upon the skull. Or most of it. The bottom part of the jaw was missing. I handed it to Ruby. She flicked the wet earth off of it, and made a sound like a cat rolling in catnip.

I felt around some more and found the missing part of the jaw. Most of the teeth were in it. We went the full hog, clawed around, found more bones, ribs and such. Some of them were very fragile. We carefully packed them all into the tow sack.

COLLECTIBLES

It wasn't until we got back to the van and put the shotgun, shovels, and the bag with the goods in it, that I began to feel true guilt. The idea of unsettling Ethel's already crumbling grave seemed way too much. Here was a woman who had run the outlaw trail, survived it, returned and led a normal life and had been buried in what must have been a decent grave-yard at one time, well-tended with regular flowers and careful weeding, but now she had been forgotten. Her grave was rich with roots and covered in tree shadow. Her stone was cracked and turned over, and in the summer weeds and poison ivy most likely grew over that grave. Until her sister's diary showed up, and some asshole wanted to give us ten thousand dollars to dig up her remains, she had at least been left alone. That made me and Ruby the real assholes.

I thought about my share of the money again, got over my feelings of ass-holism, at least temporarily. She had been dead a long time. What was the harm?

By the time we were out of the woods and the lights of the town were visible, it was past midnight and it had started to rain like a cow pissing on a flat rock. We came to Seabury Ball's house, where he had wanted us to meet him and bring the goods. I could already feel that money in my hand.

We sat in the car with the lights out, the engine humming, looking at his house through the rain. It was large enough to contain a shopping mall and a sizable number of stray livestock. It was four stories of blue and white architecture, placed on a dozen acres that were dead center of the rich part of town, and had once been on the outskirts of it. Progress had surrounded Ball, but he was tucked well away in his great sanctuary, rolling around in his money like Scrooge McDuck.

"I don't know," Ruby said.

"What don't you know? You better be talking about math after talking me into this shit."

"Math is a problem, but it occurred to me, maybe we ought to put the bones away, meet with Ball and make a deal to deliver. I have this bad feeling he might have thugs who would just take it away from us, save him the ten thousand dollars."

"For him, that's not a lot of money."

"He didn't get rich by being generous, or honest. He has a mean streak."

"You didn't put it that way when we first talked. And you had that line about how he trusted you."

"Sometimes, for a friend's own good, you have to lie. Here's the thing. I think he hired us because we're expendable. More than the tough guys he pays bigger money to. He may have thought, send out the patsies, and then whack them, take the goods. That way he'd keep his people out of it."

"So, you and Ball, you're not that close?"

"Not really."

"That's it, huh? You just now thought of that? What they might do."

"Pretty much. It's mostly instinct. Just feeling something isn't right. I may be way wrong. But why chance it when we can set this up a bit better? Meet some place that isn't his home territory. Until then, we hide the skull and bones."

"Where do we hide it?"

"I was thinking your place."

"You were thinking that, were you? How about no? How about kiss my ass?"

"Listen, dear. Ball knows me. He doesn't know you. He doesn't know I've enlisted help. Truth is, you could walk and he wouldn't know you helped me. He probably thinks I'm using my brothers. Your place makes sense, case he wants to send someone around for a look and he doesn't know where to look."

"Why do I feel like a goat at a barbecue?"

"Truth is, I'm probably being overly cautious. But I say we stay with that ticket. No conflict, then no danger. I'd rather not shoot anyone. Again."

"Again?"

This was, of course, before she wasted the three bozos.

"Forget I said that."

On the way to my place I noticed every car that was behind us or came out of streets to end up behind us. One dark SUV in particular worried me, and I told Ruby it did.

COLLECTIBLES

"They could have picked us up at Ball's house," she said, "could have been waiting on us to show up with the bones, but frankly I think you're being paranoid."

"You're the one that had an instinct that things weren't right."

Before she could comment, the car behind us picked up speed, zipped around us, and turned off.

"See," Ruby said. "Nothing."

My place is across the street from a three-story clock tower that was built in the nineteen thirties. The clock is on the top story and it still works. The mechanisms and the old clock tower are kept up reasonably well, though there has been talk of tearing it down. I can look out my window and see the huge black hands turn. The clock face is lit up from the inside and glows orange at night. You can see bats and insects making dark shapes in front of the face then. Once, it had been the tallest structure in our little city. Now it's the height, or less than the height, of nearby houses.

There's still an outside metal staircase you can use to go up to the landing. The door at the top is locked, but one time I went up there for the view, just to see what it was like. All I could see were houses and buildings, and the next time I wanted to go over there, I saw they had built a metal gate at the bottom of the stairway. It had a sign on it that said to keep out. The first time I'd gone up there, I made an extraordinary discovery. There's a rubber mat in front of the thick door that leads into the tower. I accidently budged the mat with my toe, and underneath it was a key. One of those large, old-fashioned kind that you stick in the lock and turn. I thought, really? That's your secret hiding place? Under the mat?

But considering the clock no longer had tourism, and the museum that had been there in the past was long closed, who would think to look under the mat for the key other than those who kept the clock working? Who besides the workers and me ever went up there?

I used the key. The lock clicked, the knob turned, and then I was inside, amongst shadows and the dust I had stirred. The sound of the clock's revolving gears sounded like an enormous cosmic rat gnawing at the edges of reality.

With the door open I could see inside reasonably well. I could make out a swirling iron staircase that climbed to the third floor where the brain of the clock lived. It was too dark to venture going up there, and I didn't have my penlight with me back then, so after a moment of taking it all in, I went out and locked the door, put the key under the mat, and went home.

When Ruby dropped me off, we sat in her van for a moment. She said, "Take the bag, put it in your closet or some such. I'll get in touch with Ball, see what we can set up where there will be other people around, but not too many. Deliver the goods in a way that doesn't seem curious to others."

"You mean we won't walk into Starbucks with a bag of bones?"

"We'll find some place open to the public, some place like that, but find another way to carry the skull around. Something less conspicuous. Meantime, get some sleep."

A dark SUV cruised by us. Was it the car that had passed us before, the one I was suspicious of? I couldn't tell. It went by too quickly.

Ruby sensed my worry. She looked a little worried herself, but a moment later her worry had faded like moisture on a window pane hit by the sun.

"It's cool, baby girl. I'll call you tomorrow."

I got out of the car with the tow sack, and went inside, thinking of going to bed, but I didn't. I took a shower, washed off the grave grit, slipped on my pajamas with the teddy bears on it, and climbed up my second-floor stairs and sat in a chair by the window and looked out at the slightly higher clock tower across the street.

I couldn't sleep. I was too wired. Back downstairs I made myself a cup of decaf coffee, ate a cookie, then got some tennis shoes on, stuck the penlight in my pajama pocket, took hold of the tow sack and strolled across the street with it slung over my shoulder. I was Santa Claus for the dead.

I easily climbed over the little barrier, and went up the stairs. I found the key was still under the mat. I used it and opened the door. I turned on the penlight and climbed the winding interior stairs. They squeaked like a starving mouse.

At the top of those stairs the sound of the gears was nerve-racking, and there was another sound like the beating of a heart, another like a dying man's moan. The clock seemed quite human.

Flashing the light around, I saw an indention in the wall, a kind of nook. Being careful not to fall into the gears, I slipped the bag into the shadowy nook, and departed.

I was on a spaceship to Mars, and my cabin companion was the best-looking man I had ever seen, and he was in love with me. Or it was lust, I don't know. We did some things in zero gravity, and then some things in what I guess was artificial gravity. It was great, except he started slapping me.

I was mad as hell at him, and then I woke up, and the man leaning over me, slapping me, wasn't all that good-looking, and for a moment I felt I had ended up with the worst space-traveling companion you could imagine. Then I saw there were two others equally ugly standing by my bed and I wasn't on a spaceship after all.

"Get up, bitch," said the man who was slapping me. I really didn't like him.

"Where's the skull?" said a skinny one behind him.

I like to be clever, so I said, "What skull?"

"The one you're going to give us. Put on some clothes. We like to watch."

After I was humiliated with them watching me put on jeans and a sweat shirt, tennis shoes, and finally my jacket.

To shorten up what you know, these were my friends I mentioned when I first started telling this. Ones who tore through my house looking for the skull, then when they didn't find it, took me away from my comfy home and brought me to the abandoned school, tied me to the chair in the basement, and hit me a lot. They were good at their work. They hurt me, but they managed not to mess me up too bad. They didn't want me to die before I told them the location of the skull.

You know the rest. I was about to tell them where the skull was after talking tough for a while, when Ruby came through the door with that shotgun. And now we were back in her van, riding along to somewhere or nowhere. I was as shaky as a leaf on a tree during a thunderstorm. That shotgun business was some messed up shit.

She said, "Did you give them the skull?"

"No."

"Tell them where it is?"

"No. And if I had, it wouldn't matter now."

"True enough. I left you, I got worried, so I got out of bed and cruised over, just to check on you, and that's when I saw those lugs loading you into their car. It was just luck, kid. I followed you to the school, saw you and them go in. I did a sneak. I didn't know exactly where they were keeping you, so I had to creep around a while. Then I found the basement and could hear you and them talking."

"I was about to break. I would have given them the skull, my old teddy bear, and my ATM number. I was almost done. And all of it over some old bones."

"Those guys were part of Ball's operation. It was like I worried about. Ball decided to get the skull discount."

"How do you feel about moving to Bolivia?"

"Things aren't that bad."

"You weren't tied to a chair. You don't hurt like I do. I'm getting stiff. I can hardly move. I think they might have banged up something inside me. I know this is a bad time, but can we find a bathroom pretty quick?"

Walmart is open late. They have nasty bathrooms for the most part, being as they are constantly open and constantly used. But it was a life saver. Back in the car we cruised around a bit, thinking on what to do. I was still for moving to Bolivia.

"By the way," Ruby asked. "Where is the skull and bones?"

I told her.

"That was smart play for you. Had they been in your house, had they found the bones right off, they might have killed you immediately. Listen here. I been in contact with Ball. I told him I had the goods, and then I told him that we want more than ten."

"That's pushing it."

"He knows I can sell it to another bidder. And it worked. We're now getting twenty thousand. I also called my brothers, in case we need backup. They're on their way in. I don't know when they'll arrive. They're somewhere between here and Dallas. I told them we'd be at your place."

"When do we deliver the skull?"

"I'm going to call Ball and he'll send over his people. I told him not to make it a lot of people. It might make us itchy."

"Starbucks open this time of night?"

"Got a change of plans in mind. We pick some place secluded after all, but I keep the shotgun handy. I'm in the mood to shoot someone else."

At my house we checked in case Ball had sent someone over to wait on us. He hadn't.

Ruby made coffee, turned on her cell phone, made a call to Ball, gave him the address. Just hearing her do that made my skin crawl. "We had a spot of trouble tonight, you sack of dog shit," she said. "You like to done in my girl. Guys you send over now, they need to be friendlier. Those others, they got wasted, and I'm up for doing it again. The skull isn't here, but you send some friendly folks and we'll give it over when we get the money, take them to it."

I didn't hear what was said on the other end, but Ruby seemed satisfied. "All right, then," she said.

Ruby sat in the dark in the kitchen with the shotgun in her lap. Her chair faced the front door, and the back door was off to her left. I sat by the downstairs window. We sat for a long while. Finally, I saw lights. The lights belonged to a big black van, newer than Ruby's. It parked at the curb in front of my house.

"Oh, Ruby," I said. "We got company."

Ruby came from the kitchen. She had the shotgun with her. She looked out the window. Two extremely large men were climbing out of the van. She pumped the shotgun.

"Open the door," Ruby said, "then step back, just in case things get funky."

I didn't like funky.

I opened the door and stepped back. The two men came in without invitation. Both were large, but one was much larger than the other.

Ruby said, "I got a shotgun on you, just in case you got cute up your sleeve. There's some comrades of yours that found out that I don't mind using this blunderbuss, and if they could give you advice, they'd tell you to avoid irritating me any more than I'm already irritated."

The biggest of the two, who looked a bit like a concrete bridge support, said, "No cute here."

"You can say that twice," Ruby said.

The bridge support smiled. "No cute here. No cute here."

"That's some funny shit right there," Ruby said. "Funny shit."

"Mr. Ball, he told me to tell you that those three you whacked, they went rogue. He didn't authorize that kind of stuff. He thinks they were going to make a deal with Repeat Pete."

"Be that as it may, stay cool," Ruby said.

The biggest one looked at me. "You the sidekick, honey?"

"Close enough," I said.

"Where's the bones," the smaller of the two said.

"Put away," Ruby said.

"Un-put them," said Bridge Support. "I got your money here." He moved a hand toward the inside of his coat, paused. "Point that shotgun somewhere else, will you?"

Ruby moved the barrel slightly upward.

"Make sure you don't pull anything that shoots out of that pocket and you'll do fine," Ruby said.

Bridge Support pulled out a fat white envelope. "Twenty thousand. Right here."

He tossed it to me and I caught it. I turned on a lamp and counted it.

"Yep," I said.

"All right," Ruby said. "We're going to cross the street to the clock tower and get the goods. And you two, you're going to lead the way. Keep hands by your sides. Any sudden moves and you won't remember you moved."

COLLECTIBLES

It was no longer misting. The air had turned cool, and the coat I was wearing felt thin. When we got to the top of the outside clock tower stairs, I got the key from under the mat and let us in, closed the door behind us.

I had Ruby's big flashlight, as well as my penlight in my coat pocket. I turned on the big flash. The dust was thick and it spun in the beam of the flashlight. I felt like I was trying to breathe through a blanket and see through fog. The gears chewed and the clock ticked, banging out seconds like an ape beating a bass drum.

"You better have something we want, cause you sweet little girls don't want to get clever," Bridge Support said.

"All we want is to be done," I said.

"And we're not that sweet," Ruby said. "And it's me that's got the drop on you two."

That's when the door flew open and three men stepped inside with shotguns, twelve-gauge I believe, with flashlights fastened on top of them.

Goddamn it. I hate it when nearly everyone has shotguns.

The original two thugs pulled automatics from inside their coats, and they and Ruby all wheeled and pointed their guns at the men in the doorway. I stood there with the flashlight, thinking it wouldn't be long before the undertaker was wiping my ass.

From behind the three in the doorway, a smaller figure appeared. Even in the dim glow of my flashlight I could see he wore a plaid suit. Who wears a plaid suit besides a circus clown?

The men in front of him parted slightly, and he stepped into better view. He looked as if his dark hair was well-oiled twice a day and his teeth looked to be made of polished concrete. He wore brown and white spats, like an old-time gangster. I could tell then that he was older than I first thought. He had not so much aged, as he had been well-preserved, perhaps pickled. He had what looked like a book in his hand. It seemed like a bad time for a bit of reading.

"What we got here is some business problems," he said. "Business problems."

"Repeat Pete," Ruby said. "I thought you turned into a bat when it got dark."

"Ruby, Ruby. My dear, my dear. I haven't seen you since last time I seen you."

"That is accurate," Ruby said. "Listen, Repeat. This is a business deal, not a gun deal, and we're in the process of finishing up business. You snooze you lose, and you snoozed and Ball didn't."

"Oh, Ball. Ball," Repeat said. "He's snoozing now in a ditch out near some farmland. Farmland. And his skull collection. Collection. It's now mine. Good stuff. Good stuff. I got more big guns than you. I even got the diary now."

He lifted the book. Now I knew what it was. Ethel's sister's diary.

"So," he said, "there's a new business deal can be made. Made. And you boys, you can get into a nasty gunfight, gunfight, or you can go home, because you got no boss now. Now. And I'm not hiring. Not hiring."

"No shooting then," Bridge Support said.

"Got nothing against you boys. Boys."

"We'll be clearing out then," Bridge Support said. "Good luck, girls."

Bridge Support and his Kemosabe left out of there so fast they didn't even leave body odor.

There were still three shotguns pointed at us.

"This could get unnecessarily messy. Messy."

"I can shoot you, though, can't I?" Ruby said.

"Could. Could. But, give me the skull, the skull, as Ball don't need it anymore, then I'll take it and go, and you already got paid, right? Right? Ball, somewhere between losing his big toe and his nose, he said he was sending money to you. We can all come out happy except Ball, cause he's dead. Dead."

I was liking that idea of giving him the skull and him leaving us alone with our twenty thousand dollars. Problem was, I didn't trust Repeat.

"What say my friend here gets and gives you the bones," Ruby said, "and we all play it cool down here, pointing our shotguns at each other.

She brings the bones back, and we go with your plan, and never see each other again."

"Ah, Ruby baby, baby. You done business with me before. Before. We don't have to end our business altogether, altogether. I'll have something another time, and now, with Ball gone, it's more exclusive, exclusive."

"For the moment, let's just end tonight's business," Ruby said.

"Fair enough. Fair enough. Get the goods, goods, pretty girlie."

"You mean me, right?" I said.

"I do."

"Hokeydoke then."

I trusted Pete and his gang about as far as I could throw them, but there didn't seem to be a lot of choice.

I started toward the spiral staircase that led up to the clock.

"Wait a minute, a minute," Pete said. "I'll climb up there with you. With you."

"You think I'm going to go up there and fly away?" I said.

"I just like being safe about transactions. Transactions."

"Very well," I said. "Very well."

I was starting to talk like Pete.

Repeat slipped the diary he was carrying into his side jacket pocket, which was big enough to house a kangaroo baby, and we started up the staircase, me in the lead with Ruby's flashlight.

As we climbed, I said, "You ought to take up stamps, coins, maybe rare pop bottles, unusual lingerie. You'd look cute in a pink bustier, something leather, and it'd be a cheaper hobby. Less murderous, by the way."

"But in the end, not as fun. Not as fun."

"You say."

I got to the top of the stairs. I looked down and saw Repeat Pete looking up at me. He had produced a little automatic from somewhere. He was pointing it in the direction of my blue-jeaned butt. He was also wheezing.

"Need to cut back on jacking off, Pete," I said. "It takes your wind."

"Just get the skull, the skull," he said.

I started stepping again. My mind was running a hundred miles an hour, trying to decide if there was an alternative to handing him the bag. I did that, I felt that might be his moment to jettison his agreeable plan and pop me, and that would be a cue for the guys downstairs to paint the wall with Ruby.

No brilliant strategy came to mind. I had to trust him.

When he was on the walkway with me, I slipped over to the nook where the tow sack was, took hold of it. Repeat Pete pulled the diary from his coat, said, "Slip this into the bag with the bones, the bones. So I can check the location later, see that you didn't just find a skull, any skull. I find her grave, and it's empty, then I know what I got. What I got."

I took the book, and had just taken hold of the sack and slipped the diary inside, when the door downstairs flew open and there was a bit of light and noise. Now there were two more men, and you guessed it, they had shotguns with flashlights fastened to them. It was an interesting trend.

It was Pooty and Boo-boo. They had arrived at my place and figured out what was going on across the street, probably saw flashlights moving around through the windows.

There were no introductions. As Pete's men turned toward Pooty and Boo-boo, Ruby's brothers let loose, their weapons sounding like cannons going off.

Ruby went low to the ground so as not to get a face full of buckshot, and took out one of Pete's men by shooting him in the side of the head as he was turning. He dropped his gun and the flashlight came loose of its attachment and rolled across the floor. As for the other two on the Repeat Pete squad, they were now retired. Pooty and Boo-boo do not play.

Repeat Pete glared at me. He had a look on his face that made my butt-hole suck air. I think he had decided if he was going out, he was going to take a blonde lady with him.

He raised the automatic and I swung the tow sack. The skull inside of it was heavy enough to give him a good smack, but not heavy enough to do him any real damage. Still, he staggered a little, and when he did, he said, "Shit. Shit." I stuck my foot out before he could regain his balance. He tripped over it and went into the guts of the clock like a lawn dart. He hit the churning gears and screamed as they ripped at his plaid suit and gnawed him up and made him red, and then the gears ground to a stop so violent the clock tower shook.

Later, I thought: I should have said to Pete, as the gears crunched him up, "You're out of time. You're out of time."

What I did instead was give out a little mouse squeak, turn away, and go downstairs with the bones and the diary in the bag.

My legs were shaking when I got down there. Ruby grabbed at me, said, "Hang tough, baby girl. They started it."

I thanked Pooty and Boo-boo, who were dressed in coveralls and wore baseball caps. They had fat round faces and narrow slit eyes, and it was hard to imagine that Ruby was their sister. Right then, I was damn sure glad she was. We all went out of there, closed the door and locked it up, slipped the key back under the mat like friendly neighbors who had only dropped by to water the plants.

Across the street we sat in my living room. I still had the bag. I hadn't let go of it. After a while, Pooty got up and made some drinks and put them in front of us, but I have trouble with alcohol, so I didn't drink any. I just keep it around for those who can drink.

Finally, Ruby got me up and helped me into the bedroom, pushed me on the bed, and pulled off my shoes. She said, "You might want to let go of that bag."

But I didn't. I had it clenched tight to me.

Ruby smiled, turned off the light and started out the door. I could see her shape framed there.

"Don't leave me," I said.

"Repeat and his goons are dead," she said. "Ball is dead, so no trouble there. We got twenty thousand as well. I'll put your part in the kitchen knife drawer."

"Don't leave me."

"Okay, kid. I'm sticking. Shut your mouth and close your eyes, and sleep. I'll be nearby."

When I woke up the next morning, I left the sack of bones on the bed, found Ruby was sleeping on the couch in the living room. I looked out the window at the clock tower. The clock wasn't turning, of course. It was jammed up with Repeat Pete.

I made coffee after checking to see my money was in the knife drawer. I left it there. I made some toast and put it on plates, got out the butter and the jelly, and woke up Ruby.

We ate breakfast and sipped coffee together.

"What happens now?" I said.

"We're done for now. Next time a job pops up you can do, I'll call you. Hell, baby girl. I can see you're messed over by all this, but those bastards got what they deserved. When they find them, it'll look like a gang war. Believe me, the law won't cry over Repeat Pete being chewed up by a clock."

Right then I couldn't see myself doing another job with Ruby. I was considering a career as a hair stylist in a beauty salon. But you had to go to school for that, so maybe cocktail waitress.

"I'll hang onto Ethel, if that's okay with you," I said. "I got plans for her."

"We might could sell her again."

"I don't think so."

She smiled and nodded, knocked back the remainder of her coffee. She hugged me and left.

I sat around all day in a daze hearing gunfire in my head and thinking about Repeat and his plaid suit being munched by the clock.

When it got night, I got the bones and a shovel, drove out to where Ethel had been buried. We had left the grave open when we dug her up. The gaping hole yawned up at me and made me sad. I took the diary out, but left the bones in the tow sack, as a kind of shroud, dropped her in the opening and covered her up. If I had been religious, I would have said a prayer. Instead, I said, "Sorry old girl."

COLLECTIBLES

I placed the diary on the seat beside me, gave it a pat. It had to be better reading than *War and Peace*. I drove home then and felt better about myself, about the whole mess. As far as anyone else but me, Ruby and her brothers knew, the beautiful Etta Place was still lost to history.

A Bostonian (in Cambridge)

BY DENNIS LEHANE

*T*he man who brought the letter to Nathaniel was stooped with age. Yellowed of teeth, of nails, of skin. He extended the piece of paper over the counter and asked, "How much do you pay for something like this?"

Nathaniel put on his glasses. "Well, I'd have to see what's here."

The old man handed it across the counter. "What's here is his kiss off to me."

Dear Johnny Jr.,

The most important thing a boy can learn in this world is to buck up. Because life can be quite the thing! (Why sure it can.) So I need you to buck up. For yourself, for me, and also for your Ma. She's going to need you, son. Need you to be the man around the place, to give her a strong shoulder to cry on when she has one of her sob sessions. Someday, I'll come back and check in. I expect to find a strong feller where I left a fearful boy. You wait for that day, son, and we'll throw a ball around, catch up on a few things why sure.

Respectfully,
Your father, John Sr.

"So, you're Johnny Junior?"

"Well, 'a course," the old man said with a hint of indignation. "No one's born old. I was just a kid when I got that."

Nathaniel considered him. "How old?"

"Six? Seven, tops."

The bell above the door jingled as a woman in a large winter coat and oversized dark glasses entered the store. The cold came with her. She shut the door and passed the counter on the way to the stacks behind Nathaniel. She kept her head down and the dark glasses on, but he noticed the skin along the side of her left eye was purple. The sound of her footsteps came to a stop somewhere between Ancient History and Literary Theory.

Nathaniel returned his focus to the old man.

"Did he ever," he held up the letter, "'come back and check in?'"

Johnny Junior shook his head.

Nathaniel read the man's furtive eyes. "But you know what happened to him."

Johnny Junior nodded.

"And that was?"

"He was bit in the head by a tiger at the circus. It was in all the papers at the time."

Nathaniel used the old Dell to Google it. Took all of thirty seconds. It checked out.

He bought the letter.

As he wrote Johnny Junior the check, the woman with the large glasses walked quickly to the door and let herself back out into the cold. He wondered what she'd been looking for and, given the limited profit margin associated with most of the books in the store, if it would have been worth his time to ask.

He said to the old man, "Did he ever write you again?"

The old man nodded. "But it was after he was bit in the head by the tiger, so it was a bunch of gobbly gook."

"Even so, I'd like to see the letter if you still have it."

"It doesn't make any sense." Johnny Junior took the check. "He was missing a bunch of his head."

"Let me be the judge of that."

"I'll look around for it," the old man said, "but I make no promises."

The bell over the door jingled as Johnny Junior let himself out onto Mt. Auburn Street, the bell as much a nod to an imagined past as the rest of the store. Larchmont Antique Bookshop had stood in this spot, a few blocks east of Harvard Square, since the first year of the Lincoln Presidency. Some books, not terribly valuable necessarily, had sat on its shelves almost as long. Others, not so much old as simply used, bent the description of "antique," though those were the ones—trashy bestsellers mostly with wobbly spines and pages that often smelled of sand and sunscreen—that sold most reliably. And then there were the few books of actual value that Nathaniel kept behind lock and key in a 19th Century Henri II bookcase at the rear of the store. One book, the rarest of them all, he kept tucked away in a lockbox under the floorboards beneath that very bookcase. Few of the books, rare or otherwise, had sold in some time. But it didn't matter much; Nathaniel owned the building, which housed the store and the three-story townhouse above it, and the property taxes were paid by trust.

Truth be told, Nathaniel wasn't as interested in books these days as he was in his ever-growing collection of letters. Rejection letters, in the truest sense. Goodbye letters, stay-away letters, I-don't-love-you-anymore letters. He added Johnny Junior's to the file he'd been building this year. It contained a letter to a woman from the husband who left her the day their fourth child was born, another from a woman whose fiancé left her at the airport as they were about to board a flight to meet her parents. (He said he was going to get some magazines; instead he hopped a cab, went back to their apartment, packed up his stuff, and showed back up for work on Monday at the company where they'd met. Like nothing had ever happened, she told to Nathaniel. As if their love had been something you tried out—like Pilates, like kale—before abandoning it without either prejudice or regret.) The file also contained emails—from jilting lovers, jilting parents, jilting children—as well as a photocopied screenshot of a text that a groom-to-be received while standing at the altar: ON SECOND THOUGHT, NO.

COLLECTIBLES

Nathaniel had read that text at least a hundred times in the first few days after he purchased it. So succinct! So lacking in any room for misinterpretation. The groom-to-be told Nathaniel he'd come to admire the clarity of it, the steely, no-bullshit thrust. Which, he admitted, only made him love her all the more.

Nathaniel put the file away, locked up, and walked along Mt. Auburn Street toward Harvard Square. It was a frigid windless night and his shoes snapped sharply against the cold pavement. The lack of wind could delude one into suspecting it wasn't as cold as one feared, until the chill crept under every stitch of clothing and went to work on the bones. Ankles, knees, hips, elbows, nothing was immune. They were locked in that heartless stretch of winter when the holidays and their festivities hung in the rearview but the promise of low skies, bitter winds, and icy sidewalks still stretched ahead for a few months more. He looked at the windows along Mt. Auburn and remembered a time when, on winter nights just like this one, they'd all be yellowed with lamplight and one could easily envision a collective of disparate readers, here in the intellectual capital of the Northern Hemisphere, as they consumed the knowledge of centuries. Now the light behind those windows was blue or white and small and flickering, like a match flame, as the devices—the smart phones, the tablets, the laptops—held dominion over their willing supplicants.

Nathaniel kept a computer, the old Dell, to deal with inventory. He did not own one at home. His cell phone was a flip phone, nothing "smart" about it except for its consistent ability to make and receive calls. He still looked every inch a young man, but he was an old soul.

He had a bite to eat and a single martini at his usual haunt, Ripley's on Brattle. His mind wandered to the woman who'd come into his store at the end of the evening, of the purple that fringed her left eye. He wondered where she was now and how she had come to his store in the first place and why she had stayed for such a short time before venturing back out into the cold. Nathaniel hadn't dated a woman in over a year—that curator from the Fogg who left him for a boxer who wrote free verse in Spanglish—and hadn't realized he missed it until now, in the way he was picturing the woman's cheekbones and half-imagining a life she led...somewhere. When the bill came, the bartender asked, "How goes the hunt, Nathaniel?"

Her name was Chloe and she'd worked there for years, long enough certainly to know the very few micro-facts there were to know about Nathaniel Dodson, the bookstore owner who never talked about himself.

"Which hunt?"

"Any of them." She looked around the empty bar. "It's a quiet night."

Nathaniel left cash on the small tray she'd delivered, plus his customary tip of 18%. "Not that quiet," he said and shot her a small smile as he shrugged on his coat and headed for the door. He let himself out and walked back home along the same frigid empty streets.

Despite all attempts to remain as private an individual as one could manage in the current age, three pertinent facts about Nathaniel Dodson always slipped out. The first was that he was a twin who'd been separated from his sister at birth. The second (less a fact than an inference) was that his odd interest in collecting letters of abandonment stemmed from never having received one of his own. And the third pertinent fact (more rumor than fact, but ever-persistent) was that he owned the first and most pristine copy of *Tamerlane and Other Poems* by A Bostonian. Fifty copies of this rather pedestrian collection of poems had been published in 1827. Most of these fifty copies failed to survive the next decade. Only five made it out of the century. Of this remaining five, a few popped their heads up over the next one hundred and twenty years and sold for substantial sums, the last known such sale garnering eight hundred thousand dollars back in 2005. And that copy had been dog-eared, wrinkled, several letters smudged within the text.

That comprised what was known. What was not was that Nathaniel Dodson did, in fact, own a copy of *Tamerlane and Other Poems*. But his copy looked to have just arrived from the bindery. It was also the only one to have been numbered in the upper right corner of the title page—*1*—and initialed by the author himself.

The initials were *EAP*, which was of little surprise to those who had, over one hundred and fifty years ago, ascertained that "A Bostonian" was, in fact, Edgar Allan Poe.

COLLECTIBLES

Though Poe had been born in Boston, he'd lost both parents before he was a toddler, and spent the rest of his childhood in Baltimore. Yet, in his first clumsy stab at a pen name, he'd identified as "A Bostonian," as if to say who we become to the world matters less than who we remain in our hearts.

Nathaniel reached the bookstore to find the woman waiting outside. With her dark hair, dark glasses, skin marbled white with the cold.

Somehow, he wasn't surprised.

"Mr. Dodson?"

"Nathaniel." He shook her gloved hand.

"My name is Caris."

He peered back at her, at a loss.

"Caris Jones," she said. "I believe you knew my mother?"

For a moment—maybe several moments, who knew how long exactly—Nathaniel couldn't speak. He stood on the cold street with a closed-off throat and considered this woman in her mid-thirties (or well-preserved early forties), standing before him. A gust moved through the center of his chest, and it seemed possible for a moment that all he'd ever known (and ever wished to know) of heartbreak drizzled through his soul.

"Why don't we step out of the cold?" he suggested.

Inside the bookstore, he turned on a couple of lights, and they sat in the two armchairs by the European History Pre-20th Century section. He offered her tea, which she took him up on. He made it in the back room and brought the cups back out to discover she'd removed her coat, scarf and gloves and lain them across the radiator under the stained glass window. Her skin, which had been so white in the cold, was now mottled red and pink in the warmth of the store.

She removed her glasses and as he'd suspected, the flesh around her left eye formed a mostly unbroken circle of deep purple. Black eye, some called them, though in Nathaniel's limited exposure to them, they usually came in shades of purple or brown.

"Did you fall?" he asked.

She cocked her head at the idea. Then: "Let's go with that for a bit."

He nodded in a way he suspected looked uncertain.

"My mother," she said after a few sips of the tea, "always said you'd be a smart one." She met his eyes over the cup. "She said even as a baby your eyes 'blazed.'"

"And that was a sign of intelligence to her?"

She nodded.

"You're speaking of her in the past tense," he said carefully.

"You don't," she stuttered, "you don't know."

Oh God.

"Know what?" he said.

"She passed. Died."

He went very still. "How?"

"A blood disorder," she said.

"What kind?"

"The plasma in her bone marrow overproduced protein. It killed her. That's what the doctors told us anyway."

"Amyloidosis."

Her big brown eyes grew bigger. The purple stretched around the left one. "That was it. How did you know?"

He sat back across from her and sipped his tea, holding the cup in both hands.

He rolled his eyes at the store. "I read."

"Everything?"

He thought about it.

"Yes," he said.

"She talked about you a lot near the end." She looked over her teacup at him. "Never before. Only once she knew she'd seen her last birthday, last New Year's, that sort of thing."

"What did she say?"

"It's all in the letter."

It's all in the letter. His whole life he'd waited to hear those words. He worked fluid back into his mouth before he dared speak. "She left a letter?"

"Of course. That's why I'm here."

"How do you mean?"

"If a person gets on a laptop anywhere in the world and enters 'twins sep-arated at birth' or 'twins divided' and add our birthdate, you come up. The articles about you, this store, your search for the letter you hoped your mother wrote about the day she gave you up for adoption but…" She trailed off.

"No, no," he said, "finish your thought. The day she gave her son up for adoption, *but…*"

"Kept her daughter."

"Did you read the letter?"

A nod.

"What does it say?"

"It says why."

"Why what?"

"Why she left you."

Well there it was. There it was. The thing he lived for. The need to know. To hear. To find proof that while he was discarded, he had not been discarded *thoughtlessly*. Not if someone wrote a letter to him, decades later, to explain.

"May I see it?"

"I don't have it at the moment."

"Where is it?"

"Back at my motel."

He put his teacup aside. "Well, let's go get it."

"I can't right now."

"Why?"

"I just tried," she said, "but he's still in the room."

"Who is?"

"Gerhardt."

"Who's Gerhardt?"

"My husband."

He gestured in the direction of her bruised eye. "That looks recent."

She nodded. "He gave it to me a few hours ago."

"Why?"

"I tried to leave with the letter."

"And he took it from you?"

"Yes."

"Why?"

"He wants you to pay for it."

"How much?"

"Fifty thousand dollars."

"For a *letter*?"

"Yes."

"Why does he think I'd pay it?"

"Because you want it so badly."

"Even if I did, why would he think I have that kind of money?"

Her eyes roamed the bookstore. "You know why."

"I don't."

"Because you have the book."

"What book?"

"*The* book. Everyone in the book world knows you do."

"And how would you know the book world?"

"I don't. I know the auction world. I used to work for Jardín House in San Francisco. That's where I met Gerhardt. He used to seem nice but he's grown violent. Drinks too much." She shrugged. When she looked him in the eyes, hers were moist. "I never thought this would be my life."

"Leave him."

"When I think I can leave him without him finding me and killing me for it, I will. Until then, I bide my time and mind my manners."

"What will he do if I don't pay?"

"Burn the letter."

"Take me to the motel now."

She shook her head. For a very long time she said nothing and for the same amount of time he watched her.

She raised her head and met his eyes. "Not until you tell me about my father."

Well, of course, he thought.

COLLECTIBLES

Nathaniel Dodson's biological father had not been named Dodson. His name was Moss, Arthur Moss, and when he'd discovered his girlfriend of a few months, Mary Jones of Gilmore, PA., was pregnant with twins, he took the news poorly. So poorly he left Gilmore, left Pennsylvania, and took no part in his offspring's life. Arthur was indigent at this point, not a nickel in his pocket, but that would change five years later when he invented the Wet Weasel, a handheld dry/wet vac' with a canister shaped like a weasel's face. Via *TV Guide* and infomercials, it became a sensation in the mid-80s, and Arthur Moss sold the company and the patent for an obscene amount of money, most of which he invested in cryogenics research and real estate. The former pecked away at the original fortune but the real estate holdings boomed. Mary, on the other hand, had remained destitute and, with no family to speak of, was soon overwhelmed trying to take care of two babies. So, she put one up for adoption.

Nathaniel.

For the next two years, Nathaniel grew up in an orphanage. This led to attachment issues, particularly with women, and a lifelong fascination with those who left. And those they left behind. He'd eventually been adopted and raised by the Dodsons—Nan' and Barry—for whom he always felt fondness, though never love. They were the opposite—they bathed him in love, showered him with it, baked it into his daily bread. They reminded him often that he was unique, as was his story. But he saw through that. Everyone thought his life story was unique, but it wasn't. That it had inherent value, but it didn't. The lives of the abandoned were not much different than the lives of the abandoners in that regard—they lived, and few outside their immediate circle noticed or cared; they died, and were quickly repurposed into anecdotes, cautionary tales, sentimental reveries only half felt, at best, if one were being honest with oneself.

It was the Dodsons who told him the story of his mother, scant as it was. And it would grow scanter. Mary Jones left Pennsylvania while Nathaniel was still in the orphanage; she was never heard from again. If she'd been named Philomena Pinkovich, perhaps, or Claudia Benninger, say, she may have been easier to find. But her name was Mary Jones, and when a Mary Jones decides to hide, she can stay hidden.

Even from Arthur Moss. Who'd hired a half dozen private detectives over the dwindling years of his life to find her and his daughter. He found Nathaniel, who was a high school junior at the time in Portsmouth, NH, quite quickly. He arranged with the Dodsons to have the boy picked up one fine autumn Saturday and driven to Arthur's home in Dover, Massachusetts. In that home, Arthur asked Nathaniel about his interests (books, reading, reading, and books) and informed him that he was both dying and determined to make amends for his past failings. He told Nathaniel that while it was too late to become a proper father, he hoped to prove himself an adequate benefactor.

When he died, he left the house, among other things, to Nathaniel. Nathaniel quickly sold it and purchased the bookstore and the building in which it was housed. As for the rest of Arthur's estate, what didn't sit in Nathaniel's bank account remained in trust.

"Why a trust?" his sister—sister! —asked him now. "You're over the age of 25."

"It's not for me," he said. "It's for you."

Nathaniel had never owned a car. Hadn't driven one since college. She drove, taking them west out of Cambridge toward Route 2. The tires would fail to catch here and there on patches of ice on the road; for a tenth of a second it would feel as if the car might fly off into the trees or slide into someone's front yard. It took a bit for the heat to circulate through the car, and in that time, their teeth chattered when they spoke.

"How m-m-much did he luh-leave me?"

"S-s-s-several million dollars."

"Oh, my."

They drove in silence for a bit and when she spoke again the car was warmer. Not warm exactly but they could no longer see their breath as it left their mouths. "Did he mention me? Wonder what became of me?"

"All the time." He looked at her in the car and searched for a resemblance. In the chin, maybe, and the slope of the forehead. "He searched for you."

"Not hard enough," she said with a sudden bitterness, her teeth clenched against more than just the cold.

"What about her?"

She looked over at him, and empathy flooded her face. "I'm sorry, Nathaniel. She told me at the end that it had hurt so much to give you up once, that she couldn't revisit it. She imagined you were happy, well cared for. And then…"

"What?"

"She shut you out of her mind."

A girlfriend, a nurse, had once elaborately taken Nathaniel's pulse, sighing through her nostrils the whole time. When he asked her why, she said she was checking to see if he had one. He had cultivated his existence on a removal from messy emotions, not because he was afraid of them but because he suspected he might not have any. But at the mention of his mother and her lack of interest in him, he could feel his heart. He could feel it perfectly. As it clenched. Contracted. A muscle suspended in blood. Screaming and screaming. Unheard, unnoticed, unwanted.

To turn his heart back away from the things that made it scream, he changed the subject. "It's about ten million."

"What he left me?" her eyes grew wide in the car.

He nodded. "Not counting real estate. You could get away from Gerhardt. Hire attorneys, get a restraining order."

They stopped at a red light hung by cable above the country road. It swayed in a sudden gust that whistled as it moved through the surrounding hills.

It finally sank in.

Caris turned in her seat. "I could just leave right now. I could turn the car around." She looked back the way they'd come. "Why not?"

"The letter."

Her mouth formed an 'O.' She continued to stare back down the empty road as the traffic light washed the windshield in a green glow. But they stayed put. "Maybe we could negotiate with him."

Nathaniel gave it some thought. "He'll be furious you left him. Irrational. He'll burn it." He looked at her for confirmation. "Won't he?"

She didn't have to nod. Or speak. The answer lived in her eyes.

She pulled the car over on the soft shoulder, old snow crunching beneath the tires. She looked across the seat at him. "Can you live without it?"

Could he?

If they turned the car around right now, he could go back to his life. But now with a sister. She could tell him more than any letter ever could. Yet...

It wouldn't be his mother's penmanship and it wouldn't be a permanent artifact. Just an oral history, prone to gaps of memory. No direct one-to-one connection with the woman who'd carried him in her body for nine months.

So, no, he couldn't live without it.

Except...

Caris could turn around and drive right into a whole new life. A life of comfort, free from worry, with, as he'd mentioned, access to attorneys who could make her problematic husband go away.

For the price of one letter from a woman he'd never met, he could buy his sister a whole new fate.

"Yes," he said and his stomach eddied. "I'll live without it."

She didn't seem ready for that answer. "Why? You barely know me."

"I don't know her at all," he said.

She sat very still for some time. Long enough that the heat overtook the car and grew stuffy and they had to turn it down.

When she spoke, there was new steel in her voice. "I know what it's like to spend my life with a question that might never be answered, a need that might never be met." She took his gloved hands in hers. "It's unbearable. You've given me our father tonight. You've given me our father plus a future. More than I could have ever hoped." She squeezed his fingers, her eyes glistening in the dark. "Let me give you our mother."

He could hear them both breathing. As close together in that car as they would have been in the womb.

"You want to go get the letter," he said.

"I want to go get the letter," she said.

His eyes had fully adjusted to the dark of her car. And her face loomed from that darkness in distinct colors—the white of her flesh, the red of her lips, the great warm brown of her yearning eyes.

"Then let's go," he said.

───────────

They turned into the parking lot of the Redcoat Inn in Acton, a one story, u-shaped compound of utilitarian motel rooms, each with a faded red door. Nathaniel guessed it housed about 50 units but there were only a dozen cars in the parking lot. Once the fall foliage season was over, few travelers came to Acton, a sleepy bedroom community for people priced out of Concord and Lincoln. However, the motel (calling it an inn was far too charitable) sat along a main industrial strip that appeared to have been cut out of the surrounding forests by a pack of drunks wielding scythes or driving backhoes. Across the road from the motel was a grain store and a shack that repaired lawnmowers and down the road a bit was an office park. None of it, save the motel, was lit up. The motel itself gave off the air of a place where people went to quench illicit desires and fell asleep smoking in bed. The door to unit 112, in fact, was scorched black and boarded up as if to bear out Nathaniel's suspicions.

Gerhardt and Caris had rented unit 127, first floor, in the back, facing the woods. Caris and Nathaniel parked in front of unit 123. Someone had discarded a truck trailer back there long enough ago for it to sprout weeds, but otherwise there were only four cars around back and one of them was the one they were sitting in.

"His car's not here."

"You brought two cars?"

She nodded. "In case."

"In case of what?"

"That what I asked Gerhardt. He said, 'In case of things you need an in-case for.'"

"Where could he be?"

"There's a bar about two miles down the road," she said.

He looked at the clock on the dashboard and was surprised to discover it was only 9:30. A common deception of the dead of winter, he'd long found, was that it always felt so much later than it actually was.

She removed a door key from her purse. Not a key, per se, but a white plastic card with a magnetic strip. Her hands shook, and it wasn't cold in the car. She unbuckled her seat belt and reached for the door handle.

"What are you doing?" he asked.

"I'm going in before he gets back."

He snatched the card out of her hand. "You can't. What if he comes back? He's hurt you once."

"I know he's hurt me. And it's a lot more than once." She chewed her lower lip for a moment, then turned to him with a look in her eyes that was a bizarre combination of ferocity and terror. "It's our one chance. I run in and run right back out."

"I'll do it," he said.

"You don't know where it is," she said.

"So, tell me."

She stared at him long enough that he knew what she was thinking—was he up to the task? Nathaniel was not a physically formidable man. He had no tales of bravery or wild pluck in his biography. He was a bookstore owner; he wore comfortable loafers, wool sweaters, and corduroy pants.

"Nathaniel," she said carefully.

"Just tell me where it is. Come on. He could come back any second."

Her eyes scurried back and forth. Then settled. "It's under the nightstand on the far side of the bed."

"Why did you hide it there?"

"I didn't. Gerhardt ripped the envelope out of my hand and threw it across the room. When I looked around for it later—with him never taking his eyes off me—I saw it peeking out from under the nightstand."

He looked down the line of red doors until he reached 127. He swallowed several times. "Does Gerhardt have a gun?"

"I don't think so."

That wasn't exactly a definitive answer.

"Have you ever seen him with a gun? Known him to have a gun? Entered a gun store together?"

"No."

"To which question?"

"All of them."

He could picture Gerhardt—a big blocky German, he assumed, with a blocky crewcut and a big square head and shoulders like I-beams—sitting at a bar up the road. Downing a shot and the rest of his beer as he tossed bills on the bar top and reached for his coat...

He reached for the door handle. "Be right back."

And before he could stop himself, he stepped out of the car into the bracing cold. It had dropped at least ten degrees since they left Cambridge. It found the small bones in his ears first, invaded his nostrils and froze the interior walls. As for his feet, he should have worn boots.

His hand shook when he tried to swipe the key in the door lock. Shook enough that it took him three tries, but on the third one the red light above the door handle went from red to green and he opened the door and stepped inside. The moment he was inside, he marveled at the fact that he'd done it, he'd actually done it—entered a stranger's room with a borrowed key. To steal something.

He kept his gloves on.

The room smelled of fast food and a recent shower and the faint chemical smell of ritually applied cleaning solvents used in cheap motels countrywide. (He assumed they all purchased in bulk from the same company.) Nathaniel again got an image of big blocky Gerhardt pushing off from the bar, and the thought got him moving around the bed to the nightstand. He dropped to his knees and slipped his finger under the nightstand and felt only rug. He tilted the piece back with one hand and slid his whole hand under. And felt nothing.

A shadow fell across his body.

A thought—*This is not good*—crossed his mind as he turned his head to see a somewhat slight man standing over him. The man had a face too chubby for the rest of his body, as if he stored nuts in his cheeks for the winter. He also had a stick of some kind in his left hand, which he swung down onto the side of Nathaniel's head.

It's not like in the movies, Nathaniel would have told a friend later (if he had any friends)—when you get knocked out, you don't just go to sleep and wake up with a headache. In reality, it was more like a temporary liftoff from your everyday consciousness. Your *full* awakeness. The man hit Nathaniel twice—the first blow a bit hesitant, the second more assured. The first blow landed on Nathaniel's ear and the second just above it. The room *did* spin— movies got that much right—and the walls and bed lurched as if they were being uprooted. Nathaniel felt instantly nauseous. The lights were suddenly far too bright. The man with the stick (or club, whatever it was) pulled Nathaniel to his feet by the back of his hair and Nathaniel was propelled backward, stumbling, until he landed, half-in/half-out of a chair. After a few moments, his right buttock came off the chair arm and settled into the chair with the rest of him. The man stood before him, swaying with the room, and Nathaniel worried he might throw up. He blinked several times, clenched his eyes for several seconds in which he feared he *might* pass out, and then his eyes cleared even as a pins-n-needles sensation in his face grew worse.

"Are you gonna puke?" The man seemed genuinely curious.

"I don't know," Nathaniel admitted.

The man brandished a nightstick, the kind police carried. It was wet near the tip. *With my blood*, Nathaniel realized, and a bit of bile found the back of his throat at the thought. Still, he didn't puke.

The man lifted his chin with the end of the nightstick. "What's your name?"

"Nathaniel. What's yours?"

"Gerhardt."

He didn't look like a "Gerhardt" at all. He looked like a "Cooper" or an "Aaron." He looked WASPY and a tad schlubby. Fine blonde hair thinning rapidly at 30, dad bod on its way under a plain white hoodie and charcoal sweatpants. He looked like he was hanging around the ski lodge for one more cup of hard cider before retiring.

"What are you doing in my room, Nathaniel?"

"Is this your room?" Nathaniel tried.

Gerhardt stabbed him in the abdomen with the nightstick. "Let's not be rude."

It took Nathaniel a minute to get his breath back.

Gerhardt watched him. "You came for your letter from Mommy." He poked him in the abdomen again with the nightstick, but it was much lighter than the stab. "Right?"

Nathaniel nodded.

"Did you bring my money?" Gerhardt asked.

"I don't have fifty thousand dollars on me."

Gerhardt squatted down in front of Nathaniel. "But you could get it."

Nathaniel said, "When my bank opens."

Gerhardt laughed at that. Laughed hard. When the laughs eventually trailed off, he said, "It's not the nineties for god's sakes. You can access your bank account from anywhere and wire me the money."

"Right now?"

"Right now."

"I don't have a computer."

"I do."

"Was she in on it?"

"Hmm?"

"Caris. Is she part of this?"

A strange smile. "She's not part of *this*, I can assure you."

"But of something else? Some other part?"

Another strange smile. "Let me get my laptop."

They never checked for a gun. It was quite amazing. Time after time, Nathaniel would have assumed these grifters, these hustlers, these stickup men and women, these cut-rate liars and thieves would consider the possibility—at least *one of them* over the years—that even meek and mild looking men who read Trollope by the fireplace and could quote Yeats might own a firearm.

Or several of them.

When Gerhardt turned back with the laptop open in one hand and the nightstick in the other, Nathaniel was pointing the small .22 at him. It was

Gerhardt's turn to grow pale and sickly-looking. His mouth opened to say something and Nathaniel fired the bullet straight into it. Gerhardt barely made a sound. He landed on the double bed along with the laptop. Much of his brain matter, pink as tonsils and tongue, ended up on the print over the bed, a wholly unimaginative painting of Walden Pond in the autumn. So unimaginative, in fact, that the addition of blood and bone and brain matter arguably improved it.

Nathaniel stayed where he was for a minute or so, waiting to hear any movement from adjoining rooms. There would be some kind of to-do if someone thought they heard a gunshot, the sounds of scrambling and scrabbling. But nothing. Just silence and the drips from the print above the bed.

He opened the door and looked out on the mostly empty parking lot. Caris's car was gone, as he'd expected it would be. He closed the door again and returned to the corpse on the bed. He fished in Gerhardt's sweatpants and came back with a rental car key and fob. He pressed the fob and heard a satisfying *beep-beep* from the parking lot.

He found it in a dresser drawer. It was addressed to him in a typescript that was designed to look ritzy, he supposed. He opened it and pulled out the single sheet of paper inside. Even now, some part of him hoped against all evidence to the contrary that it would be the thing he sought, dreamed of, yearned for.

It was blank.

"But don't you feel stupid?" he asked the corpse before he let himself out of the room.

———

Over the years, a few enterprising grifters had come to the conclusion—independent of one another, it bore noting—that the best way to separate Nathaniel from his copy of *Tamerlane* was to lure him away from the bookshop where it was rumored to be hidden with the promise of a letter from his mother.

Which is to say, Nathaniel had picked up a bit of an antenna when it came to grifters.

COLLECTIBLES

He'd had the first two arrested. But the third, a slippery sociopath named Harris Euclid had forced Nathaniel's hand, which is to say his heart, which was a cold, cold organ, when one got right down to it. For while his heart knew much of—and highly valued—civility, courtesy, basic decency, and even sympathy for those less fortunate, it knew nothing of empathy or love.

He could have sold *Tamerlane* and put an end to it. But he realized the grifters saw it all as a game, and so did he. He loved games. The orderly nature at the heart of them. How, in the most serious games, nothing less than fate hung in the balance. And if some of these grifters hadn't understood they were playing for mortal stakes, that wasn't Nathaniel's concern. Ignorance of the stakes was no absolution for poor game play.

Nathaniel found a classical station on Gerhardt's rental car and drove the rest of the way to Cambridge with the music playing softly. He parked the rental car on Mass Ave., alongside the red brick wall that encircled Harvard Yard, and walked toward the river and his building. He bypassed the store and entered the building through the front door. He was unsurprised to find his home ransacked—drawers open in every room, cushions removed or flipped up, the mattress half off the box spring in the bedroom. Which is where she would have found the key. Just frantic enough by that point to fail to consider why it had been relatively easy to discover.

He took the back stairs down to the bookstore.

She'd moved the 19th Century Henri II bookcase (easy enough to do; it was on wheels), and removed the loose floorboards to get to the lock box beneath. It was cemented in place so moving it wasn't an option. But she'd had the key, which still dangled from the open door.

Tamerlane and Other Poems by A Bostonian was kept in a clamshell box, the kind so commonly used to protect rare books that to find one without it would be suspicious.

Caris had dropped it after sitting down. It lay at her feet, the top corner of *Tamerlane* edging out from inside. Nathaniel nudged it back in with a gloved finger.

He was surprised to hear the tiniest wisps of breath leaving Caris's mouth and nostrils. Some part of her still struggled for life.

"Ironically," he told her, in case she could still hear, "the box is arguably worth more than the book. Not that one could legally sell such a thing." He placed a chair across from her and sat in it. "I had it made in Australia many years ago. The man who made it charged me four hundred thousand dollars. One could hardly blame him. His life was at risk from the first stage of creation to the last. He used the pulp of a stinging plant with the ridiculous name of gympie gympie, native to the region. In the smallest quantities, the gympie gympie can make a victim feel like they're being electrocuted. Sometimes the sensation lasts for months. Months! Of feeling you're being electrocuted. I can barely imagine. But, of course, you weren't exposed to a small quantity. You suffered a maximum dose." He watched twin rivulets of blood leave her nostrils. "Still hanging in there," he said and whistled.

He peered into her eyes but they were blank. Whatever piece of her still fought for breath did so like a germ or a virus. It had no conscious will, just innate selfishness.

"When I was very, very young," he told her, "my mother threw me away. I have no memories of my two years in an orphanage. People would always assure me that was a good thing. But what they don't realize is that lack of memory of facts doesn't mean lack of memory of feeling. I can remember *feeling* afraid. And discarded. And unworthy of love. And by the time someone came along to wipe those feelings away, well, it was too late. You see, those who leave take the power of those who are left. They take it with them. Somewhere, I assume, are people who care about you. But you're gone now and they'll never know what happened to you. You can trust me on that one. They'll wonder. They'll search for answers where there are none. Invent fantasies of what happened. Some of them, like your Bostonian here—" he indicated the book on the floor in front of her—"become great storytellers because of this."

Sometime in the last minute, she had stopped breathing. He removed his winter gloves so as not to ruin them and went to the small bathroom in back, where he retrieved the gloves of vulcanized rubber he used on such occasions. He returned to the room and lifted the clamshell box off the floor. She stared at him with empty eyes, her mouth open, jaw askew.

Miss Golden Dreams 1949

BY JOYCE CAROL OATES

H el-*lo!* Welcome to Sotheby's! Come *in.*

As you see, your seats are reserved. Today's (private) auction is restricted to the most elite collectors.

And I am the most prized item on the bill—*Miss Golden Dreams 1949.*

That's to say the single, singular, one-of-her-kind three-dimensional living-breathing-plasma-infused *PlastiPlutoniumLuxe Miss Golden Dreams 1949.*

Not mass-produced. Not "replicated." Just—me.

(Re)created from the authentic DNA of—me.

The most famous pinup in the history of America *and* the most famous centerfold in the history of *Playboy. And* by popular acclaim the Number One Sex Symbol of the Twentieth Century.

Do you doubt, Daddy? Approach the platform—(no, Daddy, you can't climb up on the platform!)—see for yourself.

My eyes *see.* This voice you hear is issued from *me,* it is not a spooky recording of Marilyn's hushed breathy little-girl voice but the authentic thing. *I am the authentic thing. Full-sized, anatomically correct in every crucial way.*

How am I "animated"? I am *not animated,* Daddy. I am *alive.*

In fact I am superior to the original Miss Golden Dreams. *She* was just a frightened girl, her (flat, perfect) stomach growling from hunger. Those shadowy parts of my brain that once preserved troublesome memories have been (mostly) excised. My teeth are certainly in better condition—whiter, more even, and cavity-free—than they were in 1949. A heated red liquid is circulating in my veins and arteries, serving double duty as one-third again more efficient in carrying oxygen to my brain than my old anemic blood—*and* it's an aphrodisiac, an added bonus.

Good thing you've brought your checkbook, Daddy.

How'd you like to own me, Daddy? Take me home with you? Love me? Daddy, I know I could love *you*.

All you've got to do, Daddy, is make a bid for *Miss Golden Dreams*. And keep bidding. Keep upping the ante. Up—up—up until your rivals fall behind, panting and defeated.

Lowest acceptable purchase price for *Miss Golden Dreams* today is twenty-two million. Highest—hey, there is no *highest*.

In fact, it's predicted that we will set a Sotheby's record this very day—*you*, the most elite of Marilyn collectors, and *me*, Marilyn.

Yes, Miss Golden Dreams is the original Marilyn nude. *The* nude. The one you saw as a boy and never forgot. The one that rendered all the girls, at least the girls you knew, and the women you would come to know, irrelevant.

So young! (Practically as young as your granddaughter but don't think *that*.)

Fun fact: I was paid fifty dollars to pose for this photo.

Fun fact: I wasn't "Marilyn Monroe" yet—the studio hadn't named me. I was Norma Jeane Baker.

Fun fact: already I'd been abandoned by a husband, divorced.

Fun fact: occupation *starlet* but—already—dropped by my studio.

Gaze greedily upon Norma Jeane as she was in 1949—more than seven decades ago. *That* was an era of female beauty like none before or since, and Miss Golden Dreams is the most desirable of them all—the "icon" beside which all other females fall short.

Flawless nude on red velvet. Soft sinuous velvet like the red interior of a heart. Creamy-white baby-soft skin, flawless skin, bright red-lipstick smile revealing small perfect white teeth, blond hair tumbling past (bare white) shoulders.

Pinnacle of human evolution—a female infinitely desirable yet unthreat-ening. An infant, yet a sexualized infant. Sweet-smiling, dimpled cheek, sparkly-eyed gazing coyly at *you* as a little girl would do, partly hiding her face. (For this is Daddy's girl, but a *naughty-Daddy's-girl.*)

Now in the twenty-first century human evolution has passed the point at which the species can only be reproduced by sexual intercourse—that's to say, by the powerful attraction between the sexes; in a (not-very-romantic) era of artificial insemination, sperm donors, uteruses-for-hire and surrogate moth-ers, a dazzling blond female is no longer essential but has become a luxury item like an expensive sports car or a yacht—a thirty-room mansion overlook-ing the Pacific... If you can afford these, Daddy, you can afford *me.*

My promise is that, being dazzling-blond, and nude, which means bare-foot, I will not ever demand equality from you; I will not—ever!—decide that I want to be you by defiling my perfect female body—having ghastly surgery to remove my breasts, or to remove my velvety-red vagina and replace it with...

Ugh!—I know. Just the thought is—nauseating.

(And people wonder why so many disgusting "trannies" are raped, slaugh-tered, cast aside—as if rogue females are not inviting misogyny by refusing to be *feminine.*)

Not Miss Golden Dreams! Not me.

Here before you lying naked and docile as an infant is the apotheosis of what was once celebrated as *femininity.*

Yes, I am proud of myself—this "self." Flawless creamy-white skin, moist blue eyes, girl's pointed upturned breasts and narrow (twenty-two inches!) waist and tender bare feet with toes tucked under.

What a thrill for you! (And you, and you.)

That special low-down-dirty thrill knowing that Miss Golden Dreams was paid so little to abase herself, naked; paid so little to pose for the image from which *PlastiPlutoniumLuxe Miss Golden Dreams* has been fashioned by the miracle of twenty-first century robo-technology.

It's a thrill, too, don't deny it, that *you* will bid millions to own me, in a fury of sexual competition with your brother-rivals; and once you have won me, and brought me home with you, and locked the door after me, you will keep me to yourself—for the remainder of your natural life.

You're a rich man, you have taste. You've acquired Renoirs, Matisses. Those late, erotic drawings of Picasso celebrating the elderly satyr and the always-young voluptuous girl-children who entice him.

You own silkscreens by Warhol—*Jackie, Liz, Marilyn.*

But these are flat, two-dimensional. The (ugly) Warhol *Marilyn* is a cartoon figure, no life, no breath, no soft white arms to embrace you until you cry out.

And so, your collection is not complete. Not until you acquire *me.*

Thrilling to you, Daddy, who is wealthy, and has never been desperate for fifty dollars (with which to reclaim a battered second-hand repossessed car), near-penniless since you have no employment other than *starlet* or *model* where men call the shots, pay cash and no tips; you who might if you wish scatter gold coins on the pavement for beggars to scramble after; you, a gentleman of a certain age, class, stature who will adore Marilyn as long as she resembles her young self, and never ages. And in this form, as a *PlastiPlutoniumLuxe* creation, Marilyn is guaranteed to *never age.*

Can't blame you, Daddy. No!—never blame *you.*

For as you age it's all the more crucial for you to keep a gorgeous young woman by your side, as a reminder that, though *aging,* you are (somehow) still young, indeed you are no more than my age, for a woman must be the mirror of a man's soul, otherwise—who cares for her? *Why* care for her?

No! I am *not being sarcastic.* Certainly, I am *not being shrill.*

I am breathless, breathy. My voice is a little-girl voice—feathery-soft. You must incline your head, to hear. Kingly, you lower yourself to me, that you might raise me, a beggar-maid in disguise, to your own level.

No one blames you! Of course not—no.

Marilyn understood. Marilyn forgave. Marilyn never blamed Daddy, never blamed her own mystery-Daddy who'd abandoned her mother (and her) when she was a baby, in 1926. Never bitter, Miss Golden Dreams has made a career of the opposite of bitter, for men do not like *bitter* and who can blame them?—not Marilyn!

Not bitter that I'd earned millions of dollars for strangers but not for myself. Not bitter since I've become an *icon* and a *collectible*—that's enough glory for *me*.

I was the very first *Playboy* centerfold—in November 1953. Hugh Hefner had seen pictures of me, he'd had to have me as his first centerfold—guaranteeing success for *Playboy;* but he never got around to paying me, not a penny.

(Don't believe me? That Mr. Hefner didn't give me a penny? See, he'd bought the right to the photograph from the photographer, for $500. Not a thing to do with me.)

(Which doesn't mean that Hugh Hefner wasn't crazy for me. For sure, he *was.*)

(Oh, Mr. Hefner was romantic! After I died he paid $75,000 to purchase the cemetery plot right beside me and when *he* died in 2017, at the age of ninety-one, he was buried there—right beside me. *His* Marilyn.)

(I know, it's strange. It's hard to believe. That Hugh Hefner could be crazy for me, pay $75,000 to be buried beside me, but never pay me a penny for the use of "Marilyn." You just shake your head, bemused—*men!*)

Not to boast a little but I wasn't only just the first—and most famous—*Playboy* centerfold, I was also the first *Playboy* cover. All over America on newsstands—the newest glossy magazine for men with Marilyn Monroe on the cover! Though I am wearing a low-cut dress in this photograph, though I am *not nude,* yet how gorgeous I am, and how young!—my face distended by a wide red lipstick-smile that will never, ever *go out.*

See, Daddy? Just the way I'm smiling at you, right now.

Bidding will start in a few minutes! Please take your (reserved) seat.

Please do not stand in the aisle staring at me, Daddy. I told you that I am the actual "Marilyn"—I mean, Norma Jeane. And yes, I am *alive*—I am a *living thing.*

You're blocking the way for other customers, Daddy. There will be plenty of time to stare at me once you're seated and the auction begins.

You are a special Sotheby's Platinum Plus client, Daddy. Which is why there is a name plate on your chair. Which is why I am smiling and winking at *you.*

Would you like to love me? Take me home with you? Yes?

Desperate for love all my life. Not just when I was Norma Jeane and scrambling to be a photographer's model and starlet. All my life until the last night of my life (about which we don't have to speak nor will you wish to inquire for of all things Daddy does not wish to know about his Marilyn, her final miserable days and nights) for I'd been taught by my (abandoned, scorned) mother's example that if a woman isn't loved she is nothing.

If a woman is not beautiful, desirable, glamorous, "sexy" she isn't going to be loved and if she isn't loved she is—nothing.

And if she is nothing she will be very, very unhappy; like my mother, she will end up in a lunatic asylum where the predominant desire is to wish to die.

Daddy, I have a feeling you will like this: a low-down-dirty thrill to learn that I was married while in high school—sixteen—very young for my age despite my shapely body—(but a virgin!)—and very lonely. Though my mother did not love me for more than a few fleeting seconds over the years, and could not force herself to embrace me, let alone kiss me, yet I cried and cried for her in the orphanage, where I was placed when she could not care for me, and in the (nineteen) foster homes where I was sometimes—not *always,* only just *sometimes*—sexually molested.

Well, we didn't call it by such a nasty term, then. Not *sexually molested.* So vulgar! You might say *interfered with.* You might say *drew unwanted male attention.* You might say *the way that girl looked, already at age twelve, you could see she was trouble.*

In the final foster home in L.A. my foster mother took pity on me, or maybe she was exasperated with me for my continual surprise when boys and men "interfered" with me, and she'd had enough of my crying, and didn't like the way my foster dad was eyeing me, so she introduced me to a neighborhood boy a few years older than me, who proposed to me right away—and we were married right away—except—(I never understood why, I don't understand even now)—my young husband Jim abandoned me after just a few months to join the Merchant Marines and get as far away from Los Angeles as he could.

Why was the question I asked Jim, begged him, he'd said he loved me, so why then did he leave me? Why do you say you love me but then leave me, do I need more love than you can give? More love than you are capable of? Continuous love like a radio that is never turned off? Unflagging love, relentless love, ravenous love? All I wanted was to prepare Jim's meals and cuddle with him, make love with him, bury my face in his neck and hide in his arms and—I guess—he became frightened of me—I started calling him Daddy when he was just twenty years old…

Thrilling to you, Daddy, I guess—to know that I was "suicidal." Just in my teens I'd threatened to slash my wrists when my husband shipped out (by his request) to Australia, begged him to make me pregnant before he left but he refused—abandoned me and left me and broke my heart.

You wouldn't break my heart, would you? Promise?

It's a sign how naïve I am, and how innocent I am, that men have broken my heart—*you* have broken my heart—so many times.

Yes, I am shy. Everyone said so, how shy I was. (And am.) Except when my clothes were removed my shyness seemed to melt away, too.

Why is this?—I do not know.

In this, I am unlike *you*. For *you* would be mortified to appear naked in the eyes of strangers. *You* could not bear to be stared at, assessed and judged.

I've never been ashamed of my body. I did not actually think of it as "my" body—I called it my "Magic Friend"—where I got this from, I do not know.

Of course, robo-technology has replicated Norma Jeane's skin of 1946— (perhaps it is even more dazzling-smooth than the original!—that's an extra bonus for you). Creamy-white *Plastaepidermis* covering *PlastiPlutoniumLuxe Miss Golden Dreams* snug as a glove.

My Magic Friend never let me down. She had the power to make strangers love me. I always knew—I still believe this—that if my father had seen my Magic Friend he'd have loved her, too. I mean—*me*.

Look how you're all staring at her—gosh! I guess, I'd stare at her, too.

What was wonderful was when you looked at my Magic Friend naked, you didn't see *me*. Poor sad Norma Jeane could hide inside her.

That's why deformity and ugliness scare me!—I never want to get old, wrinkled, shriveled, ugly. Always I want to be Miss Golden Dreams—just as I am right now.

(And it is a fact, this is *me*. Recreated from the "organic residue"—DNA—of my actual, authentic, certified corpse, through the miracle of medical technology reconstituted as the gorgeous nude girl lying before you in a suggestive-yet-innocent pose on red velvet.)

(Yes, it's hard to grasp. "Marilyn Monroe" officially died in 1962, aged thirty-six; born in 1926 she'd be ninety-five now. But *that's* just the old Marilyn, of yesteryear; we are living in a very different world now, where if you can afford it you can be "de-aged" while living, and "reconstituted" following your death.)

Almost, I seemed to know that I would live forever—somehow! Even as a girl, Norma Jeane had faith.

In my interviews I would say (in my little breathy Marilyn-voice with widened blue-gray eyes)—"No sex is wrong if there's love in it."

And I would say—"If I could have a baby, I would never be sad again."

You would have given me a baby, wouldn't you, Daddy? I guess it's kind of too late now, even the miracle of *PlastiPlutoniumLuxe* doesn't enable you to have children but you can do (almost) anything else with state-of-the-art *PlastiGenitalia* as you will see.

Anyway, I know that I would have been a good mother! All the mistakes my own mother made, I would not make. Not Marilyn!

Would've adored a beautiful little angel-baby, little girl-baby I'd have dressed like a doll. Cuddle, and kiss, and wrap in swaddling clothes, and bury in the cradle so we wouldn't hear her wailing, in our bed.

If her hair turned out brunette, not blond, not white-blond like my hair, that would've presented a problem, I guess—the public would look from baby girl to me and figure out that my hair wasn't "natural blond" so there'd be sniggering pieces in the media. (Easiest solution would've been to bleach the baby's hair to match my shade of blond, I guess!)

But the main purpose was to have a perfect little baby to be the momma of, Norma Jeane like she was supposed to be, not as she *was*.

Well, it didn't happen, Daddy. No need to look worried—it *won't*.
No need for you to be jealous of a kid, Daddy. Never happened.

I love you looking at me, Daddy—don't stop! Guess you understand,
most of what I say is just kidding?

Marilyn is a ray of sunshine, so *funny*. Not nasty-funny, sarcastic-funny,
but little girl-funny to make you feel good about the world.

Such fun we'll have together, Daddy!

Don't listen to the rumors, Daddy. Some people are saying, jealous people, nasty ignorant people, that I have been auctioned here at Sotheby's many
times, and that this is not the first time. Some people are claiming that fatal
"accidents" happen to the wealthy collectors who have acquired me, sometimes within a few days—falls down flights of stairs that result in broken
necks and severed vertebrae, cardiac arrest midway in vigorous intercourse,
aneurysms, glioblastomas, untraceable "organic" poisons that cause the liver
to disintegrate—but these are false rumors, and very silly rumors, pay not the
slightest heed to them, Daddy.

I vow I will adore you—only *you*. I swear, there have been no men before
you, Daddy. *You* are unique.

As I am lying in this inviting pose on the red velvet drapery with my
perfect glowing *Plastaepidermis* and perfectly coiffed blond *Plastahair* so I
will lie at your feet. I will prostrate myself before you. I will be your beautiful
bride. I will not—ever—murmur a word of sarcasm. I will not be impatient
with you though you are a foolish doddering old man; I will be respectful of
you, I will fawn over you, as only a "fawn" can "fawn"—(we have learned our
tricks young, fawns and girls, for we have learned to survive).

I vow, Daddy: I will never accuse you of not loving me. I will never accuse
you of abandoning me. I will never accuse you of exploiting or betraying me.
I will never accuse you of taking my money, hiding it in secret accounts. I will
never collapse in hysterical tears crying and screaming at you that I loathe
you—the very sight, the very touch, the *smell* of you.

I am not a madwoman. I do not cry "ugly" tears—when I cry, I am
very fetching.

I am not a nasty woman. I do not want to be your equal. I will adore *you*.

COLLECTIBLES

I am not bitter. Bitter wouldn't melt in my mouth.

Nobody wants a broody teary *Playboy* centerfold. Can't blame them! I wouldn't, myself.

Could you guess seeing me here so young, posing in the nude on sensuous folds of red velvet, so sweetly smiling, so unperturbed and unaccusing, that within a decade I would be the Sex Symbol of the Century and a few years after that I would be dead...

You could guess? Yes?

But no, don't think of *that*. Not yet—(you haven't even brought me home. Our honeymoon has not even begun).

Though it is thrilling, isn't it?—to think of *that*.

Thrilling revenge of the male, that the female is so easily destroyed. The way you can break a crystal glass under your feet. The way you can smudge a watercolor—it will never be the same again. Crumple a butterfly's wings in your fist.

Miss Golden Dream's beauty makes you sick, really. Your weakness thrown in your face—resentment, humiliation, shame that this afternoon you will be in a frenzy to bid millions of dollars for an animated *PlastiPlutoniumLuxe* doll in fierce bidding with other males in which your dread is that you will be impotent and fail—for only one of you is the most wealthy, the Alpha Male— and he will "collect" me.

For Marilyn will be auctioned—sold—to the highest bidder. Never any doubt, that is the promise—Marilyn will come into the possession of the highest bidder.

Money will go to strangers, not to Marilyn. But Marilyn is not bitter. Look at that fresh young face glowing with happiness, which is a kind of innocence! Nothing to do with money, nor with questioning the motives of others.

Love me, Daddy! I will love you.

Every man who'd ever loved me abused me. Not bitter! Just a fact.

Sometimes it was push, shove, pummel, punch. Sometimes it was cold vicious-shouted verbal abuse. *Tramp! Whore!*

Oh, yes! Piteous. But *you* will be the exception.

But *you* will not abuse me, will you? Not *you*.

188

As *you* will not topple drunkenly down a flight of stairs fleeing in terror from your *PlastiPlutoniumLuxe* bride with the hard-clamping arms and legs, fall screaming thumping against steps and break your neck. *You* will not suffer a heart attack in our marital bed as the hard-clamping arms and legs grip you like a python, you will not die of an untraceable organic toxin from the dazzling red-lipstick smile—*you* are special.

And so, *you* deserve *me*. Blond bombshell who's also girl-next-door. Ever-alive, exactly as she was in 1949—precisely replicated chromosomes, identical cells down to the teeny-weeniest organelle. See! I am breathing, my eyelids are fluttering, my gaze is fixed upon *you*.

We be happy together! Have fun together! Just you and me.

Tell me what you like best, and I will do it. And do it, and do it.

I will keep every secret of yours. I will suck you dry, the loose flabby sac of you eviscerated and your brittle bones turned to soup. And you will scream in ecstasy, I promise.

Remember, Daddy, all you've got to do is make a bid for *Miss Golden Dreams*. And keep bidding. Don't ever stop bidding. Up—up—up until your rivals fall behind, defeated. The lowest estimate for *Miss Golden Dreams* at today's auction is only twenty-two million.

Highest?—Daddy, there is no *highest*.

...from Otto Penzler's Mysterious Obsession:

LINGO DAN
PERCIVAL POLLARD

*Q*ueen's *Quorum* is an important and fascinating reference book but it is also wildly idiosyncratic. The original version was described on the title page as: *A History of the Detective-Crime Short Story as Revealed in the 106 Most Important Books Published in the Field Since 1845*. It is a good list of books that gives recognition to many of the best works in the genre and serves as an excellent guide for readers.

One might question the inclusion of certain titles, such as Mark Twain's *The Celebrated Jumping Frog of Calaveras County* (1867), which Queen credits with being the first story to feature crime and a criminal at the center of the book. A cunning stranger fills the belly of a frog with quail shot and thus wins a jumping contest with his own entry. *Maybe* it counts as a crime story...

Another title that could be questioned is *Lingo Dan* (1903) by Percival Pollard. Rightly credited as the first American serial killer in the short story form, it is safe to say that *Lingo Dan*'s historical significance far outweighs his fame or popularity. I'd go so far as to say that the vast majority of mystery readers have never heard of him, much less read the stories.

One of the reasons for the obscurity of this character is that the only book in which he appeared had a very small print run by Neale, a minor

COLLECTIBLES

Washington, D.C., publishing house. It is a black tulip—a legendary rarity known to only a handful of collectors of mystery fiction in general and of the *Queen's Quorum* list in particular. The pedestrian level of Pollard's prose did not create a frenzied demand for reprints, so the book remained essentially unread for a century until it was made available electronically.

A slim, plain volume, it does not rise to the level of even an ordinary-looking book, being merely half the size of most novels and short story collections. The publisher was so impecunious in its production that it may not even have been issued in a dust jacket. That is pure speculation, to be fair, but I have neither seen nor heard of a jacket on the book.

Lingo Dan is a title on virtually every knowledgeable collector's list of desiderata. I had seen but a single copy in more than a half-century of searching. And then, two years ago, I spotted another copy.

There was a massive auction sale of a collection of Sherlock Holmes books. It was a remarkable assemblage, numbering in the thousands of volumes of Doyle's works, as well as critical works, parodies and pastiches, and ephemera of all kinds. A collector named Daniel Poznanski had spent a lifetime dedicated to compiling it and Sherlockians from all over the world participated in a live and on-line auction.

Also in the sale were non-Holmes-related mystery first editions. The impressive auction catalogue showed about a dozen lots (groups of books) of these mysteries, usually about forty books to a lot. These lots were described as "mysteries" and listed about ten of the titles it included. Each lot was accompanied by a photograph of ten to twelve volumes, although not necessarily the same books that had been mentioned in the description.

Naturally, I read all the descriptions carefully, and then examined the photographs. At the end of the row of books in one photograph was a slim volume that I was pretty sure I recognized, though it was hard to read the type on the spine. It was a copy of *Lingo Dan*. I was certain of it.

Even though it was the height of the Christmas season, when the bookshop is especially busy (hopefully), I flew out to Los Angeles to have a look at the books. My heart beat a little faster when the lot containing that rarity was brought out to be examined and, sure enough, it was there—the real deal.

The day of the sale came and I made arrangements with the gallery to bid by telephone. I had no idea how many people had spotted the book in the photograph, or had seen it when examining books at the gallery. I checked in with my bookkeeper to see where we stood on our line of credit, as I was determined not to let it go. Besides the *Lingo Dan,* there were scores of other good books in the various lots and I coveted many of them.

The quick flight to the West Coast turned out to have been worth the time and expense when my bids secured every one of the mystery lots. When they finally showed up at the store (it wasn't long but felt like months), I made two piles of books: one for my bookshop customers, one for my personal collection.

The copy of *Lingo Dan* was in superior condition to the one that had been in my library for three decades, so I upgraded my collection and made a customer ecstatic when I offered him my duplicate—the only copy of a book he was otherwise unlikely to see in his lifetime.

The Green Manalishi (With the Two Pronged Crown)

BY THOMAS PLUCK

When Joey Cucuzza stared at the ruby copper profile of Abraham Lincoln, he clenched the abalone-handled stiletto in his pocket and imagined thrusting it into his old man's heart.

You never knew what you were going to find at a coin show. He'd learned that as a teenager, working a much smaller show on Sundays at the Nutley VFW. Wandering the Coin Expo at the convention center, he didn't expect to find the twin of the 1931-S wheatback penny that he'd bought with six weeks of summer labor from the walrus-mustached Vietnam veteran who owned Gadzooks Rare Coins, the very cent that Joey's father hocked for Yankees tickets barely a year later.

Stately, tanned Joe Cucuzza plucked the coin from the table in its lucite case. At forty-nine, his eyes couldn't discern the fine lines in the grains of wheat like they could at thirteen. He asked the coin seller—a spectacled goof in cargo shorts with hair like Larry from the Three Stooges—for a jeweler's loupe and inspected the details.

MS-67 was the certified Sheldon rating, and the rich luster of the blood-red copper was what drew his eye all those years ago, and also drew it now.

COLLECTIBLES

Minted in San Francisco, it had cost sixty dollars in 1983, paid in ten-dollar increments for minding Mr. Chundak's table while he shot Dewar's and chewed the fat at the bar, or stalked the floor in search of a deal. Mr. Chundak always wore a suit. Maybe a dull herringbone or ugly plaid, but always a suit, and that had rubbed off on young Joey; his current summer suit was tailored but discreet, not showy. It hid the eight-inch Italian stiletto in his pocket and the nickel and pearl Baby Beretta in the pancake holster under his silk shirt.

The coin was priced at three hundred and fifty dollars. Inflation. Joey took four bills off his money clip and held them out to the geek, who percolated to life and flustered through giving him change, hand-writing a receipt, and folding it up in a paper bag.

"Superb Gem Uncirculated," Aldo said at Joey's left shoulder, reading the coin's rating. His breath was rank from the sausage and peppers sub he'd bought from the truck in the parking lot. "You are a gem, but you look like you been circulated."

Aldo was his boss and partner, the red-faced capo of the Quattrocchi crime family, which ran most of northern New Jersey, and got a piece of the action at the Secaucus convention center where the coin show was held.

"I'm MS-55, Choice About Uncirculated," Joey said. "You, you're Extremely Fine. A little rough around the edges. It comes from being in so many pockets."

After a beat, Aldo chuckled. "C'mon, lemme show you something."

The table announced its presence with a large Nazi flag. It catered entirely to the losing side of wars fought by Americans from 1861 to 1945. Hitler youth daggers, Japanese swords, Kaiser helmets, Confederate currency.

"Look at this shit," Joey said. "The vets never allowed that at the VFW. Said they saw enough of it overseas."

Aldo shrugged. "Money is money, Joseph."

Joey noted that his Italian forebears rarely kept any mementos from the shameful Mussolini era. Even the ones who supported him shut up about it after he was strung up by his balls in the public square. In Germany it was illegal to sell Nazi memorabilia, but in the States, it was romanticized and fetishized by a certain kind of person.

Dry-balls, is what Joey's old man called them, among other things. Like "half a fag," which his homophobic, hyper-masculine father—a quarry truck driver who looked like The Thing from the *Fantastic Four* comic books, only hairier—said was worse than being a whole queer, because at least they "had the balls to be what they were."

Joey had realized he was of the whole cloth when he was twelve years old, watching *The Beastmaster* on their stolen HBO, and found himself more enthused with the oiled and muscled Marc Singer than the equally ripe Tanya Roberts as the duo led their menagerie against Rip Torn's tyrannical overlord. The bullies discovered it soon after. Joey was slender and fit, but had full lips that they called "dick suckers" as they cornered and beat him.

Joey's father had at least taught him to fight. He absorbed it by dodging his fast big hands, which were later fed to the crabs in a polluted lagoon in the Meadowlands. A bonding experience between a younger Joey and Aldo.

The Nazi table was run by two men—one big and heavy, the other short and muscled—and their cold little eyes excited Joey at the prospect of a new bonding experience to be had.

Aldo ignored the stack of literature that involved neither coins nor militaria, but instead shouted conspiracies and denial of history. He pointed to a Japanese samurai helmet on display next to the swastika flag.

"The Green Manalishi (With the Two Pronged Crown)," Aldo said, then air-guitared a heavy metal riff. "Judas Priest. We saw them at Garden State Arts Center, remember?"

The original was by Fleetwood Mac, but Joey didn't correct him. Aldo was more affected by eighties nostalgia than he was. He also played football for Queen of Peace and was homecoming king, and even the gay priests were none the wiser. Aldo had learned to fight out of desire, not need.

The helmet was certainly not an antique. It looked more Darth Vader than *Shogun*, and was airbrushed in metallic green like an insect. Or Aldo's garish custom IROC Camaro. Joey loved him, but his boss and partner was pure New Jersey guido, down to the gold chains and Fila tracksuits.

COLLECTIBLES

His current number was a throwback design modeled by Tony Soprano, which Aldo thought was hilariously ironic now that he controlled the turf the fictional mob boss once lived in.

Joey tolerated it. He was the jealous type, and though Aldo had jangled in more pockets and purses than he cared to think about, he kept fit, and a baggy tracksuit meant fewer old goomars grabbing his biceps and throwing themselves at him. A boss had to take a taste now and then, or people talked. And when people talked, they had to be killed.

That didn't bother Joey, but as the boss's fixer, the clean-up was his duty. Why make more work?

"Tell me that helmet wouldn't look awesome in the garage next to The Green Machine."

Joey relaxed. Better in the garage than the parlor.

"You like that, Antnee?" Little Shitler's acne-scarred face broke into a smile, and he nudged his buddy, Der Super Schwein. "Two hundred. All custom work."

Joey squeezed Aldo's forearm. He knew he was carrying the mate to his abalone-handled stiletto, and was hungering to gut the little scumbag like a bluefish after the "Antnee" crack.

"Just looking."

Der Super Schwein huffed. "Then go to a museum."

Joey's Uncle Paolo had taught him that Italians had only recently been inducted into whiteness and all its privileges. These two specimens likely considered them too swarthy to have full membership.

"We're not giving these two dry-balls a dime. They shouldn't even be here selling that shit. It's a coin show, not a Skokie reenactment."

Aldo sighed. "We're doing this?"

Joey turned to the soldiers who followed them ten feet behind. If Aldo wanted that ugly helmet, damn right they were doing it.

"Everybody's avoiding this table like a fresh turd." Everyone except Aldo, of course. "They're scaring away business. I'll give them a pro-rated refund."

Aldo's face hardened. Joey had overstepped. "They'll make a stink, and scare off more people. Just make 'em get rid of the flag and the books."

Once the apes maneuvered to their flank like two dreadnoughts, Joey leaned over the table to the proprietors. "We're the management. You have to take that flag down and put these books away."

The little Nazi pinched his face together. "We're still in America, capisce? We got the First Amendment."

"Yeah, and we're not the government. But we are in charge of this facility. If you prefer, we can have your entire table removed." Joey flashed the cracked-tooth grin that was just sharklike enough to warn off any but the stupidest. He was a mako, not a great white, but no less deadly.

"Whatever you say, Gabba Goebbels."

There was a lot of sighing and grousing and even a few muttered slurs, but they took down the swastika and put the books under the table.

"Guess you don't want me celebrating Tojo, either." Little Shitler took the Manalishi helmet from its display and set it on the floor. "No longer for sale, Antnee."

Aldo ignored them, as was his wont. He didn't get angry, not openly. The back of his neck turned a shade toward the ruby red penny in Joey's pocket. Joey patted him on the shoulder. "Let's go get some zeppoles. These assholes gave me agita."

They enjoyed the autumn air and the cattails of the northern tip of the Meadowlands. The cigar-like pods called punks—which their parents used to light up like citronella candles to keep bugs away—wagged in the breeze.

"You're all bent out of shape over those inbred fucks." Aldo stuffed one of the fried dough zeppelins into his mouth and dusted his tracksuit with a snowfall of powdered sugar.

"They'd be first in line to watch us burn."

"That's not gonna happen."

Joey tore a zeppole into pieces and ate them off a napkin so as not to sugarcoat his suit. "It did."

"That was a long time ago."

COLLECTIBLES

Aldo ate another zeppole whole. He noticed the sugar on his shirt and smeared the dots into streaks with his hand.

"Since when? Gay kids still get the shit beat out of them."

Aldo and Joey were an open secret. The operation didn't care because they were both good earners and didn't flaunt it. Among New Jersey mob bosses, they were among the least flamboyant, without even trying. The job was better camouflage than being Broadway stage directors or dress pattern makers.

"We all gotta take a beating sometime. It's one table. If they bust your balls so much, I'll tell Larry Sbarra they're banned next time."

"Please."

He patted Joey on the cheek. "I got to go meet the dock boss. Take the rest of the day. Hit the gym, or whatever. Just don't bring your work home." He walked to his Escalade.

Joey wiped his hands clean and took the 1931-S penny out of the bag.

It was almost certainly not the same coin his father had stolen, but no matter. Coins were about memories.

The first old coin Joey remembered finding was a Mercury dime in change from the Italian ice truck. Instead of Roosevelt's profile, a silver Adonis winked back at him. On the reverse side, an axe. His uncle Paolo told him that the tiny 'S' beneath the date meant it was minted in San Francisco, a city he waxed rhapsodic about, having lived in Haight-Ashbury and the Castro before settling in Greenwich Village.

Joey's uncle showed him how to be a stand-up guy, not a hot-head like his father. Uncle Paolo had married, given his mother a son, and divorced before striking out on his own, driving a Volkswagen Karmann-Ghia roadster home from out west to live the Bohemian life in Manhattan, running gay clubs for the Linn Brothers of the Jewish mob. He told Joey how they got raided by the cops despite the payoffs, and the Stonewall riots that ended the practice.

Uncle Paolo hadn't participated, but he collected bail money for the trans sisters who kicked it off. He was too much of a good worker to leave the till unless the building was on fire. Even then, he'd sell drinks with one hand and aim the fire extinguisher with the other. He'd been held up with a double-barreled shotgun to his heart, and was back behind the bar the same night, after giving the police report.

He'd survived all that, to get killed for nothing.

Joey gave the Alfa Romeo Guilia Quadrifoglio heavy pedal as he drifted around the backroad curves of the Meadowlands. The stereo thumped "The Green Manalishi (With the Two Pronged Crown)" on repeat, alternating between the rough Fleetwood Mac version and the slicker Judas Priest cover. The driving beat hypnotized him with Peter Green's haunting excoriation of a jealous god who would have no other.

To Aldo, the Green Manalishi of the title was a villain from a low-budget eighties movie, an unkillable spirit clad in samurai armor. Not much scared Aldo, except something he could not hurt.

Joey saw the Manalishi as something else. He'd read up on it, after that humid summer night at the outdoor concert where the leather-clad metal gods of Judas Priest rocked out for the first encore. For Peter Green, the Manalishi was the living personification of greed.

It was the last song he recorded with Fleetwood Mac as they rose to success. He didn't like what fame and money had done to him. Their gifts came with the price of abject worship. You couldn't coast on the highway and enjoy it. Your masters wanted more.

Joey knew the feeling.

His uncle had, too.

Running one club wasn't enough. They had him juggling three, one in Brooklyn Heights and two in the Village, sending him over the bridge every night. Uncle Paolo was exhausted after closing the bars and Joey had to wait patiently as he snoozed on his nonna's floral print couch. Once he woke up, they'd watch the Sunday afternoon creature feature on WPIX-11. Godzilla, or *The Mushroom People*, or if they were lucky, *Jason and the Argonauts* or Sinbad.

Uncle Paolo wasn't a big walrus like Mr. Chundak of the coin table, who was a Green Beret. But they were bar chums, and Unc got Joey the job to get him out of the house and away from his father's heavy hands. He'd heard them talking, deep in their cups, when he came to retrieve Mr. C for a customer dickering over the price of a Walking Liberty half dollar.

"You should carry a piece, Paulie."

"I never make the drop, what would they want with me?" He took out a money clip shaped like a dollar sign, studded with stones. "I keep a fugazi hundred in this rhinestone piece of crap. I'll toss it and run away pissing and farting like Mothra was chasing me, right Joey?" His round face lit up, reddened from his cheeks to his balding crown, combed back without vanity.

That was the last Sunday Joey saw him alive.

In Manhattan in the eighties, a mugging that went sour was barely news. Nonna howled and threw herself on the coffin, all in black. Joey's mother never recovered, like a piece had been cut from her.

In the funeral home parking lot, smoking with his buddies, Joey's father called it a fag-bashing. "That's what happens, Joey. That's why I teach you to fight." He turned to his pals. "Not that my kid's some finocchio. But he looks soft, don't he? You gotta watch out for that shit. Nip it right in the bud."

The lawyer for his uncle's killers said the deceased had flirted with his clients and their rage was justified. The jury agreed, and convicted them of provocation manslaughter. Probation and time served.

Once Joey got made, he got their names from a degenerate gambler in the NYPD. Two had died already, another hopped a merchant steamer. Joey parked outside the last guy's shithole in Yonkers, holding a throwaway piece between his ankles. When he saw the miserable prick stagger home after his shift, he decided letting him live was better punishment. He ice-picked the guy's tires and paid off a cop to ticket him once a week until the poor bastard got an ulcer, and called it even.

That had been enough, for a while.

But there was always something in the news. The kid they crucified on a fence out in cow-fucker land. The Rutgers student who jumped off a bridge after his roommate recorded him with a date. The lesbians who worked at the port, who came to Joey to get the jerks with seniority off their backs. It was a given you had to buy a job from the hiring agent, but these guys wanted a blow job with the vig. Joey made them behave. For a price, of course.

The Green Manalishi must be served.

His uncle thought juice would protect him, but he was a knock-around guy. Joey was made; killing him had consequences. At the ceremony, one hefty capo wanted to make Joey fuck one of his Russian girl whores to show fealty.

"You think that's the first I fucked?" Joey had said, and unzipped.

That homophobic fat prick was the one who dubbed Joey "The Cucuzza."

A lengthy squash prized by southern Italians, grown in every nonna's backyard garden—usually hanging from a chain-link fence in the sun like pale green Louisville Sluggers—he'd earned the name from both his daring and his endowment.

"When I got made, mine was shrunk up into my balls!" the current boss had said, and everybody laughed. After that, Joey was golden. He burned the card of Saint Sebastian, swore omerta, and never openly showed the fat capo disrespect.

He got pubes in his eggplant parmigiana every time he ate at a restaurant in Joey's territory, but he got to live. He was a made guy.

The two Nazi fucks had no such protection.

Joey wasn't a killer. He'd killed, but he wasn't a killer-killer. They had apes for that. His Baby Beretta was mostly for insurance, as Aldo's slice of New Jersey, which included the ports, was worth killing for. And made or not, there were ways. Some kid whacked a boss out in Staten Island, and blamed it on an internet conspiracy. Joey was pretty sure it was internal, set up by a captain who wanted a bigger piece.

Joey wasn't sure what set him off more. The brazen Nazis, or Aldo's reaction to them. They'd had shouting matches at Aldo's house in Essex Falls over it before. Aldo was like Uncle Paolo.

Who he loved was nobody's business.

It reminded Joey of the first time he heard the word "gay" as a slur in school.

COLLECTIBLES

He was waiting in line behind a girl for Radcliffe school to open. There were separate doors for boys and girls, with the label carved in stone above them, but they didn't separate the sexes like they had at Catholic school. His father said they couldn't pay for it anymore, so Joey changed to public school in third grade. He didn't have to wear a uniform anymore, but he didn't have regular clothes, so he showed up in a white shirt and chinos, the perfect target.

"What are you, gay?"

It was an older kid with a dusting of mustache, and two younger toadies.

"I'm happy, but I'm not gay." Joey would read the dictionary when he couldn't find a new book.

"That's halfway there, queer bait."

He asked his mother what the words meant when he walked home after classes. Her face seemed to melt.

Joey's heart raced like the Alfa Romeo's engine. He had asked a porter at the convention center to show him the Nazis' truck. They had an old white Econoline van. No swastikas, but a mosaic of bumper stickers covered the back.

Don't Tread On Me. Confederate Stars and Bars. *How's "Coexist" Working Out For Ya?*

He memorized the plate and called it in to a bought Port Authority cop. They lived in Butler. Half an hour up Route 23.

The house looked just like its neighbors.

It wasn't far from where Uncle Paolo had told him there had been an German-American Bund camp back in the thirties, where American fans of Hitler dressed in brown shirts and marched for their führer.

"The feds shut them down after Pearl Harbor, but what do you think, they disappeared? They all decided to love their neighbors?" Unc rolled his eyes so hard Joey felt it. "No. They raised little Nazi kids. Our neighbors. Never forget that. Half the people are good, one half are bad. And the other half will look the other way while the bad half kills you."

For someone who ran three sets of books on multiple establishments, his math was off, but Joey never forgot it.

What was he gonna do, burn down their shit shack?

Not after driving his shiny blue Italian sedan down their street. But it felt good to think about.

Anger issues. He'd worked hard to get a handle on them. He didn't want to turn lobster red like Aldo every time someone yanked his chain. It was unbecoming in a leader, and now that they were on top, they had to fight to stay there. Being known as a hot-head, like Joey's father, was just one way to put a target on your back when someone young and ambitious wanted your territory.

———

He drove to his uncle's grave, next to his grandparents' in a sprawling cemetery with a gorgeous view of Manhattan. Joey Ramone was buried on the Jewish side, his marker covered in pebbles from fans. The florist was closed, so he stopped at a hot dog truck and bought two with a Chocolate Cow drink. One with kraut, relish, and mustard for him, and one with hot onions, like his uncle used to get.

He set a towel down in the freshly cut grass and watched the sun burn across the glass towers of the City like God's judgment.

There was one more space in the plot. His mother would be buried with his father, and Joey had claimed this one. He had his name carved below Uncle Paolo's with his birth date and the dash hanging there like a knife at his throat.

Guys like him and Aldo usually got a free plot in the Meadowlands, but at least his name would be here until someone with enough juice had it leveled for condos.

Uncle Paolo would say to let the Nazis be.

After his uncle's bar was robbed, the Linn Brothers found the gunman and asked if he wanted to watch them cut his hand off. He knew better than to dissuade them, but he demurred from attending the punishment.

Young Joey had been excited about it. "I'd want to do the chopping!"

His uncle mussed his hair, which Joey disliked even then. "You say that now, but if you did it, you'd regret it. He scared me, that's all. He didn't pistol whip me, or even raise his voice. As far as thieves go, he was a gentleman."

COLLECTIBLES

"Then why are you gonna let them do it?"

"No one 'lets' the Linn Brothers do anything. Men like that, you stay out of their way. The thief knew what he was getting into. That doesn't mean I need to be part of it."

Joey learned, long after the Linns were found dead in the trunks of their respective Cadillacs, that his uncle had sent money to the thief's family. He hadn't made it to the hospital after his amateur amputation. He wasn't mobbed up; his crew might help his widow and kids, but like chipping into the bail fund at Stonewall, his uncle did what he thought was right, behind the scenes. It was safer, but it still mattered.

At least Joey liked to think so.

He left the hot dog with the onions in the grass, and poured out a little Chocolate Cow for his fallen uncle.

———

He filed away the Nazis' address. Someday, when he couldn't hurt some mouthy untouchable fuck in the organization, he'd send the apes to their place. And he'd feel good about it.

Anger management comes in different forms.

Projection, the book he'd read called this.

One thing he'd learned, partnered with Aldo, is you did whatever worked. They were opposites in a lot of ways, but they made it work. Sometimes that involved projection. And sometimes you went to bed angry, like he would tonight.

He hit the gym late, got a good pump, then cycled through the sauna and the cold shower until he didn't feel like emptying the Baby Beretta into two Nazi faces every time he closed his eyes.

Aldo's truck wasn't in the carport, so he parked in the garage next to the Green Machine IROC Camaro. Aldo kept it in a plastic climate-controlled cocoon like a time capsule from 1989, when he'd graduated high school. It only came out on days with zero percent chance of rain. Aldo even had a decrepit old cooler in the backseat full of mix tapes he'd made in the eighties on his boombox, and played them loud when he took it out for rides.

Glory days.

Joey went inside and set the 1931-S penny on their trophy shelf, in front of a photo of him and Aldo in Capri. It gleamed like a ruby eye.

He made a pitcher of negronis—Stanley Tucci style—and sipped on one while he waited, with "The Green Manalishi" on the stereo to wash the murder scenes out of his head. Sometimes an old song worked like a zen koan to cleanse the soul.

The green beasts, greed and jealousy.

He was jealous that Aldo put money ahead of his wishes, but Aldo was right. This was business. Just like Uncle Paolo sold drinks at The International Bar, while six blocks away, history was being made outside the Stonewall.

People gotta drink during history, too!

The ruby eye of the penny glared down on him. Killing his uncle's killers wouldn't bring him back. But maybe it would have saved someone else. Or kept them from raising more little killers. How many little Hitlers had those two inducted?

Thoughts like that kept Joey up at night.

And Aldo, who knew why he couldn't sleep.

Tonight would be one of those nights.

He took a clean phone out of a cubby and punched in the number of his favorite ape. His thumb hovered over the send button. That old Econoline van could go up in flames. He'd get pictures, and they would help block out the misshapen face of his uncle in the briefly opened coffin, that young Joey only saw because he'd sneaked out of the car while his father had a smoke.

His thumb polished the button like a bead on his nonna's rosary.

Her wails echoed through his head.

He raised his thumb.

And the door clicked open. Aldo strutted in wearing a nice linen shirt and slacks, a shopping bag in his hand.

Joey quickly closed the burner phone and stuffed it between the couch cushions. "You're late."

"I had business." Aldo set the bag on the coffee table. "You remembered! Thanks, babe." He tried to mimic Rob Halford of Judas Priest as he howled through every octave. The man had range. Aldo did not.

He patted Joey on the shoulder. "Maybe this is our song."

"We can discuss it." Joey kept a straight face. Aldo had changed out of the ridiculous tracksuit, and he had to acknowledge that.

"Whaddayoo mean? This was one of our first dates."

"That was *not* a date. I only went to see the opening band."

"Whitesnake? Here we go again…you sure you want to confess to that? Rob Halford is openly gay. I thought that meant something to you."

It was true. Halford's coming out had been a big deal. And it hadn't lost them any fans worth counting. He had dressed like a leather daddy since the early days, and drove onstage on a chromed chopper, before singing stuff like "Grinder, looking for meat" and "Hell Bent for Leather." It didn't take a genius to figure out. Most of the stoner metalheads had probably mumbled "oh yeah," and kept banging their heads to the anthems of a band that defined their youth.

"All right, it was a date."

"What about tonight? Is tonight a date? You got all gussied up at the gym, I see."

Joey wore a snug viscose T-shirt and loose shorts to show off his leg day workout. Aldo usually didn't notice. Or maybe he did?

"It can be."

"Pour me one of what you got."

Joey went to the open kitchen and made two fresh drinks. He could dig out the phone and call the hitter after Aldo conked out. Then he could sleep.

He returned with two martini glasses.

And nearly dropped one.

Aldo held up the green samurai helmet, positioning it on the shelf above the photo of them in Capri. "I just couldn't leave this behind. I know it clashes with the feng shui and all that shit."

Joey steadied the glasses. The two prongs of the helmet gouged the ceiling. The mask was like a skull, two sockets stared down as empty as he knew their souls to be.

"No, green is a good color. It brings money."

Aldo positioned the helmet, and turned with a boyish grin. "That's good. Because it's all about the money, right?"

"Right." Joey handed him a glass.

"Those two mooks made us enough. They won't be back Sunday." Aldo's face was still a little red at the edges from exerting himself.

Joey would wait until later to ask about their fate. They would both sleep well tonight.

"A drink isn't a date."

Aldo touched glasses. "I got Angelo's in the bag. Lobster oreganato, hot shrimp with the biscuit, calamari…after that workout, I was morte di fame."

Joey smiled. "Thank you."

"Anything for my jealous Manaleesh!"

They drank.

"So, how about we watch *Road House* while we eat?" Aldo sank into the couch like a yacht's anchor. "It's a Swayze night."

"Come on, *Dirty Dancing*. It's got a perfect plot." And Aldo liked Jennifer Grey.

Aldo fished the containers out of the bag and opened them. The room was flooded with the scents of butter and garlic.

"I'm afraid that tonight, I'm gonna put baby in the corner. I need to watch shit blow up."

Joey sat back and sipped his negroni. "Double feature?"

Whatever the decision, he knew they would make it work.

Devil Sent the Rain Blues (Pm 13040)

BY DAVID RACHELS

*J*ust back from the south with a backseat full of old 78s are John Fahey and Nick Perls. Most notable find was a previously unknown Charley Patton record called "Circle Round the Sun" b/w "The Devil in the Water" or something like that. It has bad chips in it, is in poor condition, and is the only copy extant.
Berkeley Barb, August 12, 1966

I hear the hotel door sliding open, so I look up from my breakfast. A woman in pink platform flip-flops shuffles in with a 78 RPM record clutched in her hands. I watch the record—ten inches in diameter, black, beautiful—as it moves toward me.

The woman stares at her feet as she moves. She seems to be worried that a flip-flop will fall off, and if it does, she won't know it if she doesn't see it happen. She peeks up at the room long enough to spot me.

I am in the lobby of the Passport Inn in Phenix City, Alabama. For several weeks running, I have placed ads in the local newspaper announcing that today I will be sitting in this spot from 8:00 a.m. to 5:00 p.m. in hopes of buying old records. I have given this notice far in advance to let the word spread and to give people time to find their old records wherever they may be, usually in a basement, attic, or garage, hidden away after the death of an elderly pack-rat relative.

COLLECTIBLES

The woman and her record eventually reach me. She looks up, but she doesn't make eye contact. She stares at my nose. Nervous. She might be thirty, or she might be fifty. She's been sunburned all her life, so it's impossible to tell.

"Mister," she says, "are you the one who put those ads in the paper?"

"Yes, ma'am," I tell her. "That's me." I am the only person sitting in the lobby. I have a 78 RPM record displayed on the table in front of me. Who else would I be?

With a glance, I see that her record is worthless. I spy a blue Paramount label, and though most of its words are too rubbed and faded to read, I recognize "Yes! We Have No Bananas" by Frank Silver and His Orchestra with vocals by Billy Jones. The record is from 1923, and if you have a copy in good condition, you might find a sucker to give you $50 for it, but this copy has been played so much that its grooves are worn flat. The disc that appeared black from a distance is actually gray. It is worth $0.

Too many people believe that everything old is valuable, and if you tell them otherwise, they think you're trying to rip them off, even when you don't want to buy anything from them at all. Their disappointment fuels their anger, and sometimes things get heated. I always start off friendly and polite. Sometimes you can let them down easy.

I say, "Show me what you've got there."

Then she says something I don't expect: "Do you think anybody would mind if I had me one of them waffles?"

I wonder for an instant—foolishly, perhaps—if she already knows that her record is worthless. Maybe her only goal is a complimentary breakfast. If a free meal will make our encounter pleasant, I am willing to oblige.

"I don't think anyone would mind," I say.

The only other person in the room is the front desk clerk, LaTanya. My visitor gestures with her head toward the desk. "She knows me, so it would be best if you made the waffle for me. Is that okay?"

"Who knows you? LaTanya?" LaTanya is outgoing, eager to make small talk, friendly in the manner of many Southerners.

"Shhhhhhh! Don't say her name!"

LaTanya has not looked in our direction, and my waffle is getting cold. "Why don't you take this one," I offer, "and I'll go make myself another one."

Her face lights up. Her morning has been made—at least for now. "Oh, thank you so much," she says. "I don't mind if I do." She sits at the table with her back to the desk. She reaches for my waffle and pulls it to her. She studies it, makes a face, and says, "Did you put any syrup on this? Maybe it's all soaked in?"

"I'll get you some more syrup," I tell her.

"Can you get me two?"

"Of course." I continue to be accommodating because it serves my mission. Another record owner might arrive, and the vibe in this room should be sweetness and light.

I get up and go to the plastic tub of syrup packets next to the waffle maker. I take two and walk them back to my table. I hand her the syrup packets, and she says, "Go on and make your waffle now. I'll wait."

Of course she will.

I go back to the waffle maker, measure the batter, pour the batter, close the waffle maker, flip the waffle maker, shut my eyes, and wait for the beep.

I picture myself riding shotgun with Nick Perls and John Fahey down a country road. We feel treasure all around us, and we don't need luck to find it. All we need are time and patience. The ghosts of Son House, Robert Johnson, and Charley Patton float above the cotton fields. I wonder how much money we have in the car. Probably not more than a few hundred bucks, if that. Nothing like the money belt I'm wearing today. In 1966, nobody was checking the internet to find out how much things were supposedly worth. If, through your own ingenuity and labor, you found a rare record to buy, then you deserved to buy it cheap because—

The waffle maker beeps.

Returning to my visitor, the first thing I notice is that she has placed "Yes! We Have No Bananas" directly on the table top, and there appears to be a drop of syrup on it. Instinctively, I gasp. All records should be protected, even if they're trash.

I put down my new waffle and reach for the record. Gently holding its edges, I lift it from the table, and it's too heavy. I am holding not one record, but two. I rotate the records to reveal the bottom disc. It's another Paramount label, but this one is black. It's PM 13040, Charley Patton's "Devil Sent the Rain Blues" b/w "Circle Round the Moon," that newsworthy record that Fahey and Perls found in Arkansas in 1966, but their copy, the only playable copy known to exist, was barely listenable. The copy in my hands looks brand new. It is the most beautiful thing I have ever seen.

"Mister," says my visitor, her mouth full of food, "why are you crying?"

———

Through the noise on the surface of that battered old record, that Arkansas miracle, I hear Charley Patton sing:

Good Lord send the sunshine, Devil he send the rain.
Good Lord, send the sunshine, Devil he send the rain.
I will be here tomorrow, on the morning train.

This is a standard blues stanza: a rhymed couplet with its first line repeated. Or is it? Is that first line repeated exactly, or is there an extra comma? Without the comma, we have facts: God sends the sunshine, and the Devil sends the rain. With the comma, we have an appeal to God: Please, good Lord, undo what the Devil has done—turn the weather from stormy to clear. And then that third line. Where is "here"? Is it Charley's point of departure? (Tomorrow he will flee the rain.) Is it Charley's point of arrival? (Tomorrow the sunshine will greet him.) It could be either, or it could be both. Or it could be either *and* both.

For listeners who want clarity, the second stanza clears up nothing:

You don't know, sure don't know my mind.
You don't know me, sure don't know my mind.
I don't show you my ticket, darling, you don't know where I'm going.

Now there is a woman. And while the first stanza refused to tell whether Charley was coming or going, the second stanza doubles down by refusing to name his destination in either case, meaning that not only do we (and the woman) not know his travel plans, but, more significantly, we do not know his "mind," which is to say, *why* he is traveling, because isn't the rain always more than just the rain?

Charley Patton toys with you.

———————

"I'm not crying," I tell her. "It's steam from the waffle maker."

I put down the records on a nearby table with "Yes! We Have No Bananas" now on the bottom. I wipe my eyes, and I begin calculating what to do. How much money will get this woman to go away? If she were thrilled to get a free waffle, will $100 be more than she had hoped for? Will $100 send her running out the door to spend, spend, spend? I've got ten times that much in my wallet. She can drive up the price quite a bit without ever learning that I have many more thousands of dollars stashed in my money belt.

She says, "Mister, aren't you going to eat your waffle?"

For all I care, she can have my new waffle, but I want to conclude this transaction as quickly as possible. I take a deep breath and sit at the table. I cut the first piece of waffle and put it in my mouth.

She says, "Aren't you going to put anything on that? I've never seen anybody eat a waffle without butter and syrup. Butter and syrup are the whole point of waffles, right? Pancakes, too. Am I right?"

I wash down the waffle with cold coffee. "I'm on a diet," I tell her, and then I just blurt it out: "What would you say to $100 for those two records?" I offer to buy both because I don't want her to think that one is any more special than the other.

She says, "$100 for *both?* I thought they must be at least a hundred years old."

"1923 and 1929," I tell her, "so not quite. Technically, that means they're not antiques, right? So $100 seems fair."

I put more dry waffle into my mouth, and I act as nonchalant as I can. I try not to choke. I feel blood pounding through my neck.

COLLECTIBLES

I hear the hotel door sliding open again, and I look. A man walks in wearing a yellow pocket T-shirt and baggy floral shorts. His hands are empty.

"Hey, there!" the man calls to me across the lobby. "I have arrived with the treasure to end all treasures!"

I must keep the mood positive.

"Good morning!" I call back. "You folks in Phenix City sure are a bunch of early risers!"

"I had to get down here before you ran out of cash," he says, and he laughs. Where are his records? In the trunk of his car? Melting in the Alabama heat?

The guy arrives at our table and says, "My name is Eugene Trainor." He extends his hand to shake, and I oblige him.

"Oh!" the woman says, blushing. "Nancy! Nancy Franklin!" And we shake hands, too.

"Bill Bracey," I tell them, though they should know my name from the newspaper. Eugene plops down in the chair next to Nancy. They exchange a sidelong glance, and I know that they know each other. Are they working some kind of hustle? My hopes of a quick and easy transaction with Nancy are gone.

"You didn't bring anything?" I say to Eugene.

"Wait for it!" Eugene says. Magician-like, he produces a compact disc and puts it on the table in front of me. *Some Gave All* by Billy Ray Cyrus. 1992. Featuring "Achy Breaky Heart." An album that has sold 20 million copies.

I am speechless. I would not have imagined that Eugene has something *more* worthless than a grooveless copy of "Yes! We Have No Bananas," but he does.

I finally manage to say, "Wow."

"And," Eugene says, "the provenance!"

The provenance?

With another flourish, he produces a piece of paper, which he unfolds and puts on the table next to the compact disc. The paper contains a typed statement, signed by Eugene Trainor, that he purchased this compact disc at Peachtree Mall in Columbus, Georgia, on Tuesday, May 19, 1992, the day of the album's release. At the bottom of the page is a notary seal.

"Can't believe your luck, can you?" Eugene says. "With all the millions of copies of this CD out there, do you realize how rare it is to find the original from the very first day? I reckon you're the expert, though. You of all people ought to know what this is worth."

Nancy looks agitated. She says, "How old is that thing? Not even thirty years? My records are damn near one hundred!"

Eugene wags a finger at her and says, "But I've got Billy Ray! Who have you got?"

"Who cares who I've got? I've got almost one hundred years! One hundred years makes an antique! Maybe I should just wait and come back. What did you say, mister—1923 and 1929? What if I keep my records until 2029? Then I'll be rich!"

Nancy is shouting, and LaTanya is looking in our direction.

"Look," I say, "you've both brought me something amazing. How about I give you $100 apiece?"

"Sold!" says Eugene.

"Great," I say. "Here you go." I take out my wallet and count five $20 bills into his palm.

"Pleasure doing business with you," he says, folding the bills in half and putting them in the pocket of his T-shirt.

"And for you," I say, and I begin counting bills onto the table in front of Nancy.

"Not so fast," she says. "You mean to tell me that 1923 *and* 1929 are worth the same as 1992? You think I'm just some dumb redneck who can't do math?"

Shouting again. LaTanya is heading this way.

"No, no, no," I say, "of course not. We can all do math here. Of course we can. I've paid $100 for thirty-two years old, and your records are about three times that, right? So I'll pay you three times as much, and you've got two records, so that's six times as much. That would be $600. How does that sound?" I should not have been honest with Nancy, and I should not have lied to Nancy. I should not have told her that her records are nearly one hundred years old, and I should not have told her that one hundred years magically makes an antique. I was being cocky, and I've made a mess of things.

COLLECTIBLES

I've paid $100 for a Billy Ray Cyrus CD, so they've hustled me. I wouldn't have thought they could do it, but they have. Therefore, when I hustle them, it will only be fair.

"Well, well, well," says LaTanya, arriving at our table. "If it isn't Nancy and Eugene. What are you two doing here? Nancy, did you just have a waffle? Isn't that what got you arrested last time?"

I need LaTanya to go away. Every moment that passes makes this more difficult.

"I'm so sorry," I say. "I gave her the waffle. It was my attempt at Southern hospitality. I was trying to fit in. You can put it on my bill if you need to."

"Are they bothering you, Mr. Bracey? Are they panhandling?"

"You wish," says Eugene. "We're making some money today." He taps on the Billy Ray Cyrus CD and says, "One hundred bucks, sister!"

LaTanya looks at me like I've lost my mind.

Nancy says, "And I'm getting $600—at least! My records are antiques."

"*Almost* antiques," says Eugene.

"Really?" says LaTanya, and her manner has changed. Nancy and Eugene have gone from freeloading ne'er-do-wells to friends of a guest, and LaTanya has gone from police mode to hospitality mode.

LaTanya steps to the table where the records are and reaches for them.

"Please don't touch them," I say.

LaTanya leans over to read the exposed label. "Charley Patton," she says. "I think I've heard of him. My granddaddy is a blues fan. This must really be worth something, huh?"

"Not as much as you would think," I tell her. "Nobody cares about records anymore, not even if they're old, seeing as how you can just stream anything you want for free."

"Hang on a second," LaTanya says, and she begins walking back toward the front desk.

"Where are you going?" I want to know.

"Just hang on."

"Come back here."

I want to chase her down and tackle her.

I look at Eugene and Nancy. Eugene has picked up the provenance letter, and he is admiring his own handiwork and smirking. Nancy is watching LaTanya, clueless but curious.

I want to grab the records and run away, but I wouldn't be hard to find. LaTanya comes back typing on her phone. "Devil…sent…the…rain… blues…value," she says.

No, no, no, no, no. If Nancy gets any idea what this record is worth, she will end up wanting a million dollars. This is crazy. If I don't end this fast, I might not get the record at all.

"Look," I say to Nancy, "I owe you an apology. The Charley Patton record is valuable. LaTanya is right. I wasn't thinking clearly. 'Yes! We Have No Bananas' is such a great song that I didn't take the other record into account. Let me pay you what I can." I reach under my shirt and unbuckle my money belt. I pull off the belt and offer it to Nancy. "Here. Take it. This is all I have to pay you."

Nancy looks at me, looks at Eugene, looks at LaTanya, looks back at me as if this is some kind of trick. She takes the money belt from me and unzips it. She fingers the thick stack of $100 bills.

"Mister," she says, still looking at the money, "I believe we have ourselves a deal." Then she hesitates and says, "What would you give me if I waited until 2029?"

"A deal is a deal," I tell her. I stand up and pick up the records to see if she will object. She looks at the records, then the money, then the records again, and she doesn't say anything. I wonder if I am capable of walking to my room without tripping and falling and breaking the Charley Patton record. Ordinarily, I would wait until the end of the day to go to my room, but this is the greatest moment of my life. I must hear this record right now. I cannot wait.

I say, "Thank you, Nancy. If you would like the rest of my waffle, you are welcome to it. Now if you will excuse me, I have a record to listen to."

Then I leave before she can change her mind.

COLLECTIBLES

As if the first two stanzas of "Devil Sent the Rain Blues" are not challenging enough, its third stanza may seem—at first—to come from a completely different song:

Followed sweet mama, to the burying ground.
Followed sweet mama, to the burying ground.
I didn't know I loved her, till they laid her down.

Stanza one: weather. Stanza two: travel. Stanza three: death of a woman. (Note: His "sweet mama" is *not* his mother!) The listener grasps for connections, and possibilities emerge. Could Charley's "sweet mama" of stanza three be the God-sent sunshine of stanza one, and is her death the Devil's rain? In stanza two, did we not know Charley's mind because even Charley would not know that he loved her until her burial in stanza three?

And then, in stanza four, there is so much water:

I been to the ocean, peeped down in the deep blue sea.
Been to the ocean, peeped down in the blue sea.
I didn't see nobody, looked like my sweet mama to me.

The Devil's rain has become an ocean, a deep sea of sorrow, and Charley can stare into the Devil's waters for as long as he desires (or rather, sapped by sorrow, weakly "peep"), but he will never see his woman again because even if the Devil's waters recede and God's sun shines, a dead woman in the ground is still a dead woman in the ground.

––––––––––

Heart racing, I make it to my room without tripping or dropping the records. I put the syrup-dripped "Yes! We Have No Bananas" on my bed, and I take Charley Patton to the desk where I have set up my phonograph. I am horrified to see that the record is wet with my sweat, and I pat it dry with a chamois cloth. I slip the disc onto the spindle, and I start the turntable spinning. When it reaches full speed, I lower the needle onto the record.

A gentle static begins. I hold my breath and wait for the sound of Charley Patton's guitar and then those immortal words: *Good Lord send the sunshine, Devil he send the rain.* I know what I will hear, but not really. No one has heard this song as I am about to hear it, clear and loud and vibrant, for nearly one hundred years. Eventually, I may let other people hear it too, but maybe not. I have earned this for myself alone.

And then the music starts, but not a guitar. I hear horns, insipid horns, the smug horns of a novelty song. I stand frozen, incredulous, mind racing, for more than a minute before the vocal finally begins: *Yes! We have no bananas!*

I want to believe that, in my excitement, I have somehow managed to put the wrong record on the turntable, but I know it isn't true. I force myself to look at my bed, and there is "Yes! We Have No Bananas" with syrup dripped on top. Looking back at the phonograph, I see a spot on the spinning record where its label is coming unglued. I pull the needle off the record, I pull the record off the turntable, and I pull the loose edge of the label. The label comes away clean, and beneath the black label for "Devil Sent the Rain Blues," I find a blue label for "Yes! We Have No Bananas."

———————

Stanza five. Whatever was clear is clear no more:

One of these mornings, you know it won't be long.
One of these mornings, baby, know it won't be long.
You going to be mistreated, and I'll have to leave your home.

Charley seems to be talking to his woman, but didn't she die two stanzas ago? Have we moved back in time, or has Charley moved on to a new woman? And what is Charley telling us about himself? Why is he so certain that he is going to mistreat her (and soon!), and why does he bother to hide behind the passive voice only to admit with his next breath that his abusive behavior will force him to leave? The song is still tragic, but Charley is no longer the victim.

And now the final stanza, the same line three times, almost:

221

COLLECTIBLES

I'm going away, mama, don't you want to go.
I'm going away, mama, don't you want to.
I'm going away, mama, don't you want to.

Charley is leaving, which suggests that he has mistreated the woman from stanza five. Why does he bother asking if she wants to go? Why would she choose to go anywhere with the man who has mistreated her? (If she's still alive, that is!) And why does Charley repeat the same line not twice but three times? He is out of arguments. He is begging, but weakly. He does not have the strength to repeat "go" after the first line, or perhaps he no longer has the temerity to suggest specifically what she might want to do. In either case, we leave Charley, abusive Charley, with the Devil having taken control of the weather, of life and death, of him. In the end, therefore, he can do nothing but helplessly, hopelessly repeat himself.

Charley Patton is not given.

Charley Patton is earned.

My own calm surprises me. Later, I can grieve over the memory of the Charley Patton record that never was, but first I have to get my money back. And not just the money I gave to Nancy. I intend to get my $100 back from Eugene, too.

I throw the bogus Charley Patton record onto the bed, and I walk to the door of my room. I take a deep, centering breath before I open the door. I walk to the elevator, press the down button, and take another deep breath. But that's it. I cannot stand here and wait.

I run to the stairwell and down a flight of stairs and down two hallways before emerging in the lobby. Of course, Nancy and Eugene are long gone, so I go to the desk where LaTanya is on the phone. She raises an index finger for me to wait, and I try to catch my breath.

As my breath slows, LaTanya smiles and nods, waiting for her caller to stop talking. She holds up a finger to me again, laughs noiselessly, and rolls her eyes. With her free hand, she mimics a mouth opening and closing and opening and closing over and over and over again. Finally, she says, "Thank you so much for calling to let me know. You have a lovely day, now." As she hangs up the phone, she says, "Is everything okay, Mr. Bracey?"

"Nancy stole my money," I tell her. "I need to know where to find Nancy."

"Who?" LaTanya says.

Did she not hear me?

"Nancy," I repeat. "The woman who was just here. The woman who got arrested for eating a waffle. The woman who sold me the records."

LaTanya smiles and says, "I'm sorry, Mr. Bracey, but I have no idea who you're talking about."

Chin Yong-Yun Meets a Mongol

BY S. J. ROZAN

Many people would not think I am the kind of person to know a Mongolian. I suppose this is not foolish. New York City is rather poor in residents from that country. Those few who come here have settled in Queens, while my home is in the Chinatown of Manhattan. Although my eldest son lives with his family in Flushing, which is in Queens, I have not to my knowledge encountered Mongolians while visiting them. Also, for many centuries China ruled Mongolia rather unpleasantly, as I understand it. Though that relationship ended a century ago, a new one involving damage to Mongolian grazing land by Chinese mining companies leaves Mongolians continuing to see Chinese people in an unfavorable light.

None of this was of any concern to me, or known to me at all, until my middle son, An-Zhang, introduced me to his friend Tomorbaatar.

Each of my four sons is quite accomplished. It is only my daughter whose work is disreputable (though in her field she is considered successful, of course). Because I am not an educated woman, the work of three of my sons in science, medicine, the law, are things I am proud of though I don't understand them.

An-Zhang's accomplishments are in a field whose very existence baffles me, however. He photographs food.

COLLECTIBLES

I opposed this when he began. I insisted it makes no sense to expect people to pay for pictures of food they will never eat. An-Zhang's roommate, Tony, assured me over an excellent dinner of whole grouper steamed with ginger that I was correct. Such an expectation was unreasonable. Nevertheless, he said, reasonable or not, people in America can be counted upon to have a particular fascination with photographs of food. Possibly, he suggested, it is because so many in America are on slimming diets that they feel they must limit their enjoyment of food to their eyes.

Tony is a fine cook. I have recently shared with him a few of my late husband's recipes, the simpler ones. He prepares them almost as well as I do, though of course my husband's cooking outshone us both. I had not previously, in the nearly twenty years since my husband passed into the next world, revealed the contents of his kitchen book to anyone. But Tony's eagerness to learn, added to the level of skill he already displays, convinced me. Plus, later in the year he is to marry my son.

My husband was one of Chinatown's legendary chefs. He looked forward to teaching our sons' life partners the fine points of Cantonese cuisine. He never got that opportunity. My two married sons have chosen wives who are wonderful women in all respects, but, being busy with their careers, neither has the time to devote to cooking on the level of my husband's kitchen book. Having recently been to my husband's grave to discuss with him the fact that in An-Zhang's case his partner will be a man, but a man intensely interested in cuisine, I now know my sharing the recipes is something he wants me to do.

In the beginning, I was unpersuaded by Tony's argument on the subject of An-Zhang's career. Nevertheless I allowed myself to agree that my son should be given a chance to see if his choice would bear fruit. Not that my agreement actually mattered, as we all knew. If I had not been able to prevent my daughter from following a career as a private detective, what chance did I have of influencing my son's choice of photography subjects? But it was kind of them to offer me the illusion of influence, as it was kind of all my children for a number of years to maintain the pretense that Tony was nothing more to An-Zhang than a roommate. They worried that the truth would upset me.

I have known for years, of course. I am not a person who likes to pry, but I am not unobservant. Many things are done in the modern world in ways clearly inferior to the old ways. I consider it my duty to point this out when necessary. Therefore my children often do not give me credit for advanced views. In this case, however, I had only to consider the needs of my son to see the suitability of this match. An-Zhang is an artist with little practical sense. He must be taken care of. Tony is well suited to this task. He seems, in fact, to enjoy it. Also, although young people often act as though they have discovered the sunrise, two young men—or two young women—making a life together is a tale as old as the Southern wind.

Happily, that mutual subterfuge is now in the past. The wedding is being planned. The young men are about to embark upon a happy future together. Which in a roundabout way brings me to Tomorbaatar.

"Very pleased to meet you, Chin Tai-Tai." Tomorbaatar used the Chinese form of respectful address, though he spoke in English. He bowed in the small entryway of my apartment. Smiling, he handed me a lovely cellophane-wrapped basket of clementines, then removed his shoes. He was a tall, handsome man, with high cheekbones.

"Hi, Ma." An-Zhang kissed my cheek. Speaking in Chinese, he said, "Tom says he's pleased to meet you."

"I understood that, thank you." Another fiction I've let my children believe is that my English is extremely poor. As a person who does not like to boast, I'm the first to admit my command of the language is not what anyone would call excellent. I don't speak English except when I must. It's not a pleasant language, full of hard-edged noises. Given a choice, who would not prefer the musical notes of Cantonese? Still, only a fool could live in America as long as I have without developing a certain level of understanding of the language. Over the years, however, it's served me well to let people assume that level to be lower than perhaps it is.

In the conversation that followed, Tomorbaatar spoke in English. To be courteous, I did the same. At the start he occasionally lifted his eyebrows, waiting for An-Zhang to translate.

"I ask son when need translation," I told him. "Please you continue."

Smiling, Tomorbaatar did so. First we spoke of the health of various family members of all concerned, as was polite. Once I'd heated the water for the second cup of tea the young men arrived at the reason for their visit.

"Tom has a situation, Ma," An-Zhang told me, settling back in his chair. "We thought you might have some advice."

Of course I'm always ready to offer advice to my children when asked. I often do it when I have not been asked, because people are frequently unaware that they're in need of guidance. But one's children—even children as filial as mine—being stubborn, I am rarely asked. When I am, I become skeptical. In this case I suspected that the true reason for their visit was something else—or something more.

"I'm Senior Cultural Attaché at the Mongolian Consulate," Tomorbaatar said, smiling as he accepted more tea. He smiled a lot, I noticed. Earlier, my son had told me it was the way of Tomorbaatar's people to face life with good cheer.

"Seems a Mongolian can always find something funny in a situation, Ma," he'd said, when he'd spoken of bringing his friend to see me. "They like to play jokes. They love it when you play a joke on them. Like Ba used to. They stick by their friends, too, the way Ba did. We've gotten pretty close. I think you'll like him."

Now, in my living room, Tomorbaatar continued, "I've been here for five years. Early on, I met…someone special. In fact, Andy introduced us." My son grinned at this use of his English name. "This special person adds to my happiness."

I sipped my tea. It was a refreshing jasmine, one An-Zhang particularly likes. I said, "But still, there is problem."

"Not with—" Tomorbaatar glanced at my son. An-Zhang nodded encouragingly. Tomorbaatar said to me, "Not with him. My friend."

"Ah. I see. An-Zhang, Tony, you, friend, all same. But still, problem. Parents don't like?"

Tomorbaatar seemed to relax. "My parents don't know. My friend is Chinese. Chinese-American, I mean. I'm not sure which would be worse, that I'm gay or that I'm seeing a Chinese man. As long as I'm here it's fine. I go home a couple of times a year, they ask me when I'll settle down and marry a Mongolian girl, I come back here. Eventually I'll have to tell them, I guess, but this has been working well."

"But you come for advice. What kind advice? About should marry boyfriend?"

Tomorbaatar laughed. "No, Chin Tai-Tai, thank you. The problem is with my new boss at the Consulate."

I waited.

"There's a book," he said. "*The Secret History of the Mongols.* Have you heard of it? It was commissioned by Genghis Khan. You've heard of him?"

"Have not heard of book but who does not know name Genghis Khan?"

"*The Secret History* was meant only for the ruling class to read. It's more than a history. It details food, clothing, customs, rules, myths, legends, folklore—it's a treasury of details about Mongol life in the period when the empire rose."

"Sound very interesting." I was starting to understand that Mongolians like to tell stories. I'm not an impatient person, but I was curious to know why my son had brought his friend to see me. "If looking for book, do not have."

An-Zhang grinned once more. Tomorbaatar laughed. "No, no, of course you don't. I don't either. That's the problem. May I have more of this wonderful tea?" He held out his cup. I poured for him. "My new boss, the Consul, doesn't like me. My first boss was great, but she's gone back. This one doesn't like that I'm gay, that I have a Chinese boyfriend. I know he wants to send me back. But I've been careful to go above and beyond in my duties, making a lot of friends in New York, finding people to sponsor Mongolian musicians and artists to come here and American ones to go to Mongolia."

"He looks good in a tuxedo, Ma," said my son. "He brings in money."

"This very American, I think. Most important looks, money."

Tomorbaatar gave a cheerful shrug. "So he hasn't been able to get rid of me. But he doesn't like it. It burns him that a gay Chinese-loving guy is the face of Mongolia to a lot of people."

I looked to my son. "Burns?"

"Makes him angry."

"Ah. Anger makes hot. Good picture."

"But now," Tomorbaatar said, "he's found something he thinks will work."

"Work to make you go back?"

"Exactly. A copy of *The Secret History* is going to be auctioned at Sotheby's. A very important copy. It's ancient and written in Mongolian."

"This is history of Mongol people. Of course written in Mongolian."

"You'd think so, but no. The original was, and the copies made from it for the Khan's family. But those have been lost. The earliest existing copies are in Chinese. They've been translated back, of course, centuries ago, but we don't have any of the originals."

"Auction one is original?"

He shook his head. "It's supposed to be one of them, but I don't think so. The provenance is murky and—"

I said, "What part of book is provenance?"

An-Zhang spoke. "Ma, 'provenance' means the history of the book's ownership. What Tom means is, the owner claims this copy can be traced back at least a century and shown to be much older than that, but Tom thinks the trail is as phony as the book."

"Yes, I do," said Tomorbaatar. "But my boss wants it. For Mongolia. He acknowledges it might be a fake, but in case it's real, as the owner claims, Mongolia can't let it go to someone else."

"Wants you go to auction, buy? But you feel bad, know not real?"

"Worse. Mongolia's policy is not to buy items of cultural heritage. We feel it's insulting to have to pay to get back what's ours. He wants me to 'find a way to get it.'"

"Hmm. Doesn't mean steal, I think. So find way mean, ask rich friends buy."

"Yes. To prove my friends are useful."

"Ah. If friends don't buy, not useful. Then who cares, you look good in tuxedo? He send you back."

"Exactly. But how can I ask someone to pay a lot of money for something I'm pretty sure is a fake?"

"No how." I looked at Tomorbaatar, then at my son. "I agree, can't ask. But if don't ask, boss sends back. So you come to me. For why?"

"Well, Ma," said An-Zhang, "we said advice, but it's more than advice."

"Know this already. Please tell, what you want me do."

"You know we want you to do something?"

"Of course, know. No advice help in this trouble. Only someone do something. You want I be someone. Yes, good. What you want me do?"

Tomorbaatar smiled his widest yet. "Andy, you were right. She's a total gem."

I have never seen a partial gem but this might have been a Mongolian saying. Perhaps it had something to do with the Chinese mines in his country, so I didn't ask his meaning.

"The thing is, Ma," An-Zhang said, "it's the owner of the book. It's Uncle Seven."

———

After the young men left I resumed work on the dress I was sewing for my youngest granddaughter. I can think best when my hands are busy.

Uncle Seven. The youngest of seven sons of the Yan family, named by his parents Yan Yi-Lun. We had known each other decades ago in Hong Kong. Yi-Lun worked in one restaurant, my husband in another, while we all tried to save for passage to America.

Even in Hong Kong, when we were all poor, Yi-Lun had been a collector of things. He would visit dusty shops, buying a clay horse or a brush painting or a pot that had sat on a shelf for years. Bearing each in quiet triumph to his room, he would clean it minutely. He would sit drinking tea, admiring the new treasure on the shelf where he'd set it. He'd invite his friends for tea, also, to do the same. More than once I went, with my husband. The room was tiny, as all our rooms were, but in Yi-Lun's case it had almost nothing in it. All Yi-Lun's clothing lay folded in a box alongside his single rice bowl. He used a Japanese-style futon, which he rolled up. His treasures sat carefully spaced on shelves. His friends exclaimed over the peaceful elegance of his room compared to the jumbled disorder of ours. We determined to emulate him but the resolve never lasted. In his case, however, the sparseness of his room was as much the result of his desire to properly display his treasures as of the poverty we all shared.

Stalking a treasure, Yi-Lun was infinitely patient. He would visit a shop many times that had so far yielded nothing. Over endless cups of tea he would negotiate with a proprietor whose price he considered high. He was satisfied when he could carry an acquisition home, disappointed but undaunted when he lost a prize. He kept track of the disposition of items he had not been able to obtain. More than once he was successful, a long time later, in securing a treasure that had for some reason returned to the market.

In all this time Yi-Lun also worked diligently at his job. He was not an inspired chef, as my husband even then was becoming, but he brought the same doggedness to his work as he did to his pursuit of a treasure.

One day, Yi-Lun's employer announced his decision to emigrate to New York. He intended to open a restaurant in the Chinatown of Manhattan. He didn't offer passage, but promised his kitchen staff he would hire any of them who came to him there. That night, in his tiny room, Yi-Lun said goodbye to his treasures. The next day he sold them all. Thus Yi-Lun, alone among the restaurant's chefs, traveled to New York with his employer. He was on the new restaurant's staff on opening day. That restaurant, a success from the start, spawned a chain of six more. Yi-Lun advanced from underchef to assistant chef, then out of the kitchen into the office to be manager of the chain. One of his responsibilities was overseeing banquets from beginning to end. During the planning for a wedding banquet he met the older sister of the bride-to-be. He courted her patiently until she accepted him.

In the course of things Yi-Lun's employer died. With his father-in-law's help Yi-Lun bought the restaurant chain from the widow, who was willing to sell all seven of the restaurants but not their name. Yi-Lun renamed them Uncle Seven's, becoming, himself, Uncle Seven. As he remains.

Before he was Uncle Seven, before he left Hong Kong, he tried to persuade me to go with him.

"My prospects are bright, Yong-Yun," he said. "I'll be proud to look after your two sons. I'll treasure you as you must know I already do. Come to America with me."

This was not the first time he'd tried to convince me to abandon my husband, to tie my fortunes, instead, to his.

His arguments were powerful. With my husband, I had arrived in Hong Kong three years before. We lived in two small rooms, cooked in the hallways with other families. In addition to my husband's work in the restaurant kitchen, I worked also, cleaning offices, yet the money mounted slowly. Life in Hong Kong was hard. In America it would be easier, especially for my sons, but that my family would be able to go to America was by no means assured. Yi-Lun's affection for me was sincere, I knew. His prospects, as he said, were bright. I had no question in my mind that he would care for my sons as though they were his own.

But they were not. They were my husband's. I loved my husband. We had started this journey together. Together we would remain. For yet one more time, I turned Yi-Lun down.

If I had any regrets about my decision, I had only to think of Yi-Lun's beloved treasures, now scattered to the winds.

My family did finally come to America. Over the years, we remained on polite terms with Uncle Seven. In fact as my husband's fame grew, I found Yi-Lun's interest in me waning, replaced by a focus on my husband—specifically, on his talent in the kitchen. Yi-Lun tried more than once to entice my husband to join the staff at Uncle Seven's, promising him the job of Executive Chef for the Uncle Seven's chain. My husband's kitchen book would raise the reputation of Uncle Seven's from excellent to outstanding. Yi-Lun dreamed of a Michelin star.

I didn't know what that was, nor did my husband, until Yi-Lun told us.

My husband had no such grand dreams. He enjoyed feeding his neighbors, his friends, first in the restaurant where he was employed, later in his own. He also preferred, where Yi-Lun was concerned, to keep his distance. I had never told him about Yi-Lun's advances, but my husband was not a fool.

Having filled my head with memories, I put my sewing aside. From the red kitchen telephone I made two calls. Although my daughter has given me a red case for my cell phone, I still consider it rather small to hold very much luck. For this job I felt I would need a larger amount.

My first call produced exactly the result I hoped for. That was a good omen. I spoke to a young woman at the Museum of Chinese in America. This is a place I do not understand the need for, as all it contains are photographs of the early, dirty, crowded days of Chinatown, plus old shop signs, dented tea tins, with very few porcelains, silks, or jades. The young woman, however, in passable Chinese, confirmed they could provide the service I required.

My second call also was successful. I changed my dress, fixed my hair. I even put on black shoes with small heels. I prefer to do my detective work in sneakers, but at certain times, a disguise is necessary. I have never been one to shirk my professional responsibilities.

Locking three of my six locks—today, the top three—I left for my appointments. First I brought my package to the Museum, where I met with the young man who would be handling my request. We had a brief discussion. I explained exactly what I wanted done. When he asked why, I told him it was for sentimental reasons. That actually made no sense but I've found it's an explanation people respect. The young man assured me my item would be in the best of hands the entire time. I was reluctant to leave it, but as I'd considered various ways of accomplishing my goal, this had appeared best.

Then I went on to my second meeting, the one for which I had changed my outfit.

Uncle Seven received me immediately in his office above the largest of his restaurants, a banquet house on the Bowery. "Yong-Yun! You look splendid! No different from the day we met. Come in, come in."

"Ah, Yi-Lun. Flattery still comes easily to you, I see." I seated myself on a red velvet sofa. In Yi-Lun's generous office, displayed even more perfectly than a previous generation had been in his tiny room in Hong Kong, a number of exquisite antiquities sat on carefully-lighted shelves. Jades, porcelains, scroll paintings—it was obvious that over the years Yi-Lun had resupplied himself with treasures to love.

I said to him, "As for yourself, you look as prosperous as I know you to be."

Sitting beside me, he poured hot water into a delicate porcelain teapot, an item, I thought, that actually did belong in a museum. "It has been my good luck to have done well since I came here," he said.

"Other men wait for good luck. You make yours out of bad luck, or no luck at all."

"I try my best." He sounded humble but his look was smug. "You'll have tea, of course? It's Jin Jun Mei. Emperor's Golden Eyebrow. Have you tasted it before?"

A ridiculous question. Of course I had not. The price of half an ounce of Jin Jun Mei would feed me for a month. Even if I were a wealthy woman I doubted I would spend my fortune on tea.

Nevertheless it is extremely impolite to turn down an offer of tea when you are visiting. I'm not a person who likes to be impolite. Therefore I agreed to take a cup.

Yi-Lun also offered a plate of Smiling Faces. These sweet dough balls were among my husband's specialties. I took two, out of courtesy. While I waited for the tea to steep I bit into one. "This is quite good," I said.

"Not as good as your late husband's," Yi-Lun smiled.

"Very nearly," I replied, though they were not.

The tea was another matter. Sweet, velvety smooth, it brought with it a faint memory of greenery as though I were breathing the mountain air near my village in China. Perhaps if I were a wealthy woman I would permit myself a cup of Jin Jun Mei on celebratory occasions, after all.

Over the first cup of tea we spoke, as I had this morning with the young men, of our families. Yi-Lun's wife was well, his children flourishing, his grandchildren small whirlwinds. I recounted my children's accomplishments, which fortunately I do not tire of doing. I didn't do this in the order of their birth, reserving my third son for the end of my report. When I spoke of him Yi-Lun said, "Oh, yes, An-Zhang. I have gotten re-acquainted with him, over the last year. What a charming young man. With such interesting friends."

"Yes, An-Zhang told me of meeting you," I replied. "You have been together at a number of cultural events, I believe."

"Yes. I have met An-Zhang's..."

COLLECTIBLES

"His fiancé," I said, offering a tranquil smile.

Yi-Lun inclined his head. "Another charming young man. An-Zhang also introduced me to two other friends, one of them a Mongolian diplomat. He was sharing the evening with an American-Born Chinese friend."

Finally, we embarked upon the second cup. It was as delicious as the first.

"Yong-Yun, I'm enjoying your company greatly, as you know I always have. I think, though, that you have not come here to reminisce, or to catch up."

I put my cup down. "No, Uncle Seven, I have not."

"'Uncle Seven?' This is a formal visit then?"

"It concerns the friends of my son An-Zhang."

"Which friends?"

"The Mongolian diplomat. The American-Born Chinese."

"I see."

"You're a wealthy man, Uncle Seven. You've risen far since our days in Hong Kong. Your restaurants enjoy an excellent reputation. I see that you continue to collect treasures, which are, as I would expect of you, quite beautiful."

We both looked at his office shelves, he in satisfaction, me with an appreciation that was not feigned.

"I understand," I said, "that among the items you seek out now are books. I see none here, however."

"I rarely am interested in books. Only when one is extraordinary."

"*The Secret History of the Mongols?* Is that one extraordinary?"

"Ah." Yi-Lun smiled. "Is that why you're here, Yong-Yun? You've heard about the book? Do you want to see it?"

"I want you to give it to me."

He lifted his eyebrows. "I'm sorry?"

"As I said, you're a wealthy man. You're about to sell this book, so it cannot be as dear to your heart as some of your treasures. Whatever price this book can bring you, you do not need. However, it has another price. If you sell it at the auction, it will literally be at the cost of two young men's happiness."

236

I told the story of Tomorbaatar, his Chinese-American friend, his superior at the Consulate. "Tomorbaatar could probably raise your price," I said. "But he's too honorable a young man. He feels he cannot ask his friends for money to buy a book he thinks is inauthentic."

"I disagree with that assumption."

"Its provenance is murky. Don't look at me that way, Yi-Lun, I'm not completely uneducated."

He smiled. "I apologize. But Yong-Yun, of course it doesn't have a spotless provenance. I found it in a tiny shop in a tiny town in Gansu Province. The proprietor only knew it had been on the shelf above the door since his great-grandfather's time. No one there could read it, or even tell what language it was written in. I suspected the script was the ancient Mongolian, but I didn't dare hope what it might be until I had it safely home."

"You've had experts look at it?"

"Of course. Also, once it's sent to the auction house, any interested buyer will be permitted to have experts examine it."

"I'm asking you once more, Uncle Seven, not to send it to the auction house. Give it to me, to give to Tomorbaatar. If it's real you'll be acknowledged as a hero by the Mongolian people for making such a priceless gift. As will Tomorbaatar for receiving it. If it isn't real you'll save yourself embarrassment. In either case, once it's in Tomorbaatar's hands his happiness will be assured. That's important to my son. Therefore it's important to me."

"Yong-Yun, what you ask is a very large favor. Very large."

"Uncle Seven, I ask it in the name of our long friendship, extending back over the years to Hong Kong."

"Ah, Hong Kong. What days those were! Of course, I asked something of you then. You turned me down."

"Things worked out very well for you, nevertheless. Better, I think, than if I'd agreed."

"It's possible you're right," Yi-Lun said readily. "I found a wonderful bride who gave me wonderful children. Even at the time I understood your decision. I've never held it against you. Still, once we all came here, there was another rejection, also."

COLLECTIBLES

"My husband, who would not work for you."

"Indeed. My restaurants, as you say, are doing exceedingly well. I enjoy a high reputation. Yet you have tasted it for yourself." He gestured at the Happy Faces. "The best from my kitchens cannot come up to your husband's work."

"I'm sorry if that's been a source of discontent for you over the years," I said. "I myself am not the cook my husband was, either."

"Nor I. Though some on my staff could be, I believe, if they had the knowledge your husband had."

"Few have that."

"But you do, Yong-Yun. Written in your husband's kitchen book."

I sat very still.

"Come," Yi-Lun said. "One book for another. A fair transaction, I think."

I looked at him. I shook my head, saying slowly, "My husband carefully guarded his book. His recipes. His methods. His secrets. That book was his life's work."

"I know. The Mongols also carefully guarded their *Secret History*. We are in a position, the two of us, to add new chapters to both of these books, if you'll indulge my flowery image."

Yi-Lun waited.

I said nothing.

"Perhaps," he said gently, "you'd like time to consider my offer. It will be a week before the *Secret History* is sent to the auction house. Unless, before that week is up…" He didn't finish, but his meaning was clear.

I returned home. While I cooked dinner I thought about my husband, laughing in the kitchen, making Happy Faces for our children. I thought of the happiness in my son's face when I told him it would please me if he married Tony. Of Tomorbaatar, hoping to stay in America with his friend. Of Tomorbaatar telling my son that I was a complete gem.

The following day An-Zhang called. I told him I'd met with Uncle Seven. We would continue our discussion in a week, I said. Of course in actuality there would be no further discussion. There would be only my answer to Yi-Lun, yes or no.

Over the next two days I went about my business. I cooked, sewed, played mah jongg. The third day I called the young man at the museum. He reported that my project was nearly complete. Could I come for it the following day?

That morning—the fifth since my meeting with Uncle Seven—I retrieved my package. Paying the young man, I hurried home. I had much to do.

I spent the day in the kitchen, working industriously. When I was finished, I found myself quite pleased with my results. I made a cup of tea, to drink as I relaxed.

The sun was setting as I called Uncle Seven.

"Yong-Yun," he said, with a smile in his voice. "I've been thinking of you."

"Yes, I know."

"You do?"

"Why would you not be? You gave me a deadline. You must have been wondering what I would do as it drew near."

"Indeed I have been."

"I'll come see you tomorrow, Uncle Seven." I added, "For tea."

Early the next afternoon, again wearing the black shoes with small heels, I walked through Chinatown to Uncle Seven's banquet restaurant. I was shown to his office where, when he saw the brown-paper-wrapped parcel under my arm, Uncle Seven gave me a very big smile.

The tea was again Jin Jun Mei. I sipped at mine while Yi-Lun examined his new treasure.

"I apologize for the tea stains, the rips, the smears," I said.

"Oh, Yong-Yun! Don't be absurd! After all, it's a kitchen book!" He smiled, turning pages. Finally he closed the wire-bound notebook. "Now to keep my word. Not that you doubted me?"

"Of course I didn't."

COLLECTIBLES

Yi-Lun opened a drawer in his desk. Removing a splintering wooden box, he handed it to me. I lifted the top. Within lay leaf after leaf of fading, browned paper covered with the tiny strokes of a strange, flowing script.

"Paper," I mused. "I would have thought parchment."

"China had invented paper a thousand years before the rise of Genghis Khan. The Mongols understood well the advances of their time."

I peered at the papers. I felt that I was holding not a box containing history, but one holding the happiness of two young men.

As to what Yi-Lun was holding—ah, well.

―――――――――

When I returned home I called An-Zhang. I used the cell phone, for I was not in any great need of luck. "I would like you to come here for tea. Please bring Tomorbaatar."

"Did you talk to Uncle Seven again?"

"Come at five o'clock." I hung up.

The young men arrived before five. From that I understood that they were anxious to hear my news. Once more, Tomorbaatar presented me with a lovely basket, this time of large oranges. I turned the kettle on.

I saw no reason to keep them in suspense. I am not the sort of person who likes to boast, but I had accomplished my mission. I'd placed the box on the chair Tomorbaatar had occupied the first time he was here. As he walked into the living room, he saw it.

"Oh! Oh, Chin Tai-Tai! Is this it? How did you do it? Andy, look!"

My son crossed the room to stand with Tomorbaatar. Together they gaped at the box, which Tomorbaatar opened.

"This what you ask I do," I said severely. "If not think I could, why you ask?"

"No—I didn't mean—but—"

"You can't win, Tom," An-Zhang grinned. "Drop it."

"Do not drop!" I said, before I realized he didn't mean the box.

"Seriously, Ma," said An-Zhang. He sat, as did Tomorbaatar. In the kitchen I poured boiling water in the teapot for the tea to steep. "How *did* you do it?"

"I want this from Uncle Seven," I called from the kitchen. "Uncle Seven want something from me. Make trade."

"What did he want?"

I walked back to the living room. "Your Ba, his kitchen book."

Tomorbaatar looked puzzled. My son went pale. "Ma! You didn't give it to him? Ba's kitchen book? You didn't."

"Stay," I said. I went back to the kitchen, returning with the teapot, plus a plate of Happy Faces. Tomorbaatar jumped up from his chair to take the tray from me.

"An-Zhang, please not be upset. One thing, happiness of your friend more important than keep your Ba's secrets secret. Second thing, did not give real book to Uncle Seven, of course. Had copy made. Hand written, kind of notebook could have bought in Hong Kong then. Uncle Seven never saw real book so easy to fool. I spend all day making dirty, torn. Tea, oil, soy sauce. Uncle Seven thinks, is your Ba's book."

"But the recipes! The secrets!"

"So what about? Real book, I going give your Tony for wedding present. He will change recipes, all cooks do. Add things, take out things, cook for longer, for shorter. If Uncle Seven have cook as good as your Ba, he will change, too. His food then delicious. If not as good, will follow recipes but food not as good."

Tomorbaatar, frowning, had been lifting the papers in the box one by one. Now he looked up at me. "Chin Tai-Tai, Andy, I'm so sorry. It was all for nothing. I don't know what idiot experts examined this, but the book's a fake."

An-Zhang said, "What?"

I said, "No experts. No one see book. Of course, fake."

"Ma! What do you mean, of course? You knew?"

"Of course, knew. Uncle Seven never collect books. None ever on shelf, Hong Kong or here. He say, only if very special, but how he know?"

"This would have been discovered right away at the auction house," Tomorbaatar said. "They never would have allowed it to be put up for sale."

"Was never going to auction house. Uncle Seven have it made when meet you, your friend. With An-Zhang. He think, now I can get Chef Chin kitchen book."

"Wait," said An-Zhang. "That was the point, Ba's book? The whole thing was a game of chicken? Him and you?"

I frowned. "What chicken? No chicken, just clever plan from Uncle Seven."

"But Ma, if you knew *The Secret History* wasn't real and Uncle Seven just wanted Ba's book, why didn't you call him on it?"

"Why call him? I go to his restaurant."

Tomorbaatar laughed.

"No, no," my son said. "Why not tell him, go ahead and send the book to auction? If the fake's as obvious as Tom says, he wouldn't have. The whole scheme would have fizzled."

"Don't know this word, but if you mean not work, only half scheme would have fizzle. Uncle Seven not get kitchen book, but boss still able to send Tomorbaatar back for have useless friends."

"She's right, Andy," Tomorbaatar said. "We knew from the get-go this might be a fake. The important thing is that I was able to get my hands on it. That was the real game of chicken. Me and my boss."

I decided all this talk about chickens must be another Mongolian saying. I asked the important question. "Can stay in New York now?"

"Yes, I do think so. Thank you, Chin Tai-Tai." Tomorbaatar stood and bowed.

"Glad could help. Now you both sit. Tea is ready. Smiling Faces, too." I lifted the cover off the plate of sweets.

"Oh, Ma," said An-Zhang, "you really are a gem. Though I hate the idea of Uncle Seven being able to serve these in his restaurants. Remember how Ba used to make them for us on Sunday mornings?" He bit into one of the sweet balls of dough.

"Don't worry. Can't."

"What?"

"Book I give him don't have that page. Everything else, not that page. This one thing, I make almost as good as your Ba."

An-Zhang laughed.

"Do you remember," I said to my son in Chinese, "how you told me Mongolians like to play tricks?"

He glanced at Tomorbaatar. "Yes."

"I think Uncle Seven may be part Mongolian. That was a good trick he tried to play on me. But I think I'm also part Mongolian. My trick was better."

I poured the two young men their tea.

An-Zhang laughed again. "Ma, you're marvelous." Then he sipped his tea. His eyes widened. In English he said, "Oh, my god, Ma! What is this?"

Tomorbaatar sipped also. He took on the same expression.

In English I told him, "Jin Jun Mei. Golden Eyebrow of Emperor. I tell Uncle Seven, *Secret History* for Tomorbaatar. If giving him Chef Chin kitchen book, want something for me."

For some time after that, very little was said. We all sat peacefully together in my living room, enjoying our tea.

The Demise
of Snot Rocket

BY KRISTINE KATHRYN RUSCH

*L*et's be honest: It was gross even before the pandemic shut everything down and made us aware of just how dirty the world—and our habits—were.

Runners, especially distance runners, didn't have time to blow their noses, so they would press one nostril closed, and forcibly exhale whatever was in the other nostril, while moving on a trail. Sometimes that exhalation worked, and sometimes it didn't. If it didn't, the runner wiped his sleeve (and yeah, "his." It was usually a guy) across his face.

Anything to prevent stopping. Anything to preclude carrying tissue or wipes, which you couldn't dispose of anyway on a trail. Sometimes you could toss the tissue into an open garbage can on a run in a neighborhood or an urban area, but that meant carrying the wet slimy thing for blocks or more, and no one did that.

Instead, they sent snot flying out their noses, and hoped no one would see it.

This happened so often that it had a name: The Snot Rocket.

Fun, right?

Not possible while wearing a mask. And afterwards—who knows? No one is confessing now. If snot rockets have returned, no one will admit to it, when they all laughed about it before.

COLLECTIBLES

This story takes place before.

Sometimes I wonder what would have happened if it had happened after. Would Snot Rocket have changed? Would he have coped? Would he have become even more obnoxious?

We will never know.

———

To clarify a few things: Yes, I knew a guy named Snot Rocket. Not named by his parents. Named by all of us in the city who raced (reluctantly) at his side. A few of us tried to have him banned from local races, but we couldn't for two reasons.

1. He was good. As in always finished in the top five good.

And...

2. Everyone did it. Even the people who lied and said they didn't do it.

I did it on one particularly long trail run when I was in the woods in the rain by myself and my nose wasn't having it. My choice was a leaf or a snot rocket and, dear readers, I chose the rocket. The leaf could've given me poison ivy or poison oak or bugs or something. The snot rocket itself was a one and done.

It did leave me feeling...curiously elated.

I'm a woman of a certain age, raised by an OCD mother in a time before anyone knew what that was. I follow (most of) the rules, and that includes not expelling snot into the wild. (It also includes not discussing snot, but I think we're beyond that in this post-2020 world, right? We discuss fluids and filth all the time now. All. The. Damn. Time.)

All those years of running track in junior high (yes, I'm old enough not to call it middle school), high school, and college—thank you very much—before Title IX funding amounted to much of anything. I wasn't good enough to go on to regional and national competitions, where you actually got a bit of money.

But, in the early days of running, I *was* good enough to compete in local races with the men, often as one of the few women. Early on, I was in the top ten, but age eventually moved me to the top twenty and then the top thirty, and finally I became Queen of my Age Group, always smoking the other women in my age range by a significant, noticeable amount.

I can't tell you when Snot Rocket joined our merry band of local runners. One day he was there, and the next day (probably) we were all discussing how disgusting he was.

It wasn't just that he expelled goobers loudly and with great enthusiasm, it was also that he seemed to have an endless supply of them. It got so none of us ever wanted to run near him. Either side was a danger zone, and in front of him, well, sometimes you didn't know you were hit until you got home and peeled off your sweaty race shirt.

He'd probably be arrested now. Arrested and charged with assault.

Back in the day, we discussed it—those of us who had to share the road with him. Half of us thought he used it as a race strategy to keep the path clear.

When I ran past him (and I didn't do it as frequently as I would have liked; he was faster than me), I would make sure I was at least a yard away from him—off trail, on the sidewalk, wherever I could go and still be on the path for the race, so I wouldn't get disqualified.

Social distancing before we ever heard the term.

Of course, that zigging and zagging added a tiny bit of distance to my run, which I resented, as it did for everyone else who used that same strategy. Some of the men claimed they didn't care. They claimed they would run past him, and not worry, because they were already sweat-covered and dirty.

But I saw them in real time: they'd pass as far from him as possible, and if they were ahead of him, they had to expend extra energy just to keep the distance.

No one wanted to get too close. And I think that extra energy cost some of Snot Rocket's competitors the race. They didn't have anything left in the tank when they got close to the finish line, and he would zoom right past them.

There was no proving it, of course.

But Snot Rocket's personal habits and his consistent wins did not endear him to the local runners. Particularly when he would brag to anyone who could stomach listening about how great he really was.

COLLECTIBLES

He had—he said—thousands of finisher medals. Some in boxes, and the best ones—the "coolest" ones—hanging from hooks on his walls.

He died, with a couple of those medals around his neck, and no other medal in the house.

But I get ahead of myself.

I'm an investigative journalist. Not the kind you're thinking of—the old-fashioned Woodward and Bernstein model, supported by a sympathetic paper filled with heroic and compassionate leaders who really didn't care about the bottom line (and yes, that was fiction, but it was a fiction we all bought). I did work for the Gray Lady once upon a time, until her D.C. rival poached me. I stayed there until I'd had enough of the insularity and constant political doublethink. Then came the rabid nightmarish shock that was the first few months of the Trump era.

My marriage of long standing broke up over (among other things) politics—his were red, mine weren't. So, I quit the day job and moved west, heading to yet another storied newspaper just in time for it to get sold and close.

I landed on my feet more or less, and became part of an online collective that partners with media outlets all over the world. We do the research and some of us also do the writing, and both organizations get the credit.

It pays less than I made in D.C., but the work is more flexible, and the cost of living here is lower.

I ran back east, so it was only natural to join running organizations here. I signed up for every race I possibly could and as a result met the other slightly obsessive runners in the community, some of whom were fast like Snot Rocket and some of whom were nice, like the bulk of the folks running the show.

I didn't get involved with anyone—wasn't that interested, really—but had a pretty fulfilling life. Research, writing, and running, plus living in a place where I didn't have to talk politics 24/7, made life a lot more pleasant than it had ever been before.

I also had the freedom to set my own schedule, which actually allowed me to run as many races as I could find. I preferred 10K because it was just long enough to challenge me, but short enough to allow me to have the rest of the day to do something else if I so chose.

It also meant that I got to meet a lot of elite runners, because 10Ks were usually attached to the big races. We had only three Boston Qualifiers in this city, but that was three more than most places.

I'd run Boston half a dozen times, including the year of the bombing. But Boston lost its allure for me, partly because I was on the team that ended up reporting the bombing. I heard stories of loss and heartache, heroism and strength, and pretended for those few years that it hadn't had an impact on me.

But after I moved, and qualified in my age group, I couldn't bring myself to go. It wasn't an east-west thing either, or the idea that I had to travel long distances. My stomach knotted and my mouth went dry even thinking about it.

Every year, the Boston Qualifiers were fraught. Runners shoved their way into separate starting corrals, yelled at volunteers, and sometimes tried to shoehorn their way into a pace group they hadn't signed up for.

I tried to stay out of their way, but that year, the year Snot Rocket died, I failed at keeping my distance.

That particular race had a new director who was a bit clueless. The corrals snaked through an industrial park, doubling back on themselves. Unlike most large races, the corrals didn't have makeshift barriers to keep runners from sliding into another grouping. The director apparently expected people to police themselves.

My corral for the 10K was across a narrow strip of parking lot away from the lead-off runners for the actual marathon. My corral was quiet. Most people in a 10K maybe cared about a personal best, but they really weren't there for a make-it-or-break-it chance to run the race of their dreams.

Those in the marathon line were there to win, or to PR and get in the race of their dreams, particularly those in that first corral. Like so many big races of its type, this one offered hefty prize money for the finishers. The qualifiers went down by age group, but the actual runners—the ones who traveled from

COLLECTIBLES

city to city collecting trophies and prizes—well, they needed to focus on their race rather than some kind of squabble about times and spots in line.

I was just trying to focus on my race when I noticed Snot Rocket was in the middle of the shoving match.

I started watching like a kid drawn to a school fight. I actually had a dog in the hunt or skin in the game or whatever cliché you wanted to drum up. Not because I wanted Snot Rocket to win, but because I was curious about what he was up to.

He was screaming at one of the runners, spraying visible spittle all over him, just from the force of his verbal outburst. The runner—a tall skinny white guy, who looked like he ran professionally—screamed back.

I couldn't make out the words, but these guys were *serious.* They were furious at each other.

Snot Rocket shoved the other guy first, right into the crowd of elite runners. They paid attention for the first time, glaring at the two of them. One of the exceptionally tall and thin runners, a man who looked vaguely familiar, raised his hand, and waved it—not to get the attention of Snot Rocket and the other guy, but to get the attention of the volunteers.

One of the volunteers responded immediately, which told me that the vague familiarity I felt actually meant something. The runner really was one of the elites, and more than that, one of the people the race was honored to have in its line-up.

That volunteer disappeared into the crowd, and I couldn't follow his yellow jersey to see where he went, because I'm not exceptionally tall or tall in any way shape or form.

Snot Rocket and his squabbling buddy didn't even seem to notice. The squabbling buddy shoved Snot Rocket. Snot Rocket tripped backwards, and probably would have fallen if he hadn't been in such good physical shape.

No one tried to break them up. No one wanted to get involved. Or maybe, no one wanted to get injured just before a race.

Finally, a couple of people wearing yellow security jerseys waded into the crowd. One of them grabbed Snot Rocket by the arm. He shook them off, and turned toward them, utterly furious. I was finally able to see his face.

"Get your fucking hands off me," he said loud enough for me to hear.

The security official said something in response, and reached toward Snot Rocket's bib. Snot Rocket stepped backwards again, only this time he backed into another security official.

Two more security officials were talking with Snot Rocket's opponent. The opponent shook them off and tried to move forward in the crowd, but the crowd closed around him. No one let him get to the front of the line.

Snot Rocket wasn't watching any of that. He was arguing with security now, only softer, so I couldn't hear.

"Never seen that before," said the woman next to me. She was thin and slight and wore the race T-shirt with an additional tech shirt underneath. It promised to be cool for this run, but I never wore the extra shirt. I always got too hot at races.

"Me, either," I said and turned away, so that I could see the rest of the fight. Only the fight was done now. Snot Rocket was being led down that strip of unmarked parking lot, walking between two security officials, his head down.

I couldn't see Snot Rocket's opponent anymore, but the crowd had closed back up, and they were all facing forward, going through their pre-race rituals while they waited for their corral's starting gun.

"I wonder what that was all about," the woman next to me said.

I could have told her about Snot Rocket, about how unpleasant he was and had always been. I could have engaged in polite speculation, since we had to wait another thirty minutes before we started moving—provided the 10K went off on time. That would depend on the full and half marathoners.

Technically, we started on a different block from the full and half folks, and went a completely different direction to stay out of their way. We'd join each other nine miles into their race—and then our group would veer off, and head toward the finish line via a different route again.

I didn't expect to see Snot Rocket again, because he was a marathoner and, I thought, had just managed to get himself disqualified from the race.

But I did see him, just before I joined the marathoners at mile marker nine (the race used the marathon numbers, not numbers for the rest of us).

COLLECTIBLES

He was loping like he always did, making it look easy. His hair flowed backwards, his arms were relaxed at his sides, and he had a half-smile on his face.

He looked nothing like the man who had been shouting so loudly that spit came out of his mouth. He actually looked content.

I watched him run as the road I was on headed toward the road he was on, and I envied his perfect stride. I didn't register anything else except a mild curiosity about how he managed to stay in the race after that egotistical display and why he was looking so content with himself.

I had been a bit unsettled from his fight; I would have expected him to be more than a bit unsettled. I would have expected him to be deeply disturbed, maybe running a bit too fast to get rid of the adrenaline from the fight itself.

And then I joined the crowd and didn't think about him at all. I concentrated on finding my lane, where I could keep a steady pace and stay out of the way of the full and half marathoners who didn't need some pokey 10K runner to screw up their PR.

That's the thing about running. People are polite, generally. And if they have conflicts, they leave them off the course. This isn't one of those confrontational sports like hockey or football. It's something most people do for themselves, including the elites. Yeah, there's money involved, but mostly, there's bragging rights. And bragging rights mean even more.

And that was all the thought I gave him that morning. Maybe I didn't even go that far. I enjoyed my race, got my finisher medal, noted that I had won my age group, and waited for the 10K medal ceremony, which was taking place long before any of the full marathoners even thought of crossing the finish line.

Then I went home, finished up an article on the impact of California fuel regulations (sometimes my job is not fun), and poured myself a glass of California chardonnay to celebrate a good day well lived.

The next day, the authorities found Snot Rocket dead. Strangled in the living room of his own house.

Of course, I didn't find out for nearly a week. I didn't know Snot Rocket's real name; I never had the desire to ferret it out. So when people talked about Dave dying, I didn't know that Dave—he of the very ordinary and forgettable name—was Snot Rocket.

I didn't learn that until the running group met at our favorite park for our seven a.m. weekend run, and were greeted by an exhausted-looking detective.

He was sitting on a concrete picnic table—on the table itself, feet on the concrete bench. He clutched an extra-large to-go cup of coffee like a lifeline. He actually wore a suit, although it was cheap and baggy, as if he had lost weight due to a serious health condition. His hair was thin, and his face was thinner. The suit called attention to him—who wore a suit to a park at this time of the morning?

We all shot him nervous looks as we mingled and talked. And when zero hour arrived—seven a.m. on the nose—he stood up and ambled over to us.

I cringed. I always do when a non-runner stranger decides to talk with our group. That person usually wants to know what running is like or if we're racing or how he can actually get into the daily habit without doing any of the work.

Only this guy flashed a badge, introduced himself as Detective Conners, and said he was looking into the death of Dave Pyron. Most of us glanced at each other in confusion, and probably would've told Conners that we didn't know any Pyron, until Roscoe Carter raised his extremely thin eyebrows and said, "You mean Snot Rocket, right?"

We all whipped our heads toward him, and a few of us expressed incredulity that Snot Rocket was named Dave. Finally, Conners hauled out a photograph—fortunately one taken from Snot Rocket's house, not the photo of him strangled—and we had to agree: yep, Dave and Snot Rocket were one.

None of us wanted to give up our morning run, so we invited Conners to join us, which he declined. Instead, he offered to interview us one by one as we returned. Apparently, he too thought this was a race, not a group venture. A few people normally would have sprinted out, but no one did this time, because no one wanted to be first to talk with the detective.

COLLECTIBLES

We left in a mass and returned in a mass. I hung back. I wanted to watch this guy work. My reporter's instinct had flared up and I found myself wondering if there was a story here I could use.

Conners got to hear stories about snot going awry, about Snot Rocket's interminable arrogance, and about his winning ways. Conners asked a few questions, mostly about Snot Rocket's relationships, which most of us knew nothing about.

Roscoe said Snot Rocket (or rather, Dave. Roscoe called him Dave) had had two live-in girlfriends over the course of the past ten years. All of the relationships had ended badly (what a surprise). And when the last one cratered three years ago, Snot Rocket swore off relationships forever—and, according to Roscoe anyway—seemed to live up to that vow.

I had taken a seat on a nearby picnic table, nursing a Gatorade that I had brought with me, as I listened to the questions. I had learned the fine art of eavesdropping as a young reporter, and it had never failed me.

Some of the questions Conners asked were routine—*Who are you? How well did you know the victim? When did you last see him?*

But one question got a snort or a half-laugh from every single person he asked it to. *Do you know anyone who disliked Dave?*

The answers seemed planned, because they were the same, almost with the same wording: *Everyone disliked Dave.*

Everyone.

Which was how I would have answered the question, given a chance.

But Conners got halfway through the scrum of runners before looking at me.

"Learn anything from your eavesdropping?" he asked.

I knew better than to be surprised at the observation powers of investigators. Much as I complain about the politics in D.C., I met a lot of career folk who saw everything. Many of those people were inspectors general or worked in the various inspectors general offices. They didn't miss a trick.

"The only thing I've learned today is Snot Rocket's real name," I said.

"Not a fan?" Conners asked, waving me over, so that I would sit near him, like all the other people he had interviewed had.

"No," I said.

"So I don't suppose you ever saw his house," Conners said.

"I didn't know he had a house until someone said he died in it," I said.

Conners nodded. He wasn't taking notes, but he had his iPhone on his knee. Even though the screen was dark, I would wager the thing was recording.

"What's your interest in all of this?" he asked.

"Curious, I guess," I said.

"Eavesdroppers are usually more than curious," he said. "So, again, what's your interest?"

"I'm not sure I have one," I said.

"Not sure," he repeated, as if he didn't understand that. "How come?"

"I'm a reporter," I said. "I have credentials in my car if you want to see them."

"When we're done," he said. "You doing a story on Dave?"

"I wasn't planning to," I said. "But there might be something here. True crime is a big beat, and this has some interesting angles."

"True crime," he said, as if I had pissed all over his salad.

"I'm always looking for stories that will help our company continue its award-winning investigative journalism," I said.

"This isn't an award-winning scoop," Conners said. "Just a squalid murder of an apparently unpleasant man."

"I wasn't thinking of it as award-winning," I said. "We have to pay the bills. True crime can do that."

"Even if you're a suspect?" he asked.

I smiled at him, condescendingly. I had perfected that smile over decades, starting during my young perky and cute decade. Then the smile let my interview subject know all those questions I had asked him—those hard-hitting ones?—they hadn't come from my bosses; those questions had come from me.

Later, that smile got me through doors that would have been closed to anyone else. I had become old enough to seem like someone, and I had that kind of face—the kind that looked like it had once been famous but was no longer.

Now, I had aged into a strong mother figure and that condescending look shamed more than one person into cooperating with me, even though they never should have.

"I'm not a suspect," I said.

"I'm the one who makes that determination," he said, maybe a tad defensively.

"I've heard enough to know your timeline," I said. "I was working—at the office—during that ten-hour window. I had been busy the day before and the day after, and once again, I never knew Snot Ro—I mean Dave—even had a house."

Conner's eyes narrowed. He didn't like my tone. I didn't really care.

"You know I'll check, right?" he said.

"Yep," I said.

Conners took a deep breath and let it out slowly, as if he were trying to control his annoyance. "So what can you tell me about your friend Dave?"

"First of all," I said, "he wasn't my friend Dave. Secondly, I can tell you the man was a pig."

"To you?"

"To everyone," I said. "You know the derivation of his nickname, right?"

"Actually, no," Conners said.

Non-runners. They weren't up on the slang. The nickname would have told him a lot had he been part of the community.

So I explained it all to him—the nickname, the behavior, the possible advantages it gave Snot Rocket in a race.

"Yet you let him join the group here," Conners said.

"If he was a member of this group, it predates me," I said. Then I had to give Conners my personal history. He got more and more tense as he heard my C.V., particularly when I mentioned which papers I had worked for.

Yeah, he'd check on me, but he was also savvy enough to know I wouldn't lie about that. Which meant I was a lot more impressive than I looked. And a lot more of a threat to his investigation. If I was going to write a story about it, I wasn't just some hack threatening to make sure he handled the case right; I was going to write something that would be *read*.

"This group run was a recurring event in his computer calendar," Conners said.

"Sounds like maybe he hadn't updated the calendar in a while," I said.

"Sounds like," Conners said, as if he agreed with me. But his tone was distracted. He was watching the rest of the group, most of whom were fidgeting. We had all budgeted time for the run and maybe breakfast afterwards, but after that we wanted to get on with our day.

He looked back at me. "When was the last time you saw Dave?"

I wanted to be obnoxious and say I never saw Dave, I didn't know a Dave, I would never socialize with a Dave, but I didn't say anything like that, because that was when I remembered the Boston Qualifier.

I got that image of Snot Rocket's perfect form, the way he glided down the road, weaving his way in and out of the other runners as if he was gifted and they were mere mortals.

I would never see that again. And that, of all things, made me just a little bit sad.

"Well?" Conners asked.

"Last Sunday," I said. And then I told him, not about seeing Snot Rocket run, but about that fight in the corral, and security dragging him off. And then I mentioned that Snot Rocket ended up running the race after all.

I finished with this. "No, I don't know who he was fighting with. No, I don't know what they were fighting about. I could tell they were really mad at each other, and their behavior was really out of bounds for any race I'd ever been part of. I have no idea what the security arrangements were at that race. I do know it had a new director, and that most people working the race were volunteers. I know they have records of everyone's times, and a lot of photographs. In fact, all of these races are well documented because not only are there official shots, but participants take a lot of pictures as well."

I stopped at that point, because I had nothing to add except speculation and while speculation was fun, it wasn't really productive, not with a detective, except maybe to indict me in a way I couldn't have anticipated.

He had a few more questions for me, none of which I considered relevant or important, and then he moved on to the remaining few. I listened

COLLECTIBLES

to the questions, heard the same or similar answers, and started packing up to leave.

He never did ask anyone if they had been to Snot Rocket's house or if they'd seen his medals or even if they had seen him be violent. It was as if the story I had told about the Sunday before hadn't registered in Conners' brain.

Or maybe he didn't want to influence anyone.

I found it curious though, and I worried that he had mentally dismissed me because of my age, my gender, or maybe even my status as a reporter.

He never looked at me again, even as he wrapped up and headed to his car. I gathered my Gatorade bottle so I could toss it, and as I did, Roscoe joined me.

"What did you make of that?" he asked.

He knew some of my history, knew that I was a reporter, and probably surmised that I had some experience with the police that he didn't have.

"I don't know what to make of it," I said, "except that they're investigating."

"He didn't seem all that invested, though, did he?"

People who read and watch a lot of television expect police detectives to work on one case at a time. Instead, they work on dozens, and never give any case much time. Except the high profile ones. That Conners spent this morning here, waiting for us, but didn't seem all that interested told me that Snot Rocket's murder was a weird death, but not significant enough for the brass to pay attention.

Conners would want to close the case to get his closure rate up, but that was all. It was going to be hard for anyone to care about Snot Rocket. He wasn't the most charming of men alive, and there was no family that I knew of to clamor over solving his death.

"He spent a lot of time with us," I said, not liking being in the position to defend Conners.

"Yeah." Roscoe frowned. "I just get the sense this one is going to just slide into the unsolved pile."

I nodded. "I suspect you're right."

I didn't ask Roscoe why he cared. At that point, I wasn't sure I did either. But as time went on, I found the murder niggling at me. The fight. The medals. The pointed message of the strangulation.

It wasn't that I cared about Snot Rocket as much as I cared about something else: Someone had murdered a person I knew.

I'd met a lot of people connected to murders over the years, but only after the fact. I never knew the victim. I was never involved in the early stages. I only got involved later on, when the death became a story.

My reporter brain was noodling this one. We were always being admonished to take the initiative, to look for something that might make the company money as well as something that would *cost* the company money.

All of us, the investigative reporters, were good at spending money so we could chase the best stories, the kind that won Pulitzers and Edward R. Murrow awards. But I noted that the reporters who stayed with the company weren't just the award winners. Unemployed award winners were thick on the ground these days.

The company held onto the reporters who could do both—win awards and make money. I hadn't had a moneymaker in a while.

I figured this story might do the trick.

I pitched it that Monday with the title "Death of a Weekend Warrior," about a lonely guy with no social skills who spent all his time running and collecting medals, a guy who ended up dying horribly. I told my boss that this might be an *Unsolved Mysteries* kind of thing, and he reminded me that we were in early days. Maybe it would end up being a series.

In that conversation, I learned he was also flirting with a new podcast, one that would capitalize on the true crime podcasts that were getting turned into books and films and cultural conversations at the time.

My boss also pointed out, in that cold dispassionate way journalists had of discussing uncomfortable (and often unsaid) things, that Snot Rocket didn't have any family to object to his portrayal. My boss reminded me to document, document, document, but he also told me that speculation was possible in this instance—and he said so in a way that encouraged it.

COLLECTIBLES

I wasn't comfortable with that, at least not at the time, but apparently I can be persuaded. The deeper I got into the case, the more I found my way to the dark side.

I started, as I always do, with what the internet could tell me. Snot Rocket did not have a public-facing Facebook account. He didn't seem to be on Twitter or Instagram or any other social media site that I could find. He did have several professional accounts with places like LinkedIn, but those looked corporate, as if his bosses had mandated them and he had to follow a template.

From them, I learned that he worked in some engineering field with a technical specialty that I didn't really understand. The corporation he worked for spanned the globe, doing all kinds of building and other projects. On none of these sites was it clear what kind of work he did—whether it was building something or back-up work or design. He didn't seem to travel for the job, which made some kind of sense, because this city is big enough to have all sorts of engineering and construction work, enough to keep an entire flood of people busy for years.

I looked up his ex-girlfriends, but they didn't have much of a social media presence either. The one who did keep her photographs current seemed to delete her past with regularity. If I wanted to track her relationship with Snot Rocket—or, um, Dave—I could do so, but that would require a lot of digging into the Wayback Machine Internet Archives or other places that kept track of the world as we once knew it.

I nearly gave up there. I mean, why write a story about a man that no one liked, a man who had filthy personal habits, and did his best to shove people away from him, a man who was murdered for his efforts?

And every time I got to that last bit, I realized that was why. Snot Rocket had pissed off a whole slew of people. This was rather like a game of *Clue*. Who hated him enough to finally off him—and in the most personal way possible?

I sat at my desk with a yellow legal pad after doing my preliminary search, and doodled what I did know, not just about Snot Rocket, but about the killer as well.

I knew that the killer knew Snot Rocket. The killer clearly hated Snot Rocket. The killer used Snot Rocket's most treasured possessions (I assumed) to actually kill Snot Rocket. Then, the detective thought, the killer stole those possessions, except for the ones that had strangled the life out of Snot Rocket.

I also figured that the killer was tall—at least as tall as Snot Rocket. I couldn't imagine someone short standing on a chair, with his (her?) hands clutching a ribbon around a medal and pulling that ribbon tight enough to strangle Snot Rocket. I figure that the killer had to be strong as well, because Snot Rocket—well, anyone, really—would have fought like hell to avoid being strangled like that.

Unless he was unconscious. Since I did not, at the moment anyway, have any access to Snot Rocket's autopsy report, I did not know if he was drugged or unconscious when that medal (those medals?) got wrapped around his neck.

I would need that information eventually, but first, I was going to work on who Snot Rocket was.

I was about to give up on the internet side of Snot Rocket's life when I realized I hadn't even gone near the entire treasure trove of internet research that would give me everything there was to know about Snot Rocket. Not Dave the Engineer, but Snot Rocket, the runner.

As I had told Detective Conners, most of racing had gone online in the last twenty years. From race results to photographs to vanity selfies (with other people in the background), the internet held a virtual wealth of information about runners, racing, and more.

Hell, I'd been in Boston after the bombing, and between the video surveillance from stores and official cameras, and the cell phone photos and videos of the race, the authorities were able to track down the bombers in record time. I had contributed a handful of photos to the authorities at their request—after the suspects were caught, but as the prosecution was putting their case together.

Even though I was a reporter, I had been *in* the race, and had no trouble parting with what could have been key evidence, something I might not have been able to do had I actually been a reporter on the story.

I learned though. I learned the value of other people's moments, the way that those moments captured one whole hell of a lot more than the photographer realized.

It took three full days of work, searching for races with Snot Rocket's real name in them. Some of those races weren't easily searchable—especially later races. Early on in the century, the internet was a lot cruder than it is now. If a race wanted to post results, they did so on a page on their website.

Sometime around 2010, those pages became private. You had to be part of the race or someone who knew how to get into those private pages to see them. Fortunately, I'd hacked a number of them, not because I was trying to get a story but, for one reason or another, my own listing in a race didn't give me access to those pages. So I learned how to get access without waiting for one of the organizers to give me permission.

Now the race pages were on some dedicated site, one that you only learned if you actually paid for the race. Those would have been tough to find except that innovation had only come about in the last few years, and in the last few years, I had met Snot Rocket, and we were often in the same race together.

I worked from those backwards, developing a system: I looked up Snot Rocket—Dave—by name to find out where he finished. His finisher spot— almost always near the front—then provided his bib number. In the more recent races, I could search official photos by bib number, catching a glimpse of Snot Rocket throughout the race.

The later photos usually showed a man running alone. One of the photos actually caught him launching a snot rocket, and I marked it. I wanted Detective Conners to see it. There was no one else in the frame, though, so I doubt that particular loogie was heading toward anyone else.

Photos of these races showed him at the starting line, usually standing by himself, sometimes holding one of his ankles as he stretched. The photos at the end of the race showed him grabbing his medal from the volunteer handing them out—no graceful bow of the head so the medal could go around his neck, no smile. Just a *gimme that now* kinda yank.

Then Snot Rocket would walk away, usually out of the frame. Some photos at various races caught him on the way to the parking lot, medal clutched in his fist. A few showed him in the crowd. Often, it seemed, he went to the timer's tent to see where he placed. If he was first, second or third, the spot that would give him an award, he would grab that early so that he could leave.

He almost never climbed on the podium—if, indeed, there was a podium. He always walked to his car, medals clutched in his hand as if he had stolen them.

He didn't seem to get any joy out of collecting those medals. He had the same grim look of determination on his face that he had had at the start of the race, as if whatever prompted him to run hadn't been satisfied by the simple act of completing the race.

The photos started to change four years back. He looked less Snot Rocket and more Dave. His hair was lighter, trimmer, and once in a while, he grinned as he crossed the finish line, pumping a fist or slapping someone else—a guy I didn't recognize—on the back.

A closer look at some of the finisher photos showed Snot-Dave talking with people as he got a bottle of water out of the ice chest or waited to get on the finisher podium.

Eventually, I started to recognize the people around him. A dark-haired thin-faced woman, who was not wearing racing clothes, and another couple, both of whom seemed to be runners. They had bibs, usually wore the race's T-shirt, and often wore compression pants. They talked and laughed with the thin-faced woman, who didn't seem to smile all that much.

Indeed, her eyes had a wary, tired look, but I couldn't see the source until I went farther back.

Farther back, she too wore racing clothes and an extra twenty to thirty pounds. That weight looked good on her. She smiled more, and that made her pretty. Often, she looked up at Snot—well, Dave. He looked more like a Dave here—with something like love and affection.

He usually had an arm around her, pulling her close. They would share water bottles, pose with their finisher medals, holding them up to the camera or mug with them on their foreheads or wrapped around their arms like matching bracelets.

COLLECTIBLES

Even farther back, there were the photos of young love, the meet-cute that every rom-com has, only here, the couple would have that awkward leaning into each other stance that people who were attracted but hadn't yet committed to anything often had.

Before that—about ten years back—Dave ran with a group of young men, none of whom looked familiar. And before that, he would show up at races with a young woman (who had to be his age) who would stand at the sidelines, arms wrapped around herself, mouth a thin displeased line, as if she didn't want to be anywhere near sweaty runners so damn early in the morning.

Roscoe had said Snot Rocket had two girlfriends. I wagered I had seen them both. Only one had been serious, and the other had been a flirtation, something that young people got into before they knew themselves well enough to know in the space of a conversation or two or three that the attractive person they were talking with wasn't really right for them.

I made a list of all the people he seemed to socialize with, and if they had a bib number, I wrote those down too. Then I worked recent to less recent, trying to figure out who his associates were.

They weren't as good at running as he was, that was for certain. They were recreational runners who usually ended up in the middle of the pack. Except for the final woman, the woman with the thin face, who lost twenty to thirty pounds. She did well in her age group, often placing first by a long distance.

Her name was Noelani Kahale, and, as her name suggested, she was originally from Hawaii. She had a huge social media presence, but it confused me. Her photographs were full of Dave. Noelani and Dave, running on the beach. Noelani and Dave, laughing before their sunrise run. Noelani and Dave, entwining their matching finisher's medals at the end of races.

It wasn't until I looked at the dates that I realized the posts I was seeing on all her platforms were five years old.

There was nothing new.

Some people vanished because they closed or abandoned their online accounts. Others watched their lives to go hell and didn't want to chronicle that.

I suspected something else though. Noelani had gone from a healthy tanned woman to a too-thin rail of a person who did *not* participate in runs.

I searched for her on the internet, and found the obituary almost right away.

Noelani Kahale, dead of lung cancer at thirty-five. The obituary mentioned that she hadn't been a smoker, and there was no obvious cause of the disease. It urged everyone to give to various cancer organizations and research foundations that were searching for causes of lung cancer in non-smokers.

She had no children, and was not married. Her parents had brought her back to Oahu, and buried her there.

There was no mention of Dave or running or anything personal about her.

The friends had a big social media presence as well, and, it seemed, they had moved onto triathlons. They did not seem to participate in any of the local runs.

But I had found them, and I knew they might be helpful.

So I called, and left messages, asking for an interview, not mentioning Dave. Three of them never returned my call.

The fourth, the woman in the shot with Dave and Noelani and another friend, called, and set up a meet at a local coffee shop for the following day.

She assumed I was interested in her recent triathlon finish which was good enough to qualify for one of the bigger races in the fall. I let her hold that assumption. It was always easier to talk with people when they were unprepared.

I also set up an appointment with Detective Conners—only I told him that I was officially covering the story, and that I would want whatever information he could give me. I would, I said, let him know what I had discovered as well.

He hadn't sounded happy, but he hadn't told me to stop investigating either. My sense that he was overwhelmed and not that interested in this case persisted, just in the ways that he addressed me or seemed to need reminding about the case itself.

I put my annoyance at him aside, and focused on the first interview. My subject, Jenna Wasserman, also had a large social media presence, with lots of friends and lots of activities. The man she had been with in those photos with Dave had vanished from her social media pages a few years back, so I assumed a break-up.

But I made notes, just in case.

I wrote those on paper, because I planned to use my phone to record the interview, just as I had done for more than a decade.

If she didn't like that, I would record anyway, and call it all deep background.

The early morning meeting came after both of our runs. We were both rosy cheeked and bright-eyed, but we had both changed into business casual— khakis and somewhat dressy shirts.

She was on her way to the bank where she worked in the loan department, and I would go back home to make notes after the interview was over.

The coffee shop we met in was a wannabe Starbucks not far from my place. The baked goods were sinful and delicious, but the coffee was always watery and unimpressive. I liked the blueberry muffins, and had learned to order an ice tea with them.

Jenna ordered her standard coffee drink, took one sip, made a face, and set it aside. She said nothing about the quality, though, for which I gave her silent props.

She looked even more fit in person, and she had that glow that distance athletes often had, that sense of comfortable athleticism that gave her a grace with every single movement.

I asked if I could record, and told her I would take notes by hand as well. She had no problem with that. And because she was so cheerful and pleased about an interview, I did ask her about her athletic career—her recent success at triathlons, and the upcoming big race. I liked her enthusiasm.

I was sorry that I was going to have to squash it.

"I'm not just here about the triathlon," I said to her. "I assume you heard about Dave Pyron."

"No," she said, with a slight frown. "What did he do now?"

Whatever I had expected her to say, it wasn't that.

"He died three weeks ago," I said. "I thought you would have heard."

"Died?" Her frown grew. "No, I hadn't heard. Why did you think I would?" I decided to save the *well, he was murdered. It was all over the news* for a little later. Instead, I said, "Because I saw photos. I thought you were friends."

She shook her head ever so slightly. "We were never friends," she said. "He was friends with my ex-boyfriend, Calvin."

"You didn't like him?" I asked.

"Calvin?" she said, deliberately misunderstanding me.

"Dave," I said.

Her lips thinned. "I liked him a lot that first year. He took great care of Noelani."

"When she was so ill," I said, guessing.

Jenna nodded. "He did everything for her. He made sure she had everything she needed, he worked with home health care, he even paid for hospice when she lost her medical insurance."

That was not the man I had expected. "But...?" I asked.

"Her parents," Jenna said. "I blame them."

"For what?" I asked.

"They did nothing." There was anger in her voice, and her eyes flashed. *"Nothing.* They wouldn't help financially, they didn't come out for her surgeries, and when she was dying, they didn't come to visit."

I felt that tingle I both loved and hated, the journalist moment—the one that says, *This is a great story,* and I loved great stories. But I also knew that this was someone's life we were discussing, and someone's pain, and for that reason, the tingle irritated me.

"Then," Jenna said, her voice getting louder, "they commandeered her body, and they could. Because she didn't have a will or anything, and they were her next of kin."

I nodded. I didn't want to interrupt the flow.

"They took her to Hawaii and buried her there, even though she wanted to be cremated. Dave told them—hell, we *all* told them she wanted to be cremated, but they didn't listen. They didn't even acknowledge Dave. He went out for the funeral only to find out that they didn't even hold one. Just some ceremony at the grave site *that she didn't want."*

Jenna leaned back, and let out a small "whew," then gave me a tiny smile. "Sorry," she said. "I guess I'm still mad about it all."

She sipped the coffee and winced.

"I'll wager Dave was too," I said.

"He was *livid*. And not just at them. At *everything*." She shook her head. "Everything was unpleasant with him. *Everything*. We would go to races, and he got viciously mean. Noelani had made him promise he would keep going. They were collecting medals from races all over, especially the ones you had to qualify for."

"Like Boston," I said quietly.

"Yeah, like Boston, which they did, and New York, which has some weird system that they couldn't get through. And they were going to hit every Rock N Roll Marathon around the world, so now he was assigned to do that, and he just got angrier and angrier." She wrapped her hands around that coffee cup, and then seemed to recall that she didn't like it, and shoved the cup aside.

"So the medals were…?"

"Theirs," Jenna said, threading her hands together on top of the table. "I kinda got the sense he resented it all, but he couldn't get out of it." She shrugged. "We all tried. We talked to him, and that didn't do any good. It just made him madder. We suggested that he quit running for a while, and that really infuriated him. We suggested therapy—or I did—and jeez, I've never had anyone yell at me like that in my entire life. It was awful and scary, and for a minute, I actually thought he would hit me."

That did not surprise me, given the level of anger I had seen at the Boston qualifier. It had seemed as if Snot Rocket had a deep well of anger that looked like it was infinite.

"That was the last time I saw him," Jenna was saying. "I refused to go to runs if he was there, and that pretty much destroyed my relationship with Calvin."

"He continued to go to the runs?" I asked.

"For a while," she said. "Then even he gave up. I think I could've handled that, but he told me that I overreacted to Dave, that Dave wouldn't hurt anyone, and I disagreed. I *hate* it when people tell you you're overreacting and they weren't even there."

"He was nowhere around when Dave challenged you?" I asked.

"We were at a run, so Calvin was *there,* but he wasn't right next to me. He couldn't hear anything. And later, after we broke up, he called to apologize. I didn't take the call but here...you can hear it for yourself."

She took out her phone, opened it, and scrolled through the screen with her thumb. I didn't say anything, not even to comment on the fact that she had saved a message from someone she ostensibly was no longer interested in.

"Here it is." She set the phone between us, and clicked on a voicemail message.

Hey, Jenn, it's me. I owe you a major apology. You said Dave was scary, and I told you that was an overreaction, but I was wrong. I should've listened to you. I just wanted to say that I'm really sorry.

Then there was some phone noise, as if he half-expected her to respond. And finally, he hung up.

"Did you call him back?" I asked.

She shook her head. "I learned long ago that guys like that think they've wised up, but they never do. He'd make the same mistake. He did make it a few times earlier, usually on smaller stuff. This was one that made me scared, and he dismissed it, and I decided that he wasn't for me."

I made some sympathetic noises, which were not fake. I was sympathetic, just not as interested in that part of her story.

"Would you mind giving me Calvin's number?" I asked, just in case it was different from the one I had.

"It doesn't matter," she said. "He moved out of state nearly a year ago. He wouldn't know what happened to Dave any more than I do."

"But Calvin can give me some background," I said.

Her lips thinned. "I suppose. Just don't tell him you got the number from me. I don't want him to think I hung onto it or anything."

I almost said, *But you did hang onto it,* and then I changed my mind. It was her business, and it had nothing to do with the story I was working on.

I thanked her, and ended the meeting. Then I got into my car and checked my notes on my laptop. The number I had for Calvin was the same one that Jenna had given me. He hadn't answered before, and I doubted he would answer now. But I called and left another message.

Then I drove home. I had two hours before my meeting with Detective Conners. I needed some think time. Something about my meeting with Jenna bothered me.

I had just lugged my laptop and purse into the kitchen when my cell rang, with the ringtone I reserved for people I don't know. I set everything on my already overcrowded table, and then found the phone inside my purse, barely managing to answer before the call went to voicemail.

"Hey," said an unfamiliar voice. "This is Calvin."

I sank into a nearby chair. I hadn't expected him to call. I thanked him for his call, then asked if I could record our conversation.

He paused for just a moment, then said, "Ah, what the hell."

So I hit the record button and put the phone on speaker. He asked a few questions about Dave's death, which I answered, and then he confirmed Jenna's information, almost verbatim.

"So, here's the weird thing," Calvin said. "I don't talk to him for years—I mean, we're in separate towns, you know? Then he calls me out of the blue."

Calvin was using present tense. Dave's death hadn't registered with him yet, even though he had known about it before he called.

"I'm all like green," Calvin said. I wasn't sure I understood him, and was about to say so, when he added, "I mean, I even work in the industry. We're both engineers but on different sides of the environmental divide, if you get me."

I finally did. I made an affirmative noise.

"So, he says, you always wanted me to get rid of the medals, melt them down. Can you give me the name of the company that does that? So I do." Calvin sounded reflective. "I thought it was weird, you know. But I also figured he was finally moving on from Noelani. And maybe it was time, since he'd been so angry for so long."

"Did you ask him about that?" I asked.

"Naw," Calvin said. "We're not that kind of friends, never really were. And besides, he hung up right after. It felt...I don't know...abrupt, weird, off somehow."

"When was this?" I asked.

"About a month ago," Calvin said.

Not long before Snot Rocket died. That seemed odd.

"Can you give me the name of the company?" I asked.

"Yep," Calvin said. "That's the only reason I called. I was looking online at the stories about the murder and they mentioned that someone stole his medals. No one stole them. He'd gotten rid of them."

"How do you know that for sure?" I asked.

"I got a friend who works there," Calvin said. "I asked him to watch out for them."

"Because you wanted to keep track of the medals?" I asked.

"Because I didn't believe Dave would go through with it," Calvin said. "But he did. It was one of the bigger hauls of medals that the company ever got."

We talked a bit more, and then we ended the conversation. The medals weren't stolen. They had been melted down. Snot Rocket was redesigning his life—whatever that meant.

I called Detective Connors and told him what I learned about the medals. He was already ahead of me on that. They'd found a receipt in Snot Rocket's office for the medals, sent by the company shortly after they arrived.

"Still leaves us at square one, though," Detective Conners said.

"Not really," I said. "Let's still meet in an hour. Bring me photos of the medals that strangled him."

"They weren't used to strangle him," Conners said. "They were just hung around his neck."

The way someone did when they finished a race.

"Bring them anyway," I said. "I'll bring my computer."

"And what good will that do?" Conners asked.

"You'll see," I said.

COLLECTIBLES

We met at a different coffee shop, one he had chosen that wasn't far from the precinct. The coffee shop was a lot more utilitarian. It clearly predated Starbucks. There was a menu for specialty coffees, but the menu itself seemed to discourage trying them. I got a bottle of water, which seemed safest, considering the filthy state of the yellow walls and linoleum floor.

I found one table that didn't have crumbs, but I still wiped it off before I sat there. I put a napkin underneath my laptop. I'm not usually that fastidious, but some places just inspire extra precautions.

Conners came in, ordered "the usual," and sat down across from me without picking up anything from the counter, clearly expecting someone to bring his order.

He slapped some pictures at me. They had been printed on a high quality printer, showing the medals front and back. One medal was a finisher medal, the kind everyone got. The other was a third place medal from the same race. And the third wasn't from any race at all. It just looked like a race medal. Someone had engraved *World's Biggest Asshole* on the back.

That detail hadn't made the news, and I could see why.

I raised my gaze to Conners.

"We figure they're all fake," he said.

"They're not," I said. I recognized the first two. They were from a Boston qualifier nearly a year ago. I had the same finisher medal on my wall. I'd actually fingered the age group medals before the race, hoping I'd make my time, because those medals were pretty.

These weren't medals you could find easily, and I knew, because I had researched it, that Snot Rocket hadn't received any age group medals in that race at all—which was odd. He'd been placing well in other races at that point.

I looked up third place in all the male age groups first, just on a hunch, but I didn't recognize anyone.

Then I stopped. "How did Dave die?" I asked. "I thought you said he was strangled with the medals."

"That's what the officers who answered the call thought. We let it stand, figuring we'd release cause of death when we had our suspect in hand."

I nodded. "You haven't answered my question," I said.

"Blunt force trauma to the side of the head," Conners said. "He fell or was pushed and banged his temple on a table. Whoever was there didn't call for help—which might've actually saved him. Instead, they propped him up, put the medals around his neck, and left. He wasn't found for three days."

"You're saying he was alive when that person left?" I asked.

Conners nodded. "Probably not conscious though. The ME thinks he lived another five, six hours or more."

I couldn't help myself. I shuddered.

"So," I said, thinking about all that calculation I had done for strength and height, "it could've been a woman, then."

"Hmmm," Conners said noncommittally. Which was a confirmation, in its own way.

I spun the laptop around and went through the podium photos, showing him the third place finishers in all of the age groups. He stopped me after I had shown him the forty-to-forty-five age groupers.

"Can you email me the link to all of this?" he asked.

"Sure," I said, and did it as we were sitting there. "You know who did it."

"Maybe," he said, slapped down a five for his nonexistent "usual," and left.

I studied the pictures. I didn't recognize anyone. But I went through the names, and scanned social media, just because I was feeling a tad off. What I had thought I knew, I hadn't known, and what I hadn't known turned out to be important.

I found her in the thirty-five to thirty-nine age group. McKenna Granchester. She mentioned on several of her sites that she'd discovered someone new, that he was kinder than the other men she had known, and he was a runner.

And the real tell? She said she was helping him overcome a big loss. She tried to convince him to get rid of the past—to Marie Kondo it, in other words, get rid of all the clutter, stop hanging onto the loss, and move forward. He refused.

She wrote on Facebook: *Some people just need to be pushed. He found the service that would recycle his stuff. I just mailed it all off one afternoon. He'd said he was going to do it; now he's mad that I did. That's weird, right?*

People weighed in. They always did. And I didn't care what they said.

I was just imagining the conversation. She'd gotten rid of his possessions, his memories of Noelani, the one thing Noelani had made him promise to continue.

He had a terrible temper, one that had scared Jenna, one that had upset the entire running group, and half the people who raced with him.

I couldn't imagine what he would have done when he discovered that McKenna had sent his memories to be recycled.

The argument was for the cops to figure out, if they could. Had Snot Rocket pushed her first? Or just screamed in her face, like he had done with Jenna? Had McKenna pushed him away, which was what people seemed to do with him?

He probably tripped, fell sideways, and hit his head. And if she had called 911 right there, everything would've been all right.

But she had to put the medals on him—*her* medals, as a kind of fuck-you. And then she left him to die.

I got up, brought Conners's five to the cash register, and left, feeling vaguely sick to my stomach.

I knew how to write this, once I got the information I needed from Conners, once she got arrested and the case started wending its way toward trial.

An angry man fell in love, lost the woman he loved, tried to rebuild but got angrier and angrier. Met another woman, thought maybe she was the one, and instead, she proved how very wrong she was.

He'd been trying to move forward—and that attempt failed.

Which is how I wrote the story. Without a mention of his nickname, although I did mention the snot rockets. I had interviews with a number of people, including the guy who pushed him at that last race. They'd gotten into a fight over starting position. Snot Rocket believed the guy had cheated and moved up several slots.

After I talked to him, I believed the guy had too.

That didn't make Snot Rocket likeable. He had been an arrogant asshole, and he remained one. I empathized with a lot—the loss of medals, the loss of control—but not the way he responded.

And the anger, the anger was problematic.

I wrote the story, McKenna not only got arrested and immediately pleaded to manslaughter (from Murder 2), and she went away, and the story caused enough of a blip that I was able to keep my job through the next round of layoffs.

All of that, a month or two before the pandemic shut down everything, including racing. Everything except the media company I worked for. Suddenly, I had more to do than I had ever planned—none of it weird click-bait homicide stories.

With so much death in the U.S., no one really cared about strange little murders anymore. We were all trying to survive.

And yet…I find myself thinking about him. Snot Rocket. Not who he really was, but who he presented as at the races.

That filthy habit of his, the one that brought his nickname, has become something else in this post-COVID world. People are getting arrested for spitting on others.

And had races resumed, and had he not reformed, and had he been murdered then, think of all the people who would have had motive. He might have made them sick. He might have killed their loved ones.

And the way his grief had taken him, he might not have cared.

Not that it matters, because he died in the pre-COVID world. Along with his filthy habit.

The demise of the snot rocket came after the death of Snot Rocket. But not long after.

And neither, I must report, caused the slightest ripple in the world we find ourselves in. No one misses them. I get the sense that no one thinks of them, besides me.

We actually lived that way—with free-floating snot rockets and spittle and petty jealousies and shoving matches over medals. We lived that way, and saw nothing wrong with it.

COLLECTIBLES

In a world we no longer recognize as our own. In a land so far away it feels like another century.

I can't say as I miss it.

But I think about it.

All the damn time.

...from Otto Penzler's Mysterious Obsession:

RED HARVEST AND
THE MALTESE FALCON
DASHIELL HAMMETT

About fifty years ago, *The Booklover's Answer*, an amateurish literary magazine, was published irregularly. It was a labor of love for the editor/publisher, as it was for contributors. No one made any money from it but that was never the idea.

Before collecting mystery fiction, I mainly bought books in two fields: British adventure fiction (H. Rider Haggard, Rudyard Kipling, Robert Louis Stevenson) and poetry (mainly World War I poets, such as Joyce Kilmer and Rupert Brooke).

I had written an appreciation of Rupert Brooke, submitted it to that very nice periodical, and it was published, which pleased me enormously. A few weeks later, the mail delivered a gracious letter from a gentleman in the Detroit area who told me how much he enjoyed the essay and asked if I was a collector and, if so, what did I collect.

We became active pen pals and I soon discovered that C. E. Frazer Clark, Jr., was perhaps the country's greatest Nathaniel Hawthorne collector. Later, when there was so little for him to collect because he had acquired pretty much everything, he decided to collect Ernest Hemingway as well; he called it his Hem & Haw collection.

COLLECTIBLES

I had come to learn that it wasn't possible to afford to collect very much in the two areas in which I had focused and had made the decision to specialize in mystery fiction, a genre that I loved to read and for which there was very little competition. With my paltry book budget of five or ten dollars a week (if I skipped a lunch or two), I could buy several excellent volumes.

Frazer told me he was coming to New York and would like to meet for dinner, an enticing proposition, and I found him to be just as bright and witty in person as he was in his letters. I later recalled that he happened to mention that his wife adored pistachio nuts.

A year or so later, he invited me to his home in Bloomfield Hills for the weekend. I'd planned to go to Homecoming at the University of Michigan and so combined the two for a glorious few days. As a trivial house gift, I had bought a three-pound tub of shelled pistachios for his wife. We talked of books most of the time, much of the conversation devoted to collecting. One piece of advice he gave me was that the stature of a collection depended on the amount of original material it contained—letters, manuscripts, presentation copies, etc.—not merely the books.

When it was time for me to go, he asked if I had a little room left in my suitcase, as he had a small gift for me as a remembrance of the happy time we'd had together. He handed me two books: first editions of Raymond Chandler's *The Big Sleep* and Dashiell Hammett's *Red Harvest*, both superb copies in dust jacket. Among collectors of detective fiction, it is *The Maltese Falcon* that is often regarded as the Holy Grail but, in fact, fine copies of *Red Harvest* are ten times rarer.

"It's not every day," Fraser asked, "when you get a gift of the first book by the two best mystery writers of the twentieth century, is it? But I had to reciprocate your generous gift," he said—not at all sarcastically.

My "generous gift" was a tub of pistachios. His diffidently-offered going away presents, in their fresh, bright dust jackets, still (metaphorically) take my breath away when I recall that remarkable day. Frazer was not a man one was likely to hug but he deserved one and I regret that I wasn't confident enough to do it.

While I have long considered Chandler the finest stylist of twentieth-century mystery writers, it is Hammett to whom every hard-boiled private eye writer must genuflect. Yes, it was Carroll John Daly who invented the private detective in the pages of *Black Mask* magazine, but it was Hammett who brought the genre into the realm of serious literature, raising the level of the prose to such heights that it was well-received by critics and became hugely popular, opening the door for Chandler and the other tough guy authors.

Not only is *Red Harvest* Hammett's first novel, it is the first private eye novel of any importance to have been published in the United States (which means anyplace in the world, as it was such a uniquely American literary form for decades after its invention).

The Big Sleep eventually moved on when I had the opportunity to get a signed copy to take its place on the Chandler shelf, but that copy of *Red Harvest*, essentially as new, remained in the collection ever after as there never has been one to compare. And it's been impossible to look at it without thinking of my long-lost friend and his generous gesture.

THE MALTESE FALCON

The early years of my bookshop on West Fifty-Sixth Street were a struggle in several ways. The workload was dramatically greater than I ever dreamed possible. Carolyn, the woman I was to marry, had moved to New York from Southern California only a few months before and helped build the store, working more closely with the contractors than I did because (a) I was trying to run the Mysterious Press, my very small publishing company, and *The Armchair Detective*, a little magazine; and (b) she knew a lot more about design, plumbing, electrical work, and every other question the contractor asked. He would direct his questions only to me, man-to-man, I'd look at her, she would make the decision or answer the question, tell me, and I'd tell him.

The financial struggle was enormous. I knew nothing about running a bookshop, assuming that customers would stream in as soon as we opened the doors. They did at first, then the stream became a trickle, and it remained fairly dry for months to come. We finally discovered a bit of a customer base

COLLECTIBLES

when *New York Magazine* ran a feature on us and the wonderful street fair called New York Is Book Country had its first annual festivities in the fall. Our booth had a lot of authors signing books, we made some money but, most important, hundreds of people found the bookshop as we handed out flyers and bookmarks.

By the third year, it wasn't dire anymore but we continued to have trouble paying bills. Still, whenever good rare books were offered to us, I knew I had to buy them. "Gotta buy books so I can sell books" is what I told my horrified bookkeeper.

A call came into the store one afternoon from a fellow who wanted to sell some outstanding private eye books, including a nice, fresh first edition in a bright dust jacket of the iconic classic, *The Maltese Falcon*. I *had* to buy them, writing a check that I couldn't afford to write. There are times when being sensible is a bad decision. This book is one of the Holy Grails (well, there's only one possible Holy Grail, but you get the point), for collectors and here it was, handed to me as if on a platinum platter.

Probably the most famous detective novel ever written, *The Maltese Falcon* had been serialized in *Black Mask* magazine and immediately captured the public's imagination. Its fame and popularity were doubtlessly helped by having three films made of it, the first in 1931 starring Ricardo Cortez and Bebe Daniels; the second (titled *Satan Met a Lady*) in 1936 with Warren William and Bette Davis; and the memorable 1941 version with Humphrey Bogart, Mary Astor, Sydney Greenstreet, and Peter Lorre.

The capitalist principles of supply and demand are exemplified by this beautifully produced book. It would be hyperbole to call the first edition a rare book, as there are usually two or three copies available for sale at most times if you know who to call. But it is an expensive book because it is so desirable. Many—many!—collectors want to own a copy, even if they don't particularly collect mystery fiction. Any collection of American literature would be incomplete without this masterpiece.

In those days, my office (the most beautiful in New York, honestly) was about a thousand square feet with twelve-foot-high ceilings and shelves that completely covered the walls. My personal collection filled most of those shelves.

Once a book was on those shelves, it was not for sale. Period. When books came in, I'd price most of them and put them out for sale, or call a customer who I thought would like one or more. Sometimes, I'd put one or two on my own shelves. And then there were times when I'd leave a book on my desk while I decided where it was going—the bookshop or me. Purgatory, as I decided its fate.

The Maltese Falcon was on a corner of my desk when Carolyn saw it and asked if it was mine or the bookshop's. I told her I didn't know because it was very expensive and we couldn't afford to keep it but I didn't have the heart to sell it just yet. She asked if I had a copy in my collection. I didn't. She said, "Well, how can you have a good collection without *The Maltese Falcon?*" This is known as an understanding wife.

It was rash, it was foolish, it was not at all sensible, but I immediately picked it up and carried it to the shelves that held my collection and added it to the small but growing accumulation of Dashiell Hammett's works. Although I went on to sell another half-dozen copies during my bookselling career, this is the book that even people who were only casually interested in first editions looked for when browsing the shelves, the one that had the "wow!" factor.

First Appearance

BY ALEX SEGURA

Carlos Avila knew he'd seen it. He must have, he told himself.

No way had he imagined it.

You didn't just will those things into existence.

More on that in a second, though.

He'd walked into Frank's Comics and Cards a few times a week. The shop was teeny-tiny—maybe the size of Carlos's tiny bedroom inside his mom's cramped three-bedroom house on 28th Street in the Westchester neighborhood of Miami. Frank's was a dump, too. Dusty, loaded with junk, a back room of stacked longboxes stuffed to the gills with old comic books in no realistic order. It was heaven for someone like Carlos. A fan. A real fan.

It was a place where he could lose himself—wander the tiny, precariously stacked aisles, his fingers dancing over the bagged-and-boarded single issues crammed in bloated boxes, looking for a deal or anything that might be of interest. The possibilities were endless. Some days he'd find an issue that could complete his run of *Justice League International,* or an errant install-ment of *Web of Spider-Man.* The thrill of the hunt was part of the high, Carlos knew. The roll of the dice that could go big or small, but either way, he'd win.

If he had more than two tens burning a hole in his pocket, he might splurge on a box of DC Cosmic Cards or the Impel Marvel ones, the ones that had gotten him hooked on comics to begin with.

283

COLLECTIBLES

Carlos remembered his first moment with the trading cards. He was at his dad's girlfriend's house—well, girlfriend at the time. Marissa? Maribel? She smelled of old flowers and her skin was soft, like a clean pillow sheet. She'd place her hand on the back of his neck and just leave it there, the warmth of her palm warming him. No, he didn't remember her name. But he remembered the cards. Black costume Spider-Man. X-Factor. Beta Ray Bill. The New Mutants. Every little piece of paper told a story, loaded with information on the opposite side—stats, like a baseball player. First appearance. Strength, agility, dexterity, and other attributes. A brief origin. A few cards in and Carlos was hooked. An obsession was launched. He'd been only a few days older than ten then.

Now it was August 1996 and Carlos had just finished up his sophomore year at Columbus High, an all-boys private school across 87th Avenue from his house. He hated it there. He didn't fit in, or feel part-of. Carlos wasn't deluded. He knew his faults. He had braces at an age when most kids were getting them off, had some serious acne, and seemed more inclined to spend time jerking off or reading his comics and Star Trek novels than playing football or (trying to) mack to girls. Carlos was fine with his lot in life, he really was. He loved cracking open the new issue of X-Men or Batman, or spending the afternoon reading about some lost story of the Enterprise. It was the other kids who didn't seem to get it. They just wouldn't leave him the fuck alone.

One kid in particular had cemented his role as Carlos's main nemesis—Edwin Delacruz. His pre-college CV was already loaded with a litany of Great Things: QB on the junior varsity team, cross-country champ, point guard on the basketball team, and so on. When he wasn't scoring points on the field, he had his hands up the head cheerleader's skirt. He had it made. No problems. His dad was a local city commissioner and his mom, well, suffice to say Carlos really enjoyed when Edwin's parents were around. It was one of the few positives Carlos could assign to Edwin Delacruz.

So why wouldn't he leave Carlos alone? Carlos, lonely Carlos, who just wanted to get through his school day with the bare minimum of anguish so he could get home, rip open another bag of Chewy Chips Ahoy! cookies and lock himself up in his room—reading a stack of *Flash* comics or finding out if Mr. Spock really had a son born in an alternate dimension.

Edwin's torment of Carlos ran the entire spectrum. From the typical shoving-into-lockers to the much more cruel: like a charley-horse before chemistry class, or, the one thing that broke Carlos. The one that he kept thinking back to and couldn't seem to shake. Not because it was particularly original, mind you, but because it hurt. Because for a brief second, Carlos thought he'd suffered through so much shit at Edwin's hands, that the bully had finally deemed Carlos worthy of friendship—or at the very least of some kind of grudging respect.

It'd been toward the end of the day and Carlos was heading out the back door toward the intersection of 87th Avenue and 30th Street. He saw Edwin step in front of him and felt his entire being sag. This wasn't new. It'd become a ritual of sorts, Carlos knew. If Edwin was in a sour mood, he'd take it out on Carlos at the end of the day. It might be a passing, cutting insult—"Where you going, shithead?" or "Do those pimples burn your face, Carlos?" No artistry, of course. Just a bludgeon of meanness. It might be a punch in the stomach. It might be a full-on beating. It varied. Most days, Carlos could ride it out and get home fast. If he just accepted it was coming and steeled himself, he'd be fine. Or so he'd come to accept. But this time it'd been different, remember?

Edwin pulled his black JanSport backpack around, so it was draped over his chest instead of his back. He unzipped the main compartment and pulled out a book. Carlos looked at the cover. A book? Edwin wasn't a reader, Carlos knew. What the fuck was this?

Edwin raised a hand as Carlos approached.

"What's the rush, asshole?" Edwin said. Carlos stopped short. He was sure he looked confused, because he was. Was Edwin going to hit him with the book? Make him eat it?

Carlos mumbled something in response, but Edwin was already on to the next thing, shoving the paperback into Carlos's chest. The thick book fell into his hands. Carlos held the cover up to his face as Edwin rambled on.

"Thought you might like this book, you know," he said. "Since you read all the time and shit."

COLLECTIBLES

"Read all the time and shit." Carlos knew what this was in reference to. Another low point in a series of low points. They'd all been seated in Social Studies class, listening as Ms. Delgado prattled on about the pocket veto or how the War of 1812 started, when the school librarian walked in. Carlos actually loved social studies. He loved presidential history. Loved biographies and learning about how the world worked. But at school, he tried to keep a low profile. Tried to just power through it and get home. Not that day.

The librarian whispered something to Ms. Delgado then turned to leave—but before she did, she caught sight of Carlos, seated in the front row, trying desperately to hide his face somehow. She almost squealed when she saw him. She grabbed Ms. Delgado's arm and pointed at Carlos.

"You have Carlos in your class?" she asked the teacher, who seemed confused and proud all at once. "What an honor. He comes into my library every day after school. Every day he checks out three or four books, then brings them back the next day. It's amazing. He just loves to read."

Carlos could hear the hissing laughs and insults bubbling behind him before the librarian, a wispy old woman named Lin, finished her story. Carlos hated her now, hated how she'd thrust his private world—his private love of reading and books—and shoved it into the spotlight for all to see. To laugh at. But how could he hate Mrs. Lin? That day had been a full-on beating day from Edwin. For once, Carlos felt he deserved it.

The memory flashed before Carlos as he looked at the paperback—the author's name, Christopher Pike, emblazoned over the cover in a jagged, pink font. The cover featured a realistic painting of a girl—probably a year or two older than him—splayed out on the floor, clearly dead. Under her was the title: *Remember Me.*

"This is for me?" Carlos asked. He'd never read Pike before. He wasn't big into teen supernatural dramas, but Carlos was also at an age where he'd read anything. New books were in short supply, and he could read and reread comics fast. So a novel? That was a treasure, no matter what it was about.

"Yeah, yeah, hope you enjoy it, bro," Edwin said, a strange, flickering smile on his face—like he was trying hard to stop from breaking out laughing. The thought had been fleeting then, Carlos recalled, but would be proven right in a few days time. Then he turned away and left. No insults. No punches. No pain.

Carlos had rushed home, his hand coating the book's cover in sweat as he navigated the humid Miami afternoon and made a beeline for his room. He didn't remember much else about that night except the book.

In terms of story, it wasn't anything great—a teen girl goes home and wonders why her parents and brother don't talk or react to her, only to realize she's actually dead—a presumed suicide. She's a ghost. Then she has to take it upon herself to become an astral detective of sorts, solving her own murder. It was at about the middle of the novel when Carlos discovered it.

The novel itself, from the moment Carlos really looked at it, felt off. Beat up, bent, not well kept. Certainly not the way Carlos treated his books. But he ignored it, too caught up in the potential of not only the novel, but of the bigger narrative—the fact that Edwin had made a gesture of friendship. That if Carlos read this book, perhaps the two sides could put down their arms and become, if not friends, then at least respectful allies in the trench warfare that was high school. It'd been a foolish thought. He learned why a few pages later.

He was sitting in the school cafeteria, the next day, reading the book. Lunch was ending and Edwin and his two stooges, David and Nestor, were flanking him, trays in hand. Edwin turned to catch a glimpse of Carlos, immersed in the novel. He couldn't stop himself from smiling.

"Hey Carlos," Edwin said, that sneer now fully formed on his face. "You like that book, buddy?"

Carlos didn't, really. I mean, it was fine, but he did like that Edwin was asking him about it—creeping doubt be damned.

"Yeah, definitely," Carlos said, nodding eagerly. "It's great. Thanks again."

The trio walked off, Edwin looking back for one last parting word.

"I hear it gets really good soon," he said. He turned to his friends and shared a long chuckle. Carlos's stomach turned.

This was no olive branch, he realized. But he wasn't sure *what* it was. Not yet.

He returned his attention to the book.

COLLECTIBLES

As the story careened toward the second act, and Shari Cooper began to get acquainted with being dead, Carlos discovered he was having trouble turning the pages. Some were stuck together. It sent a chill through him. He knew the joke before he got to it, like a poorly choreographed blooper. Which, in retrospect, this was. By the time he flipped forward and reached the greenish, dried out hunk of spit that decorated the middle section of the book, Carlos knew what was coming. He didn't stare at it long. Tried not to breathe or memorize the disgusting present Edwin had left for him. In the years that would follow, Carlos would take pride in how he reacted. The calm that overtook him as he gently closed the book, stood up, and walked toward Edwin's table.

The three jocks saw him and giggled with anticipation, as if waiting for Carlos to break down in tears or run out of the school into traffic. Carlos did neither and did nothing in between. He merely walked by them, reached a nearby waste basket, and tossed the book in. As he walked back to his own seat he turned to Edwin, a genuine, placid look in his eyes.

"Thanks again for the book," Carlos said.

He'd never forget the angry confusion smeared across his face.

But it'd taken everything Carlos had to keep it together. To stop from falling to his knees and falling down. To think he'd even thought Edwin wanted to be his friend? Or that this sign of peace might signal a few days of peace and tranquility? A reprieve from the insults and beatings and hate that seemed to populate every minute he spent at this shithole school? It was enough to break you, he thought. Life was a collection of realizations like this, Carlos would soon learn. Moments when your innocence was taken and shattered one more time, a reminder that there were few good, pure things, and not everyone in the world cared for you or even thought of you the way you might think of them.

The door chime at Frank's Comics and Cards jarred Carlos from the memory.

Anyway, yeah. Carlos was sure he saw it. That was when the plan formed in his brain.

He knew it was wrong, of course. Carlos had been raised right. Sure, his parents were divorced—but his mom worked hard and they never wanted for anything. His abuelo and abuela lived with them and he never felt alone, ignored, or unloved. He knew even thinking about this would be wrong. But God, it felt so damn good.

The comic was in a hard plastic case, atop the shop's main counter. *The Legendary Lynx #11*. It'd been published by Spectrum Comics, one of those tiny publishers that populated the sixties and seventies, when there was more than just Marvel or DC. Spectrum had published a bunch of great comics, like the vigilante noir *The Black Ghost* to the all-star super-team *The Freedom Alliance* to the chilling horror anthology *Blood Oath*. But no one talked about Spectrum anymore. The company had folded a few short years after it was founded, and many of the characters and ideas faded into anonymity. Except one.

Carlos didn't know much about the Lynx, the street vigilante heroine that starred in the series. The comics were rare and most collectors knew what they had when they found them, so they weren't in wide circulation. But Carlos knew about the series—knew that the first dozen or so issues were some of the most influential superhero crime comics of the era. He also knew that this issue, in particular, was worth more than what his mom made in a year at her nursing job. Maybe two.

The cover called out to him. The dark-clad hero leaping toward the reader, a grim, focused expression on her face. Carlos looked around the small shop. Frank was at the other end of the counter, talking to a customer complaining about the store not having the new Dungeons & Dragons Dungeon Master's Guide.

"We're a comic shop, Mike," Frank said. "Not a gaming store, all right? Quit it with this shit, kid."

"It's just, it, like, doesn't make any sense," the kid whined. "Gaming and comics go so well together."

"Go home, Richie," Frank said, pointing to the door.

Richie gathered his box of 20-sided dice and the stack of comics he just bought and left.

Frank turned his attention to the television screen on the counter. It was plugged into the local news. Carlos heard something about a teacher in

Seattle being arrested for hooking up with her student. He didn't look at the television. His eyes were locked on the comic.

It'd be easy enough for Carlos to slip the book into his backpack. There was no alarm at Frank's. No security cameras. This despite the fact that the store boasted a fairly impressive collection of high-end comics: from *The Amazing Spider-Man* #32 to *Giant-Size X-Men* #1 and a handful of notable *Superman* issues, Frank's was well-stocked. But those comics were, smartly, behind protective glass. If you wanted to steal them, you'd have to break some shit.

But why not this issue? Carlos wondered.

The sound of a toilet flushing. That was the answer. Albert, Frank's sole employee and someone who would never be classified as sharp and organized, was on the can. Even Carlos knew Albert's bathroom journeys were epic—hours spent reading some of the new comics before Frank or he would even shelve them. It added a touch of grit and nausea to any shopping experience. So, Albert had been shelving the high-end stuff. He'd left this copy of *The Legendary Lynx* on the counter, like the dumb shit he was. It was destiny, Carlos thought. If stuff like that existed.

The story unfurled. He'd take the comic and make his way back home, sliding the thick plastic case under his bed. He'd wait until Monday, Ms. Wooten's home room period. Then he'd wait until Edwin—who was seated in front of him—would inevitably get up to shoot the shit with Nestor and David across the classroom. Then he'd slide his hands under his desk, reaching his fingers out until they grasped the zipper of Edwin's backpack and opened it just enough to weave the comic inside. He'd cover his tracks, zipping the bag up as he finished.

Then Carlos would lean back and wait. For the bell to ring. For Edwin to get up, watching carefully to see if he'd notice the additional weight. But of course he wouldn't. He was a big, strong dude. Plus, he didn't think about what was in his backpack. Books were for losers.

Then Carlos would wander down to the lobby and step outside, to the bank of payphones stationed near the school entrance. He'd pull out the change he'd saved just for this, and he'd ring Frank.

"Frank's Comics and Cards, Frank speaking."

"Hey, uh, Frank?"

"Yeah, who's this?"

"I'm a, well, I'm a—uh, a concerned customer."

Silence.

"I think I know who took your *Lynx* comic."

"How did you know about that?"

"Well," Carlos would stammer. He hadn't expected this to be so complicated. "I saw it there, then I didn't see it there."

"Someone coulda bought it," Frank would snap back. Frank wasn't a nice guy. Hell, he was an asshole. Carlos wasn't even sure he liked comics, to be honest. "Did you take the book, kid? 'Cause it sure sounds like you did."

"Ask Edwin Delacruz," Carlos would spit. "He's got it. He had someone steal it for him. He's about to sell it. Better come get it. He goes to Columbus."

Then Carlos would hang up. It wouldn't feel as good as he'd hoped but it'd feel pretty good.

He'd watch as their third period class, Mr. Tuohy's English, would be interrupted by one of the school administrators—a ramrod military-style assistant principal, Mr. Morris. Morris would talk to Tuohy, then turn and point to Edwin, who would stand up, not a care in the world. He was often taken out of class, you see—to get in an early practice, to go to a team event, that sort of shit. He was blessed. Not this time.

He'd catch a glimpse of the cop car pulled up in front of the school. The officer gently handcuffing Edwin and leading him out of Columbus and toward the waiting vehicle, Edwin's classmates and teachers lining up and watching, heads shaking, stern frowns. Carlos would laugh. The sound would cut through the buzz of noise, and Edwin would look back—catching Carlos's eyes. Then he'd know. But he'd also know there was nothing he could do about it. His pristine little life was over, you see. He was a thief. A thug. Derailed by someone who just wanted to be left alone.

"You all right?"

Frank's question felt like a slap in the face. Carlos blinked and spun around.

"Huh?"

COLLECTIBLES

"You all right, kid?" Frank said again. "You looked like you were in a fucking trance, dude. You gonna buy anything or just stare into space? You looking for something in particular? Origin story? First appearance? What? We got it all."

Carlos shook his head. No. He wasn't going to buy anything. The fantasy faded from his brain, like a particularly vivid dream.

"No, no," Carlos said, hastily stepping toward the exit. "You don't have what I'm looking for. Not anymore."

The door chimed as Carlos walked out, feeling the bright Miami sun eradicate the fleeting darkness that almost threatened to consume him.

Collecting Ackermans

BY LAWRENCE BLOCK

On an otherwise unremarkable October afternoon, Florence Ackerman's doorbell sounded. Miss Ackerman, who had been watching a game show on television and clucking at the mental lethargy of the panelists, walked over to the intercom control and demanded to know who was there.

"Western Union," a male voice announced.

Miss Ackerman repeated the clucking sound she had most recently aimed at Charles Nelson Reilly. She clucked this time at people who lost their keys and rang other tenants' bells in order to gain admittance to the building. She clucked at would-be muggers and rapists who might pass themselves off as messengers or liverymen for an opportunity to lurk in the hallways and stairwell. In years past this building had had a doorman, but the new landlord had curtailed services, aiming to reduce his overhead and antagonize longstanding tenants at the same time.

"Telegram for Miz Ackerman," the voice added.

And was it indeed a telegram? It was possible, Miss Ackerman acknowledged. People were forever dying and other people were apt to communicate such data by means of a telegram. It was easier to buzz whoever it was inside than to brood about it. The door to her own apartment would remain locked, needless to say, and the other tenants could look out for themselves. Florence Ackerman had been looking out for her own self for her whole life and the rest of the planet could go and do the same.

COLLECTIBLES

She pressed the buzzer, then went to the door and put her eye to the peephole. She was a small birdlike woman and she had to come up onto her toes to see through the peephole, but she stayed on her toes until her caller came into view. He was a youngish man and he wore a large pair of mirrored sunglasses. Besides obscuring much of his face, the sunglasses kept Miss Ackerman from noticing much about the rest of his appearance. Her attention was inescapably drawn to the twin images of her own peephole reflected in the lenses.

The young man, unaware that he was being watched, rapped on the door with his knuckles. "Telegram," he said.

"Slide it under the door."

"You have to sign for it."

"That's ridiculous," Miss Ackerman said. "One never has to sign for a telegram. As a matter of fact they're generally phoned in nowadays."

"This one you got to sign for." Miss Ackerman's face, by no means dull to begin with, sharpened. She who had been the scourge of several generations of fourth-grade pupils was not to be intimidated by a pair of mirrored sunglasses. "Slide it under the door," she demanded. "Then I'll open the door and sign your book." If there was indeed anything to be slid beneath the door, she thought, and she rather doubted that there was.

"I can't."

"Oh?"

"It's a singin' telegram. Singin' telegram for Miz Ackerman, what it says here."

"And you're to sing it to me?"

"Yeah."

"Then sing it."

"Lady, are you kiddin'? I'm gonna sing a telegram through a closed door? Like forget it."

Miss Ackerman made the clucking noise again. "I don't believe you have a telegram for me," she said. "Western Union suspended their singing telegram service some time ago. I remember reading an article to that effect in the *Times*." She did not bother to add that the likelihood of anyone's ever sending a singing telegram to her was several degrees short of infinitesimal.

"All I know is I'm supposed to sing this, but if you don't want to open the door—"

"I wouldn't dream of opening my door."

"—then the hell with you, Miz Ackerman. No disrespect intended, but I'll just tell 'em I sang it to you and who cares what you say."

"You're not even a good liar, young man. I'm calling the police now. I advise you to be well out of the neighborhood by the time they arrive."

"You know what you can do," the young man said, but in apparent contradiction to his words he went on to tell Miss Ackerman what she could do. While we needn't concern ourselves with his suggestion, let it be noted that Miss Ackerman could not possibly have followed it, nor, given her character and temperament, would she have been at all likely to make the attempt.

Neither did she call the police. People who say "I am calling the police now" hardly ever do. Miss Ackerman did think of calling her local precinct but decided it would be a waste of time. In all likelihood the young man, whatever his game, was already on his way, never to return.

And Miss Ackerman recalled a time two years previously, just a few months after her retirement, when she returned from an afternoon chamber music concert to find her apartment burglarized and several hundred dollars' worth of articles missing. She had called the police, naïvely assuming there was a point to such a course of action, and she'd only managed to several hours of her time making out reports and listing serial numbers, and a sympathetic detective had as much as told her nothing would come of the effort.

Actually, calling the police wouldn't really have done her any good this time, either.

Miss Ackerman returned to her chair and, without too much difficulty, picked up the threads of the game show. She did not for a moment wonder who might have sent her a singing telegram, knowing with cool certainty that no one had done so, that there had been no telegram, that the young man had intended rape or robbery or some other unpleasantness that would have made her life substantially worse than it already was.

That robbers and rapists and such abounded was no news to Miss Ackerman. She had lived all her life in New York and took in her stride the possibility of such mistreatment, even as residents of California take in their stride the possibility of an earthquake, even as farmers on the Vesuvian slopes acknowledge that it is in the nature of volcanoes periodically to erupt. Miss Ackerman sat in her chair, leaving it to make a cup of tea, returning to it teacup in hand, and concentrated on her television program.

The following afternoon, as she wheeled her little cart of groceries around the corner, a pair of wiry hands seized her without ceremony and yanked her into the narrow passageway between a pair of brick buildings. A gloved hand covered her mouth, the fingers digging into her cheek.

She heard a voice at her ear: "Happy birthday to you, you old hairbag, happy birthday to you." Then she felt a sharp pain in her chest, and then she felt nothing, ever.

"Retired schoolteacher," Freitag said. "On her way home with her groceries. Hell of a thing, huh? Knifed for what she had in her purse, and what could she have, anyway? Livin' on Social Security and a pension, and the way inflation eats you up nowadays she wouldn't of had much on her. Why stick a knife in a little old lady like her, huh? He didn't have to kill her."

"Maybe she screamed," Ken Poolings suggested. "And he got panicky."

"Nobody heard a scream. Not that it proves anything either way." They were back at the station house and Jack Freitag was drinking lukewarm coffee out of a Styrofoam container. But for the Styrofoam the beverage would have been utterly tasteless. "Ackerman, Ackerman, Ackerman. It's hell the way these parasites prey on old folks. It's the judges who have to answer for it. They put the creeps back on the street. What they ought to do is kill the little bastards, but that's not humane. Sticking a knife in a little old lady, that's humane. Ackerman, Ackerman. Why does that name do something to me?"

"She was a teacher. Maybe you were in one of her classes."

Freitag shook his head. "I grew up in Chelsea. West Twenty-fourth Street. Miss Ackerman taught all her life here in Washington Heights just three blocks from the place where she lived. And she didn't even have to leave the neighborhood to get herself killed. Ackerman. Oh, I know what it was. Remember three or maybe it was four days ago, this gay boy in the West Village? Brought some other boy home with him and got killed for his troubles? They found him all tied up with things carved in him. It was all over page three of the *Daily News*. Ritual murder, sadist cult, sex perversion, blah blah blah. His name was Ackerman."

"Which one?"

"The dead one. They didn't pick up the guy who did it yet. I don't know if they got a make or not."

"Does it make any difference?"

"Not to me it don't." Freitag finished his coffee, threw his empty container at the green metal wastebasket, then watched as it circled the rim and fell on the floor. "The Knicks been stinking up the Garden this year," he said. "But you don't care about basketball, do you?"

"Hockey's my game."

"Hockey," Freitag said. "Well, the Rangers stink, too. Only they stink on ice." He leaned back in his chair and laughed at his own wit and stopped thinking of two murder victims who both happened to be named Ackerman.

Mildred Ackerman lay on her back. Her skin was slick with perspiration, her limbs heavy with spent passion. The man who was lying beside her stirred, placed a hand upon her flesh and began to stroke her. "Oh, Bill," she said. "That feels so nice. I love the way you touch me."

The man went on stroking her.

"You have the nicest touch. Firm but gentle. I sensed that about you when I saw you." She opened her eyes, turned to face him. "Do you believe in intuition, Bill? I do. I think it's possible to know a great deal about someone just on the basis of your intuitive feelings."

"And what did you sense about me?"

"That you would be strong but gentle. That we'd be very good together. It was good for you, wasn't it?"

"Couldn't you tell?"

Millie giggled.

"So you're divorced," he said.

"Uh-huh. You? I'll bet you're married, aren't you? It doesn't bother me if you are."

"I'm not. How long ago were you divorced?"

"It's almost five years now. It'll be exactly five years in January. That's since we split, but then it was another six months before the divorce went through. Why?"

"And Ackerman was your husband's name?"

"Yeah. Wallace Ackerman."

"No kids?"

"No, I wanted to but he didn't."

"A lot of women take their maiden names back after a divorce."

She laughed aloud. "They don't have a maiden name like I did. You wouldn't believe the name I was born with."

"Try me."

"Plonk. Millie Plonk. I think I married Wally just to get rid of it. I mean Mildred's bad enough, but Plonk? Like forget it. I don't think you even told me your last name."

"Didn't I?" The hand moved distractingly over Millie's abdomen. "So you decided to go on being an Ackerman, huh?"

"Sure. Why not?"

"Why not indeed."

"It's not a bad name."

"Mmmm," the man said. "This is a nice place you've got here, incidentally. Been living here long?"

"Ever since the divorce. It's a little small. Just a studio."

"But it's a good-sized studio, and you must have a terrific view. Your window looks out on the river, doesn't it?"

"Oh, sure. And you know, eighteen flights up, it's gotta be a pretty decent view."

"It bothers some people to live that high up in the air."

"Never bothered me."

"Eighteen floors," the man said. "If a person went out that window there wouldn't be much left of her, would there?"

"Jeez, don't even talk like that."

"You couldn't have an autopsy, could you? Couldn't determine whether she was alive or dead when she went out the window."

"Come on, Bill. That's creepy."

"Your ex-husband living in New York?"

"Wally? I think I heard something about him moving out to the West Coast, but to be honest I don't know if he's alive or dead."

"Hmmm."

"And who cares? You ask the damnedest questions, Bill."

"Do I?"

"Uh-huh. But you got the nicest hands in the world, I swear to God. You touch me so nice. And your eyes, you've got beautiful eyes. I guess you've heard that before?"

"Not really."

"Well, how could anybody tell? Those crazy glasses you wear, a person tries to look into your eyes and she's looking into a couple of mirrors. It's a sin having such beautiful eyes and hiding them."

"Eighteen floors, that's quite a drop."

"Huh?"

"Nothing," he said, and smiled. "Just thinking out loud."

Freitag looked up when his partner entered the room. "You look a little green in the face," he said. "Something the matter?"

"Oh, I was just looking at the *Post* and there's this story that's enough to make you sick. This guy out in Sheepshead Bay, and he's a policeman, too."

"What are you talking about?"

Poolings shrugged. "It's nothing that doesn't happen every couple of months. This policeman, he was depressed or he had a fight with his wife or something, I don't know what. So he shot her dead, and then he had two kids, a boy and a girl, and he shot them to death in their sleep, and then he went and ate his gun. Blew his brains out."

"Jesus."

"You just wonder what goes through a guy's mind that he does something like that. Does he just go completely crazy or what? I can't understand a person who does something like that."

"I can't understand people, period. Was this somebody you knew?"

"No, he lives in Sheepshead Bay. Lived in Sheepshead Bay. Anyway, he wasn't with the department. He was a Transit Authority cop."

"Anybody spends all his time in the subways, it's got to take its toll. Has to drive you crazy sooner or later."

"I guess."

Freitag plucked a cigarette from the pack in his shirt pocket, tapped it on the top of his desk, held it between his thumb and forefinger, frowned at it, and returned it to the pack. He was trying to cut back to a pack a day and was not having much success. "Maybe he was trying to quit smoking," he suggested. "Maybe it was making him nervous and he just couldn't stand it anymore."

"That seems a little far-fetched, doesn't it?"

"Does it? Does it really?" Freitag got the cigarette out again, put it in his mouth, lit it. "It don't sound all that far-fetched to me. What was this guy's name, anyway?"

"The TA cop? Hell, I don't know. Why?"

"I might know him. I know a lot of transit cops."

"It's in the *Post*. Bluestein's reading it."

"I don't suppose it matters, anyway. There's a ton of transit cops and I don't know that many of them. Anyway, the ones I know aren't crazy."

"I didn't even notice his name," Poolings said. "Let me just go take a look. Maybe *I* know him, as far as that goes." Poolings went out, returning moments later with a troubled look on his face. Freitag looked questioningly at him.

"Rudy Ackerman," he said.

"Nobody I know. Hey."

"Yeah, right. Another Ackerman."

"That's three Ackermans, Ken."

"It's six Ackermans if you count the wife and kids."

"Yeah, but three incidents. I mean it's no coincidence that this TA cop and his wife and kids all had the same last name, but when you add in the schoolteacher and the gay boy, then you got a coincidence."

"It's a common name."

"Is it? How common, Ken?" Freitag leaned forward, stubbed out his cigarette, picked up a Manhattan telephone directory and flipped it open. "Ackerman, Ackerman," he said, turning pages. "Here we are. Yeah, it's common. There's close to two columns of Ackermans in Manhattan alone. And then there's some that spell it with two n's. I wonder."

"You wonder what?"

"If there's a connection."

Poolings sat on the edge of Freitag's desk. "How could there be a connection?"

"Damned if I know."

"There couldn't, Jack."

"An old schoolteacher gets stabbed by a mugger in Washington Heights. A faggot picks up the wrong kind of rough trade and gets tied up and tortured to death. And a TA cop goes berserk and kills his wife and kids and himself. No connection."

"Except for them all having the same last name."

"Yeah. And the two of us just happened to notice that because we investigated the one killing and read about the other two."

"Right."

"So maybe nobody else even knows that there were three homicides involving Ackermans. Maybe you and me are the only people in the city who happened to notice this little coincidence."

"So maybe there's something we didn't notice," Freitag said. He got to his feet. "Maybe there's more than three. Maybe if we pull a printout of deaths over the past few months we're going to find Ackermans scattered all over it."

"Are you serious, Jack?"

"Sounds crazy, don't it?"

"Yeah, that's how it sounds, all right."

"If there's just the three it don't prove a thing, right? I mean, it's a common name and you got lots of people dying violently in New York City. When you have eight million people in a city it's no big surprise that you average three or four murders a day. The rate's not even so high compared to other cities. With three or four homicides a day, well, when you got three Ackermans over a couple of weeks, that's not too crazy all itself to be pure coincidence, right?"

"Right."

"Suppose it turns out there's more than the three."

"You've got a hunch, Jack. Haven't you?"

Freitag nodded. "That's what I got, all right. A hunch. Let's just see if I'm nuts or not. Let's find out."

"A fifth of Courvoisier, V.S.O.P." Mel Ackerman used a stepladder to reach the bottle. "Here we are, sir. Now will there be anything else?"

"All the money in the register," the man said.

Ackerman's heart turned over. He saw the gun in the man's hand and his own hands trembled so violently that he almost dropped the bottle of cognac. "Jesus," he said. "Could you point that somewhere else? I get very nervous."

"The money," the man said.

"Yeah, right. I wish you guys would pick on somebody else once in a while. This makes four times I been held up in the past two years. You'd think I'd be used to it by now, wouldn't you? Listen, I'm insured, I don't care about the money, just be careful with the gun, huh? There's not much money in the register but you're welcome to every penny I got."

He punched the No Sale key and scooped up bills, emptying all of the compartments. Beneath the removable tray he had several hundred dollars in large bills, but he didn't intend to call them to the robber's attention. Sometimes a gunman made you take out the tray and hand over everything. Other times the man would take what you gave him and be anxious to get the hell out. Ackerman didn't much care either way. Just so he got out of this alive, just so the maniac would take the money and leave without his gun.

"Four times in two years," Ackerman said, talking as he emptied the register, taking note of the holdup man's physical appearance as he did so. Tall but not too tall, young, still in his twenties. White. Good build. No beard, no mustache. Big mirrored sunglasses that hid a lot of his face.

"Here we go," Ackerman said, handing over the bills. "No muss, no fuss. You want me to lie down behind the counter while you go on your way?"

"What for?"

"Beats me. The last guy that held me up, he told me so I did it. Maybe he got the idea from a television program or something. Don't forget the brandy."

"I don't drink."

"You just come to liquor stores to rob 'em, huh?" Ackerman was beginning to relax now. "This is the only way we get your business, is that right?"

"I've never held up a liquor store before."

"So you had to start with me? To what do I owe the honor?"

"Your name."

"My name?"

"You're Melvin Ackerman, aren't you?"

"So?"

"So this is what you get," the man said, and shot Ackerman three times in the chest.

———————

"It's crazy," Freitag said. "What it is is crazy. Twenty-two people named Ackerman died in the past six weeks. Listen to this. Arnold Ackerman, fifty-six years of age, lived in Flushing. Jumped or fell in front of the E train."

"Or was pushed."

"Or was pushed," Freitag agreed. "Wilma Ackerman, sixty-two years old, lived in Flatbush. Heart attack. Mildred Ackerman, thirty-six, East Eighty-seventh Street, fell from an eighteenth-story window. Rudolph Ackerman, that's the Transit Authority cop, killed his wife and kids and shot himself. Florence Ackerman was stabbed, Samuel Ackerman fell down a flight of stairs, Lucy Ackerman took an overdose of sleeping pills, Walter P. Ackerman was electrocuted when a radio fell in the bathtub with him,

Melvin Ackerman's the one who just got shot in a holdup—" Freitag spread his hands. "It's unbelievable. And it's completely crazy."

"Some of the deaths must be natural," Poolings said. "Here's one. Sarah Ackerman, seventy-eight years old, spent two months as a terminal cancer patient at St. Vincent's and finally died last week. Now that has to be coincidental."

"Uh-huh. Unless somebody slipped onto the ward and held a pillow over her face because he didn't happen to like her last name."

"That seems pretty like a stretch, Jack."

"You think? Is it any more of a stretch than the rest of it? Is it any crazier than the way all these other Ackermans got it? Some nut case is running around killing people who have nothing in common but their last names. There's no way they're related, you know. Some of these Ackermans are Jewish and some are gentiles. It's one of those names that can be either. Hell, this guy Wilson Ackerman was black. So it's not somebody with a grudge against a particular family. It's somebody who has a thing about the name, but why?"

"Maybe somebody's collecting Ambroses," Poolings suggested.

"Huh? Where'd you get Ambrose?"

"Oh, it's something I read once," Poolings said. "This writer Charles Fort used to write about freaky things that happen, and one thing he wrote was that a guy named Ambrose had walked around the corner and disappeared, and the writer Ambrose Bierce had disappeared in Mexico, and he said maybe somebody was collecting Ambroses."

"That's ridiculous."

"Yeah. But what I meant—"

"Maybe somebody's collecting Ackermans."

"Right."

"Killing them. Killing everybody with that last name and doing it differently each time. Every mass murderer I ever heard of had a murder method he was nuts about and used it over and over, but this guy never does it the same way twice. We got—what is it, twenty-two deaths here? Even if some of them just happened, there's no question that at least fifteen out of twenty-two have to be the work of this nut, whoever he is. He's going to a lot of trouble to keep this operation of his from looking like what it is. Most of these killings could pass for suicide or accidental death, and the others were set up to look like isolated homicides in the course of a robbery or whatever. That's how he managed to knock off this many Ackermans before anybody suspected anything. Ken, what gets me is the question of why. Why is he doing this?"

"He must be crazy."

"Of course he's crazy, but being crazy don't mean you don't have reasons for what you do. It's just that they're crazy reasons. What kind of reasons could he have?"

"Revenge."

"Against all the Ackermans in the world?"

Poolings shrugged. "What else? Maybe somebody named Ackerman did him dirty once upon a time and he wants to get even with all the Ackermans in the world. I don't see what difference it makes as far as catching him is concerned, and once we catch him the easiest way to find out the reason is to ask him."

"*If* we catch him."

"Sooner or later we'll catch him, Jack."

"Either that or the city'll run out of Ackermans. Maybe *his* name is Ackerman."

"How do you figure that?"

"Getting even with his father, hating himself, *I* don't know. You want to start looking somewhere, it's gotta be easier to start with people named Ackerman than with people not named Ackerman."

"Even so there's a hell of a lot of Ackermans. It's going to be some job checking them all out. There's got to be a few hundred in the five boroughs, plus God knows how many who don't have telephones. And if the guy we're looking for is a drifter living in a dump of a hotel somewhere, there's no way to find him, and that's if he's even using his name in the first place, which he probably isn't, considering the way he feels about the name."

Freitag lit a cigarette. "Maybe he *likes* the name," he said. "Maybe he wants to be the only one left with it."

"You really think we should check all the Ackermans?"

"Well, the job gets easier every day, Ken. 'Cause every day there's fewer Ackermans to check on."

"God."

"Yeah."

"Do we just do this ourselves, Jack?"

"I don't see how we can. We better take it upstairs and let the brass figure out what to do with it. You know what's gonna happen."

"What?"

"It's gonna get in the papers."

"Oh, God."

"Yeah." Freitag drew on his cigarette, coughed, cursed, and took another drag anyway. "The newspapers. At which point all the Ackermans left in the city start panicking, and so does everybody else, and don't ask me what our crazy does because I don't have any idea. Well, it'll be somebody else's worry." He got to his feet. "And that's what we need—for it to be somebody else's worry. Let's take this to the lieutenant right now and let him figure out what to do with it."

———

The pink rubber ball came bouncing crazily down the driveway toward the street. The street was a quiet suburban cul-de-sac in a recently developed neighborhood on Staten Island. The house was a three-bedroom expandable colonial ranchette. The driveway was concrete, with the footprints of a largish dog evident in two of its squares. The small boy who came bouncing crazily after the rubber ball was towheaded and azure-eyed and, when a rangy young man emerged from behind the barberry hedge and speared the ball one-handed, seemed suitably amazed.

"Gotcha," the man said, and flipped the ball underhand to the small boy, who missed it, but picked it up on the second bounce.

"Hi," the boy said.

"Hi yourself."

"Thanks," the boy said, and looked at the pink rubber ball in his hand. "It was gonna go in the street."

"Sure looked that way."

"I'm not supposed to go in the street. On account of the cars."

"Makes sense."

"But sometimes the dumb ball goes in the street anyhow, and then what am I supposed to do?"

"It's a problem," the man agreed, reaching over to rumple the boy's straw-colored hair. "How old are you, my good young man?"

"Five and a half."

"That's a good age."

"Goin' on six."

"A logical assumption."

"Those are funny glasses you got on."

"These?" The man took them off, looked at them for a moment, then put them on again. "Mirrors," he said.

"Yeah, I know. They're funny."

"They are indeed. What's your name?"

"Mark."

"I bet I know your last name."

"Oh, yeah?"

"I bet it's Ackerman."

"How'd you know?" The boy wrinkled up his face in a frown. "Aw, I bet you know my daddy."

"We're old friends. Is he home?"

"You silly. He's workin'."

"I should have guessed as much. What else would Hale Ackerman be doing on such a beautiful sunshiny day, hmmmm? How about your mommy? She home?"

"Yeah. She's watchin' the teevee."

"And you're playing in the driveway."

"Yeah."

The man rumpled the boy's hair again. Pitching his voice theatrically low, he said, "It's a tough business, son, but that doesn't mean it's a *heartless* business. Keep that in mind."

"Huh?"

"Nothing. A pleasure meeting you, Mark, me lad. Tell your parents they're lucky to have you. Luckier than they'll ever have to know."

"Whatcha mean?"

"Nothing," the man said agreeably. "Now I have to walk all the way back to the ferry slip and take the dumb old boat all the way back to Manhattan and then I have to go to…" he consulted a slip of paper from his pocket "…to Seaman Avenue way the hell up in Washington Heights. Pardon me. Way the *heck* up in Washington Heights. Let's just hope *they* don't turn out to have a charming kid."

"You're funny."

"You bet," the man said.

"Police protection," the lieutenant was saying. He was a beefy man with an abundance of jaw. He had not been born looking particularly happy, and years of police work had drawn deep lines of disappointment around his eyes and mouth. "That's the first step, but how do you even go about offering it? There's a couple of hundred people named Ackerman in the five boroughs and one's as likely to be a target as the next one.

"And we don't know who the hell we're protecting 'em *from*. We don't know if this is one maniac or a platoon of them. Meaning we have to take every dead Ackerman on this list and backtrack, looking for some common element, which since we haven't been looking for it all along we're about as likely to find it as a virgin on Eighth Avenue. Twenty-two years ago I coulda gone with the police or the fire department and I couldn't make up my mind. You know what I did? I tossed a coin. It hadda come up heads."

"As far as protecting these people—"

"As far as protecting 'em, how do you do that without you let out the story? And when the story gets out it's all over the papers, and suppose you're a guy named Ackerman and you find out some moron just declared war on your last name?"

"I suppose you get out of town."

"Maybe you get out of town, and maybe you have a heart attack, and maybe you call the mayor's office and yell a lot, and maybe you sit in your apartment with a loaded gun and shoot the mailman when he does something you figure is suspicious. And maybe if you're some *other* lunatic you read the story and it's like tellin' a kid don't put beans up your nose, so you go out and join in the Ackerman hunt yourself. Or if you're yet another kind of lunatic which we're all of us familiar with you call up the police and confess. Just to give the nice cops something to do."

A cop groaned.

"Yeah," the lieutenant said. "That about sums it up. So the one thing you don't want is for this to get in the papers, but—"

"But it's too late for that," said a voice from the doorway. And a uniformed patrolman entered the office holding a fresh copy of the *New York Post*. "Either somebody told them or they went and put two and two together."

"I coulda been a fireman," the lieutenant said. "I woulda got to slide down the pole and wear one of those hats and everything, but instead the coin had to come up heads."

———

The young man paid the cashier and carried his tray of food across the lunchroom to a long table at the rear. A half dozen people were already sitting there. The young man joined them, ate his macaroni and cheese, sipped his coffee, and listened as they discussed the Ackerman murders.

"I think it's a cult thing," one girl was saying. "They have this sort of thing all the time out in California, like surfing and est and all those West Coast fads. In order to be a member you have to kill somebody named Ackerman."

"That's a theory," a bearded young man said. "Personally, I'd guess the whole business is more logically motivated than that. It looks to me like a chain murder."

Someone wanted to know what that was.

"A chain murder," the bearded man said. "Our murderer has a strong motive to kill a certain individual whose name happens to be Ackerman. Only problem is his motive is so strong that he'd be suspected immediately.

COLLECTIBLES

So instead he kills a whole slew of Ackermans and the one particular victim he has a reason to kill is no more than one face in a crowd. So his motive gets lost in the shuffle." The speaker smiled. "Happens all the time in mystery stories. Now it's happening in real life. Not the first time life imitates art."

"Too logical," a young woman objected. "Besides, all these murders had different methods and a lot of them were disguised so as not to look like murders at all. A chain murderer wouldn't want to operate that way, would he?"

"He might. If he were very, very clever—"

"But he'd be too clever for his own good, don't you think? No, I think he had a grudge against one Ackerman and decided to exterminate the tribe. Like Hitler and the Jews."

The conversation went on in this fashion, with nothing contributed by the young man, who went on eating his macaroni and cheese. Gradually the talk trailed off and so indeed did the people at the table, until no one remained but the young man and the girl next to whom he'd seated himself.

She took a sip of coffee, drew on her cigarette, and smiled at him. "You didn't say anything," she said. "About the Ackerman murders."

"No," he agreed. "People certainly had some interesting ideas."

"And what did you think?"

"I think I'm happy my name isn't Ackerman."

"What is it?"

"Bill. Bill Trenholme."

"I'm Emily Kuystendahl."

"Emily," he said. "Pretty name."

"Thank you. What do you think? Really?"

"Really?"

"Uh-huh."

"Well," he said, "I don't think much of the theories everybody was coming up with. Chain murders and cult homicide and all the rest of it. I have a theory of my own, but of course that's all it is. Just a theory."

"I'd really like to hear it."

"You would?"

"Definitely."

Their eyes met and wordless messages exchanged. He smiled and she smiled in reply. "Well," he said, after a moment. "First of all, I think it was just one guy. Not a group of killers. From the way it was timed. And, because he keeps changing the murder method, I think he wanted to keep what he was doing undiscovered as long as possible."

"That makes sense. But why?"

"I think it was a source of fun for him."

"A source of *fun?*"

The man nodded. "This is just hypothesis," he said, "but let's suppose he just killed a person once for the sheer hell of it. To find out what it felt like, say. To enlarge his area of personal experience."

"God."

"Can you accept that hypothetically?"

"I guess so. Sure."

"Okay. Now we can suppose further that he liked it, got some kind of a kick out of it. Otherwise he wouldn't have wanted to continue. There's certainly precedent for it. Not all the homicidal maniacs down through history have been driven men. Some of them have just gotten a kick out of it so they kept right on doing it."

"That gives me the shivers."

"It's a frightening concept," he agreed. "But let's suppose that the person this clown killed was named Ackerman, and that he wanted to go on killing people and he wanted to make a game out of it. So he—"

"A game!"

"Sure, why not? He could just keep on with it, having his weird jollies and seeing how long it would take for the police and the press to figure out what was going on. There are a lot of Ackermans. It's a common name, but not so common that a pattern wouldn't begin to emerge sooner or later. Think how many Smiths there are in the city, for instance. I don't suppose police in the different boroughs coordinate their activities so closely, and I guess the Bureau of Vital Statistics doesn't bother to note if a lot of fatalities have the same last name, so it's a question of how long it takes for the pattern to emerge in and of itself. Well, it's done so now, and what does the score stand at now? Twenty-seven?"

COLLECTIBLES

"That's what the paper said, I think."

"It's quite a total when you stop and think of it. And there may have been a few Ackermans not accounted for. A body or two in the river, for instance."

"You make it sound—"

"Yes?"

"I don't know. It gives me the willies to think about it. Will he just keep on now? Until they catch him?"

"You think they'll catch him?"

"Well, sooner or later, won't they? The Ackermans know to be careful now and the police will have stakeouts. Is that what they call it? Stakeouts?"

"That's what call it on television."

"Don't *you* think they'll catch him?"

The young man thought it over. "I'm sure they'll catch him," said, "if he keeps it up."

"You mean he might stop?"

"I would. If I were him."

"If you were him. What a thought!"

"Just projecting a little. But to continue with it, if I were this creep, I'd leave the rest of the world's Ackermans alone from here on in."

"Because it would be too dangerous?"

"Because it wouldn't be any fun for me."

"Fun!"

"Oh, come on," he said, smiling. "Once you get past the evilness of it, which I grant you is overwhelming, can't you see how it would add up to fun for the right sort of demented mind? But try not to think of him as fundamentally cruel. Think of him as someone responding to a challenge. Well, now the police and the newspapers and the Ackermans themselves know what's going on, so at this point it's not a game anymore. The game's over and if he were to go on with it he'd just be conducting a personal war of extermination. And if he doesn't really have any genuine grudge against Ackermans, well, I say he'd let them alone."

She looked at him and her eyes were thoughtful. "Then he might just stop altogether."

"Sure."

"And get away with it?"

"I suppose. Unless they pick him up for killing somebody else." Her eyes widened and he grinned. "Oh, really, Emily, you can't expect him to stop this new hobby of his entirely, can you? Not if he's been having so much fun at it? I don't think killers like that ever stop, not once it gets in their blood. They don't stop until the long arm of the law catches up with them."

"The way you said that."

"Pardon me?"

"'The long arm of the law.' As if it's sort of a joke."

"Well, when you see how this character operated, he does make the law look like something of a joke, doesn't he?"

"I guess he does."

He smiled, got to his feet. "Getting close in here. Which way are you headed?"

Coincidentlly, they were both headed in the same direction. Halfway up the block she said, "I'll tell you something, I'm glad my name's not such a common one. There aren't enough Kuystendahls in the world to make it very interesting for him."

"Or Trenholmes. But there are plenty of Emilys, aren't there?"

"Huh?"

"Well, he doesn't have to pick his next victims by last name. In fact, he'd probably avoid that because the police would pick up on something like that in a hot second after this business with the Ackermans. He could establish some other kind of category. Men with beards, say. Oldsmobile owners."

"Oh, my God."

"People wearing brown shoes. Bourbon drinkers. Or, uh, girls named Emily."

"That's not funny, Bill."

"Well, no reason why it would have to be Emily. Any first name—that's the whole point, the random nature of it. He could pick guys named Bill, as far as that goes. Either way it would probably take the police a while to tip to it, don't you think?"

"I don't know."

"You upset, Emily?"

"Not upset, exactly."

"Well, you certainly don't have anything to worry about," he said, and slipped an arm protectively around her waist. "I'll take good care of you, baby."

"Oh, will you?"

"Count on it." They walked together in silence for a while and after a few moments she relaxed in his embrace. As they waited for a light to change he said, "Collecting Emilys."

"Pardon?"

"Just talking to myself," he said. "Nothing important."

ABOUT OUR CONTRIBUTORS...

JUNIOR BURKE's most recent novel is *Cold Last Swim*. As a young musician, he opened for many blues luminaries including Muddy Waters and John Lee Hooker. He owns nine gorgeous guitars and would love to figure out how to play more than one at a time.

S. A. COSBY, award-winning author of *My Darkest Prayer* and *Blacktop Wasteland*, has a collection of knives and swords that includes a katana he once used to slice a birthday cake. He has not been back to that restaurant since.

JANICE EIDUS's books include the novels *The War of the Rosens* and *The Last Jewish Virgin;* her short story collections are *Vito Loves Geraldine* and *The Celibacy Club*. It could be said of her that she collects friends, but only in the most loving of ways—i.e. by gathering them together for hours and hours to schmooze, kibbitz, and share confidences both large and small.

LEE GOLDBERG is a #1 *New York Times* bestselling author (*Lost Hills, True Fiction* etc.), TV series writer/producer (*Diagnosis Murder, SeaQuest* etc.), and a lifelong TV geek who is frighteningly similar to the protagonist of his story. Lee has been collecting videos of unsold pilots (first episodes of proposed-but-unproduced TV series) since he was a kid and has written several nonfiction books on the subject.

COLLECTIBLES

ROB HART is the author of *The Warehouse,* which sold in more than twenty languages, as well as the Ash McKenna crime series, the short story collection *Take-Out,* and *Scott Free* with James Patterson. His work has been included in *Best American Mystery Stories,* and his next novel is *Paradox Hotel.* He is an avid collector of ice cream but you wouldn't know it if you looked in his freezer.

ELAINE KAGAN is a Los Angeles-based actress, journalist (*Los Angeles Magazine, Los Angeles Times*), and novelist (*The Girls, Losing Mr. North*). She is working on a collection of short stories (*The Picture Business*). When she can once again visit New York she'll be at the Viand on Madison having a tuna melt. On rye.

JOE R. LANSDALE: "Can't say as I collect skulls, but I've both enjoyed and fought the collecting bug all my life. My lifetime horde of books and comics, as well as odds and ends, though less criminal, allow me to understand the impulse. It should also be noted that much of my collection deals with dark deeds as well as criminal activity, therefore giving me, at least once removed, a connection to the shadier aspects of humanity."

KASEY LANSDALE has been accused of collecting mugs. As a traveling musician and performer, she owns enough "places I have been" mugs to know it's time to stop. She now has a Pinterest board where she hoards interesting & bizarre article clippings, as well as all things pertaining to Italian culture. Her most recent collection is *Terror is Our Business.*

DENNIS LEHANE: "I don't collect things myself but the story was inspired by my wanderings through the used and antique bookstores of Cambridge when I was a kid in the early eighties. It feels like a vanished world now, but back then, when there were twenty bookstores in a single square mile of Harvard Square, I would wander from store to store, sometimes for hours, and soak up an atmosphere that felt lost in time. I'd find myself deep in the stacks of some musty old store that had been there for decades and feel as if I was in London in the 1800s. It felt alive and mysterious and slightly haunted. Dickensian, believe it or not. I'd step back out the door and sometimes be shocked to see cars where I'd expected horse drawn carriages. I think I decided to become a writer sometime in all that wandering, with the sun going down and the winter chill taking hold, and a long subway ride back home still ahead of me."

JOYCE CAROL OATES has long been a 'collector' of Norma Jeane Baker/ Marilyn Monroe tales, since researching her epic *Blonde* (2000).

OTTO PENZLER: "I lied when I said *all* my books went to auction. I kept my Raffles and E.W. Hornung collection. Mostly not very valuable or desirable, as I tried to collect every edition of every book, when the only ones of value are the first editions and the inscribed copies, and most people don't even know who Hornung is these days—he was Conan Doyle's brother-in-law—but it fills a nice corner of my otherwise barren library."

THOMAS PLUCK collected American coins until shifty movers stole his collection, which he never replaced. Now he collects handmade knives, focusing on Master Smith Bowies and recurve folders. Keller and LB have lured him, but Tommy has yet to commit philately. He is the author of the Jay Desmarteaux crime thriller *Bad Boy Boogie,* which was nominated for an Anthony award, the adventure novel *Blade of Dishonor,* which MysteryPeople called "The Raiders of the Lost Ark of pulp paperbacks," and over fifty short stories, published everywhere from *Hardboiled* to *The Utne Reader.*

DAVID RACHELS is the author of the poetry collection *Verse Noir,* and he has edited four volumes of short stories by the classic noir writer Gil Brewer. He collects blues CDs, which are substantially less valuable than blues 78s— but far more antiquated.

COLLECTIBLES

S. J. ROZAN is not a collector of anything. She is, however, a lover of and frequent visitor to Mongolia. Possibly this is because she's from the Bronx, which to many New Yorkers is kind of like Mongolia. Her most recent book is *The Art of Violence.*

New York Times bestseller KRISTINE KATHRYN RUSCH has won the *Ellery Queen Reader's Choice* award twice, been nominated for the Edgar, the Shamus, the Anthony, and many other mystery awards, not to mention what she does in her science fiction and romance careers. An award-winning editor and a recreational runner, she's not a collector, but she lives with one—writer Dean Wesley Smith, whose collector friends "tell Dean that he's not allowed to have more than three of anything, because that'll be a collection. Which is why we now have only two cats."

ALEX SEGURA is the author of *Star Wars Poe Dameron: Free Fall,* the Pete Fernandez Mystery series (including the Anthony Award-nominated crime novels *Dangerous Ends, Blackout,* and *Miami Midnight*), and the upcoming *Secret Identity* (Flatiron Books). His comic books include the superhero noir *The Black Ghost,* the YA music series *The Archies,* and the "Archie Meets" collection of crossovers, featuring real-life cameos from the Ramones, B-52s, and more. He is also the co-creator/co-writer of the *Lethal Lit* crime/YA podcast from iHeart Radio, named one of the best podcasts of 2018 by *The New York Times.* A Miami native, he lives with his wife and children in New York, where he spends his days as co-president of Archie Comics.

LAWRENCE BLOCK, whose response to encroaching senescence has led to a second career as an anthologist, has been described as a man who needs no introduction—and that's precisely what he's going to get here.